Greek Mythology

Fascinating Myths and Legends of Gods, Goddesses, Heroes and Monster from the Ancient Greek Mythology

By Simon Lopez

Table of Contents

Part 3   The Trojan War and Odysseus' Voyage Home

Conclusion 359

Introduction

Since the dawn of time, humans have created myths to explain the wondrous world around them. All ancient civilizations concocted stories that eventually became legends, told and retold throughout the ages. The myths brought order to chaos and explained the unexplainable. In modern days, our explanations of the seasons, the weather, natural disasters, or the movement of the stars are driven by science, but there was a time that man relied on their cultural myths to explain such things.

The ancient Greeks wove one of the richest and best-preserved collections of stories of all the early civilizations. The stories explain the creation of the world and man. They illuminate the lives and intrigues of the gods of the ancient Greeks. As society evolved, so did the stories to include great epic poems, such as the *Iliad* and the *Odyssey*, where the focus shifted to tales of heroes among men.

These entertaining legends have been compiled here in story form and take you from the dawn of creation to the bloody siege at Troy. You'll learn how Zeus came to rule supreme and how mortal man emerged to walk the earth. You will also experience the machinations and intrigues of the gods and their tumultuous court upon Mount Olympus. From Olympus, you will walk the earth with the heroes Peleus, Theseus, and Hercules. Finally, you will survive the Trojan War at Odysseus' side and fight the decade-long battle to return to his home shores of Ithaca. Adventure awaits as only the Ancient Greeks could tell it!

Note: these tales have been compiled from various ancient Greek and Roman sources to tell the most entertaining and captivating version of the stories. There are numerous variations of each and every myth. If you've heard a story a bit differently elsewhere, likely it came from a different source and is just as valid as what is recorded here! The gods also have multiple names and titles. For ease of reading, only the main Greek form has been used. For a list of reference that informed this work, please see the end of the book.

Part 1 The Gods and Godesses

Creation of the World

Civilizations throughout the ages have endeavored to answer one of the greatest questions known to man: "Where did we come from?" The ancient civilizations created rich mythologies to explain the origins of man and the world on which he walked. The ancient Greek creation myth was recorded by one of the earliest Greek poets, Hesiod. This shepherd-turned-poet claimed that the Muses gifted him the poet's speech and staff while he watched his herds at the base of Mt. Helicon. They also revealed to him the origin of the universe, the earth, and the gods, bidding him sing the song of the blessed immortal gods. Dated to around 700 BCE, Hesiod's earliest and best-known work, *Theogony*, compiles the origins and histories of the gods and is one of the earliest works of Greek mythology.

Before getting started in exploring the creation of the world and man according to the Greeks, it is important to note that when you're an immortal god, the usual rules of procreation and modern morality don't apply. The original immortals were capable of creation without involving anyone else in the process. Children created from a single parent are referred to as parthenogenic and add some very interesting twists and turns in the Immortal Greek Gods' Family Tree! Immortals also have the option of procreating with other immortals and later, once they are created, mortal men and women. Just remember, traditional rules of reproduction and family relations aren't applicable in the myths. To add another layer of confusion to the myths, multiple versions of the stories by the early poets often contradict each other or take great liberties with any kind of chronological order. It's best to enjoy the stories of the myths without attempting to plot them out on a timeline or fit them neatly together in a larger picture. Keep an open mind and enjoy the imagination and legends of the ancient Greeks.

According to the ancient Greeks, the universe began with Chaos, but not the same chaos we know today. Here, Chaos represents a void, a nothingness. It has nothing to do with disorder or confusion. It was the complete absence of anything. From this void, Chaos brought forth Gaia, the Earth. Described as broad-chested and unshakeable, Gaia was to be the home of the immortals. Chaos also created Eros, Tartarus, Erebrus, and Nyx. Known as the most beautiful of all primordial gods, Eros embodied love and desire that would eventually cloud and confound the minds of gods and men alike. Tartarus was sent to dwell deep in the dark recesses of the earth, creating the Underworld. With Erebrus and Nyx, Chaos made Darkness and Night.

As in all creation myths, balance sought to establish itself throughout the universe. Together, Erebrus and Nyx created Brightness and Day and named them Aither and Hemera. Nyx and Hemera were given a home in Tartarus to share, but they could never be in it at the same time. One had to wait for the other to cross the bronze threshold before they could enter, thus establishing the cycle of day and night.

Gaia brought forth from herself an equal and opposite god, Uranus, who became the sky and the starry heavens to cover and engulf her. She also bore Pontus, the mighty sea, and created the rest of the physical world by pushing up mountains and carving out rivers. With the help of Uranus' life-giving rain, she covered herself with flora and fauna.

During this time of creation, a multitude of gods were born. Nyx, in keeping with her dark nature, generated the shadows in the world. Thanatos became death. Moros brought doom, and Hypnos brought sleep to the world. Eris and Nemesis were created as Strife and Retribution. Finally, Nyx brought forth the Moirai, or the Fates, Clotho, Lachesis, and Atropos, to control the destinies of both gods and man.

Gaia continued to produce offspring as well. She lay with Uranus and had three monstrous children who each had 100 arms, 50 heads, and were so tall, they reached the heavens. These creatures were followed by three formidable cyclops, Brontes, Steropes, and Arges. Finally, Gaia brought forth the Titans, six goddesses and six gods who would become the foundation for the most legendary pantheon in the world.

Uranus despised all his children. He had been told by an oracle that one of his children would one day take his power from him. When the multi-headed giants and cyclops were born, Uranus cast them down into Tartarus and imprisoned them in its darkness. As Gaia birthed each of the Titans, Uranus shoved them back into her womb, trapping them in the dark corners of the world. Uranus gloried in his power and felt no remorse for his unfatherly actions.

Gaia, feeling like she was going to burst and incensed with Uranus, fashioned a sickle with a wicked serrated blade. She called to her children, begging them to act against their father, but none would stir until Cronos agreed to her plan. Gaia hid him in her mists and waited. When Uranus came to her next, she seduced him. When Uranus was fully aroused, Cronos sprang from his hiding place and cut off his genitals, dripping blood all over Gaia. From the blood sprang the Goddesses of Vengeance or the Furies, along with an army of fully armored giants with spears in hand and a collection of tree nymphs with an affinity for ash trees. Uranus, wounded and unmanned, allowed his children to emerge from their mother's womb and resigned himself to his fate.

Cronos cast his father's severed organ into the sea where it drifted and collected a dense white foam around it. From the foam, a maiden emerged and became the Foam-born Goddess, Aphrodite. From the moment of her birth, Eros, the god of love and desire, was never to be separated from her. Radiant and beautiful, Aphrodite held the power to beguile gods and men alike.

Gaia was yet not done bearing offspring. She lay with Pontus, the god of the sea, and had several more children in the form of minor sea gods and goddesses, sea nymphs, and even terrifying sea creatures. Gaia was not the only one producing children. Nyx's daughter, Strife, gave rise to a multitude of unsavory characters, including Famine, Murder, Sorrow, Quarrel, and Ruin, to name a few.

The children of the gods proved to be prolific. However, they did not only create more gods and goddesses. They created monsters as well. Ceto, Gaia's sea monster daughter, lay with the sea god, Phorcys. Together, they created three sisters, known as the Graeae, who were born ancient with gray hair, withered skin, and stooped with age. They also made the terrifying Gorgons, snake-haired goddesses who were beautiful nymphs from the waist up and a slithering serpent from the waist down. The Gorgons turned anyone who looked upon them to stone. Ceto also gave birth to Echidna, another half-snake, half-woman beast, and she went on to mother a brood of monsters of her own, most notably the multi-headed dog, Cerberus, the Sphinx, the Hydra, and the Chimera.

Free from their banishment, the Titans began to establish themselves as the rulers of the world and nominated Cronos as their leader. They paired off among themselves and began to reproduce. They also freed their giant, multi-headed brethren and the cyclopes from their prison in Tartarus. However, the giants proved to be unruly and would not respect the authority of the Titans. In the end, Cronos banished them back to Tartarus.

Several of the unions between the Titans resulted in notable offspring. Sun Goddess, Theia, and Sun God, Hyperion, produced Helios, who would eventually replace them as the main sun god of the Greek pantheon. Selena, goddess of the moon, and Eos, goddess of the dawn, became Helios' sisters and balanced his daytime brightness. The Titans of the sea, Tethys and Oceanus, created over 3,000 rivers and a god to watch over each of them. They also created an equal number of female Oceanids, making them by far the most prolific pair of Titans. There were other children and creatures conceived during this time of procreation, but the most illustrious union within the Titans was that of Cronos, the king, and Rhea, a goddess of the earth.

Cronos and Rhea had six children: Hera, Poseidon, Hestia, Hades, Demeter, and Zeus. Cronos received a prophecy from his mother, Gaia. She told him that he would be deposed by one of his children, just like he did to his father. Of course, Cronos was not keen to allow history to repeat itself, so he swallowed each of his children as soon as they left Rhea's womb. While heavily pregnant with Zeus, Rhea sought out her parents, Gaia and Uranus, to help prevent her baby from sharing the fate of his brothers and sisters.

"You must hide, my daughter. Go now to the Isle of Crete, and I will help conceal you from your husband's sight," Gaia counseled her daughter. Deep in a cave surrounded by Gaia's enshrouding mists, Rhea gave birth to Zeus.

Gaia spirited the infant away while Rhea wrapped a stone in swaddling clothes. She presented it as if it was her newborn son to her husband and wept as Cronos swallowed it like he had done to the rest of her babies. Despite her heartache, Rhea returned with Cronos to their court.

Baby Zeus was entrusted to the Tender Goddess, a nymph named Amaltheia. Hiding in the caves of Mt. Aigaion, Amaltheia raised Zeus. She became a goat to provide him milk as an infant. A troop of warriors, the Curetes, protected them and played their drums and banged their shields to disguise the infant's cries from Cronos' ears. Like all immortal children, Zeus grew quickly. While still a child, he broke off one of Amaltheia's goat horns. From it, the first cornucopia was created, and Amaltheia became the world's first unicorn.

Fully grown, strong of body and cunning of mind, Zeus emerged from the mountains of Crete. Gaia knew it was time for him to free his brothers and sisters from his father's stomach.

"Seek out the Oceanid, Metis. She is prudent, wise, and cunning. She will know how you can save your brothers and sisters."

Zeus found her in her grotto on the edge of the sea. "Young Zeus! It was foretold that you would be the mightiest among your siblings. You must go now to your parent's court. Insinuate yourself in their inner circle as your father's cupbearer. Your mother will know you. She is gifted with the ways of the earth and knows many herbs and plant lore. Tell her to make an emetic potion that you will give to your father. He will liberate your siblings but beware. Cronos will not willingly step aside for you."

Zeus followed Metis' instructions and Rhea, overjoyed to see her son again, happily concocted the needed potion.

"My lord," Zeus told his father, who hadn't the slightest notion that his son was standing before him. "Your Lady Rhea has created a fine drink for you this day. It is ambrosia most sweet!" Cronos greedily drank the potion and immediately vomited up the stone he had swallowed all those many years ago. His five other children quickly followed, fully grown, unharmed, and more than a little cross with their father. They banded together behind their brother and unanimous leader, Zeus.

Zeus and his siblings fled from their parent's court and began to prepare for war. They knew their father would never allow them to live in peace. Cronos called the Titans to arms, but only his five brothers and some of their children answered his call. All of the female Titans and several of the second-generation Titans, notably Prometheus and Epimetheus, sided with Zeus. The Titans amassed on Mt. Othrys, and Zeus's army made Mt. Olympus their base. Thus, the Clash of the Titans began.

Evenly matched, the armies of the gods fought bitterly. Over the span of a decade, they met daily on the battlefield, but neither side was able to gain the advantage. Finally, Gaia received inspiration.

"Zeus, you must go to Tartarus. My children, the Hundred-Hand Giants, and the Cyclopes, were imprisoned there by Cronos. If you set them free, they will fight on our side and will tip the scales in our favor," Gaia told her grandson.

Zeus traveled to Tartarus and freed the monsters. Grateful for their freedom, they eagerly agreed to fight for Zeus. The Hundred-Hand Giants with their massive size and strength hurled a relentless stream of boulders at the opposing army. The Cyclops created three magical weapons in their gratitude. To Hades, they gave the Crown of Darkness, which made him invisible - even to other gods. Poseidon was given a mighty trident that could stir the seas and shake the ground. Zeus received the power of thunder and lightning which he could pull from the sky at his command.

While the Hundred-Hand Giants rained down rocks, Poseidon engaged Cronos with his new trident. The earth shook with the force of their blows. Hades donned the Crown of Darkness and snuck into the Titan's camp. Hidden from their sight, he stole their weapons, causing an uproar within the Titan camp. The Titans accused each other of stealing the weapons and turned the camp upside down searching for them, all the while dodging the hailstorm of rocks being relentlessly fired by the Hundred-Hand Giants. Cronos continued to duel with Poseidon, but neither could gain the upper hand. The earth rolled and shook under the furious forces until Zeus harnessed thunder and lightning and struck Cronos. In a blinding flash of light and roar of thunder, the Titan's leader fell, and the war finally drew to a close.

Following the battle, the conquered Titans were banished to Tartarus, and the Hundred-Hand Giants were assigned as their eternal jailers. Atlas, a Titan general who had given Zeus much grief throughout the war, was spared the pits of Tartarus but was punished by having to bear the world on his shoulders for all eternity. The victorious Olympians now reigned supreme.

The Division of the World

Once the Titans were taken care of, Zeus and his fellow gods were free to set up the world the way they wanted it. Zeus, Poseidon, and Hades were the mightiest of the gods. They cast lots to see who would reign over the three kingdoms - the heaven, the sea, and the underworld. They all agreed that the Earth itself would be the domain of no single god. Zeus won the draw and chose the heavens. Poseidon came in second and took the sea. Hades was left with the underworld, but he was not unhappy with his lot. Hades had long shunned the company of the other gods and preferred to live in solitude. He had never minded the darkness when they had been trapped for those long decades within their father's belly. So, back to the darkness he went, this time to rule as the king of the Underworld.

It was also unanimously decided that Zeus would be supreme over them all. Zeus claimed his throne and began to organize the stars, moon, and planets. Once they were set to his satisfaction, he turned his attention to the sky and created the clouds, rain, and snow. Finally, as the supreme ruler, Zeus implemented the concept of law and order. He decreed if a law was not obeyed or if an oath was not upheld, he would levy punishment.

Poseidon was also quite happy with his lot. He had a natural affinity for the water and quickly began to put his kingdom in order. His first order of business was to assign all the creatures in his domain to the various seas, rivers, lakes, and streams, building an extensive hierarchy among his subjects based on their loyalty to him. He also erected an opulent underwater palace. Poseidon was notoriously fickle and impulsive. He sent sea monsters to topple cities or temples that displeased him. He flooded lands with great tidal waves for any perceived offenses. He quickly became known as the Earth Shaker for throwing tantrums underwater, hammering his trident on the ocean floor when he was in a temper.

Below the Earth, Hades made his home. He had never cared for court politics or had an interest in socializing with the other gods. He arranged his kingdom of the dead to his liking. The river Styx served as its border, dividing it from the land of the living. He placed the multi-headed dog, Cerberus, to guard the gates and keep the shades of the dead confined. The souls of the living were delivered to the Underworld via a ferry that was captained by Charon. He would name the price to each shade requesting passage. If unable to pay, the soul was forced to roam the Earth for 100 years before being allowed to cross to their final rest. Hades also inherited the role of enforcer. Whenever a law or oath was broken, Hades was sent to dole out whatever punishment Zeus decreed. Between being the ruler of the dead and the muscle of the gods, Hades' became the most feared and dreaded of all the gods.

The world had been set to order, jurisdictions assigned, and the Olympians had established themselves as masters of the universe. The next phase of the world had begun.

The Creation of Man and Beasts

Prometheus and his brother, Epimetheus, fought beside the Olympians in the Clash of the Titans and therefore, were not bound to Tartarus. After Zeus and his brothers divided the world into thirds, Prometheus was instructed to create man. From clay and fire, Prometheus sculpted man in the rough image of the gods. During this time, the other gods were making their own creations to populate the earth. Soon, there was a collection of assorted beasts, including man. But they were unrefined and dumb. They lacked consciousness or ability. Zeus saw this collection and ordered Prometheus and Epimetheus to endow the creatures with skills and characteristics.

Epimetheus was often thought of as the lesser of the brothers. Prometheus was renowned for his cunning wit and had been blessed with the gift of foresight. He was a powerful seer, and the Fates whispered in his ear. Epimetheus, on the other hand, was rash and impulsive. He was the embodiment of afterthought and lived only for the moment. When Zeus handed down the assignment to the brothers, Epimetheus saw it as a chance to stand equal to his brother.

"Prometheus, you are too busy with your sculpting of the bronze ones to be bothered with this. I will dispense the features to the featureless and grant capabilities to the incapable. It is a task below your skill and cunning. You can inspect my work when it is done," Epimetheus begged his brother.

Prometheus saw how much his brother wanted to do the job on his own, and he was very busy, so he relented. He told Epimetheus he would be back later to see how he was getting on.

Elated with his opportunity, Epimetheus set to work. One by one he bestowed features, skills, and awareness on the beasts. To provide protection from the elements, cloaks of feathers, fur, or scales were distributed. Hooves, calloused feet, and wings provided a means to travel the earth. Some creatures were made large and some small; some were swift while others were slow; some had many young at once while others had only a few. All these things Epimetheus divided among them, working hard to maintain balance among all things. Remembering that all creatures needed to eat and that they couldn't all eat the same thing, he made some animals eat plants and herbs, while others ate insects, and some ate only the flesh of other animals. He made some of the beasts mighty with weapons and armor while others he left defenseless, though he always provided them with a means of escape. Soon, there were no capabilities or features left to assign, and the beasts of the world were created. Victorious, Epimetheus beckoned them into the light with pride swelling in his breast. His brother and the other gods were going to be so impressed with the way he had outfitted their creatures.

However, Epimetheus saw that he had missed one. There was man, waiting in the dark for his gifts. Frantically, Epimetheus looked around for something to adorn his brother's creation. All he found was a few hairs and nails. He gave them to man, but it remained pitiful and dumb. Nervously, Epimetheus sat next to the clay creature and feverishly tried to think of what to do.

Epimetheus was still sitting there, racking his brain for a solution, when Prometheus came to inspect his work. Prometheus admired the animals with their fur and feathers. He delighted to see them soaring, running, swimming, and slithering everywhere. Then, he saw his brother and his creation still apart in the dark. With a sigh, he went to them, already knowing what happened.

"Oh, my dear brother, when will you learn," he asked wearily as he dropped to the ground next to Epimetheus. "This will not do. Man cannot go into the light like this. He has no armor, no way to defend himself. He has no cleverness or cunning. He cannot provide for himself. No, this will not do," Prometheus murmured as he turned the problem over in his mind.

Ever cunning and clever, it didn't take long for Prometheus to dream up a solution. "Wait here," he told his brother and leapt to his feet, "and do not let it into the light. I will return as quickly as I am able."

Ideally, he would go straight to the great citadel of Zeus atop Mount Olympus. However, he had been banned from the high court for his refusal to tell Zeus the one thing he wanted to know above all else. The Fates had whispered in Prometheus' ear the name of a child and his mother that would dethrone the Father of All. Zeus desperately wanted to know which of his children posed a threat to his reign. Prometheus had sealed his lips against the knowledge and would not unseal them for any reason. He had no delusions that he would be able to slip past Zeus' guards, State and Violence, to steal what he needed. The thought of those two creatures bearing down on him made him shiver in fear. Obtaining divine wisdom and political understanding was beyond his reach at the moment.

Instead, he set his sights on something more immediately necessary and far more useful at this stage of man's development. Prometheus went by stealth to Hephaestus' workshop. He breathed a sigh of relief when he found the smithy empty, save for the ever-burning forge fire. Knowing that he must not be seen, he quickly scooped fire from the forge and stole many of craftsman's talents as he could before fleeing the grotto.

Prometheus stashed his ill-gotten gains in a sea cave and began the next and most dangerous part of his plan. He held his breath as he crept toward the palace of Athena. He needed just a dash of her strength, wisdom, and cunning for his creations. He couldn't help but smile when he found her palace just as empty as Hephaestus' grotto. The Fates were obviously aligned with him, but he didn't want to tempt the fickle sisters by dallying or growing too confident. He knew all too well how quickly they could change their minds. Moving swiftly, he stole into the palace and, in a blink of an eye, gathered what he needed.

Time was truly against him now. He must finish his creation with his stolen talents before their owners noticed they were missing. With all the speed he could muster, he returned to the sea cave before hurrying to where he had left his brother and the creature. Epimetheus helped him to finish the creature called man. When they were done, he stood upright in the manner of the gods and in his mind, he held the knowledge to build and to destroy. He knew how to protect himself and to provide for himself. Prometheus bestowed his last and greatest gift, the ability to make and control fire, just a roar shook the foundations of Mount Olympus. His theft had been discovered.

Prometheus stepped into the bright rays of Helios and brought his creation forth. Zeus, Athena, and Hephaestus appeared moments later. The goddess of war seethed with indignation. Before she could launch into accusations, Prometheus proclaimed, "Mighty Zeus, Queen Athena, and Nimble-fingered Hephaestus! See the last and greatest creation for the Earth. It is the race of man, and he shall honor us. See how he stands straight, and his face is turned to the heavens? He will know and worship your benevolence," he said with a nod to Zeus. With a nod to Athena, he continued, "He is clever, cunning, and strong, and he will thank the Mighty Athena for these gifts." The goddess of war looked slightly mollified and gave the slightest inclination of her head in return. Prometheus turned to Hephaestus, but the god of fire was examining the new creation closely. He moved it this way and that and spoke before Prometheus could offer him pretty words.

"It is a good thing you have given it fire and craftsmanship. It is puny and has no natural defenses. You should have made it better," Hephaestus said before he limped away from the group, apparently finished with the lot of them.

Zeus, happy now that Athena's ire had been cooled, spoke to the new creation. "Hear me now, First of Man. You have been given divine gifts. Use them well and remember where they came from. Be diligent in your gratitude, lest you lose them!" With that proclamation, Zeus and Athena gathered the clouds around them and ascended back to Olympus.

The brothers looked at each and smiled. They had completed their task, and all the creatures of the world were well appointed.

Prometheus needed to make more men. The other creatures had been created in multitudes, but he had made only a single man. So, he set to work, making men from clay and giving them their gifts. Man was quick to learn. He learned to speak, construct a house, and feed and clothe himself. However, he lacked the knowledge of how to interact with others of his race. Each man lived apart and often fell prey to the wild beasts of the world. Prometheus was having a difficult time making men fast enough, so they didn't disappear entirely from the Earth.

Zeus quickly grew to like the way that man paid homage to him, and so did the other gods. They did not want to see the bronze-skinned creations eradicated, so Zeus sent them Shame and Justice. He dispatched Hermes to take these traits to the race of man.

"Mighty Zeus, do I give only a few of these traits or do I give them to all men," the messenger asked before leaving on his task.

"Give them equally among all men that they may know how to form the bonds of friendship and community," Zeus instructed. "You will tell them that anyone who does not obey Shame and Justice will be killed. It is my law, and they must obey."

Hermes left on his winged sandals, and soon, it was done. Villages formed, followed by cities. Order and structure were established, and the race of men took root on the Earth.

The world was still very fresh and new at this point. Prometheus taught the race of man many things. At the order of Zeus, he instructed the mortals about the path to freedom versus slavery. To explain this concept, Prometheus created two tracks. One path was steep and rocky with brambles covering the trail. The other was smooth and level and lined with flowering bushes. He told man to choose his path. Those who chose the more difficult path soon found it opened into a lush valley that was more beautiful than anything they had ever seen. The way easy and the reward was great. The men on the path that was easy at the beginning soon found themselves fighting through thickets of thorn bushes and crawling up rocky, impossibly steep slopes. The trail led to a deep, dark abyss. And thus, the race of man learned that the road to freedom is often difficult, to begin with, but the ultimate destination is worth the work. However, man had to walk the path of slavery many times before they learned that an enticing entrance did not always lead to a beautiful journey.

Prometheus had several apprentices to assist him in making more of the bronze-skinned men for the world. As they crafted more men, they often times endowed them with more characteristics that the gods wished them to have. Prometheus and his new apprentice, Dolos, were crafting a new man in the shape of Veritas, or Truth. Just as they had finished sculpting Veritas, Prometheus was called away and left Dolos in charge in his absence.

Dolos wanted to create something of his very own, so while his master was away, he created another man. However, he ran out of clay as he reached its feet. Before he was able to get more, Prometheus returned. Dolos sat down at the base of the statue, hiding the unfinished section.

Prometheus was astounded by the craftsmanship of his apprentice, and he didn't want anyone to know that he hadn't personally made each creation. So, he quickly fired them in his kiln and imbibed life into them. Veritas stood proudly and walked forward steadily. The copy stood frozen, for he had no feet to carry him forward. He was named Falsehood, and this pair taught man that while things might look the same at first glance, Truth will always show itself in the end.

Prometheus was also often waylaid by his creations with complaints or comments about their characteristics or lot in life. One creature was particularly critical of the way he had been made. Every time Prometheus saw the mighty lion approaching, he cringed inwardly. Lion had been made the king of beasts, and he still wasn't satisfied! One day, Lion accosted Prometheus as he journeyed across the land.

He fell into step next to his creator and said, "I am greater than all the animals. My claws and teeth know no rival, and my wit and cunning are unmatched. Yet, I am terrified of roosters! I cannot abide by them! Why did you make me like this? Why did you give me this terrible burden?"

Prometheus had heard this complaint many times and finally had had enough. "Lion, why are you wasting your time complaining about roosters? You are the king of beasts! You got every good trait we could give you! It is a simple thing. If you don't like roosters, stay away from them. They cannot hurt you anyway, you silly lion. Now, go away before I make you as meek as a field mouse!"

It wasn't long after that that Zeus took away the beasts' ability to speak.

The world continued to take shape as the Olympians added more creations and set down the laws of nature and man. Man became more and more unified and progressed from simple beings to creatures who were cunning, strong, and increasingly independent of their creators. However, they did not forsake their creators and regularly sent up prayers of gratitude to the heavens. Zeus, nevertheless, felt they were not paying enough homage to him and the other gods. He felt that man was beginning to see themselves on par with residents of Mount Olympus. Zeus summoned Prometheus to court to discuss the matter.

"You gave them too many divine traits," Zeus grumbled when Prometheus answered the summons. "They walk upright in our image. Their minds are clever, and now they create cities and communities. They are becoming bold and are not paying homage as they ought."

Prometheus listened to Zeus' complaints in silence with his mind racing through the possible solutions that would appease Zeus. Before Prometheus could answer, Zeus continued, "From now on, the mortals must offer us sacrifice in addition to their prayers. Nothing but their best animal will do. They must make these offerings often lest our wrath be stirred."

Prometheus frowned. This would cause great hardship on the mortals, particularly the poorer ones who did not have as many animals as others. "Mighty Zeus, Father, and Wisest of all. The mortals are yet simple creatures. What you demand will cost them greatly. What do you need entire animals for? You have the greatest herds in all the world! Surely, we can compromise."

Zeus regarded Prometheus for a moment and tried to see if he was being played by the clever god. It was true that he had no need for the sacrifice. He merely wanted the mortals to pay proper homage to their creators. "What do you have in mind, Clever One? Do not be deceitful and play me false, for I warn you, I am in no mood to be toyed with."

Prometheus bowed low to hide his grin. Zeus was all-powerful and omnipotent, but he wasn't as smart as Prometheus - and they both knew it. "I shall return very soon with something that I hope will be to your liking," he said as he swept from the chamber, not waiting for Zeus to dismiss him.

From his own herds, Prometheus selected two of his finest oxen and killed them. From their carcasses, he prepared two offerings. He took them both back to Olympus and laid them at Zeus' feet. "Mighty Cloud Gatherer! I agree that the mortals should offer sacrifice to you and all the gods who bless them with such bounty! Instead of the entire animal, they should offer you the cuts of your choosing and observe the rituals you set forth. What say you, Mighty Zeus? Would that not be sufficient homage? Choose which cut you prefer, and it will be so!"

Zeus looked down at the offerings. One was a bulging stomach and guts of the oxen, and the other was wrapped in a sumptuous hide that was almost bursting at its seams. The stomach of the beast and its entrails held no appeal to him. The choice was obvious. "Bring me the hidden bundle. It is best of the offerings, and I deserve nothing less than the best."

With a graceful bow, Prometheus bore the bundle reverently to Zeus, but before giving it to him said, "Do I have your word that this is the cut the mortals will be required to offer you? You will not demand more?"

Zeus was quickly growing weary of Prometheus and his troublesome mortals. "Yes, I swear by the dark depths of the Styx that this is the offering the mortals shall give and I shall be content with it. Now, let us get this business done!"

Prometheus handed the bundle to Zeus and quickly stepped back. Zeus' face fell and darkened with rage as he unwrapped the beautiful hide to reveal a bunch of bones and gristle. With a flick of his wrist, he opened the stomach to show the prime cuts of meat and fat that had been stuffed inside it.

It didn't take profound forethought to predict Zeus' reaction. Prometheus had already vanished from the court before Zeus had figured out the trick. Once he had Zeus' solemn oath, that was all he needed.

With Prometheus out of reach, Zeus took his anger out on the mortals. With a vengeful wave of his hand, he swept the land and gathered all the fire of the mortals. Not a spark was left. Without it, man suffered greatly. They regressed to living like animals without ways to cook, to warm themselves, or to fend off the wild beasts. Eating raw meat decivilized them, and soon their communities broke down.

For an omnipotent being, Zeus could be incredibly short-sighted. As man fought for survival, they no longer offered up prayers or sacrifices to the gods. They were intent on one thing - staying alive. Prometheus watched his beloved bronze-skinned man fighting among themselves and falling prey to the elements and beasts. Anger burned hot in his belly at Zeus. He would not stand by and let his creations be destroyed.

Prometheus couldn't simply waltz back up Mount Olympus and steal fire from Hephaestus' forge as he had done before. He was the equivalent of an outlaw, and everyone was looking for him. So, clever and cunning as always, he crafted the most luscious pear ever seen. The pale green skin was perfect, and its sweet smell was intoxicating. He tied a scroll to the stem that said, "For the most beautiful and powerful goddess," and with a mighty throw, he threw it all the way into the middle of Zeus' court on top of Mount Olympus.

As expected, each of the goddesses laid claim to the pear, and an intense squabble broke out amongst them. While the goddesses bickered and fought, the other gods looked on with amusement. Prometheus used the distraction to sneak to the highest peak of Mount Olympus and concealed a bit of Helios' bright sun-fire within a fennel stalk. He sped back down the mountain and flew from village to village lighting torches and community hearths as he went. With fire restored, man soon came back together and began to live as civilized beings once more.

Pandora - The First Woman

Zeus was once again furious with both Prometheus and the race of man. He called Hephaestus to him. The crooked-legged god answered the summons as quickly as he was able and stood before Zeus warily, for the Father of All was in a foul temper.

"Master of the Forge, you will create something for me. I wish to send a plague to the mortals. I will send to them something they will embrace with all their hearts that will destroy them even as they cling to it." He gave Hephaestus his instructions and laughed at his own cleverness as the god of the forge lurched away to do his bidding.

The God of Craftsmanship fired his forge and gathered his materials. He mixed clay and water and fashioned it in the form of a maiden. Comely in shape and features, Hephaestus created the first woman. Fresh from the forge, Athena took her and saw her fitted out in beautiful robes. She showed her how to weave and be clever. Aphrodite then instructed her on the ways of a woman and how to seduce and please a man. She taught her to be haughty and cruel as well as sweet and guileless. Hermes tutored the creature on deception and lies, and she was given the gifts of grace, charity, and eloquence.

Zeus oversaw the project with satisfaction. Once the gods had finished bestowing their gifts upon her, she was everything that Zeus had intended. He named her Pandora, meaning All Gifts.

"Behold," Zeus said to the assembly as he brought Pandora into court, "the loveliest creature we have ever made. There shall be nothing more beautiful in the world to the bronze-skinned man than this creature - the woman." The assembly murmured their amazement. She rivaled the beauty of Aphrodite, but she unsettled them with her obvious cunning and guile. Zeus smiled at their reaction. "She will be a plague to man. Woman-kind will bring the race of the bronze-skinned man to their knees. She will never be happy, no matter what man gives her. Her tongue spews forth lies and deceit while she lulls him with her beauty and womanly ways."

It wasn't enough for Zeus that he had created Pandora and the race of women. He wanted to ensure that man would have no escape from them. So, he set a decree that every man should marry a woman. An unwed man would have his property divided among his kinsfolk upon his death, and no one was to observe burial rights for him. He would go to the Underworld without means to pay the ferryman, and his spirit would be doomed to roam the earth for 100 years.

To set the proper example, Zeus arranged Pandora's marriage. He sent Hermes to bring Epimetheus to court. The scatterbrained god quickly answered the summons and was awed with the beautiful creature presented to him. He completely forgot the parting words his brother, Prometheus, had told him only days before, "Accept nothing from Zeus. His ire is stirred, and he cannot be trusted!"

"What say you, Epimetheus? I offer this beautiful maiden to you. Will, you wed her," Zeus asked.

Epimetheus couldn't believe his good fortune. He had never been a favorite of the court, and this was an unexpected boon. He bowed and scraped as he stumbled through words of gratitude.

They were married immediately in the high court. Before the happy couple left Mount Olympus, Zeus spoke to Pandora in private.

"Pandora, I have a wedding present for you," Zeus told her as he presented her with a beautiful lacquered box.

"My thanks, Mighty Zeus," Pandora gushed and beamed a beguiling smile at him.

Zeus felt himself reacting to her smile and quickly stepped away from her. She was indeed the perfect weapon against the simple minds of man, but he had one more blow to deliver. "This box must never be open. It contains powers beyond your imagining. I am trusting you to protect it with your life. Can you do this for me?"

Pandora assured him that she would never lift the lid and went to rejoin her new husband.

Pandora and Epimetheus got on well, and they had a daughter, Pyrrha. Other women came among men, and the bronze-skinned race flourished. Their numbers multiplied, and soon the earth grew crowded.

Marital bliss was not to be found for Pandora and Epimetheus, despite their happiness over the birth of their daughter. The lacquered box sat in the corner, looming like a dark shadow over everything in the house. Epimetheus wanted to open the box. After all, it had been a wedding present. He never could understand why they couldn't open it. Pandora steadfastly refused, though her curiosity pricked her continually to just peek inside. She had begun to wonder if Zeus had been serious about great powers within the box. It probably was nothing more than a pretty trinket.

Finally, after a particularly heated argument, Pandora could no longer withstand the temptation. She would open the box if only to silence her husband's whining. She slid her fingers over the box's smooth surface and flicked open the delicate latch. With a deep breath, she opened the box the smallest fraction.

A roar filled the room like a torrent of darkness spewed from the small box. War, Strife, Famine, Hate, Envy, Poverty, Hunger, Greed, and many more escaped from their confines. Every bad thing known to the gods had been set loose on the world.

Pandora managed to snap the lid shut just before the final thing escaped. Hope lingered in the box, and Pandora clutched it tightly to her breast. She felt the dread around her heart ease a bit as Hope filled her. The world was now full of terrible and destructive forces. However, safe in her box, Hope would always be there for people when they needed it.

Zeus' Revenge

Once Zeus had launched Pandora into the world, he turned his attention to his revenge on Prometheus. He sent out his guards and had the whole host of Olympus watching for him. Prometheus, despite his cunning foresight, wasn't able to evade capture for long. He stood before Zeus and glared at the Cloud Gatherer. He had seen what Zeus had sent into the midst of man and feared for their future.

"And here is the Lofty-Minded One," Zeus sneered at Prometheus. "You see that your precious mortals are on the road to destruction. He will cling to his harbinger of death even as she smiles while feasting on his bones. Are you all out of tricks, Prometheus?"

Indeed, Prometheus didn't have any more ideas to save his skin. He had known when he stole fire from Helios that he would eventually end up here. The Fates had whispered it would be so. However, he had given man a chance to live and even though Zeus believed it only a matter of time before the race of man fell, Prometheus had more faith in their cleverness and resiliency. After all, they were his creation.

When Prometheus said nothing, Zeus continued, "You must be punished for your interference. I have shown leniency with you in the past, but this time you've gone too far. Hephaestus," Zeus bellowed, and the crippled god shuffled forward. "Take Prometheus to the mountains of Caucasus and in their desolation, bind him there with bonds that no man or god can break."

Zeus' guards, Force and Power, flanked Prometheus and together with Hephaestus, went to the Caucasus Mountains. Rocky crags with sparse vegetation fill the peaks of the unforgiving mountains. Force and Power found a particularly gloomy spot with a large boulder. They held Prometheus as Hephaestus bound first his arms and then his legs in heavy chains.

"Hurry up," the guards groused at Hephaestus who seemed to be fiddling with the chains and fetters.

"Why hurry? Can you not see that his wrists and ankles are secure and done so properly," Hephaestus shot back. Prometheus had been his friend and companion for a long time. "I am sorry for your suffering, old friend," he murmured to Prometheus as he drove the first spike into the boulder.

"You had better not let Zeus hear you talking that way," Force growled. "The Thunderer has no patience for fools."

Hephaestus continued his work slowly and methodically. "Have you no mercy? Do you not know what comes for him? You would be in no rush to meet it, I can assure you!"

"I have nothing to fear, for I am not a traitor," Power said easily and prodded Hephaestus with the tip of his spear. "Make haste! It is his own fault for thinking he could outwit the mightiest of all gods."

With a heavy heart, Hephaestus drove home the last spike, and Prometheus was bound inexorably to the boulder. An eagle's screech broke the heavy silence, and they stepped back as the enormous bird landed with a thud on Prometheus' chest. Its talons dug cruelly into the flesh and with lightning precision, its razor sharp beak struck deep into his abdomen to feast on his liver. Prometheus' cries of agony haunted Hephaestus and the guards all the way back to Mount Olympus.

And, thus, Prometheus was bound, and his daily torment of the great eagle eating his liver began. Every night, the eagle would leave, and his body would heal. Every day with the sunrise, he waited with dread for the cry of the eagle as it came to torture him.

After a time of cruel suffering, Hermes alighted in front of the ill-fated god. "Prometheus, Father Zeus sends me with a message. Take heed! You can end your torment, and I will set you free this very day. You will be restored to favor in the court and be welcomed back to Olympus with Zeus' fatherly embrace."

Prometheus was no fool. He knew that Zeus was not benevolent and would not simply set him free. "At what price, Hermes of the Silver Tongue? You speak your pretty words, but I know them to be laced with poison."

Hermes smiled, "Here now, Prometheus. There is no need to be insulting. See where your cleverness has gotten you. You still speak as if you walked freely on the earth. Father Zeus will hear from you the name of the woman who will bear the child that will end his reign. Tell me the name of the usurper to the throne!"

Prometheus wearily shook his head. Zeus had asked for this information countless times over the years. He answered as he always did, "My lips have been sealed against the knowledge in my mind. I shall not speak the name for it is not mine to say."

"Bend your neck, you stubborn fool," Hermes cried in frustration. The morning sun rose higher in the sky, and both gods looked to the sky as the faint cry of the eagle was carried on the breeze. "I knew this to be a waste of my time. Know this, Prometheus, this is just the beginning. Zeus will rain down lightning on your head. He will cast you into the darkest corner of Tartarus. He will entomb you in flames and watch you burn. You can end it all with a simple name!"

The shadow of the eagle glided across the land, heralding its approach. "My fate has long been written and resolved. Zeus will not be the death of me. Go now, you silver-tongued serpent. Slither back to your master and leave me in peace!" Prometheus glared at Hermes and awaited his fate.

The winged messenger shot the bound god one last look of loathing before he disappeared into the sky.

Despite their creator's fate, the race of the bronze-skinned mortals thrived. The addition of women to their ranks allowed them to reproduce and the additional skills led to even more refinement of their society. Their cities grew, and the world found its stride, settling in with an ebb and flow of life. It was a time of bounty and stability, but as with all things, it couldn't last forever. The mortals spread in vast numbers, and Zeus once again became concerned that they felt they were equals with the gods. Threatened by their numbers and unhappy with their arrogance, Zeus decided to walk among them to really learn what was in the hearts and minds of men.

In the Kingdom of Arcadia, he was welcomed to the court of Lycaon. King Lycaon boasted 50 sons and pompous manner that greatly irritated Zeus. As he spent time in the court, he learned that the princes were despised for their cruelty and conceit. Even more disturbing were the rumors of cannibalistic rituals. Whispers flew about human sacrifices and pagan gods. Unsettled by the information, Zeus lingered in the court to discover if there was any truth to the rumors. The Father of All hid his true nature from the king and his court but offered plenty of hints that he was no normal visitor.

King Lycaon noticed his guest might be more than he seemed. To test him, Lycaon ordered the death of a prisoner and mixed his raw entrails into the visitor's supper. Zeus, of course, knew at once that his food was tainted and was enraged by the audacity of the king. With a roar, he upended the table, scattering the feast and dinner guests everywhere.

"You dare serve me the flesh of man? Lycaon, question no further my divinity!" Zeus called down 50 simultaneous bolts of lightning, striking each of the king's sons. Lycaon watched his legacy turn to cinders in front of him.

Terrified and fearing for his life, the king fled. Zeus, disgusted with the man's cowardice, turned him into a wolf and said, "Since you like to serve your guests raw meat, you shall thirst for it for the rest of your miserable life. May the unerring bow of Artemis never give you peace."

Zeus assumed his divine form and returned to Olympus. In his fury, he decided that the race of man was flawed, twisted, and beyond saving. He condemned them all to death.

Prometheus, bound and tortured though he was, still heard the whispers of the Fates. From his distant prison, he feared for his creations. He summoned his mortal son, Deukalion, through the Oceanids, who were his kin and could hear his calls.

Deukalion heeded his father's summons and toiled through the long journey across the mountains of Caucasus. Once he arrived, Prometheus told him what the Fates had whispered to him. "Go forth and build the strongest boat you are able. Take your wife aboard with as many provisions as you can. Make haste, for there is little time."

Deukalion knew better than to doubt his father's words, even though building a boat seemed a foolish thing to do. He hurried back to his home and did as he had been instructed. Just as he and his wife, Epimetheus and Pandora's daughter, Pyrrha, finished filling it with provisions, rain began to fall.

It soon became apparent that this was no ordinary storm. Zeus, from his throne high on Mount Olympus, stirred the clouds furiously, sounded thunder that shook the foundations of the earth, and flung down massive bolts of lightning. Mortals cringed in fear and cried out to the heavens for mercy, but there would be no mercy from the dark-faced Cloud Gatherer. Relentlessly, he poured rain from the sky until a great deluge covered the earth. The bronze-skinned mortals all perished, save Deukalion and Pyrrha, who rode out the storm in their boat.

They wrecked against the very top of Mount Parnassus in the violence of the tempest. There, they cowered as the floods raged but never covered their precarious perch. Finally, the waters began to recede, and Deukalion and Pyrrha made their way down to the temple at Themis. In the ruins of the sanctuary, they made an offering to Phyxius, one of the many faces of Father Zeus and the god of fugitives. As sacrifices go, it was pitiful, taken from their meager provisions, but it pleased Zeus, nonetheless. His anger had abated, and he whispered winged words to them to seek the counsel of the Oracles of Delphi.

Together, the two remaining mortals traveled to Delphi and offered their final provisions in sacrifice that the mighty oracle would grant them wisdom.

The Oracle regarded the mortals and their offering. She was moved by their plight and knew the desire of their hearts. "Go forth with veiled faces and open your robes. Cast behind you the bones of your mother, and humanity will rise again!"

Pyrrha was filled with fear, and she dropped to her knees, bowing so low she touched her forehead to the ground. "Oh, gentle goddess, do not ask this of us! We will vex the spirits of the departed, and they will bring us grief! Tell us another way, oh seer of all!"

The Oracle made no reply. True to the nature of oracles, once they speak on a subject, they will say no more.

Deukalion and Pyrrha spoke on it for a long time. Deukalion concluded that oracles did not seek to trick or harm the seekers who came to them begging their knowledge. "If this is so, then the mother of whom she speaks cannot be our mortal mothers. She must be speaking of the mother of all and the bringer of all life, Gaia, Mother Earth," Pyrrha speculated excitedly.

"Exactly," Deukalion agreed, "and her bones must be stones, for they are the foundation of the world."

Without any better ideas, they veiled their faces and opened their robes. As they walked away from the Oracle, they cast stones behind them. Much to their amazement, every stone they dropped began to soften and shift its shape. From the smallest pebble to the largest rock they could carry, each stone grew into a person. Every rock Deukalion cast became a man, and every stone that fell from Pyrrha's hands formed a woman. In this miraculous way, the human race was reborn, and the silver age of man began.

Zeus's Love Life and Hera's Jealousy

Zeus was quite possibly the greatest philanderer of all time. However, this isn't unusual for mythological figures who are considered the All-Father figure in the pantheon. In Zeus' case, he seemingly embraced this role with gusto. His amorous conquests were legendary, and his libido knew no bounds.

Zeus had a total of seven wives, countless lovers and paramours, and dozens of offspring. His wives were taken simultaneously, and as you can imagine, seven wives at once cause more than a little contention on Mount Olympus! His first wife was Metis, the wise and beautiful Oceanid who counseled him on how to liberate his siblings from Cronos' body.

After Zeus banished the Titans, he sought a wife to help rule his new kingdom. He decided that Metis, with her sage wisdom and cunning mind, would be the perfect wife for a king. However, being the wisest of all the gods, Metis knew that Zeus would never be a faithful, loving husband. She spurned his advances. Like most kings, Zeus was not one to take "no" for an answer, and ultimately through his power and persistence, Metis relented and became his wife. It didn't take long for Metis' fears to be realized. She often observed her husband switching to an animal form to sneak off for a rendezvous with another woman. Metis, clever as always, began to use his same tactics against him. Whenever he sought her out, she transformed into an animal and slipped away.

"Wife, I grow tired of this," Zeus groused. "I challenge you to a shape-shifting duel. I want you to promise me that if I best you, you will never again avoid your wifely duties."

Metis took up the challenge, confident she could outwit him. Every time Zeus changed into an animal, Metis anticipated his choice and transformed into something bigger and nastier. As animals, they fought and wrestled with each other until they finally both collapsed, exhausted.

"You are too smart for me," Zeus praised his wife. Metis preened under the compliment. "Give me one more chance, my love," Zeus cajoled. "You are clearly superior as a mighty beast, but what about a wee insect? Do you think you can best me on a smaller scale?"

Metis, emboldened by her victory, promptly turned into a tiny but very quick and agile fly. Instead of turning into an insect, Zeus snatched Metis from where she was buzzing in his ear and swallowed her. Satisfied, Zeus patted his stomach and enjoyed his victory.

Zeus actually hadn't been upset about Metis' reluctance to warm his bed. Rhea had whispered a prophecy to him saying Metis would bear two formidable children and the second would be a boy who would ultimately overthrow Zeus. And so, like his father and grandfather before him, Zeus acted to secure his throne. However, he didn't know that Metis was already with child. Deep in Zeus' belly, Metis raged at being outsmarted. Her pride was stung, but she knew that the babe in her belly must live. She built a forge and crafted an impenetrable suit of armor for her daughter. As you might imagine, all this activity caused Zeus much discomfort until the pain intensified in his head to unbearable proportions. Crazed with agony, Zeus tore at his hair and ordered Prometheus to split his head open with an ax to release the pain. When Prometheus struck, Athena, the goddess of war, sprang from Zeus' head fully clad in the armor made for her by her mother.

As for Metis, she had grown to care for Zeus and knew that he needed her council. So, she stayed within him to guide and counsel him throughout his reign. She never bore her second child, and the prophecy went unfulfilled. Zeus would claim that he alone bore Athena, but Metis was most assuredly Athena's mother.

A king needs a queen, so Zeus sought out another wife. This time he chose Themis. Themis, the goddess of justice and prophecy, was actually two goddesses in one. Mother Tethys and her daughter, Themis, merged together, became known by the daughter's name, and embodied the strengths of each. Themis was born of the sky, sea, and earth and was always in perfect harmony. She offered Zeus advice as he set laws governing the world. Often, she stayed Zeus' hand when his vengeance clouded his judgment. When thieves attempted to steal the sacred honey of Diktaion, Zeus wanted to destroy them with his thunderbolts. Themis tempered his rage and would not allow him to sully the sacred space with death. Heeding her counsel, Zeus turned the thieves into birds instead.

Themis bore Zeus several children. Together, they brought forth Horea, the goddess of law and order; Irene, the goddess of peace; Dike, the goddess of justice; and Eunomia, the goddess of order. They all became the wardens of the gates to Mount Olympus. Though Zeus moved onto subsequent wives, Themis was never far from his side. Steadfast and unbiased, she maintained balance and order in his court.

After Themis, Zeus took to wife Eurynome, another Oceanid and daughter of the Titans Oceanus and Tethys. Goddess of the watery pastures, Eurynome was what we would recognize today as a mermaid, meaning she was a woman from the waist up and a fish from the waist down. Eurynome mothered the three Charities: Aglaea, goddess of beauty; Euphrosyne, goddess of mirth; and Thalia, goddess of good cheer.

Zeus' fourth conquest was his sister Demeter. Demeter was the goddess of grain and harvest. With flowing golden hair and surrounded by the sweet smells of grain and the essence of the earth, Demeter was one of the most desirable of all the goddesses. In an epic coupling, Demeter and Zeus came together in the form of giant serpents to mate. The result was Persephone, who would one day rule as the Queen of the Underworld. Neither Demeter nor Zeus seemed to worry much about fidelity within their union. Though their relationship was fleeting, Zeus often remarked about Demeter's beauty and the passion they shared.

Zeus was not yet done taking wives. His fifth wife was Mnemosyne, the goddess of memory, and one of the original Titans. For nine nights, Zeus and Mnemosyne lay together. They produced the nine Muses. These sisters were the goddess of art, literature, and music. Tutored by Apollo on Mount Olympus, they each developed a special talent. However, they often performed together and bewitched gods and mortals alike with their beauty and song.

Calliope was the eldest and their leader. The Muse of epic poetry, eloquence, rhetoric, she often whispered advice and ideas to kings and rulers.

Clio, the Muse of history, recorded and celebrated events and was never without a scroll upon which to write.

The muse of lyrical poetry, Erato, was often accompanied by Eros and Cupid and had her own quiver of golden arrows of love.

Euterpe was the muse of music and carried an aulos, a double-headed flute, that she used to make the most beautiful melodies.

Melpomene was the muse of tragedy. She wore a theatrical mask and was known to move even the most hardhearted man to tears.

Polyhymnia, the goddess of hymns and sacred poems, rarely spoke and always wore a veil. She was the most serious of the sisters and often frowned upon their revelry.

Her sister Thalia, the muse of comedy, had a quick wit and sharp tongue and learned at an early age to ignore Polyhymnia's disapproving glares. Every day was an endless joy to Thalia.

As the muse of dance, Terpsichore could hypnotize an audience with her movements and often played the lyre while she danced.

The final sister, Urania, had a unique gift that was very different than her sisters' talents. Urania was the muse of astronomy, and her eyes were often fixed heavenward. Closest of all Muses to their father, Zeus, Urania learned to read the future in the stars.

These nine gifted women entertained the Olympians, inspired mortals, and recorded the histories of gods and men.

Leto

The sixth wife of Zeus was Leto, who was a second-generation Titan. Legendarily beautiful, her parents tried to disguise her beauty so she would escape the notice of the philandering Zeus. Even though she kept her face covered by a veil, her cascades of dark hair and sweet disposition caught the king's attention. Leto, goddess of modesty and motherhood, had been endowed with kindness and gentleness to all men. When Zeus took her to wife, she did not object. The only trouble was that Zeus' seventh wife, Hera, was exceedingly jealous of Leto with her shy smiles and unassuming nature. Once she learned that Leto was pregnant with twins, Hera became consumed by her jealousy. She cursed Leto that she would not bring her babes into the world on the mainland, or island, or anywhere under the sun.

Not content with her curse, she whispered to the great serpent, Python, "See the lovely Leto of the shy smiles and dark curls. Her belly grows heavy with a son and a daughter. Her son will be the death of you, so sayeth the oracle."

Python immediately began to hunt Leto, intent on killing her and her unborn children. Pursued by the giant snake, Leto fled from Mount Olympus but found no sanctuary anywhere she roamed. Hera threatened any land that welcomed Leto, and everyone knew that Hera's wrath was nothing to be toyed with. From island to island and across the mountains and plains, Leto wandered relentlessly even after her labor set upon her. As her pains increased, she frantically sought refuge and finally found the floating island of Delos.

Delos had been created when Leto's sister, Asteria, transformed into a quail and flung herself into the sea to escape Zeus' seduction. She became an island that fell like a star from the heavens, but she never rested in the sea. Heaven sent, she hovered above the surface. Since Delos floated above the sea, it was exempt from Hera's curse. Rocky and unwelcoming, it had a single palm tree to protect Leto from the sun and allow her to escape Hera's curse. Zeus, who could not openly defy Hera, secretly called the North Wind to cloak the island and hide Leto from the relentless pursuit of Python. It was the only thing he could do to help her.

Leto spoke to the island, "Great Delos! Will you welcome me? I carry in my womb Apollo, the Archer Prince, and he will be mighty among the gods. No other gods want you. You have no cattle or fields of grain. If you let me rest here, Apollo will build a temple here, and his faithful followers will call you home."

Delos answered the weary Leto, "Gentle Lady, you would be welcome here, but I confess that I am afraid. I am afraid that the prince will take one look at my rocky soil and barren hills and seek out fertile land and lush forests to build his temple. He will leave me to be battered by the waves and riddled with caves inhabited by sea monsters. Nay, lady, unless you swear a holy oath that the first temple of Apollo will be built on my shores, you cannot tarry here."

Leto smiled and didn't hesitate to answer, "Mighty Delos, I swear by steadfast Gaia and boundless Uranus that the temple will be built here, but hear me, Delos, I swear by the inky depths of the Styx that my son, Apollo, the Archer Prince, will honor you first above all." Delos welcomed Leto, for by invoking the River Styx, she had made the gravest of all oaths.

Leto's time was upon her, and she barely made it to the palm tree before she gave birth to Artemis, goddess of the hunt. For the next nine days, Leto's labor stretched on and on. Her pains were unspeakable, but her second babe did not come. Other goddesses attended her in her confinement. Rhea, Themis, and Amphitrite, Poseidon's wife, all did what they could, but none of them knew how to help poor Leto. They waited for Eileithyia, the midwife to the gods, to come and ease Leto's suffering. When it became obvious that something, or someone, was preventing Eileithyia from hearing Leto's cries, the goddesses summoned Iris, the goddess of the winds and a messenger of Zeus. They made a stunning necklace from gold and gems to pay her to take a message to the midwife.

Iris went to Mount Olympus where Hera was distracting the midwife and masking the cries of Leto. Iris sent words on the wind to Eileithyia so Hera could not hear. Upon hearing of Leto's distress, Eileithyia left straight away for Delos. Soon, with the wise midwife's help, Apollo was brought into the world, and Leto in her joy and gratitude cause four large pillars to erupt from the ocean, anchoring Delos to the sea and making it a proper island. Both Apollo and Artemis were strong babies and grew rapidly. They would reach full maturity in a matter of days.

After her labor, Leto began to journey with her children back to Mount Olympus, but the young mother's troubles were not yet over. Leto crossed the province of Lycia, and the summer sun beat down on her relentlessly. Her throat was parched, and her small children were weary. When she came upon a lake at the edge of a village, she knelt gratefully to drink. The villagers rushed forth and forbid her to take even a sip of water.

"Why can't I drink? I'm so thirsty, and my children are so tired. We just want to refresh ourselves, and we will be gone," Leto pleaded with the hardhearted villagers. They still adamantly refused to let her quench her thirst and threw mud at her and the children.

"How dare you block the way to what belongs to everyone! The water in this lake is not yours any more than it is mine! I'm not asking to bathe in it. We simply want a drink," Leto tried to reason with the mob.

They were having none of it and began to threaten Leto and the children with their pitchforks and scythes. Finally, Leto had had enough. In a rare show of temper and strength, Leto drew herself up. "Since you are so very fond of your mud and your water, let me make it so you will never be separated from it again!" With a wave of her hand, she transformed all the villagers into frogs.

With a satisfied smile, Leto bent to drink her fill and let the children refresh themselves while the frogs raised a croaking chorus around them.

The small family traveled on, but they soon encountered another obstacle. As they crossed the land of Pytho, Hera whispered words on the wind to the giant Tityus who dwelt there. Tityus was the son of Zeus and a mortal woman named Elara. He was one of the largest of the giants and had grown so large in his mother's womb, he split it in two. Zeus then gave him to Gaia, the mother of all, to carry until he was ready to be born. Tityus possessed a nasty temper, a lustful nature, and a volatile personality. Hera's words told him about Leto's beauty and her demure disposition. Inflamed with lust and desire by Hera's words, Tityus hid among the high hills to wait in ambush.

Leto, Artemis, and Apollo worked their way across the valleys and hills of Pytho, unaware of the lurking danger. Without warning, Tityus leapt from his hiding place and grabbed Leto by her robes. With a couple of his giant strides, he stole Leto away from her children. Artemis and Apollo gave chase. They were fully grown by this point and had full command of their talents and powers. Even though he was a giant, Tityus had the Archer Prince and the Goddess of the Hunt on his tail. He didn't get far before they caught up with him. Leto called out to her children to save her as Tityus tried to force himself on her. Apollo and Artemis let their arrows fly. The giant dropped Leto and advanced on the twins.

49

They emptied their quivers but could not kill Tityus. He was born of a god and was immortal.

Zeus, furious about the attack on his wife and children, intervened and struck Tityus down with a thunderbolt. He banished him to the Underworld. In punishment, Hades staked the giant to a patch of ground. Tityus was so big, he covered nine acres worth of land! Unable to move, Tityus suffered day after day as vultures and snakes ate his liver and other soft juicy bits.

Leto and the twins finally returned to Mount Olympus. However, it was not a happy homecoming for Leto. Even as she once again took up her place in Zeus' court, she heard murmurings from the city of Thebes, where she had a large temple of faithful followers. The queen of the city, Niobe, was growing increasingly proud and was demanding the citizens worship her as opposed to Leto.

Niobe entered the temple of Leto as the faithful made offerings and exulted their goddess. She was draped in the robes like a goddess with jewels and gold thread. Her skin glowed creamy white, and her golden hair trailed down her back. Niobe looked about her with scornful disdain. She ripped down the laurels that adorned the head of Leto's statue. Tossing them aside, Niobe stood on the dais as the crowd quieted and looked up at her in terrified awe.

"What fools you are! Why do you raise your voices and make your offerings to an invisible god? You have never seen her, yet here I stand in front of you, as much a goddess as the one you bend your knees for. I hear no prayers to my name. I see no offerings for me.

My father was favored by the gods and sat at their table. My mother was one of their blood. My husband is the king of this great city, and I am your queen. Everywhere I look, I see evidence of my power and my will. I see nothing here of from the god you grovel before. Leto, the goddess of motherhood, has only two children. Bah! I have fourteen children - seven strong boys and seven beautiful girls. She is practically childless. I could never be as pitiful as her! Fortune smiles on me and shall continue to. Do any of you deny this?" The petrified worshippers said nothing as they cringed in fear at Niobe's feet.

Leto observed this speech from Mount Olympus, and it was the final straw. She called to her children and told them to remind Niobe who the true goddess was. Artemis and Apollo immediately cloaked themselves in clouds and descended to Thebes. Apollo delivered swift vengeance and killed all the sons of Niobe.

Witnesses of the carnage screamed and fell to the ground in the face of Apollo's wrath. Niobe heard the tumult and left the temple to find her sons dying in the street. She fell to her knees and crawled from son to son, kissing them and crying over their bodies.

The citizens of Thebes shook their heads and whispered among themselves, "See Niobe now! Look what her pride has brought her."

Niobe pulled herself from the blood and the dirt and shouted to the heavens, knowing Leto would hear her words. "Oh yes, cruel Leto! Are you enjoying your victory? Are you reveling in my grief?

Still, even as I set the night alight with seven pyres, I am still richer than you! You cannot steal my triumph!"

Artemis showed her how very wrong she was. Before the final words left Niobe's lips, Artemis' bowstring sung as arrow after arrow flew. Within minutes, none of Niobe's children continued to draw breath. Niobe's husband was overcome by the devastation and plunged a dagger into his heart. Niobe crumpled under the weight of her grief and collapsed in the street. Zeus, who had been watching, took pity on her. He turned her into stone and cast her high in the mountains where she could look down over the city. Even as a rock, Niobe could not contain her tears. Water leaked from her stony face and has never ceased.

Hera

Hera, Zeus' seventh wife, held the title of the Queen of the Heavens and sat on a throne on Zeus' right. Sister to Zeus, Hera's cunning and desire for power made her one of the most feared and vengeful of the gods. Her abilities were almost on par with Zeus, who often went through great lengths to avoid her wrath.

Hera wasn't at all interested in marrying Zeus when he first pursued her. She knew of his other wives and his philandering nature. Every time Zeus would approach her, she would flee. They engaged in this immortal's game of tag until Zeus tricked her. He appeared to her as a cuckoo bird with a hurt wing. As Hera cuddled the poor bird close to her breast, Zeus transformed back and ravaged her on the spot. Hera decided to marry Zeus rather than have the stigma of being one of his conquests that he cast aside.

They were married by Eros, the primordial god of love and desire, in a grand celebration that went on over 300 years.

As the goddess of marriage, Hera adhered to a high marital standard and never strayed from the bounds of her union with Zeus. Zeus, as we know, held no such convictions. His numerous dalliances and affairs infuriated Hera. As with Leto, Hera tormented Zeus' conquests and offspring, causing Zeus to go through great lengths to hide his indiscretions.

Semele, a princess of Thebes, learned first-hand about the jealous nature of Hera. She was an exceedingly beautiful woman and caught the eye of Zeus from his heavenly throne. He seduced Semele in the form of a mortal man but confided in her his true identity and swore her to secrecy. Their liaisons did not escape the ever-vigilant eye of Hera. Hera disguised herself as the princess' childhood nurse, Beroe, and sought out Semele in the court of Thebes. Semele was overjoyed to see her old friend and was brokenhearted that she couldn't confide her greatest secret to Beroe.

"Oh, faithful Beroe! If only you knew what wonderful tidings I hide behind my lips. It is a secret, and I cannot tell even a trusted friend such as you. You would be so jealous of me," Semele whispered as she embraced her friend.

Hera, in the guise of Beroe, smiled at the young princess with a knowing look. "Oh, you do not have to tell these old ears anything, for my eyes can see plainly the blush of love on your cheeks. I wonder what lucky young suitor has caught your fancy."

Semele smiled back and looked around them anxiously. No one else was paying them the least bit of attention. Unable to hold such momentous news back, Semele spoke close to her nurse's ear. "The King of Heaven, the Mighty Zeus himself has taken me to his bed. Oh, Beroe! He says that I am the loveliest of all the creatures in heaven and earth, and I am carrying his child." Semele's eyes danced with excitement as she confided her secret.

Hera's jealousy burned white hot in the depths of her dark heart. Not only had Zeus lain with a mortal woman, but he had also told her that she was more beautiful than Hera and had gotten her with child. She shook her head at the young woman. "Bah! The King of Heaven? It is more likely a young upstart with a pretty face that has bewitched your mind. How do you know he is the mighty Zeus? What proof has he given?"

Semele's excitement dimmed slightly. It was true that she had no proof beyond his word that her lover was actually the king of the gods.

Hera saw the uncertainty in the girl's eyes and pressed her advantage. "Next time he comes to you, demand that he offers you a boon. Make him swear an oath and when he does, ask him to reveal himself to you in all his glory. Ask him to come to you as he would his wife, Hera. If he is who he says he is, this should be a simple request."

Semele frowned. "I trust him. He doesn't need to prove anything to me," she retorted and stomped out of the court.

The seeds of doubt had been firmly planted in Semele's mind, however, and when next Zeus came to her, she decided that she had to know his identity for sure.

"May I ask a boon of you, my love," Semele asked sweetly as she eagerly went to his embrace.

Zeus raised an eyebrow but didn't hesitate. "If it is within my power, then by the dark waters of the Styx, you shall have it!"

Semele took a deep breath and before she could lose her nerve, blurted, "I want you to show me you are a god. I want you to come to me in your full glory as if I were Hera, Queen of the Heavens."

Zeus frowned at the request and encouraged her to choose something else. But Semele would not be dissuaded, and he could not break his oath. Knowing the consequences of his actions, he let his mortal disguise fall away, and Semele beheld him as a god. Thunder and lightning swirled around them as his magnificence overwhelmed her. Unable to withstand such an assault, she was consumed by it. In the split second, before she was incinerated to dust, Zeus took the babe from Semele's womb and stitched it into his thigh, effectively hiding it from Hera.

When it was time for the infant to be born, Zeus undid the stitches and Dionysus was brought into the world. Dionysus was the only Olympian who was born of a mortal parent. He became the god of wine and celebration. Zeus entrusted him to a trio of nymphs to raise far from Olympus and his spiteful wife.

Hera didn't reserve her ire only for her husband's mortal lovers. Goddesses, like Leto, also felt her wrath if they let themselves be seduced by Zeus. Another goddess who fell afoul of Hera was one of her own priestesses, the nymph, Io. Zeus became enraptured by the beauty of Io and true to form, attempted to seduce her. Io, knowing Hera's temper all too well, refused him. Every night, Zeus sent erotic dreams to Io until, at her wit's end with desire and lack of sleep, she succumbed to Zeus' advances. Hera heard court whispers about the affair. When she confronted Zeus about it, he blatantly denied ever laying with Io. Hera accepted his words, though she didn't believe them.

After a time, Hera sought out her husband and found him in a lavish garden within the palace. He had with him a beautiful white cow. Hera knew instantly that it was no ordinary cow.

"Here now, my husband, my King! What a fine cow you have. She is above all other cows in every way." Hera walked around the beast, admiring her from every angle.

Zeus, who had turned Io into the cow to hide her from Hera, answered his wife, "You are mistaken, my Lady Queen. She is just an ordinary cow and is far beneath your notice." Zeus desperately wanted Hera to lose interest so he could spirit his lover away from the palace.

"Will you do something for me," Hera asked sweetly, looking at Zeus with beguiling innocence.

"Of course! If it is within my power, I swear by the murky water of the Styx, it is yours," Zeus answered. Apparently, he hadn't learned his lesson about swearing unbreakable oaths.

"I want that cow," Hera said simply. "I think she will make a fine addition to my herd."

Zeus had no choice but to give his wife the cow. Even as Hera led the beast away, he began to plot how to steal her back. However, Hera wasn't going to make it easy. She summoned the all-seeing one, Argos. A giant who was covered with a hundred eyes, he was one of Hera's faithful servants and her key informant. Nothing escaped his keen gaze. She asked Argos to take the cow away and to watch over it.

Away from the high court, Argos and Io in her cow form roamed the pastures of Mount Olympus. Zeus knew he would not be able to sneak past the all-seeing gaze of the giant, so he called Hermes to his side. "Follow this bird," he said, indicating a small falcon-like bird called a hyrax. "She will take you to where Argos watches over my beloved Io. I want you to kill Argos and bring Io back to me."

Hermes dutifully followed the bird and came upon the cow and giant. Careful to stay out of sight, he played a gentle lullaby on his flute. Soon, all one hundred eyelids began to droop. Hermes played until the giant was sound asleep. Silently, he threw a rock that struck Argos' head and killed him on the spot. Hera, who had been keeping tabs on the pair expecting something like this from her husband, took the eyes of her faithful servant and set them into the tail feathers of the peacock, her favorite bird. She then created a gadfly from the shade of Argos and possessed it to ceaselessly torment the flesh of the cow.

Hermes watched in horror as the cow, driven mad by the stinging fly, began to rampage through the hills. In a matter of moments, the cow had disappeared, and Hermes was forced to return to Zeus empty-handed. Io wandered for years and years. She covered all the corners of the known world, never able to stop lest the fly began his never-ending torture. During her wanderings, she happened upon Prometheus, one of the Titans, where he was bound to a boulder in punishment for offending Zeus.

"Please tell me, Clever One, what I am to do," Io asked the bound god, who had not acknowledged her presence. "I have wandered for years and years and...Ouch! Oh, the fly! It never leaves me! Dear Mother Earth, open beneath me and swallow me! Consume me by fire - anything! Just, please, end my torment! I have learned many lessons, but I have not discovered how to escape this misery! Can you hear my words, Bound One?"

"Yes, I hear the word of the maid that stirs the fire of passion in Mighty Zeus. I hear the words of the daughter of Inachus, the one who Hera hates above all others," Prometheus replied from his rock. "I can tell you how to end your torment, but you must first tell me how you came into this trouble."

"Please, don't make promises that you cannot keep! I will tell you of my wretched state, for what can that hurt?" Io told Prometheus her story. "And, so, now you know my shame. Now tell me, as you promised, how can I be free of this punishment?"

"You must head east toward the land where the sun rises. Avoid the nomads of Skythian, for they are not friendly to strangers and stay to coast away from the savage Chalybes. Over the mighty peak of Caucasus, you must travel until you come to the land of the Amazons. There they will guide you to the channel of Maeotis. You must have courage and ford the mighty river. The Amazons will sing hymns to your name once you have crossed it!" Prometheus paused and looked at Io, who was shivering in terror. "Why are you shaking and crying? What I have told you is but an introduction!"

"Oh, I should just throw myself off a cliff or dash my head against the rocks. How am I to do all of that? Ouch! Oh, this cursed fly," Io moaned as she thrashed about trying to escape the incessant stings.

"Be still and listen," Prometheus snapped. "You must remember all I tell you. Once you leave the mighty river, you will cross the plains of Cisthene. Heed me well, child. Beware the three sisters who share a single eye among them. They will end you if they see you. So too will Medusa and her sisters, the Gorgons, with their serpent tresses and gazes that turn mortals to stone. Past these terrors, you must go, but they are not the worst of them. You must escape the notice of the fearsome cyclopes and sharp-beaked griffins as well. Travel on to the fathomless cataract high in the Bybline Mountains. Here you will find Nile, who will see you safely across to the land of Neilos. There, dear Io, will you be allowed to rest. On shores of the mighty river, you shall find the peace you seek."

Io stared at Prometheus in wonder. How could he think that she would ever be able to survive such a journey? Of course, what choice did she have? She could either stay a cow tormented by a biting fly forever or find this new land. Resigned to the fact that either way she would likely die a miserable death, Io thanked Prometheus for the information.

"I wish you well, daughter of Inachus. Heed all that I have told you. Do you remember it all? I can retell any part you need, for I have far more leisure time than I desire," Prometheus said as he looked gloomily at the bonds that held him firmly to the bolder.

Io bade him farewell and began her long journey. Her travels were arduous, but she finally rested on the banks of the Nile. As foretold, Io finally found peace. Changing back into her human form, she gave birth to Zeus' son, Epaphos. Hera heard of the birth of Io's son and sent the Curetes, the same band of warriors who guarded Zeus as a child, to murder the baby. Zeus heard about the plot and killed the Curetes to allow Io and her child to start a new life in peace.

Hera was not the only jealous party in the marriage. Even though Hera never offered to stray from her marriage vows, she still had numerous admirers. The king of Lapiths, Ixion, had been given asylum by Zeus on Mount Olympus after he murdered his father-in-law. While he was a guest in Zeus' court, he fell in love with the beautiful Hera. When she rejected all his advances, Ixion attempted to force himself on her. Hera escaped the attack and told Zeus about their guest's bad behavior. Zeus didn't totally trust his wife and wanted to confirm the report. He fashioned a group of clouds in Hera's likeness and laid them next to Ixion. The ex-king was fooled and attempted to take advantage of the Hera look-alike. When Zeus saw this, he was furious that his hospitality had been so poorly repaid. He cast Ixion into the sky like a wheel that stretched across the heavens, turning endlessly while being scorched by the fires of the sun.

The court of Hera and Zeus was often tumultuous as the pair frequently argued about everything from who was the most powerful to which sex enjoyed the pleasures of the flesh more - man or woman. Zeus claimed that women enjoyed the act more, and, of course, Hera said it was just the opposite. The argument finally got so heated, they had to call in a mediator to help settle it. Teiresias, a priest in the house of Apollo, had a unique viewpoint on the subject, and was one of the few people who had ever experienced the act as both a man and a woman.

Once, Teiresias had seen two snakes mating. He killed the female snake and was changed into a woman. After living and loving as a woman for a time, he saw a second set of snakes mating and this time killed the male, changing himself back into a man. As he knelt before the King and Queen of Heaven, he listened to the arguments of each. Once they had both presented their case, the priest spoke, "A man can enjoy only one of the ten pleasures, but a woman can enjoy them all."

Hera, with her typical flash temper, blinded the priest for taking Zeus' side. Zeus, feeling magnanimous after being given a rare victory over his wife, granted Teiresias the prophet's sight and he became one of the greatest clairvoyants of the age.

Another time, Hera became so enraged with her husband, she left the court on Mount Olympus all together. No matter how sweetly Zeus pleaded, she would not return. Zeus, despite Hera's hateful disposition, wanted his wife by his side, so he sought out the wise god of the mountains, Kithaeron. Kithaeron told him to carve a woman from wood, wrap it in fine garments, and put it in a wagon. Zeus was to drive the wagon blatantly down the road of Euboia, announcing his impending marriage to the lovely daughter of Asopos. As Kithaeron knew she would, Hera heard of Zeus' upcoming nuptials and flew down from her mountain hiding place. She tore the garments from the wooden woman and made to strike her down. When Hera realized that the woman really wasn't a woman, she knew that she had been tricked. However, she was pleased that Zeus had gone through so much trouble to bring her home. With her pride assuaged, she and Zeus returned to their court in Mount Olympus.

Despite the marital strife, Zeus and Hera managed to have several children together. First born was Ares, the god of war. Ares differed from Athena's role in the war. He loved violence and strife. Ares reveled in bloodshed and tumult. He often stirred up conflict among the gods and men just so they would fight and then prolonged the battle by aiding both sides. Unsurprisingly, he was little loved by his parents or his fellow gods.

After Ares came Eileithyia, goddess of childbirth and midwife to the gods. She was worshipped devoutly by expectant mothers. Eileithyia's favor could mean the difference between short, painless labor and a lengthy, miserable ordeal. Eileithyia greatly valued chastity and monogamy. A laboring mother who did not meet her expectations would be punished by an especially cruel and painful labor.

Finally, Hera and Zeus had Hebe. Hebe, the goddess of youth and vitality, became the cupbearer to the gods. She poured ambrosia and often helped her brother, Ares, ready himself for war. She was the counterbalance to Geras, the demon that embodied old age. Personified as a feeble old man, Geras was the offspring of Nyx, the goddess of the night. Hebe was brought forth to maintain balance. She would eventually go on to become the wife of Hercules.

Hephaestus

Hera had one other child, but Zeus was not the father. In fact, no man or god fathered this child. Zeus claimed that Athena was his daughter by no woman, despite the role of Mitis in the process. Not to be bested by her husband, Hera decided to create a child all on her own and brought forth Hephaestus. Unfortunately, Hephaestus wasn't a glorious goddess of war like Athena. His legs were malformed, and he was puny and weak. Disgusted and embarrassed, Hera flung the infant off Mount Olympus into the sea. The Titan, Thetis, found the baby and fostered him in her grotto deep within the sea. There, Hephaestus came into his powers as the god of fire and forge. From his labors at the forge, his arms and chest grew strong and stout, but his legs were forever crippled. Thetis refused to tell him who his parents were, but Hephaestus had heard the whispers of the other gods. Frustrated by the lack of answers, he created a magnificent chair of gold and sent it as a gift to Hera. Crafted with unequaled skill, the chair gleamed and was covered with intricate designs. Hera was immensely pleased by such an opulent gift and didn't hesitate to take her place upon it. The instant that she sat down, fetters sprang forth and bound her to the chair. No matter how she struggled, she could not get free.

Hephaestus made his slow, lurching way up the slope of Mount Olympus. The other gods watched his shambling, stooped walk and laughed at the poor misshapen creature. As he passed the gods, he offered them ambrosia, and they were surprised to see his muscular broad chest and arms. They began to wonder if they had underestimated Hephaestus. Finally, he came to a stop in front of the throne he had made for Hera.

His mother glared down at him. "You are responsible for this? How dare you treat me thus! Release me this instant," she demanded.

Hephaestus shook his head. "My Queen, you have but to ask one question and the fetters will fall away. Who are my parents? What gods created and discarded me?"

Hera looked wildly around at the assembly who were all listening intently. They all suspected they knew the truth, but Hera had never publicly acknowledged Hephaestus as her son. "You think you are born of the gods? Look at you! Crippled and twisted; ugly and hated! How could you have come from divinity?"

Hephaestus nodded and turned to leave. He had not expected Hera to answer. With the patience born from living with a constant struggle, he left the court while Hera shouted for him to return and release her.

Zeus watched the entire scene and did nothing to help his wife. Hera pleaded with her hard-hearted husband to free her. Finally, the King of Heaven decreed that whoever brought Hephaestus back to the court would have Aphrodite's hand in marriage. Aphrodite agreed to Zeus' plan because she had long nurtured a desire for Ares, the god of war, and knew if anyone would be able to catch Hephaestus, it would be him. For his part, Ares had little use for love or marriage, but he did want to show that he was unequivocally the strongest of all the gods.

Ares donned his armor, took up his arms, and went down to the cave where Hephaestus had built his vast forge. Confident that the cripple would put up little resistance, Ares marched straight up to the mouth of the cave. As soon as his foot crossed the threshold, fire and lava rained down on him, causing him to beat a hasty, undignified retreat to Mount Olympus. After Ares' defeat, none of the other gods felt bold enough to take Hephaestus by force. Even the promise of the lovely Aphrodite was not enough to entice them to make another attempt.

Dionysus, the god of wine, had a different idea. Never accepted among the gods on Olympus since he was half mortal, Dionysus dwelt on the fringes of the heavenly court, mostly ignored by everyone. No one noticed when he slipped away and went to Hephaestus' cave. Instead of brandishing weapons, he brought only a bottle of his very best wine and humbly asked to be invited inside.

"Enter, Dionysus. For you and I share the enmity of our fellow gods," the god of fire said from deep in the gloom of his cave.

Dionysus went forward and poured them both a glass of the finest wine ever made. They drank appreciatively and in companionable silence for a time. After the wine had time to do its work, Dionysus put forth his plan. Hephaestus, his anger dulled by wine, listened and saw the wisdom in his visitor's words. With a toast for luck, they drained the bottle and set off back up the slope of Mount Olympus.

Together, they entered the court. Dionysus led a donkey that carried Hephaestus. Hera glared at the pair, and before she could start shouting about being set free, Hephaestus slid from the donkey's back and stood as tall as his crippled legs would allow him.

He addressed the assembly, "I have come to free Hera from the chains that bind her. Dionysus has helped me see the errors of my ways. My Lady Queen, I beg your patience for a moment longer," Hephaestus bowed to his mother before turning to Zeus. "Father Zeus, I believe you promised Aphrodite's hand to whoever brought me back to the court of Heaven. As you can see, I have brought myself back, so I deserve the hand of the fair Aphrodite."

A cry of shock rippled through the assembly, and Zeus held up a hand for silence. "Indeed, I did, and so it shall be. Hephaestus, I give you Aphrodite in marriage and offer you my blessings. You are indeed your mother's son."

Hephaestus smiled broadly and turned back to Hera, who was looking at him like she was seeing him for the first time. "Mother," Hephaestus murmured and bowed as low as his twisted body would allow. With a lazy flick of his hand, the bonds holding Hera to the chair disappeared. Hera looked down at her son and nodded regally before she looked past Hephaestus at Dionysus, who had been overlooked by everyone else.

"Dionysus, I believe it is you I have to thank for my release. I want all here to bear witness that from this time forward, Dionysus is welcome and equal in this court. To treat him otherwise will incur my wrath." With those parting words, she swept from the court, leaving her entourage scrambling to follow.

Hephaestus took Aphrodite home to wed, and Dionysus took up his place among his fellow Olympians. Neither of them was thought of as a lesser god ever again.

Hestia's Story

Hestia was the first-born of Rhea and Cronos. Thusly, she was the first child her father swallowed and the last child he regurgitated, earning her the nickname, Hestia, First and Last. Often an overlooked goddess, Hestia's domain was the hearth, home, and all things domestic. Soon after she was liberated from her father's stomach, she gained the knowledge of how to build a structure. She showed gods and mortals alike how to build their houses and temples.

It didn't take long for Hestia to realize that she was very different from the other gods. She didn't feel the need for adventure, conquest, or intrigue. She was happiest at home, running the house and seeing to the needs of guests. Many of the gods forgot all about her because she was so quiet and withdrawn. It suited her perfectly.

Though she was shy and remote, she was quite beautiful. She was a goddess after all, and her beauty didn't go unnoticed. The god of the sea, Poseidon, saw her always standing apart from the crowd. Her unassuming, docile nature appealed to him, but every time he sought out her company, Hestia would slip away.

Young Apollo watched his uncle's failed courtship of the lovely Hestia. He didn't blame the goddess, for who would want to marry such a volatile tyrant as Poseidon. As the god of poetry, he wrote beautiful verses praising Hestia's virtue and beauty. Written in an elegant hand on scented scrolls, he presented them to Hestia and waited for her praises and declarations of love.

"Silver-tongued Apollo, great honor you give me with these words, but I will not receive any god or man to me," Hestia said simply, handing the scrolls back to Apollo and slipping away from the great hall.

Poseidon's laughter rang throughout the hall, and Apollo's blood boiled with indignation. Inspiration struck them both at the same moment, and they raced to find Zeus. If anyone could persuade Hestia to wed, it would be the Father of All.

Zeus heard each suitor's case and was concerned. He could not favor one over the other without causing a war between two of the mightiest of the gods. Unsure of what to do, he called Hestia to come to stand before them. "Hestia, with all your domestic wisdom and prowess, you would make a fine wife. You have two admirable suitors seeking your hand, yet you have refused them both. Do you not wish for a hearth and home of your own?"

Hestia bowed low to Zeus and to her would-be husbands before she made her way up the dais to Zeus' side. She laid her hand on his head to show herself to be in earnest and spoke quietly to her youngest brother. "I will wed no man or god. I shall remain a maiden for all my days. Force me not into a union that I do not desire."

Zeus understood her oath to be a solemn truth, and he had an idea of how to avert disaster. "Hestia, goddess of hearth and home, free from the embrace of man you will remain for all your days. Not even the fair Aphrodite or her disciple Eros with his golden arrows can touch your heart or stir your lust. I give you the keys to my home that you may keep the hearth and fire of our court on Olympus. You will be the first among all in the ways of women."

With this decree, Hestia was officially off the marriage market. As the keeper of Zeus' house, she had been given an extremely high honor and neither Apollo nor Poseidon had been spurned over the other. As keeper of the First Hearth of the Gods, Hestia was also entitled to a portion of all hearth offerings made to any of the gods. This made her a powerful and wealthy goddess in her own right.

Just because Hestia had joined the ranks of Artemis and Athena as virginal goddesses, it didn't mean that she wasn't admired and sometimes pursued by amorous gods, who cared little for vows of chastity. One year in celebration of the arrival of spring, Rhea, Cronos' wife and a powerful goddess of the earth, held a feast. She invited all the gods, minor and major, and Dionysus supplied vast quantities of his best vintage. The nymphs and earth spirits as well as Dionysus' Satyrs, erotic spirits of lust, also came. As the wine flowed, Eros, Dionysus, and the Satyrs stirred the party to a frenzy by spreading love and desire among the host.

It was forbidden to recount all that happened that day, but part of the story has been told. Hestia, in a rare appearance away from Mount Olympus, enjoyed the party and while she was not affected by the amorous atmosphere, she caught the eye of many gods. Priapus, the god of fertility, was particularly smitten. Eventually, the party broke up as couples and groups drifted away to private places. Hestia took herself away from everyone else to a small secluded glen and made a bed in a soft patch of spring grass.

Having drunk more wine than she was used to, she fell into a deep sleep.

Priapus had watched Hestia all night, and he couldn't believe his luck when she went off by herself. Silently, he tiptoed toward the sleeping goddess. The night was very dark, and Priapus didn't see Selinus, Dionysus' old tutor, leaving on the far side of the glen. Selinus had arrived late to the party because he was old and slow, and he rode a donkey that was as old and slow as he was. It had taken him all day to travel to the party. Priapus had his attention fixed on his sleeping prize and didn't see Selinus' old swayback nag until he walked right into the creature, who let out an ear-splitting bray in indignation.

Hestia woke with a start at the donkey's noise, and she screamed down the night when she saw Priapus with his enormous penis advancing on her. Her screams brought the gods running, and Priapus scampered away in the confusion. Hestia returned immediately to Mount Olympus and never left it again.

Rebellion on Olympus

The court of Olympus was rarely peaceful for long. Powerful gods and goddesses in close quarters were never content with the status quo. Hera, in particular, constantly chafed under Zeus' philandering ways and utter disregard for her and her opinions. She eventually decided that the only way to be free of Zeus' tyranny would be to depose him. As with most rebellions, it started with whispers and veiled comments. Hera bided her time until she had a chance to speak privately to Apollo. She despised the younger god, who was far more powerful than he had a right to be, but he was always complaining about how his father ran the court.

"Swift Apollo," Hera spoke sweetly to the Archer Prince. "You are the mightiest of Zeus' sons, and though you are not of my loins, I see your strength and potential. You would be a great and mighty leader, wise and clever."

Apollo looked at the Queen of Heaven, clearly surprised and disconcerted at her words. Typically, Hera barely contained her disdain for him and tolerated him at court only because Zeus insisted on it. He humbly bowed his head to acknowledge her words and murmured, "My Lady Queen, I confess your words surprise me. However, I must agree that the Cloud Gatherer is increasingly difficult to abide. Is it not time for a new regime?"

Hera's eyes glittered with malevolence as she smiled at Apollo, who felt a moment's pause at the naked malice he saw in her beautiful face. "Leave it to me, for now. It is enough to know you are of a like mind." She drifted away to speak to others in the assembly, leaving Apollo wondering if he had imagined the whole thing.

Hera chose her next ally carefully. One wrong step would bring the whole thing down around her ears. Zeus couldn't hear a whisper of what was brewing. With the utmost caution, Hera leaned in close to her brother's ear. "Poseidon, it really isn't fair that you ended up as the second son. Your wave and winds are so much more powerful than your brother's claps of thunder and sparks of light. Should you not be ruling on high?"

"My Lady Queen, I am glad you think so. I have grown weary of late with Zeus and his heavy-handed ways. Tell me what is churning in that wicked mind of yours."

And so, it went. Hera worked her way through the assembly, stroking egos and whispering in ears. Soon, all the court was aligned behind her. Zeus made her work easy by throwing his weight around and making ceaseless demands for one thing or another. When she judged the time was right, Hera put her plan into action.

Always comely in face and form, Hera approached her husband with a seductive smile and a goblet of wine. Surprised, since his wife so rarely withdrew her spite long enough to offer affection, Zeus opened his arms to her and accepted the cup. He drank deeply as he drew her down on his lap. Zeus drained the goblet and was going to ask for more when he noticed that his eyes were growing heavy and his limbs refused to obey him. Understanding dawned as the poison worked through his veins, but the sleep of the dead stole over him before he could do anything about it. The great king slumped unconscious on his throne.

Hera called her key allies, Poseidon and Apollo, to help secure the slumbering god. Working quickly, they tied him to his bed with strips of rawhide. When they were done, Zeus was bound with one hundred knots and couldn't move as much as his little finger. As an extra precaution, they stole his thunderbolts and tucked them safely away.

Zeus, being the mightiest of all the gods, did not sleep for long. When he awoke, his outrage at the betrayal of his wife, brother, and son shook the very foundations of Mount Olympus. He struggled and raged at them but to no avail. Impotently, he seethed as he heard his court buzzing with excitement over the turn of events.

"Each and every one of you who has tied a knot to bind me will pay dearly," he shouted.

"Do be quiet, Husband," Hera snapped. "We are electing a new king since our old one is too tied up with affairs at the moment." The court's laughter at her jest rang in the halls and only served to infuriate Zeus further.

However, the merriment didn't last for long. Hera sat upon the high throne and ignored the dark glances from Poseidon and Apollo, her erstwhile allies. They took a leaf from her book and began to work through the court, forming alliances. Athena, daughter of Zeus and leader of the war, also felt she had a claim to the throne. Soon, the court was divided, and tempers were growing ever hotter. Only humble Hestia abstained from the machinations of the court.

Wise Thetis, a goddess of the sea, watched from her watery abode as the court fought amongst themselves. She felt the balance of the world shifting and knew it would be catastrophic if order was not restored. Having been raised as one of Hera's handmaidens, she had little love for Zeus. However, she knew he was the only god capable of restoring order. She also knew it would take too long for her to undo all of the bindings one by one without being discovered. She needed someone who could do it all at once.

And so, she undertook the long journey to the gates of Tartarus. There, she spoke to Briareus the Strong. He was one of the one-hundred-hand giants who guarded the gates to the deepest parts of the Underworld.

"Mighty Braireus! You must come quickly! Father Zeus needs your help," Thetis told the giant.

"I have work here to do, and I care nothing for the goings-on at court. Now go away!"

Thetis was not so easily dismissed. "Great one! Stout heart! Hear my words! Have you forgotten who freed you? You and your brothers would still be on the other side of these gates if it weren't for the Cloud Gatherer! Come now, I am in earnest! You must help!"

Braireus heard her words and wisdom, and together, they hurried to the court of Olympus.

The situation had deteriorated. The gods' squabbling and bickering could be heard from miles away. Thetis and the giant snuck into Zeus' bedchamber where the god lay with a murderous countenance as he listened to his fellow Olympians. On Thetis' command, Braireus pulled all one hundred knots free in the same instant, and Zeus leapt from his bed.

At his summons, his thunderbolts flew to his hands, and he rained them down on the court. All arguing ceased. A deathly silence filled the hall. The Olympians might have been immortal, but they all feared the wrath of Zeus.

Zeus strode into the hall and went straight to his wife where she sat regally on his throne. Rage twisted his face, and Hera cringed back into the luxurious cushions of the chair. Without so much as a word, he cast her into the sky with her wrists bound by golden fetters and heavy anvils pulling at her feet. Her cries of pain and outrage shook the court, and the other gods were quick to bow low before their king.

Seeing the punishment of Hera, Poseidon and Apollo both began to work their way toward the back of the court, intending to slip away unnoticed. Zeus, however, wasn't about to let them off so easily.

"Brother! Son! Where are you off to in such a hurry," Zeus called from his throne. "Come before me. I would speak to you before you leave."

With uneasy glances, the two gods approached the high throne. They hadn't missed the edge to Zeus' genial tone. Only Hera's cries of fury broke the silence as the assembly parted to let them pass. Bowing low, the God of the Sea and the Archer Prince held their breath as they awaited their fate.

"I understand how difficult it must be for both of you. You are both powerful and yet, you find your lot in life unjust with your hearts' desires just out of reach. It must be difficult to live in such a state." Zeus spoke with the utmost sympathy in his voice. "I imagine it must be as difficult as managing a court of traitorous gods!" All traces of sympathy vanished. Zeus' words lashed out over the entire assembly. In a voice of thunder, he continued, "I am the one and only supreme ruler among gods and men!" Every member of the court dropped to their knees in acknowledgment of their king. Appeased slightly, Zeus softened his tone and once again addressed the two gods who still bowed low at his feet. "Since you find me such a tyrannical ruler, perhaps you would benefit from some time in another kingdom. Apollo, Archer Prince, and Poseidon, God of the Sea, for the next year, you shall don your mortal forms and serve King Laomedon of Troy. I understand that a wall is needed around the city. Perhaps manual labor will adjust your perspective on your lot in life! Now, get out of my court!"

The two gods wasted no time finding the exit, and the other gods waited to see what their king would do next. His anger appeased,

Zeus allowed the rest of the court to resume their normal activities. However, no one at court could be easy. Hera yelled and screamed day and night from her torment in the sky. No one could console her, and everyone's nerves were frayed from her constant caterwauling.

Hephaestus was most distressed at his mother's situation. Though Hera never expressed any maternal feelings toward him, Hephaestus had grown quite protective of her over time. As evening fell and the court attempted to enjoy the after-dinner entertainment, the god of the forge quietly slipped from the assembly to gather his tools. First, he tried to loosen the anvils from Hera's feet, but he could not break Zeus' chains. Frustrated, he turned his attention to the golden cuffs at her wrists. He pounded and pried, but they were just as impenetrable. While he debated what to do, Zeus glanced up to see him trying to free Hera. In a fit of temper, he grabbed the crippled god and flung him from Mount Olympus.

It was not Hephaestus' first flight off of the mountain, and he had allies in the sea. Kind Thetis, who had raised him, caught him and set him safely on the shore. It would be an arduous journey back to the top on his crooked legs. Hephaestus sighed wearily and began his long walk.

After Hephaestus' unceremonious ejection from the court, Hera's wailing increased ten-fold. Even the mortals could hear her torment as she cried and pulled against her bonds. The gods all begged Zeus to free her. They assured him that she had learned her lesson.

Zeus looked down at his court. "Perhaps you are right. My Lady Queen, have you learned what comes of crossing your king?"

Hera nearly choked on the words, but she managed to say, "Yes, Mighty Zeus, Husband and Father of All! As sure as the dark waters of the Styx flow, I shall never endeavor such a thing again! Now, free me!" She rattled the anvils at her feet impatiently.

"In good time, Hera. First, every god in this court will come forth and swear an oath on the inky waters of the Styx that they will never again challenge my rule."

And so, Zeus sat high on his throne as one by one each of the gods bowed low and swore fealty to him. Finally, he released Hera, who ungraciously swept from the court without another word to her husband.

Zeus sat back with satisfaction. Olympus was an unruly court, but he was their undeniable king.

Demeter and Persephone

Demeter, the goddess of agriculture and harvest, loved her daughter Persephone above all her children. Persephone ruled at her side as the goddess of spring and growth, and Demeter was determined that she would stay there always. She sheltered Persephone from the ways of the world and kept her in childlike innocence even after she grew into a woman. Radiant and youthful, Persephone rivaled her mother's beauty. She roamed the meadows of the earth in the playful company of nymphs.

Unbeknownst to mother or daughter, Persephone had caught the eye of the Lord of the Underworld. Hades had long ago foregone the sunshine and the company of the living. Over time, he grew more and more powerful. His role as judge of souls made him feared by mortals and immortals alike. Thanks to the duty paid by all the souls that cross into the Underworld, he was also very wealthy. Despite all this, Hades was isolated and lonely. When he saw Persephone, the embodiment of life and growth and his exact opposite, he was instantly enraptured. After watching her for days and days, he finally went to Zeus with a request.

Zeus was surprised to see his brother when he entered his court on Mount Olympus. Hades rarely left his dark domain. He didn't have long to wonder what had prompted the visit since Hades got straight to the point.

"Brother, I am ready to take a wife."

This was the last thing Zeus expected. "Indeed! This is wonderful news. Who is to rule as Queen of the Underworld?"

Hades didn't hesitate. "Your daughter, Persephone."

Again, Zeus was surprised, and he took a moment to consider. While Hades did not have a significant presence at court, he was one of the most powerful of all the gods. Besides, the girl would be a queen. What father could ask for more? However, he knew that Demeter would not have the same opinion. "This pleases me, Hades. You may have my lovely Persephone - provided you can convince her mother."

"I will think on it. Remember your oath when it is time," Hades said as he left the court.

One day, Persephone's eye was caught by the most beautiful field of wildflowers that she had ever seen. A riot of violets, daisies, narcissus, roses, and irises carpeted the ground. Their sweet scent beckoned to the young maiden, and she excitedly ran into the heart of the meadow. Bending to pick a particularly beautiful blossom, the ground shifted beneath her feet, and before she could cry out, a crack in the earth opened, swallowing her.

She fell down into the Underworld where Hades waited in his chariot. He caught Persephone and stole her away to the depths of his kingdom. She cried out for help over and over, but no one could hear her. True to his promise to Hades, mighty Zeus stopped up the ears of man and gods to the girl's cries. However, Hecate, the goddess of magic and witchcraft, heard Persephone's pleas for help, despite Zeus' interference. She recognized the maiden's voice and went immediately in search of Demeter.

For her part, Demeter watched bright Helios give way to Nyx as she blanketed the world in darkness. Persephone had not returned home, and Demeter's stomach churned with anxiety. Her daughter was never late. Trusting her mother's intuition, she set out in search of her beloved daughter.

Demeter wandered over the valleys and glens where her daughter spent her days but found no trace of her. On the tenth day of her search, she met the witch, Hecate.

"Can you hear her, my lady Demeter," Hecate asked, brandishing her torches and looking around her like she was expecting to see someone else joining them.

"Do you speak of Persephone? Speak clearly, Witch, for I have no patience for riddles!"

"I hear her cries, my Queen, but I know not who has taken the fair Persephone. She cries most piteously in the night," Hecate said, bowing low.

Demeter said no more. She marched up to Helios and blocked the way of the horses that pulled his chariot across the sky.

"Ho, Bright One! Seer of all! Ten days hence, my daughter, the bringer of spring and growth, was taken from me. With your wide arching beams, you oversee the deeds of gods and man. Tell me what has happened."

Helios looked down at Demeter with pity etched on his face. "My Queen of the Seasons, I am sorry to tell you, but the fair Persephone was taken by the Ruler of Many to the Kingdom of Darkness. Hades bore her away in his chariot as she cried out for help, but it was his brother, the Great Cloud Gatherer, who gave him leave to take the girl," the sun god paused at the look of fury on Demeter's beautiful face. "Check your anger, mighty Queen. There are far worse matches to be made among the immortal gods. Hades is the ruler of a third of creation and is powerful. He will take good care of his wife." With these final words of counsel, Helios twitched his reins, and his winged horses once again resumed their daily trek across the sky.

Demeter tore at her hair and beat her fists on her breast in her fury. Since Zeus had sanctioned the deed, she was powerless to undo it. She could not stand the thought of returning to Olympus and facing Zeus and the other immortals with her grief so fresh. She disguised herself as a mortal woman. Her golden tresses turned to gray and her delicate skin sunk in deep wrinkles. As a bent-backed old crone, she wandered the valleys and plains of mortal men.

Without design or direction, Demeter found herself sitting by the Maiden's Well when the four daughters of Keleos came to draw water from the well. Though they were not goddesses, they were all exceedingly beautiful, and each was in the full bloom of her youth. They saw the gnarled old woman sitting next to the well and did not recognize her as a goddess.

"Dear Mother, who are you? How did you come to sit by this well? You are a long way from a village where you could find your ease among the shady halls meant for women your age."

Demeter smiled at the maids and answered, "Dear Children, I thank you for your concern and shall share my story since you asked. My name given to me by my stout and worthy mother is Doso. Across the sea from Crete, I have come, but I did not come of my own plan. Pirates took me from my home and forced me into the belly of their ship. When we came ashore in Thorikos, I snuck away into the night while my captors and fellow slaves were occupied making camp. They will never miss one such as I. I have wandered for days and days over this land, but I know not where I am. Have pity on an old woman and may the gods on Mighty Olympus bless you with husbands and children aplenty. Do you know of a house where I could do the work of women my age? Is there a house that needs one such as I to tend to the babes or make the beds or teach the other women their work?"

The loveliest of the maidens, Kallidike, knelt in the dust near the old woman. "Old Mother, what the gods send, we men must endure, and it sounds like you have had a terrible journey. Let me tell you of this land and the people in it." She told Demeter all the names of the great houses in the city. "But, good Mother, if you will wait here, we will go and tell our own mother of your travels. There is something very special about you, and I know that she would welcome you into our home. She has newly brought a babe, a boy - praise Zeus - into the world and needs someone who can nurse and care for him. Our house is strong and sturdy, and my father is the king of the city."

Demeter nodded her agreement to this proposal, and the four girls hurriedly filled their vases before returning to their home. They told their mother about the strange old woman at the well, and their mother told them to bring her back straight away.

The girls raced with the nimble legs of young deer and led the old woman back to their home. Demeter plodded along behind them, the sorrow in her heart making her feet heavy and slow. Excitedly the girls threw open the door of their home to reveal their mother seated on a high seat with her precious babe to her breast. They eagerly went to her and bade their visitor join them. But Demeter did not enter the house. She stood upon the threshold and for a moment allowed her radiance to shine forth and fill the doorway.

Metaneira, the mistress of the house, quickly stood from her high seat and offered it to Demeter. "Lady Mother, I think you are not of common birth and have come to this house bringing great blessing and power. Please take my seat here as it is the most comfortable." Demeter didn't move or speak. She cast her eyes down and stayed like a statue.

A clever courtier in the house, known for her wit as well as her wisdom, Iambe, brought forth a stool and covered it with a shimmering fleece. Satisfied, Demeter sat but still said not a word. Distraught with her grief, she clutched her veil to her face and sat lost in her misery.

Metaneira offered her wine and food, but Demeter sat, unmoving. Demo and Kallithoe, two of Metaneira's daughters, sang sweetly, but Demeter gave no sign of hearing. It was clever Iambe, granddaughter to Hermes and endowed with the power of laughter and verse, that coaxed Demeter from her grief. She made bawdy jokes at the expense of the gods, but the one that finally cracked Demeter's stony facade was when she raised her skirt and farted into the wind. Iambe blew a kiss to follow it and said, "That's for you, Zeus! Take it to your lover's bed!" Demeter couldn't hold back her mirth and dissolved into a fit of giggles.

With the tension broke, Metaneira poured the goddess a glass of red wine, but Demeter again refused it.

"I cannot drink wine from grapes. It is forbidden to me. Bring me mead and water flavored with mint that I might cleanse myself."

Metaneira scrambled to make it so, and once the draft was gone, she made bold to speak to the strange old woman. "It is obvious you are nobly born, my lady. Your radiance is plain to see, and justice shines from your eyes. We are but mortals here and must bear what the gods see fit to give us. I haven't much to offer you, but I have my son, given to me late in life as an answer to endless prayer. I would trust him to your guidance and wisdom. Help him grow into manhood, and I will give gifts that will make you the envy of any who would see you."

This pleased Demeter for the babe helped ease her grief at losing her own precious child. "Dearest Lady, your son I will most humbly take to my breast and raise him to be good and true. He will know no fever or pain, for I know the spells of the wild worlds that will keep them at bay. May the gods bless this home and all who dwell here!"

And thus, Demeter became the nurse of Demophoon, the prince of the royal house of Eleusis. Since she was not a mortal, Demeter did not care for the child in the ways of mortal men. She did not feed him bread or milk. Instead, she dropped ambrosia between his lips and breathed sweet divinity across his face as she held him to her breast. At night, she placed him in the flames of her fire to purify him and make him immortal. Demophoon grew as if he were a god-child, and those who beheld his maturity were amazed.

His mother, however, was concerned at the abnormal progress of her son and spied on Demeter one night. When she saw Demeter cast her precious son into the flames, she cried out and demanded Demeter save her son.

The goddess looked at the queen as she stood with her breast heaving and her hands firmly on her hips. Angry at being spied on and interrupted, Demeter snatched the child from the flames and dropped him at the feet of his mother.

"You foolish mortals have no foresight, no sense!" Demeter threw off her disguise and let Metaneira see her as the goddess she was. "I am Demeter, Queen of the Harvest, and by the deep flowing river Styx, I would have made this child one of my own. The years would have never turned his hair to gray. He would have lived immortal and greatest among all men. But, with your meddlesome nosiness, you have ruined everything. He will age, and he will die. For that, he can thank you! Mortal though he is, Demophoon will always be blessed and honored, for he has lain in my arms and been nurtured at my breast. Hear these words, for they will come to pass - when your son reaches his prime, the men of Eleusis will have no peace for war and strife will reign and rage among them!" With this prophecy, Demeter's ire cooled ever so slightly. "Now, gather your carpenters and smiths and build me a temple on the high hill. I will cure you and your city of their ignorance of how to properly observe my rights and sacraments so you may find favor once again in my heart."

As the goddess swept from the chamber, Metaneira collapsed, overcome with what she had just experienced. So gone were her senses, she didn't even pick up her crying child. Her daughters heard the cries and found her and Demophoon in the dirt. They cradled and rocked the young boy and splashed their mother's face with sweet, fragrant water. The boy refused to be comforted for he was used to the embrace of a goddess. When their mother was revived and told them what had happened, they went straight to their father. Fearful of Demeter's vengeance, the king ordered every able-bodied man and woman to begin construction of the temple immediately. Day and night, the people of Eleusis toiled and raised a gleaming temple in the name of Demeter, Queen of the Harvest and Goddess of Grain. They made offerings and prayed for her favor.

Demeter sat on the dais of her temple and grief consumed her once more. Helios marched across the sky again and again, but no warmth came to the earth; no grain shot forth from the ground; no rains fell from the sky. Demeter sat cruelly brooding and held them all clutched tightly to her. For a year, she sat thusly, and the mortals suffered. They plowed fruitless fields and watched helplessly as their livestock died from starvation. Soon, empty storehouses led to empty bellies, and ultimately, a great famine swept over the land. Mortals died in droves until Zeus noticed their plight.

With fewer mortals to worship him, Zeus' power had begun to diminish. He had to put a stop to Demeter's stranglehold on the world. He dispatched the lovely Iris to take a message to Demeter.

Fleet of foot, Iris descended from on high and found Demeter wrapped in gloom and grief, sitting as if she was a statue in her temple. The sweet winds of Eleusis bore only the stench of death and decay, and Iris' heart ached at the cruel destruction.

"Lady Demeter, the Great Cloud Gatherer beckons you to the court on high. He would have you attend him in Olympus. Come now, my lady, and heed his command."

Demeter said nothing to the divine messenger and stirred not an inch to obey the summons from Zeus. Iris returned with Demeter's refusal. Zeus sent the rest of the immortal gods, one after the other, to bring back Demeter back to Olympus. They promised her favors and gifts. They spoke sweetly and tried to coax her from her black mood. Through it all, Demeter sat, unmoving, and spoke only these words, "Until my daughter stands before me and I see her with my own eyes, I will not stir from this spot. I will never set foot on Olympus or allow a sprig of grass to grow until I behold my daughter in all her beauty returned to me."

Zeus realized he was not going to move Demeter, so he sent Hermes with a message to the Underworld.

Hermes stood before Hades as he sat on his throne with Persephone seated as an equal next to him. Surprisingly, Persephone looked happy and healthy. Hermes swept a low bow to the King and Queen of the Underworld and delivered his message.

"Powerful Hades, King crowned in darkness, Zeus, Father of All, has bid me come here to take the Lady Persephone back to the realm of the living. Her mother, the mighty Demeter, has locked the seeds in the earth, and the mortals have begun to perish. She means to end them all, and therefore, end the offerings to all the gods. Demeter demands that her daughter be returned to her or she will carry out this dark deed."

Hades heard the message and smiled a gruesome smile at the messenger. He rose from his throne and offered his hand to his wife. "Walk with me, my Queen."

Persephone didn't hesitate to take his hand and let him escort her away from the heavenly messenger. "My dearest, you must go to your mother and appease her anger. She cannot be allowed to erase the mortals in a fit of hatred and wrath. But while you are gone, I hope you think kindly on me. Remember that here you rule as one of the greats among the immortals and that anyone who does not pay their offerings and rights to you accordingly will be punished forevermore." Hades embraced his wife and kissed her deeply.

What no one realized was that Hades and Persephone had fallen in love. Hades, after his rather rude abduction of her, treated

Persephone with tender kindness, but more importantly, as an equal. Her mother had always sought to keep her a child wrapped in innocence and ignorance. Hades treated her like a woman. He gave her powers on par with his and showered her with gifts. He didn't hesitate to grant her request that a section of the Underworld be designated for those who had led an exemplary life. Here the sun's light penetrated, and ambrosia flowed freely. Hades gave it to Persephone as her own, private domain. Delighted with the gift, she named it Elysion, and it became the goal of mortal and immortal alike to live out their days in its paradise.

Despite her affection, Hades wasn't sure that Persephone would return to him once she rejoined the land of the living. As he kissed her, he slipped six pomegranate seeds into her mouth. Up until then, she had not eaten or drunk anything in the Underworld. To do so would mean that she could never leave the realm. Surprised, she swallowed the seeds before turning to Hermes where he waited patiently.

"Take me to my mother and let us end this dark deed." Persephone climbed aboard Hades' chariot, and Hermes took up the reins. Together, they ascended from the dark depths of the earth into the warmth of Helios' rays.

Persephone noticed at once how very wrong the world felt. There was no life under her feet as she stepped down from the chariot outside Demeter's temple. No flowers bloomed, and the breeze held no sweetness. Frowning, Persephone climbed the stairs to where her mother sat wrapped in darkness, brooding and full of hate.

Demeter raised her eyes to see who came to disturb her and saw her fair-faced daughter. With a cry of joy, she leapt from the dais and wrapped Persephone in her embrace. Persephone buried her face in her mother's shoulder and clung to her. She had missed her mother desperately and had thought she would never see her again. The two women embraced, and the clutch of anger loosened around Demeter's heart. With a mother's intuition that all was not as it seemed, she held her daughter away from her that she might look upon her.

"Tell me truly, daughter," Demeter demanded earnestly, "did you eat anything while you were in the world of darkness? Did a sip of water pass your lips or a drop of wine hit your tongue?"

Persephone couldn't hold her mother's gaze. Hades had tricked her, and Persephone feared her mother's anger once she found out. Demeter saw the truth in her daughter's face.

"Come with me," Demeter said, grabbing Persephone's wrist as if she was a child. Demeter commandeered Hades' chariot that still stood outside the temple. She whipped the horses into a frenzy, driving them as fast as they could go to the heavenly court of Olympus.

"Zeus," Demeter cried as she entered the court. "You stole my daughter from me once, and here she is returned to me, only to be torn away again. Hades forced her to eat the food of the dead. You must fix this!"

Zeus regarded Demeter with her countenance as dark and ferocious as any of his storm clouds. He did not want to anger her further, for the mortals were dwindling rapidly. With a kindly look at his daughter, he beckoned her forward. Persephone left her mother's side to embrace her father with a kiss on each of his cheeks. In her ear, he whispered, "What did you eat, child?"

Persephone spoke quietly, "Six pomegranate seeds. He slipped them in my mouth when he kissed me farewell."

Zeus nodded, and as Persephone went back to join her mother, who was silently seething, he considered what could be done. Having consumed food of the underworld, Persephone was now irrevocably tied to it. However, there might be a compromise that would keep Demeter from killing everything.

"Hermes, return to the Underworld and bring Hades before me," Zeus commanded his messenger, who hastened to obey.

Hades came straight away and stood calmly before Zeus while Demeter showered him with hate-filled glances. Persephone smiled at her husband and waited to see what the fates decreed.

"Persephone, you have eaten the food of the Underworld, and there you must return," Zeus began. Demeter cried out in indignation, but Zeus, weary of her tantrum, silenced her with a clap of thunder. "Silence, Demeter, before I change my mind! The child cannot escape her fate. Since she ate but six seeds, she will stay six months of the year in the Underworld. The other six months, she will walk among the living at her mother's side. Now, Demeter, unclench your fist around the earth. Let the shoots of grain come forth that the mortals might thrive, and their offerings flow freely once again!"

Demeter acknowledged it was a good compromise. She had seen the smile her daughter had for her husband, and her anger toward the Dark God cooled slightly. He was obviously a good husband, and Persephone was happy with him. Feeling joy blossoming in her chest, Demeter spread fertile seeds across the lands. With Persephone by her side, they brought growth and abundance back to the fields, forests, and glens.

In six months, Persephone returned to the Underworld to take up her throne next to her husband. Demeter's heart grew heavy with loneliness, and the earth went dormant in her neglect. From that time forward, the cycle of the seasons was set. The earth slept in fall and winter as Demeter mourned the annual separation from her daughter. With Persephone's return to the land of the living, spring and summer reigned, and the earth's bounty was brought forth.

The War with the Giants

After centuries of banishment, Gaia felt that the Titans had punished enough for the war against the Olympians. Zeus, however, disagreed and refused to release the Titans from Tartarus. Furious at her grandson's obstinance, Gaia roused the giants who had been created from the blood during Uranus' castration. Her army of giants numbered over one hundred strong and was a fearsome lot with reptilian-like armored scales, wild eyes, and streaming manes of scraggly hair. In her ancient wisdom, Gaia knew of an old prophecy that decreed her army of giants could defeat the gods unless the gods aligned with a mortal man. She doubted the Olympians would deign to seek out assistance from a mere mortal but wanted extra protection for her army. There was a rare herb that would make her army truly invincible, and she set off to gather it before leading her troops into battle.

Zeus heard of her plan, and to buy himself time to beat Gaia to the plant, he trapped Helios, the god of the sun, Eos, the goddess of dawn, and Selene, the goddess of the moon, so they were unable to rise or set, thus suspending time. He found the plant sought by his grandmother and chopped it up, scattering it so she could not find it. Now that the Giants would remain vulnerable, Zeus sought out Hercules to fulfill the prophecy by enlisting the help of a mortal man.

The Giant War was no less brutal than the war with the Titans. Even though they were not gods, the Giants were cunning and fierce warriors. Hercules met their leader, Alkyoneus, on the battlefield. After a vicious fight, Hercules prevailed, and Alkyoneus lay dead at his feet. However, the giant didn't stay dead but leapt to his feet. Hercules gave ground, unsure of what to do with an opponent who wouldn't stay dead.

"This is the land of his birth," Athena told Hercules. "As a creature of the earth, he will not die as long as he stands upon it!"

Hercules taunted the giant until he gave chase. Hercules ran and ran until he crossed the mountains, all the while hurling insults at Alkyoneus. Finally, on the other side of the mountains, he turned and engaged the giant in battle again. Away from his home soil, when Hercules struck him down, he stayed down for good.

Athena had her hands full with her own giant opponent, Enkelados. She battled relentlessly. Her armor was caked in filth and gore. Her horses foamed at their bits, but she whipped them forward from her chariot as she fought the giant. Enkelados knew he could not beat her and attempted to flee. Enraged at his cowardice, Athena crushed him under the mass of Mt. Etna and made a shield from his skin.

Poseidon called mists to roll in from the sea to confuse the battle, and when the giant, Polybotes, fled across the sea, Poseidon gave chase. Of course, as the god of the sea, Poseidon, had no trouble catching up with Polybotes. With a flick of his hand, he tore a chunk off the Isle of Cos and threw it, flattening Polybotes beneath it.

The other Olympians were similarly engaged. Hercules, who had returned to the main battle, and Hera fought the mighty Porphyrion. Zeus cast a spell on the giant and made him mad with lust for Hera. Driven by desire, he focused all his attention on Hera, forgetting about Hercules and Zeus. Hercules felled him with an arrow, and Zeus finished him with a bolt of lightning.

Elsewhere on the battlefield, Dionysus, the god of wine, beat down a giant with his thyrsos, a magical staff made from grape vines. Hekate destroyed one with fire while Hephaestus killed another with molten iron. Hermes used Hades' Crown of Darkness and with a golden sword, ended Hippolytus. Artemis and Apollo also fought bravely and conquered their opponents. Aphrodite beguiled and distracted the giants, luring them into caves where Hercules waited with his arrows. Even the Fates fought. Using maces cast of bronze, the triplets vanquished a pair of mighty giants. As the Olympians finally gained the upper hand, Zeus pulled down bolt after bolt of lightning to finish the rest.

With the Giants beaten, the Olympians once again returned to their court. Gaia, however, was angrier than ever. With her giants dead, she turned to Tartarus, the Titan of the Underworld, and with the help of Aphrodite, seduced him. Channeling her vengeance and the darkness of Tartarus, she brought forth the vilest creature the world had ever known, Typhon, the storm monster. Larger than a mountain, his head scraped the stars. Instead of hands at the end of his arms, he bore one hundred serpent heads. His legs were coils of snakes, and his matted, dirty hair swirled from the massive winds he held in his breast. His eyes glowed red, and fire spewed from his mouth. Enormous wings beat from his back as he roared his fury over the word.

The gods, Olympians and Titans alike, were afraid of this new and terrible creation. Even Gaia trembled under his gaze. With every move the great beast made, the world shook and great chasms opened in the ground. Storm winds raged and fed fires that ravaged the land. The gods fled Mt. Olympus, changing into animals to hide from the monster's sight. Hermes transformed into a black-headed bird called an ibis, and Apollo took to the skies as a hawk. Ares dove deep in the ocean as a lepidotus fish while Artemis ran streaking along the land as a sleek jaguar. Dionysis was nimble and quick in his goat form, and Hephaestus charged boldly across the plains as a bull. Leto changed into a tiny field mouse and hid deep in the earth. The rest of the gods chose whatever forms they could and fled over land and through the seas and skies in terror of Typhon.

Zeus confronted Typhon with Athena at his side. Raining down lightning, he tried to weaken the monster so he could strike with his mighty sickle made of iron. He landed several blows before Typhon flew back in retreat. Zeus pursued him relentlessly until he was close enough to attempt a killing blow.

Typhon was not so easily killed, however. When Zeus came close to strike him, Typhon trapped Zeus in the coils of snakes that served as his legs and tore out the sinew from Zeus' arms and legs. Unable to move, Zeus was powerless, and Typhon cast him aside in a cave. Deep in the lair of the half-girl, half-beast, Drakaina, Typhon hid Zeus' sinew and ordered the creature to guard them.

Faithful Hermes and the goat-god, Aigipan, stole into the lair of the Drakaina and retrieved the cords. Unbeknownst to Typhon, they found Zeus and restored him to health. Aigipan distracted Typhon by creating an enormous pit full of fish.

Intent on his fishy buffet, Typhon did not see Zeus coming with his chariot pulled by mighty winged horses. Zeus took aim and cast down several thunderbolts, but Typhon took flight, avoiding the attack. He fled to the mountain of Nysa.

"Mighty Typhon," called the three Fates. "Come here to us. We have a gift for you!" The triplets enticed him to eat the enchanted fruit of Dionysis. "You must be so weary of being chased over hither and yon. Come and take your ease. This fruit will make you hale and strong. None will be able to challenge you!" Typhon gobbled up the fruit and was instantly intoxicated.

Zeus pressed his advantage and again caught up with the beast. Befuddled though he was, Typhon still put up a fight. He hurled mountains at Zeus, who bounced them back at Typhon with his thunderbolts until he buried the monster beneath the rubble. Trapped beneath his own weapons, Typhon could no longer take flight but was still very much alive and very angry. Zeus didn't waste his opportunity. Lightning scorched the sky as Zeus threw bolt after bolt onto the monster until he melted the scaly hide of Typhon, and the beast surrendered. To make sure he could cause no further trouble, Zeus cast him into the deepest pit of Tartarus where his agonized, angry breath became the tumultuous East Wind.

Thus, ended the final uprising of the Titans. The Olympians would remain the masters of the universe, unchallenged and supreme until the end of time.

Part 2   **Stories of the Heroes**

The Adventures of Perseus

As Greek mythology evolved, the poets shifted their attention from stories of the gods to create tales that celebrated heroes among men. As with many of the ancient civilizations, these tales told of the cunning and strength of man and served as society's guides to morality and values. They sought to level the playing field between gods and man and signified an evolutionary shift in civilization. Over the ages, the stories have morphed a little with each telling, but no matter the version, the literary concept of a hero's journey played out again and again. In this tradition, the hero is given a quest which he accepts and must overcome multiple obstacles to achieve. Along the way, he'll receive divine help, fight a life and death battle, and return home triumphant but fundamentally altered forever. Ancient Greek heroes are often partially divine in nature and can trace the roots of their family tree back to Mount Olympus. Let's begin with Perseus and his epic adventure with the snake-haired Medusa.

Before we can get to Perseus, we must first meet his grandfather, Acrisius. He had a twin brother, Proetus, with whom he fought from the moment they left their mother's womb. As princes of Argeia, a wealthy and prosperous kingdom, they should have had a blissful childhood. However, jealousy and petty rivalries drove the brothers apart. Acrisius finally succeeded in forcing his brother out of the kingdom and was quite pleased with himself for coming out the victor in their sibling rivalry. Proetus didn't stay gone, however, and returned to the realm married to a beautiful princess and backed by an army of cyclopes. The brothers met in many years of bloody battles before they decided to split the kingdom down the middle, and peace was finally found in Argeia.

Acrisius had a daughter, Danae, who was exceedingly fair. Acrisius was proud of his daughter and knew that she was prettier and smarter than any of his brother's daughters. Danae for her part was sweet-tempered and spread joy throughout her father's kingdom and court. One evening, a ragged old fortuneteller presented himself at the palace gate. As was the custom of the day, every evening ended with entertainment. The fortuneteller offered to entertain the court with a story in exchange for a place to stay the night. The king accepted and instructed his daughter to make ready the old man's chamber.

While she was gone, the old soothsayer told a story that held the entire court rapt. The king beckoned the man to sit next to him for a glass of wine as the court began to break up for the evening. "Tell me, old one, what do you know of my future," Acrisius asked the traveler.

The old man stared deeply into his goblet. He indeed knew the king's future, but Acrisius was going to be none too happy to hear it. "Good king, the Fates have sent winged words to my ears about your future. They were displeased that you raised your hand to your brother and expelled him from the kingdom. The years of war have soured the Fates to you, I'm afraid. Thus, they have told me that you will be deposed by your daughter's first-born son. He alone can mend the rift in this country and see the kingdom of Agreia reunited."

The king's face darkened with anger, and he was about to banish the man from his presence when Danae returned.

"Father," she exclaimed, seeing the look on his face. "What has happened?" She looked from her father to the old fortune teller, who was staring intently into his wine.

King Acrisius considered his situation for a moment and then rose solemnly from his chair. He embraced his daughter and kissed her forehead before grabbing her arm and dragging her toward the door. Confused, she looked at the old man, who shook his head sadly and dropped his eyes back to his wine.

"Father! What are you doing? Where are we going," Danae pleaded as the king towed her inexorably behind him. Up the crumbling tower steps, they went until they reached the single prison cell at the top. Without a second thought, King Acrisius pushed his daughter inside, locked the door, and threw the key out the window into the river. She could not produce a child from behind a locked door for which there was no key.

Confused and angry, Danae wept piteously for days and days. She had no idea why the Fates had been so cruel to her. Her cries reached the ears of Mighty Zeus. He peered down to see Danae's beautiful face covered in tears and resolved to help her. That night as she slept, Zeus came into her tower prison in the form of golden rain. He fell gently on the roof of the tower and soaked through.

He tracked down the walls, across the floor, and into Danae's womb where slept on her straw pallet. He whispered in her ear that she was carrying his son before he left her. When she woke, Danae was more confused than ever by dreams full of golden light and whispers in the night.

Danae soon realized that it hadn't been merely a dream. Impossible though it seemed, she was carrying Zeus' child. Her body grew heavy, and she could no longer hide her secret. She bore her son alone in her cell and named him Perseus.

King Acrisius, of course, couldn't allow this child to live. His daughter had never wavered in her story about the baby's father, and no mortal had passed through that door since the day he had locked it. This left him with another problem. One didn't just kill a son of Zeus without significant repercussions. So, he did the next best thing. He fashioned a small boat, put Danae and her newborn in it, and set them adrift in the sea.

For days, they were tossed about on the waves. Hungry, thirsty, and exhausted, Danae clung to her babe and prayed to gods for help. Poseidon did not like to see such a lovely face in such distress. He calmed the seas and called for a gentle north wind to carry her to a friendly shore.

The little craft washed up on the shores of the Isle of Serifos. There the young mother and her infant were taken in by Dictys, a fisherman and brother to the king of the island. He took them into his home, and Danae kept the house and did needlework for him in return for their keep. Perseus grew to be a strong and handsome young man. He and his mother lived a quiet, unknown existence on the edge of the sea for many years.

They could not hide forever, and eventually, Danae's beauty caught the eye of the king, Polydectes. The king resolved to have Danae for his wife, but Danae had no interest in the proposition and Perseus blocked his every advance.

Realizing he would need to take a different approach, Polydectes called together all the young, strong men of his kingdom, Perseus included. He told them he wanted to wed the princess of a neighboring country but needed to gather an impressive wedding present so her father would consent. The other young men offered their best horses since the princess was famous across the land for her love of all things equine. Of course, Perseus had nothing to offer, having never owned anything beyond the clothes on his back. Polydectes saw him standing awkwardly as the other men brought horse after horse to him.

"What's this, young Perseus? Have you nothing to contribute," the king asked in mock surprise.

Embarrassed, Perseus spoke with the bravado of youth, put forth the only thing he had - his courage. "Nay, Great King. I have no horse to add to this impressive herd. Besides, you don't need any more horses to woo the princess. What you need is something truly spectacular. Name the object you think most precious in the world, and I will fetch it for you!" Perseus finished his speech with a bow and a cocky smile.

Polydectes couldn't believe his luck. The boy had played right into his hands. "An excellent point! Thank you for volunteering your services. I have heard of a prize beyond all others. To the land of the Gorgons, you must go and bring me the head of the once beautiful Medusa!"

A stunned silence fell over the assembly at the king's request. It was a suicide mission, which, of course, was precisely why Polydectes picked it. It would get Perseus out of the way once and for all, and he could take Danae as his wife, whether she liked it or not.

Perseus' stomach clenched in fear at the proclamation, but he had no choice. "A fitting choice, my lord," he said and stood as straight and proud as he was able. "I'll fetch it for you directly." He turned on his heel and strode away from the group without another word.

The story swept through the court like wildfire, and soon, Danae heard of her son's quest. She pleaded with the king to withdraw his demands, but he refused. With dread in her heart, she rushed to find Perseus as he prepared for his journey.

"My son! You cannot do this! I will marry Polydectes. Do not throw away your life for me," she begged.

"I have taken an oath and cannot break it. Goodbye, Mother. I will return, and you will be free of the king once and for all!" He embraced her, trying not to think it was for the last time, and set out on his quest.

Perseus had grown into a strong, fit man, but he had never left the island. When he reached the first crossroads, he realized he had no idea how to go about finding the land of the Gorgons, let alone chopping off the monster's head. He had been running on pride and bluster, and now that they had ebbed and his head cleared, he understood the enormity of his folly. Crumbling under the weight of his responsibility, Perseus sank to the ground on the side of the road and tried to think of what to do.

As a son of Zeus, Perseus had long been watched by the various deities on Mount Olympus. As he sat on the road, unsure and overwhelmed, two of those watchers decided to help him. Athena and Hermes loved to champion heroes, and they felt Perseus was worthy of their aid. And so, they came to him on the side of the road, and Perseus stared at them in wonder for a moment before he scrambled to his feet to bow to them. He knew beyond a doubt they were gods, even without Hermes floating inches off the ground on his winged sandals.

Hermes looked down at the stunned mortal and said, "Son of Zeus, fear not. Long have we watched you and know you to be worthy of the divine blood in your veins. Your feet are set on an impossible path. We would offer our aid. First, your father sent his sword." The messenger god presented a fine sword made of polished metal with a gold hilt. "This sword is unbreakable and is the only sword capable of killing the Gorgon, Medusa."

Perseus accepted the sword in awe. He had never held such an impressive weapon. He was surprised when Hermes bent to take off his winged sandals and handed them to him.

"You stand no chance on human legs. Medusa's sisters will not stand idly by. These sandals will give you the speed and agility to escape once the deed is done."

"Thank you, My Lord Hermes, Great Messenger to the Gods! I will use them well!" Perseus bowed again and flicked an uncertain gaze at Athena, who had been standing back and observing with a stony expression.

The goddess of war regarded Perseus for another long moment before stepping forward to hand him a large shield she had slung over her shoulder.

"Perseus, Son of Zeus, I give you a shield of my own making. Heed my words. You must not look at Medusa or her sisters. They will tempt you and beguile you with illusion. Only look at their reflection in the shield. If you do not, you will be turned to stone."

Again, Perseus bowed low to the beautiful goddess and murmured his thanks. "I have no words equal to the gifts given to me. I will do my best to honor them," he said and hoped it was enough.

The gods nodded and began to leave. Over her shoulder, Athena said, "Do not hesitate! Be bold! Be clever! For no number of gifts can save you in their absence. Seek out the daughters of the sea monster Ceto. The three gray-skinned sisters live far to the north. They have but one eye between them but see all. They alone know the location of the Nymphs of Hesperus. Your quest starts here. Good luck, Perseus."

Before Perseus could thank them again, they were gone. He struck out to the north, grateful to have at least the beginning of his journey mapped out for him. Days of travel finally brought him to the northern shores and home of the Graeae, the gray-skinned sisters. As he had traveled, Perseus had heard stories of these gray women. Borne with bent backs and stringy gray hair, they had been ancient since their conception. They not only shared one eye but one tooth as well. Their pallid gray flesh clung loosely to their skeletal bodies and reeked as if it was decomposing on their bones. If they touched a mortal, it was said that the mortal would instantly age until they too became like the walking dead. People on the road advised him to turn back, for the gray sisters did not like company and never ventured into the light of day. The closer he got to their lair, the fewer people he saw until he traveled the final day of his journey in complete isolation.

From a deep crevasse on the rocky cliff face, Perseus could hear the sisters cackling and bickering. He peered into the entrance to the cave and shivered with dread. Not a glimmer of light could be seen, and the stench of rotting flesh made him gag. He would need to draw them out if he were to stand a chance of beating them.

Perseus banged his sword on the shining shield and bellowed, "My Ladies Graeae! I am Perseus and am on a quest to seek out the most beautiful of all women. I have heard of your legendary beauty and beg you now to come forth that I might behold it for myself!"

The bickering in the cave ceased at once, replaced by hushed, rasping whispers. From deep in the cave, rustling movements sounded like leaves blowing across the forest floor. "Perseus," a voice hissed, drawing out his name in low, menacing tones. "We do not welcome visitors here, particularly ones who come to mock us. You will pay for your insolence."

The rustling sounds grew louder, and Perseus forced himself to hold his position just to the side of the cave entrance, standing in a patch of morning sunlight. The smell slammed into him a moment before the sisters appeared in the gloomy half-lit mouth of the cave. His gorge rose as the skeletal women leered at him with their robes hanging in tatters around them. The leader had the eye and squinted in his direction. Her sisters held fast to each of her hands. Their empty eye sockets opened, revealing dark, gaping voids. Perseus shuddered but held his ground.

"I see the rumors were true," he said, sweeping them a courtly bow. "I have never stood in the presence of such radiance."

In unison, the sisters hissed in fury at the obvious falsehood. "He has a shiny sword and shield, sisters! Perhaps he thinks to slay us," the hag with the eye rasped.

"I want to see! Give me the eye," the one on the left demanded.

"No, I get it next," the one on the right argued.

"Neither of you will take it before I am done with it," the leader screeched and clapped her hands over the eye.

In an instant, they forgot all about Perseus as they began to quarrel and bicker over the eye. One sister managed to gouge it from its socket, but before she could use it herself, it was snatched from her fingers. Perseus watched for his opportunity, and when the eye fell to the ground in the tumult, he darted in, grabbed it, and scaled up the rocks, high into the bright sunshine.

The hags screamed in frustration but would not pursue him beyond the shadows of the cave. Perseus let them rage and shriek until they finally quieted enough for him to be heard.

"My Ladies Graeae! I am afraid I have not been truthful, and for that, I apologize. However, I will be happy to restore your eye in exchange for a bit of information."

"Restore our eye, and we will share it amongst us as we watch you writhe in agony as your body wastes away. One touch, Perseus, is all it takes." They spoke in harmony, and when they drew out his name into a long hiss, a shiver of dread ran down his back.

"If you try to touch me, I will toss your eye into the sea! I seek the Nymphs of Hesperus. Tell me where I can find them, and I will give you back your eye."

The sisters growled in frustration. They coveted their knowledge as much as they did their eye, but they had little choice but to give the hero the information he asked for. Again, the trio spoke in their disconcerting harmony. "You seek the daughters of the Evening Star. They live under the protection of Hera, Queen of Heaven. At the edge of the western world, you'll find Hera's garden and Nymphs of Hesperus. Now return what belongs to us!"

Perseus quickly tossed the eye down in the middle of the small huddle in which the sisters stood. As he knew it would, their unity broke, and they instantly began to fight over the eye. He slipped away unnoticed and oriented himself to the west.

The next leg of the journey took Perseus to the farthest reaches of the world. He traveled across seas, mountains, and deserts before he finally came to a lush paradise. The small group of nymphs welcomed him to their garden and offered him refreshment and rest. After he was fully recovered from his journey, the daughters of the Evening Star asked him why he had come to their garden.

"I am on a quest to save my mother. I must slay the monstrous Medusa and bring her head to King Polydectes of Serifos. If I do not, my mother will be forced to wed the king against her will. The wise and mighty Athena told me to come here," Perseus said, stating his case plainly. Now that he was recovered from his arduous journey, he was eager to be back on his way.

"Medusa and her sisters are vile creatures, though Medusa was not always a monster." Perseus raised his eyebrows in surprise at this revelation, and the nymphs explained, "She was once a woman, comely in shape and fair of face. She was a handmaiden to Athena. Like her mistress, Medusa had taken a vow of chastity, but the master of the sea, Poseidon, saw her and desired her. He seduced her in the Temple of Athena, and as punishment, Athena banished her to live out her days as a Gorgon." After they shared Medusa's story, they gave him two gifts to help him complete his quest. First, they gave him a sack made of silver to carry the head inside, for even severed from her body, Medusa's curse would live on. Second, they presented him with the Helm of Darkness which would render him invisible.

"Go now, Perseus, Son of Zeus, and may your sword not hesitate in the moment of truth! Follow the path south, and you will find the lair of the snake-haired sisters. Use your gifts! Be bold and clever! Good luck," the nymphs called to him as he left the garden.

Perseus dutifully followed the southerly path into the mountains. After days of difficult travel, he came to the lair of the Gorgons. Helios had just pulled the sun down for the night, and Nyx led darkness across the land. Perseus listened intently at the mouth of the cave that the Gorgons called home. It sounded like someone was sliding boulders back and forth across the stone floor. He realized the Gorgons were snoring! It was the perfect opportunity to sneak up on them.

Perseus knew that even a sleeping Gorgon was not an easy foe, so he donned the winged sandals of Hermes, the Helm of Darkness, and held Zeus' sword in one hand and Athena's shield in the other. As prepared as he would ever be, he floated silently into the cave.

Perseus found the sisters lying around a small fire in a large cavern. Careful only to look at the shield, he watched them a moment. Two were much larger and much more hideous with thick serpents growing from their heads and horrible scaly flesh over their bodies. The third, who lay on the far side of the fire, was the size of a mortal woman and still bore the comely shape and features that had led to her downfall. Snakes squirmed and writhed around her lovely face as Medusa tossed and turned in a fitful sleep. Remembering the Nymphs' story, Perseus felt a pang of pity for her as he saw her punishment with his own eyes.

One of the other Gorgons shifted in her sleep and let out a deafening snore. Perseus forced himself forward, floating well over the sleeping monsters until he hovered over Medusa. He raised his sword and staring at her reflection in the mirrored surface of his shield, brought it down. In the split second, before it struck, Medusa's eyes snapped open and stared in his direction, though he was hidden by the cloak of invisibility. His swing stayed true, and he thought he saw a flicker of gratitude before her head parted company with her body. From her neck erupted a mighty giant, Khrysaor, and the winged horse, Pegasus. Both were products of her liaison with Poseidon.

Of course, the giant and the horse made a great deal of noise. The other Gorgons were awake in an instant, and even though they could not see him, thanks to the Helm of Darkness, they could clearly see their murdered sister. Their shrieks turned Perseus' guts to water as he wasted no time scooping Medusa's severed head into the bag. Keeping his eyes firmly averted, he fled the cave. The Gorgons were hot on his heels bearing their fangs and screeching their rage.

Perseus pelted through the night and didn't stop, even when the Gorgons gave up the pursuit and returned to their cave to wail their grief into the night. He didn't dare slow down until he couldn't hear even a whisper from the Gorgons. Finally, he stopped and removed the Helm of Darkness. He had done it! He had the head of Medusa. Now, all he had to do was return home.

Using the magic sandals, Perseus began the long trek back to his home and his mother. He flew until his fatigue dragged him to a stop. He saw below him a bountiful forest that glittered with golden leaves. It looked like a perfect place to rest for a while. Gliding down, he noticed the branches of the trees bending low, laden with heavy golden apples.

"Who comes into my forest," a thundering voice that seemed to come from everywhere at once demanded.

"I am Perseus, a weary traveler. I seek only a place to rest my tired body!" Perseus finally saw the owner of the voice and stared in wonder. Bigger than a mountain with his shoulders stooped by the heavy weight of the heaves, the Titan Atlas stood looking down at him. Perseus hurried on, hoping to ensure his welcome, "I am Son of Zeus and would tell you my tale! I have bested the Gorgon Medusa and am traveling home in triumph!"

Atlas' eyes narrowed. Long ago, words on the wind told him that a descendant of Zeus would rob him of his golden apples. "Be gone from here! You are no son of Zeus, and if you had even but glimpsed the Snake-haired Sisters, you would be stone. Take your bravado and move along!"

Perseus' temper flared. Refusing hospitality to a traveler was one thing but calling him a liar was quite another. "Bravado, you say? Look here Mighty Atlas and behold my truth!" He opened the ties of the silver bag and carefully looked away.

Atlas stooped down to inspect the contents of the bag and immediately turned to stone. Keeping his eyes resolutely away, he pulled the bag closed and laid down to take a much-needed rest.

Perseus didn't tarry long in the golden forest and soon resumed his journey. He had traveled for many days, flying over the lands of the Amazon women and into Ethiopia. There he found a kingdom under siege by a terrible sea monster. The creature roared and lobbed boulders into the seaside town. The earth trembled as Poseidon, the Earth Shaker, let his anger be known. As he skirted the edge of the sea, thinking to go around the troubles, he spotted a maiden chained to a rock on a high cliff.

Perseus flew to the lovely young woman and shouting over the roaring beast asked, "Beautiful lady! Tell me your name, and what fate has brought you to this terrible end?"

The woman looked at him with wide, terrified eyes. "My name is Princess Andromeda, daughter to King Cepheus and Queen Cassiopeia. Please help me! My mother's folly has led me here! She boasted that I was more beautiful than Poseidon's sea nymphs. The Master of the Sea sent that beast, Cretos, to destroy the kingdom lest I am offered in sacrifice!"

Perseus personally agreed that the woman before him was more beautiful than any other creature in the world but wisely kept his opinion to himself for the moment. He didn't even have time to reassure her because they had caught the sea monster's attention. It dropped the boulder it was preparing to throw at the town back into the sea, causing a massive wave to roll over the shore. In two quick strokes of its many tentacles, it closed the distance to the cliff and rose out of the water to its full height. Cretos' many arms came at Perseus from all directions. Ducking and dodging, he flew straight for the creature's torso. With the infallible Sword of Zeus, he jabbed and cut, piercing flesh time and time again. The beast roared in pain and annoyance but was too slow to inflict more than a glancing blow to Perseus as he darted about on the winged sandals. Finally, the multitude of cuts and slashes began to take their toll on the monster, slowing it even further, until Perseus was able to land a death blow through its heart. The sea ran red with the creature's blood while the inhabitants of the city cheered from the cliff's edge.

Perseus flew straight to Andromeda where she trembled with relief and tears coursed down her cheeks. His sword swung once more and cleaved the chains that bound her. He swept her into his arms and flew to the castle where her parents had been watching.

There, over hugs and tears and much rejoicing, the king offered his daughter to Perseus in marriage.

"I am deeply honored, King Cepheus. If the lady will have me, I could ask for nothing more," Perseus said, looking anxiously at the princess who rewarded him with a bright smile and bashful kiss on the cheek.

They were married immediately and together continued Perseus' journey back to his homeland. Back on the Isle of Serifos, the young couple hurried to the court of Polydectes. Perseus frowned as he entered the hall. His mother was on her knees, scrubbing the floor while Polydectes sat on the dais lazily watching.

"You missed a spot, Danae," the king sneered and deliberately emptied his goblet of wine on the floor.

Perseus' rage erupted when he saw his mother crawl toward the tyrant to clean up the mess. With a cry of protest, he came fully into the hall and crossed it in several swift strides. He reached his mother and pulled her to her feet. "You'll never bow to him again. Leave this hall now and no matter what, do not look back," Perseus whispered Danae's ear and pushed her gently toward the door, where Andromeda waited anxiously.

Polydectes lumbered to his feet with his face purpling with indignation and intoxication. "Perseus! How dare you enter my court and give orders! You've been gone a long time, boy. Many things have changed. Danae, my wife, come back and sit at my side while we tell Perseus of all the things that have happened in his absence."

Perseus' blood ran cold when he heard Polydectes refer to Danae as his wife and he realized how completely he had been manipulated. "King Polydectes! I have something to give you before you share your news. You sent me on an impossible quest, but I stand before you today as proof that all things are possible!"

With icy resolve, Perseus carefully lifted the bag with Medusa's head in front of him. After a quick glance to make sure his wife and mother had left the hall, he squeezed his eyes closed and peeled back the bag, revealing the head of Medusa to the king and all his courtiers. Once the court was eerily silent, he closed the bag and opened his eyes. A court of stone stood around him with frozen expressions of horror and shock.

Perseus turned and left the hall of statues and didn't look back. He had one last thing to do to see his quest complete. With a quick reassurance to his wife and mother, he went to Athena's temple. On the altar, he solemnly placed the shield and sword. He added the winged sandals and the Helmet of Darkness. Finally, he laid the silver bag with its monstrous contents on top of the pile and dropped to his knees in supplication.

Athena and Hermes appeared to accept the offerings. "You've done well, Son of Zeus," Athena said. "Your cunning and courage did not falter. I accept the head of the Gorgon. She will adorn my battle shield, and armies will flee from her stony gaze! I am well satisfied."

The goddess of war gathered the offerings and disappeared as abruptly as she arrived. Hermes lingered only a moment longer to say, "Your father is impressed with you, Perseus." Then, he too was gone, and Perseus' quest was officially complete.

With his perspective of people and the world forever changed, Perseus wearily went to find his wife and mother and begin the next chapter of his life.

The Life of Theseus

In ancient times, Greece was divided into many kingdoms, each striving for supremacy over them all. King Aegeus and his brothers ruled the southern empire of Attica, which included the powerful city of Athens. Aegeus was the eldest of the brothers and had two wives but no children. He feared that his brothers would usurp the throne if he did not produce an heir. Aegeus undertook the long journey to the Oracle at Delphi for a solution to his problem. The Oracle, as always, spoke in riddles and told him, "Do not open the mouth of the wineskin until you have once again reached the heights of Athens, lest you come to everlasting grief."

King Aegeus mulled over the prophecy but could make no sense of it. As he traveled back to Athens, he had the inspiration to consult a fellow ruler, King Pittheus of Troezen, who was known for his cunning wisdom. Pittheus welcomed Aegeus and listened to his tale.

"What can you make of this, Pittheus," Aegeus asked as they sat drinking wine.

Pittheus' reputation was well-earned, and he understood the prophecy well enough. If Aegeus lay with a woman before returning to Athens, he would come to grief. The king of Troezen also knew an opportunity when he saw one. He'd just been offered a chance to undermine the most powerful kingdom in the region and possibly set it up for conquest.

"I will need to think on it, Aegeus, but in the meantime, have more wine," Pittheus said, smoothly refilling his visitor's goblet. "Have you met my lovely daughter, Aethra?" He presented his daughter and proceeded to get Aegeus very drunk.

Aethra, at the instructions of her father, seduced the drunken king and lay with him. As she slept, Athena appeared to her in a dream and commanded her that she should walk along the shore of the sea and embrace anyone she should meet. Puzzled but wise enough not to question the goddess' instructions, she left the sleeping king and waded along in the warm waters of the sea. Poseidon saw her there, fresh-faced and beautiful. He desired her and came to her as a mortal man. Remembering the goddess' words, Aethra embraced him, and they lay together in the surf. Thus, Theseus was conceived of two fathers, one mortal and one divine.

Aethra's pregnancy proceeded rapidly, and King Aegeus was torn. He could not stay in Troezen. He had his own kingdom to run, but here was his longed-for child. He told Aethra to keep his identity as the baby's father a secret until the baby was old enough to retrieve the gifts he left for him. Aegeus then hid a pair of sandals, a sword, and a shield beneath a large rock. "When my son comes of age and moves the rock aside, send him to me. I will know him by these things." Reluctantly, Aegeus made his way back to Attica to tend to his responsibilities.

Aethra raised their son, Theseus, and told him nothing of his father, despite his persistent questions. Finally, he was old enough to move the rock, and Aethra told him the entire story. Theseus, like most young men, was ready for an adventure and eagerly struck out for Athens to meet his father and claim his birthright as the prince of Athens.

Theseus had to choose which route to take to get to Athens. The sea route was by far the easiest, but it took longer. The overland route took him precariously close to the six entrances to the Underworld where terrible monsters and beasts lurked, but it was considerably shorter. With the confidence of youth, he chose the short route, sure that he could handle anything he might encounter.

It wasn't long before that conviction was put to the test. Periphetes, a giant born of the god Hephaestus and the cyclops, Anticleia, roamed the route between Troezen and Athens. The hideous monster with his crooked legs and single eye carried a huge bronze club that he used to pound unsuspecting travelers into the earth. Theseus encountered him outside of Epidaurus when the giant waylaid him. Theseus taunted the giant. "I like your little club! What's it made of," he called.

Periphetes, who was quite proud of his club, was instantly insulted. "It was made by my father, God of the Forge, from the finest bronze in the world. Come here, and I will show it to you up close!"

Theseus shook his head. "Bah! It's a simple wooden club with a bronze cover! Prove that it isn't," he insisted.

Periphetes' pride was genuinely wounded, and he was distracted from smashing Theseus to bits by his desire to prove the quality of his weapon. He handed Theseus his club. "See for yourself! There is no seam or hint of wood about it," he challenged.

Theseus carefully inspected the club and said, "My apologies. It is indeed pure bronze," and with that, he swung the club down on the giant's head, driving him down deep into the ground.

Carrying on the giant's club, Theseus continued along the road. Next, he encountered the dreaded Pine-Bender, Sinis. Sinis menaced the road by luring travelers off the path by asking for their help before robbing and killing them.

As soon as he saw Theseus approaching, Sinis called to him. "Young man, come help me! You look fit and strong! I need to hold this pine tree down."

Theseus thought it was a rather odd request but got a good grip where the giant indicated he should hold. Without warning, Sinis let go, and the tree tried to spring up. Anyone else would have been flung into the nearby rockface, but Theseus pinned the tree to the ground with his extraordinary strength. Sinis scratched his head. He'd never had anyone hold the tree down before. He bent down to peer at the trunk of the tree, thinking it had broken. Theseus released his grip. The tree whipped up and knocked Sinis unconscious. While the giant was stunned, Theseus bent down four pines and tied them to the giant's arms and legs. When he let them go, they tore the giant into pieces.

Theseus heard a scream and turned to see a beautiful woman, watching with horror. He rushed to console her. "My Lady! Fear not, I've killed the monster who harried the travelers along this route."

"You killed my father," the woman shouted and then, much to Theseus' surprise, threw her arms around him. "Thank you for freeing me from him!"

Theseus lingered there for a while, and as heroes do, he lay with the beautiful woman whose name was Perigune. She later bore Theseus his first son, Melanippus.

Traveling on, Theseus heard about a huge sow terrorizing the region. Phaia, the Krommyonian Sow, slaughtered anyone unfortunate enough to cross her path. Theseus stayed alert, and it wasn't long before he heard the beast coming for him. Snuffling and grunting, she lumbered toward Theseus, who drew his sword in one hand and the giant's club in the other. Though strong and filled with meanness, the sow was not agile. Theseus easily evaded her charge and had no trouble vaulting onto her back. With a strike of his club and a stroke of his sword, Phaia, killer of man, lay dead in the road.

After he cleaned his weapons, Theseus continued down the road, wondering what was going to be next. As he walked along, the passage narrowed as it twisted and turned along the sea. Theseus rounded a bend to come face to face with another giant. His face bore deep furrows and leathery skin from facing the spray off the sea day after day. Massive and at least twice Theseus' size, he blocked the path.

"Hello, I am Sciron," the giant boomed genially over the waves of the sea. "You'll pay the toll if you want to pass. It isn't much, a trivial thing really."

Theseus raised a brow. He was quickly learning that nothing was ever trivial with giants. "Name your price, sir."

"Oh, it is but a little thing. Help me wash my feet. They're so hard for me to reach, you see?" Sciron bent and reached vainly for his feet but couldn't much past his knees.

Sensing there was probably more to it, Theseus proceeded cautiously. "What if I don't do it?"

The giant shrugged his boulder-like shoulders, "I'll toss you into the sea."

"Well, when you put it that way, where's the pool to wash your feet?" Theseus asked and followed the giant over the rocks to the edge of the cliff. While the waves and wind whipped around them, Theseus bent to wash Sciron's enormous feet. Using the stones in the pool, he scrubbed the mud away and straightened up once his task was finished.

"Am I allowed to pass now," he asked, wary of a trick.

"Of course, just head along there and you'll come to the path." The giant pointed with a hand that was bigger than Theseus' head to a small rocky ledge that wrapped around the cliff.

Sensing that the trap was about to be sprung, Theseus took a couple of cautious steps toward the ledge when he felt the giant move behind him. In one swift motion, Theseus spun and caught the foot that was about to kick him off the shelf and into the sea. With a mighty heave, he threw the giant off the cliff and watched in fascination as a massive turtle surfaced just in time to catch Sciron in his jaws. With its prize, the turtle disappeared below the waves.

Theseus picked his way back to the path and was relieved when it looped back into the main road. Of course, it wasn't long before he came to another spot of trouble. As he reached Eleusis, the guardian rumbled out from behind a large pile of rubble. Cercyon had been given dominion over the area and challenged everyone who passed through to a wrestling match. Growing weary of giants and their tricks, Theseus met him head-on.

"Come, Cercyon, but I warn you, I have bested three giants already!"

Cercyon said nothing but lowered his shoulder and charged Theseus. They came together in a clash of mighty arms and legs that sounded like a landslide. As they wrestled, the earth trembled and quaked. Finally, Theseus gained the advantage, and while Cercyon was down, he buried him under a pile of boulders.

Theseus continued down the road, hoping that he was getting close to Athens. He noticed a well-lit house in the distance. The night was coming on, and after the day's exertions, Theseus didn't fancy sleeping outside on the ground. He hoped the people in the house would show him hospitality for the night and give him a bed to sleep in.

Darkness had closed in before he reached the house and knocked on the door. It opened immediately, and a hulking man opened the door. He took a moment to survey Theseus before speaking. "You look tired, sir! May I offer you a bed for the night? I have the most comfortable bed in the world. It adjusts to fit every person just perfectly. I am Procrustes, and you are welcome in my home."

He drew the door open all the way and stood back to let Theseus inside.

Theseus' hopes for a restful night evaporated. He had heard rumors about this magic bed. Anyone who slept in it never woke up. If the rumors were true, Procrustes adjusted the person to the bed as opposed to the bed adjusting to the person. He sawed off any appendages that were too long. Anyone who was too short he would stretch and flatten with hammers until they filled the bed from end to end. Theseus had no intention of becoming Procrustes' next victim.

Theseus accepted a seat at the table while Procrustes lumbered around the kitchen and brought him wine and bread. Inspiration struck Theseus. "I hate to eat alone. Won't you sit and have a drink with me. The road is lonely, and I would enjoy some company," he said to his host.

Procrustes was surprised but figured his victim would go easier to the bed if he was put at ease. Theseus struck up a light conversation and poured the man a cup of his own wine. As the evening wore on, Theseus kept the wine flowing into Procrustes' goblet but took none himself. Soon, the large man was bleary-eyed and sleepy with a drink.

"Good sir! We have talked the night away, I'm afraid. Do lay down in your bed. I'll be perfectly fine on the floor," Theseus said, steering his swaying companion to the bed despite his drunken protests.

"Nonsense! I would not deprive you of a good night's sleep, Procrustes," Theseus assured him as he tucked him in under the blankets, wrapping him up tightly so he couldn't move. He ignored hammers and straps hanging on the wall. As much as the villain deserved it, Theseus had no stomach for torture. Procrustes struggled feebly, dimly aware something was amiss. With one swift swing of the bronze club, Procrustes was dispatched, and Theseus wearily traveled on through the night.

With the rising sun, Theseus finally came to the great city of Athens. The city buzzed with anticipation. The Panathenaia festival was in full swing, and King Aegeus was to send the champion, Androgeos, prince of the kingdom of Crete and son of King Minos, against the great Cretan Bull that was menacing the countryside. It was to be a celebration as the final game of the festival and the solution to a difficult problem. The unholy creature had been sent as a plague by Poseidon against King Minos of Crete after he had offered unsatisfactory sacrifices.

Minos was a son of Zeus and felt because of that divine parentage, he felt he should be exempt from the laws that governed other mortals. Poseidon, of course, disagreed and to reinforce the lesson, not only did he lose the Cretan Bull on Minos' kingdom, he had Aphrodite, the goddess of love, cast a spell on Minos' wife, Pasiphae, that she lusted after the bull. The bull, of course, had no interest in a human woman, and the poor queen was driven mad with her desire. She ordered Daidalos, an ingenious craftsman, to construct the frame of a cow that would conceal her. The ingenious inventor covered the structure with a cowhide, and Pasiphae disguised herself inside. The great bull was fooled and mated with Pasiphae, who then bore the monstrous Minotaur as a result.

The bull had been driven out of Crete and had turned its attention on the kingdom of Attica and the city of Athens where it had been wreaking havoc and causing widespread devastation. Everyone was excited to see the culmination of the games and the end of the bull.

Theseus listened to the stories humming in the crowd about Androgeos, the champion of the games. They praised his skill and strength, and they were certain he would best the creature. Everyone said how fitting it was that a son of Crete would vanquish the beast. Theseus joined the throng of people crowding into the stadium to watch the spectacle.

The bull charged around the arena. Spectators close to the ring shrank back in fear as it crashed into the barricades. The mighty beast slung its head and bellowed its frustration at being confined. Silence settled on the crowd when Androgeos entered the ring. He carried a shield and sword and stood confidently in the center of the arena.

The bull fixed his malevolent stare on the young prince and lowered his head. His hooves shook the ground as he thundered toward Androgeos. The warrior raised his shield and set his feet. Theseus and the rest of the crowd watched in dismay as the bull hooked his horns under the protection and ran his horns through Androgeos' soft belly. The screams of Androgeos were drowned out by the panic of the crowd. The bull flung the corpse off his horns and leveled its head at the far barricade. The crowd began to surge and push, trying to get out of the stadium. They knew the wall would never hold the enraged creature. Theseus fought against the tide of people until he reached the edge of the arena. Club in one hand and sword in the other, he leapt the wall and screamed at the demon bull to get his attention.

The bull swung his head and fixed his gaze on Theseus. The bellow of fury shook the stadium and the crowd, despite their desperation to get away, stopped in their tracks and held their collective breath. High in the stands, far out of any danger, King Aegeus and Queen Madea looked on in fascinated horror and silently dared to hope that this unknown warrior could deliver them from their troubles.

Theseus stared at the bull as it flung its head. Gore and blood streamed down its horns. It stomped its massive legs, leaving deep furrows in the earth, and it bellowed its displeasure. Without warning, the bull charged, and Theseus ran straight toward him. The beast lowered his head, ready to gore Theseus just as he had Androgeus. Just as the lethal horns began to sweep upward, Thescus vaulted himself over the bull and landed behind it. In the next heartbeat, as the massive beast wheeled around for another charge, Theseus went on the offensive and launched himself onto the creature's back. With a stroke of the club and the slash of the sword, he killed the beast and threw himself free as its momentum carried it into the barricade, shattering it.

Theseus got to his feet to the roar of the crowd. They spilled into the arena, giving the giant beast wide berth, and bore him out on their shoulders. They presented their champion to their king and queen.

Theseus swept a bow and said, "I am Theseus from Troezen. I have come to speak to King Aegeus."

Aegeus nodded and beckoned the young man forward, but Queen Madea whispered in his ear, "Husband, wait a moment. We do not know this man. He is clearly powerful. Be wary until we know his intentions." Madea was a sorceress and exile from Corinth. She had bewitched the king and had him firmly under her control. If her suspicions were correct, this newcomer would threaten all she had so carefully arranged. Moreover, he could threaten her son, Medus' claim to the throne.

Despite his wife's warnings, Aegeus welcomed Theseus and took him back to the palace. Over the coming weeks, Theseus and Aegeus grew close, but Madea poured a constant stream of doubt and deception into Aegeus' ears. Aegeus decided to throw a feast in Theseus' honor, and Theseus knew it was time to reveal his true identity. Through her sorcery, Madea divined Theseus' relationship to the king and his plan to take his place as successor to the throne. Of course, this would set aside her son, and she couldn't allow that.

"Husband," she said to Aegeus as they were dressing for the feast, "I feel Theseus is hiding something, don't you? It is as if he is not exactly who he pretends to be."

Aegeus, who was still under her influence, thought on it. There always had been something slightly off about the boy. "I agree, but he has done us a great service. I have no real reason to doubt anything he says. What do you propose we should do about it?"

Madea smiled sweetly at her husband and pulled a vial of poison from her robes. "Tip this into his goblet. If he is true in intention and word, it will not harm him. If he has played you false, he will lay dead at your feet."

Aegeus took the vial, and that evening during the feast, he poured it into the glass of wine he handed Theseus. There was something different about the young man that evening. As Aegeus handed him the poisoned goblet, it finally snapped into focus. Theseus was wearing the sword and sandals Aegeus had left buried under a rock all those years ago.

With a cry of surprise and delight, Aegeus knocked the goblet from Theseus' hand, spilling the wine and Madea's dreams onto the cobblestones. "My son! Oh, my son, you are returned to me," the king exclaimed and threw his arms around Theseus' neck.

Madea watched the happy reunion with despair. She knew her time as Queen of Attica had come to an end. True to her nature, she and her son fled the court that very night.

Theseus claimed his birthright as a prince of Athens, and he and his father ruled together in harmony. However, peace was short-lived. Word came from the lookout tower on a bright summer's day that a ship with black sails approached. Aegeus' stomach clenched. He knew those sails. The ship was from King Minos of Crete. News of Androgeos' death had apparently reached his homeland and here was the reply.

Theseus accompanied his father to the docks where they received the emissary from Crete, who wasted no time delivering his message. "King Minos sends his thanks for your sympathy in the death of his son. However, he demands recompense since he was killed on your soil. You will send seven young men and seven young women with me to Crete to be offered as a sacrifice to the Minotaur. Great King Minos will not attack your shores in retribution for his son's life if you do this."

Theseus frowned. Minos had no right to ask for anything, let alone threaten attack because his son was killed fighting a monster that had been spawned in Crete, to begin with. He drew Aegeus aside and shared his plan. He would go as one of the seven young men, and he would defeat the Minotaur. If all went to plan, none of the Athenian youths would be killed. Aegeus didn't like the plan, but Theseus would not be dissuaded.

The next day, Theseus boarded the ship with the other young men and women. Aegeus reminded him before he left that if he were successful, he must turn the sails to white before returning home. On the journey to Crete, the guards on the ship took all their weapons, but Theseus concealed his sword beneath his tunic. When they arrived in port, King Minos and his court met them.

"Young men and women of Athens, your lives will bring honor to your kingdom and maintain peace in the land," King Minos proclaimed as they were herded off the ship and down the path.

"I am the son of Poseidon and Prince of Athens," Theseus proclaimed, striding up to Minos. "I killed the beast that gored your son. That should be enough vengeance. Return us to our home."

"If you are a son of Poseidon, return my ring to me," Minos instructed as he pulled a gold ring from his finger and threw it out into the sea.

Theseus dove in after it. He was immediately surrounded by creatures of the sea and taken to Poseidon's palace in the depths of the ocean. In a court of merpeople, Oceanids, and sea nymphs, he was greeted by Poseidon's wife, Amphitrite, and made welcome. She wrapped him in a beautiful robe of rich purple and gifted him with a crown that had been given to her by Aphrodite on her wedding day.

"Theseus, my son," boomed Poseidon as he joined them. "You have grown to be brave and strong. Here is the ring you seek," he said and dropped the signet in Theseus' hand. The master of the sea continued, "I grant you three boons to ask of me when you are need. Return to the surface now and show that son of Zeus the power of those born of the sea!"

Just as quickly as he had arrived, the creatures bore Theseus back to the surface with the ring and crown. Minos laughed as he put the ring back on his finger. "Sea-born you may be, Theseus, but this debt will be paid." Without any further discussion, the procession resumed its course away from the docks.

They traveled into the hills under the watchful eyes of the guards. A young woman fell into step next to Theseus. She was the most beautiful woman he had ever seen.

"My name is Ariadne, daughter of King Minos. I do not want to see you die at the hands of the Minotaur. He is an unholy creature and a blight on our land. My mother bore him as a result of an evil trick played by Poseidon. To protect the people, he has been locked away in the middle of the great labyrinth created by the most cunning inventor, Daidalos. The Minotaur's bellows shake the earth and make us tremble in fear."

"My lady, I will do my best to rid you of this beast and save both of our people," Theseus promised, though he was at a loss as to how he was going to accomplish such a feat. Even if he managed to slay the Minotaur, he still had to find his way out of the labyrinth.

"The moment I saw you, I knew you would be the one to save us all," Ariadne said and slipped a ball of twine into his hand. "Daidalos told me the secret of the labyrinth. Tie the twine on the door when you enter. Unwind it as you go, and you'll be able to follow it out once you've killed the beast." She turned to go, but Theseus held her hand and pulled her back to him.

"If I succeed, I'll take you away with me as my wife - if you like. You'll be the Queen of Athens one day." Ariadne kissed him quickly and slipped away.

Feeling more confident with at least part of a plan, Theseus boldly led his fellow Athenians into the labyrinth. Carefully, he let out the twine as he wound his way deeper into the maze. The Minotaur's earth-shaking bellows echoed off the walls and grew ever louder. Finally, Theseus stepped out into the opening in the very heart of the labyrinth. The Minotaur stood as still as a statue. Only its eyes darted all around the clearing, watching for its next victim. Theseus scarcely had time to take in the heavily muscled legs and arms of a man that supported the grotesque head of a mighty bull before it was upon him. Long horns sprouted from the bull's forehead, and the beast lowered them as it charged. Nimbly, Theseus spun away from the attack and drew his sword. Eyeing the weapon, the Minotaur trumpeted his displeasure, but Theseus only grinned.

"It's not so easy when your opponent can fight back, is it," Theseus taunted the beast. "You couldn't best a girl armed with a sewing needle, could you?"

Enraged, the Minotaur lowered his head for another charge. Theseus anticipated this and dodged the lethal horns, but the Minotaur's mighty hand caught his tunic and pulled him into a crushing hold. They fell to the ground, wrestling viciously. Finally, Theseus broke free just enough to get his sword up between them and with a desperate thrust, shoved it through the beast's throat. The Minotaur's life's blood spilled across the ground.

Theseus retrieved his sword and began to follow the string back out of the labyrinth, gathering his fellow Athenians as he went. He knew that King Minos would not be happy that they had survived the challenge, so he hurried his small band straight to the ship that had carried them to Crete. His faithful Ariadne was waiting there for him and had brought her sister, Phaidra. They all worked together and were under sail before their escape was discovered.

As predicted, Minos was furious that his son's blood had not been repaid. When he discovered that the labyrinth's creator, Daidalos, had assisted Theseus, though indirectly, he banished Daidalos and his son, Icarus, to the center of the maze. Daidalos fashioned wings of feathers, wax, and glue for both him and his son. He warned Icarus not to fly too high or too close to the sea, for the heat from the sun and the spray from the sea would weaken the wings. Icarus took flight and lost himself in the joys of soaring through the air. He forgot his father's advice and flew too high over the sea. His wings failed, and he fell to his death. His father made it safely to the shores of Sicily where King Cocalus made him welcome in his court.

Minos became obsessed with finding Daidalos. He searched the surrounding kingdoms by presenting them with a conch shell and a thread. He asked the leaders to send word if they had anyone in their court who could get the shell onto the thread. King Cocalus gave the shell and thread to Daidalos, who used an ant to bore a hole in the shell and pull the string through. King Cocalus sent word to Minos that he had found the man Minos was looking for.

Minos rushed to Sicily, and King Cocalus welcomed him to his court. King Minos wanted to see Daidalos straight away, but Cocalus persuaded him to refresh himself with a bath and some rest. Cocalus sent his daughters to tend to his royal visitor. Following their father's instruction, the daughters killed Minos by pouring boiling water over him in the bathtub. By murdering Minos, King Cocalus had rid himself and the region of the heavy-handed tyrant Minos and secured the most clever craftsman a permanent spot in his court. After Minos departed from the earthly world, he was made a judge of the dead in the Underworld, sitting next to another son of Zeus, Rhadamanthys.

While the drama of Minos' murder was playing out in Sicily, Theseus and his fellows made haste back to Athens. They were forced to stop at the island of Naxos to take on fresh water. The entire crew went ashore in search of water. Theseus and his new bride, Ariadne, availed themselves of a cozy grotto among the rocks and spent the afternoon making love. Unknown to either of them, the island belonged to Dionysis. From the moment the God of Wine saw the lovely Ariadne, he coveted her and planned to claim her for himself. As everyone was gathering to head back to the ship, Dionysis revealed himself.

"How dare you defile my island with your lust? I did not give you leave to stop here, take my fruits and water, and rut in my sacred caves like animals," he thundered at the small band of travelers, who quailed in the face of his anger.

Theseus stepped forward and bowed low in an attempt to appease the angry god. "Great Dionysis! We did not know this island belonged to you! Please, let us make an offering to you that all might be forgiven!"

"You speak the smooth words of diplomacy. I ask for only one thing, and then you may be on your way with my blessing."

"Of course! Name it! We will gladly give it," Theseus replied with the rashness of youth. He had no experience negotiating with gods and was about to learn a valuable lesson.

"That fair lady will stay with me and become my wife." The God of Wine pointed at Ariadne. A collective gasp went up from the group, but no matter how they begged, Dionysis would not be swayed. Ariadne had to go with him, or the entire group would be punished. And thus, she became the immortal wife of Dionysis and sat among the gods on High Olympus from that day forward.

With a heavy heart, Theseus set sail back to Athens without his bride. Her sister, Phaidra, accompanied him, and they were both inconsolable in their grief. So lost in his misery, Theseus forgot to reverse his sails as his father had instructed. King Aegeus had been keeping an anxious watch over the sea ever since his son had left for Crete. His heart sank in despair when he caught sight of the black sails coming into port. He flung himself from the top of the Acropolis in his grief and fulfilled the prophecy from so long ago. He lay with a woman before returning to Athens, and it ultimately brought him to ruin.

Theseus' homecoming was not the triumph he had planned it to be. He lost his love and his newly found father in the space of a few days. Nonetheless, he took up the reins of leadership and managed to do something no other king of Attica had done. He unified the entire region under his direct control.

Peace, however, took effort to maintain. Theseus crossed paths with the famous Hercules during this time. Hercules was going about his labors and had spirited away the sister of Hippolyta, Queen of the Amazons. Theseus gave Hercules refuge in his kingdom and by doing so, brought the Amazons to his doorstep. Together the two heroes led the armies to fight off the Amazons. Hercules and Theseus made a treaty with them after the battle, and Theseus was so taken with Queen Hippolyta, he had a brief affair with her. She later bore him a son, Hippolytos.

During another adventure, Theseus' bosom companion, Prince of Lapith and son of Zeus, Pirithous, was to wed Hippodamia, a mistress of horses. Even in the age of the Ancient Greeks, the wedding of a prince was a huge production. All the nobles for neighboring kingdoms attended and at Hippodamia's request, the herd of centaurs was invited as her special guests. The wedding vows were exchanged, and the feast began. As the festivities went on, the centaurs got very drunk and decided to steal all the women at the party - including the bride! Theseus and Pirithous led their warriors against the centaurs and in a bloody battle that left most of the centaurs dead, retrieved all of the women. Pirithous and Hippodamia settled down to enjoy their lives, but their happily ever after was cut short when Hippodamia died in childbirth less than a year later.

Theseus needed a wife as well, so he wed Phaidra, who had stayed a loyal friend to him all these years after fleeing from Crete. They had several happy years together that bore the fruit of two sons. While the boys were still in their infancy, Hippolytus, Theseus' son by the Amazon Queen, came to stay with his father at court. Phaidra took one look at Hippolytus and fell in love. Unfortunately, the young Hippolytus did not return his step-mother's affections and threatened to tell his father. Spurned and angry, Phaidra decided to take preemptive measures.

With hair streaming behind her and her robes ripped open, Phaidra burst into her husband's study. "Theseus," she cried and threw herself at his feet. "Hippolytus has forced himself on me!" With dramatic flair, she sobbed in a huddle on the floor.

Enraged, Theseus sought his son. Hippolytus had left the palace in his chariot, so Theseus called out to his father, Poseidon, "Father of the Sea, I call in a boon that you granted me many years ago. A grievous wrong has been done to my wife and me. I would see my son punished for his treachery. May he not see another sunrise!"

These words caught on the sea breeze and reached the Lord of the Sea in his watery court. Poseidon stirred the currents and caused the waves to form a mighty bull that charged out of the surf as Hippolytus' horses pulled his chariot along the beach. The horses screamed and reared as the sea creature erupted from the waves. They broke their traces, and the chariot careened out of control. In the chaos, Hippolytus became tangled in the long reins and was dragged over the rocks to his death.

News traveled quickly to the palace that the Amazon son of the king had been killed. Phaidra and Theseus received the message. Much to Theseus' surprise, Phiadra tore at her hair and wailed in grief. Thinking she was overwrought with the experiences of the day; Theseus had her attendants take her to her rooms. They left her to rest, and when they went back to check on her later, they found her hanging by the bedclothes, dead by her own hand. She had written a full account of her lies and broken heart before she committed suicide. Theseus never did use his other two boons that Poseidon gave him.

With their marital bliss spoiled, Theseus and Pirithous decided to go fetch the wives of their dreams. They agreed that as sons of gods, they deserved to marry a woman of divine birth. Theseus, in the tradition of Greek heroes, set his sights on Helen, who would later become the famous Helen of Troy. However, at this time, she was only a little girl of about seven years old. Theseus and Pirithous snuck into the Spartan court and abducted the young princess. They stole her away to Athens and left her in the safekeeping of Theseus' mother, Aethra.

It was then Pirithous' turn to choose a bride. After much consideration, Pirithous settled on Persephone, Queen of the Underworld and the wife of Hades. The two heroes traveled deep into the Underworld where no living man ought to go. Hades, omnipotent of everything within his realm, watched them as they journeyed and listened to their plans to steal his wife.

When they reached his court, Hades bade them welcome and offered them food and drink. Of course, neither of Theseus or

Pirithous touched a drop of wine or crumb of food, for to do so would trap them in the Underworld.

"If you will not accept my hospitality, then you must at least make yourself comfortable," Hades offered and conjured two luxurious chairs. "Do sit and tell me what brings you into the darkness."

The heroes looked at each other. They hadn't concocted a story since they hadn't expected to be welcomed into Hades' court. With no good reason not to, they sat in the chairs.

The moment their flesh hit the seat, snake-like coils wound around their feet and arms, binding them to the chairs. Hades smiled a terrible smile. "Do you know what becomes of thieves," he asked in a deathly quiet voice. Before either man could answer or plead for their lives, a band of furies descended on them and bore them out of the court.

The furies dropped them on the edge of the Underworld. Their luxurious chairs turned to solid rock that engulfed them and changed their bodies to stone. There the heroes sat in darkness until Hercules came upon them as he journeyed to the Underworld in his labors. Recognizing Theseus and remembering how Theseus had given him refuge in the past, Hercules cut him free of the rock. He tried to free Pirithous, but the ground shook violently every time he tried. The furies appeared and surrounded Pirithous, who screamed in anguish. Hercules and Theseus cringed as the furies dug their claws into Pirithous' stony flesh and carried him away into the darkness.

Theseus and Hercules parted ways, and Theseus returned to the land of the light and the living. He hurried to Athens but found his young bride stolen back by her brothers, Castor and Pollux. They had besieged Athens in his absence and had succeeded in not only taking Helen back to Sparta, but they took Theseus' mother with them. To add insult to injury, his crown had been usurped by Menestheus. He was no longer welcome in his own kingdom. Forced into hiding, Theseus fled to the Isle of Scyros and sought asylum with his old friend, King Lycomedes.

Lycomedes welcomed Theseus to his home. Once his visitor was recovered from his journey, Lycomedes offered to show Theseus around the island. As they walked along the high cliffs, Lycomedes, who had allied himself with the new King of Athens, unceremoniously pushed Theseus over the edge to his death. And thus, our hero, Theseus, Son of Poseidon, King of Athens and all Attica, met his rather ignominious end.

The Life and Labors of Hercules

Hercules was probably the most iconic of all Greek heroes. As with most heroes, his life from the moment of his conception onward was influenced by the gods. His story begins in Thebes with a woman called Alcmene.

Alcmene was said to have dark eyes that were so beautiful they rivaled Aphrodite's. She possessed uncommon wisdom for a mortal woman and was famous throughout the land for her devotion to her husband, Amphitryon. Alcmene was patiently waiting for her husband to return home from leading a campaign against a neighboring kingdom when he surprised her by appearing at the door to their house.

"You're home," Alcmene exclaimed and threw herself into his arms. As a soldier's wife, she never knew if or when her husband was going to return home.

Passion erupted between them, and they spent the entire day closeted away in their bedroom, reacquainting themselves with each other. The next morning, Alcmene sent her husband off about his day with a kiss and smile. As she went about her work, she thought about the wondrous night she had spent with her husband, who had seemed very different. She supposed that weeks at war could change a man.

The day grew late, and Amphitryon finally returned home, looking tired and battle worn. Alcmene welcomed him with open arms and an amorous embrace. Amphitryon looked at his wife with surprise. While she was always receptive to his advances, she rarely took the initiative. He was exhausted from weeks of fighting, but with such a warm reception, he felt rejuvenated. Willingly he followed her to the bedroom, where she proceeded to shock him some more.

The next morning Alcmene embraced her husband. "I wish you could stay home with me today, though I suppose I should let you rest. You've only been home from the battlefield two days."

"Two days? My wife, I have only been home since last night. Have I loved you so well that you have lost track of time," Amphitryon teased.

"Nay, husband. Do you not remember the way you surprised me at our door? You looked like a god standing in sunlight." Alcmene smiled at her husband, but it quickly slid from her lips at the look on his face.

They soon realized that something was not right. The couple sought out Tiresias, a prophet at Apollo's temple. "Amphitryon, do not be angry with your wife. The Father of All tricked her by wearing your appearance and manner. Zeus has lain with your wife, and we must wait to see what the outcome of his actions will be."

The outcome soon became apparent as Alcmene grew heavy with child. From high on Olympus, Zeus proclaimed that the next descendant born of the great hero Perseus would become the future king of Mykenai. Alcmene was the granddaughter of

Perseus, but she wasn't the only descendant of Perseus who was pregnant. Perseus' grandson, Sthenelos, and his wife were also expecting a baby. The prophecy enraged Hera, whose jealousy over Zeus' infidelities still burned hot. She refused to allow one of his illegitimate children to ascend to the throne. As the women's bellies swelled, Hera sent her daughter, Eileithyia, the midwife to the gods, to stall Alcmene's labor. In the meantime, she brought on Nicippe's labor at seven months so she would bring her child into the world first.

Alcmene labored for days and days. Her body fought against an invisible force to bring forth the child. Alcmene writhed in agony for over a week. Her companion, the faithful Galanthis, suspected divine interference, and she finally found Eileithyia saying her spell to delay Alcmene's baby. Clever Galanthis exclaimed loudly, "A boy is born! A son for the mighty Amphitryon!"

Eileithyia was so surprised, she stopped muttering her spell, and Hercules and his brother, Iphicles, were finally born. Eileithyia, furious with Galanthis' trickery, turned her into a weasel. In her new form, Galanthis stayed on as Alcmene's companion for the rest of her days. Through Hera's machinations, the history of the mortal world was once again altered and the son of Sthenelos, Eurystheus, was destined the next king of Mykenai.

Hera wasn't satisfied by simply taking away Hercules' birthright. Her jealousy knew no bounds. As the infants slept, she cast two vipers into their cradle. His nurse cried out in terror, but before she or his parents could intervene, baby Hercules grabbed each of the snakes and strangled them. He sat up in his bed and played with them while his brother wailed in fear.

Alcmene was terrified for her baby's life. The concerned parents took the baby to the prophet Tiresias. He laid a hand on the baby's face while his unseeing eyes closed in concentration. "Be glad of heart, young mother. Your baby is strong and has been blessed with many gifts. He is threatened by a mighty foe. He must be hidden from her view until he is older. He will fight many monsters and conquer many battlefields in his future."

With a heavy heart, Alcmene took Hercules into the forest. She had to hide him if he were ever to have a chance of survival. Her tears flowed as she tucked him into a hidden nook, well off the path.

"Pallas Athena, goddess of wisdom and war, I give you my young warrior. Protect him that he might grow strong and fight many battles in your name," Alcmene prayed and left an offering of bread and milk by the baby. She straightened her back, blocked her ears to her baby's sweet babbling, and hurried away.

Athena heard the young mother's prayers and came to the forest. Immediately, she recognized the divine strength in Hercules. She took the babe and the offerings and returned to Olympus. Athena presented him to Hera. "Mother Hera, see what I found in the woods. This child was abandoned. He needs nourishment and care. Will you take him?"

Hera did not recognize the baby as the same one she had attempted to kill only hours before. As the goddess of women, childbirth, and family, she felt a strong urge to care for the child. She took him and offered her breast. The hungry baby latched on and bit down furiously with a far stronger hold than any mortal baby should have. Hera cried out in pain and pulled the babe from her breast. Her mother's milk spilled across the night's sky and created a swath of stars they called the Milky Way.

"You found him, Athena. Let him suckle at your breast and be responsible for him," Hera said and waved a hand in dismissal. What Hera didn't realize was that she had just reinforced Hercules' divinity by allowing him to nurse from her.

So, Athena cared for the infant. She had no children of her own since she followed a path of abstinence and chastity. Hercules grew quickly, and Hera's attention was diverted to other nefarious plots. It was safe for him to return to his mortal family. He had grown into a gangly young boy when Athena escorted him back to the city of Thebes to his parents, who were overjoyed to welcome him home.

Hercules matured into an exceptional young man. His strength was unequaled by man or god. His handsome face turned the head of every maiden in the area. His days were filled with learning. His father taught him to drive a chariot and wield a sword. He was tutored by some of the greatest Greek warriors of the time in fencing, archery, wrestling, and boxing. He honed his mind as well. He learned to read and write, play music, and recite poetry by the direct descendants of the Muses.

When he came of age, Hercules was sent to Mount Cithaeron in Thespiae to tend his father's herds. A fierce lion prowled the area, ravaging the sheep, cattle, and people. The villagers sent offering after offering to the gods asking for deliverance from the beast. Hercules decided that he would take matters into his own hands. He fashioned a huge club from the trunk of a wild olive tree and began to hunt the beast. For fifty days, he tracked the lion until he finally had a chance to make his move. With swift efficiency, he killed the giant creature and skinned it. He donned the pelt and presented himself to Thespius, the king of Thespiae.

The king and his people showered Hercules with gifts of gratitude. Thespius was so impressed with the young hero, he insisted that Hercules lay with each of his daughters - all fifty of them! He left the court some days later to journey back to Thebes, leaving fifty pregnant princesses behind.

On the road to Thebes, Hercules encountered the heralds of Erginus, king of Orchomenos, on their way to collect the annual tax from Thebes. A long-ago war between Orchomenos and Thebes had resulted in a treaty between the two kingdoms, stating Thebcs would pay Orchomenos one hundred oxen every year. Thebes paid the tribute, despite the hardship it placed on the country. When Hercules saw the men of Orchomenos coming to take his countrymen's oxen, he decided it was time for the treaty to end.

Hercules hid among the boulders on the side of the road until the group of travelers drew even with him. With a war cry that echoed for miles and still wearing his lion pelt, he fell onto the small group in a fury. One by one, Hercules cut off their ears and noses and hung them on a string around their necks. He bound their hand behind their backs and told them, "This is my tribute to King Erginus. Henceforth, Thebes owes you nothing."

King Erginus flew into a rage when his mutilated emissaries returned. He rallied his troops, and his army was marching toward Thebes before the sun was out of the sky.

Hercules sat on the boulder on the side of the road, waiting for the army from Orchomenos. Athena appeared on the road in front of him. "Hercules, you have grown strong," the goddess of war commented as he bowed to her. "But, you have not grown wise, I'm afraid. You have prodded a sleeping bear without a sword in your hand."

Hercules shrugged, unconcerned. "I have my club and my two hands. No army can get past me."

Athena shook her head but couldn't help but smile at the arrogance of the young warrior. "No warrior goes into battle unarmed. I have gifts for you, Son of Zeus. Let us make you ready for war." Athena strapped on a bronze breastplate forged in the fires of Olympus by Hephaestus. She handed the young hero a sword from Hermes, a bow and quiver of arrows from Apollo, and an impenetrable cloak made by her own hands. In the distance, the rumble of hundreds of men on the move could be heard. Athena glanced toward the sound before fading into nothingness with these final words, "Fight well, my warrior. Remember, be as cunning as you are strong."

More confident than ever bearing the Arms of the Gods, Hercules stood in the middle of the road and waited. The rumbling grew louder and louder, and a large dust cloud appeared on the horizon, heralding the arrival of the army. King Erginus led the column of men and pulled up in front of Hercules.

"You must be the monster my men told me about. They spoke of a man wearing the skin of a lion who fought like ten men. I see now that you are nothing more than a boy playing dress up in his father's armor. Offer your life in repentance of your actions, and I will turn my army around."

Hercules lifted his chin defiantly. "Your army will turn about and run home before I am done with them. The kingdom of Thebes is free from any obligation to you. Accept that and return to your court alive. Press forward on the road, and you will all die."

King Erginus shook his head at the young man's bluster. Without any further words, he signaled his men to move forward. The first wave of soldiers surged ahead but were forced to narrow their ranks as the road squeezed in between great boulders left scattered about from a long-ago landslide. Hercules had chosen the spot purposely. No more than ten men could come in at one time. He stood his ground and engaged wave after wave of soldiers, waiting for them to enter the tight confines. Soon, corpses hid the ground and slowed the onslaught of the soldiers even further. Hercules leisurely picked them off with bow and blade. King Erginus led the final wave of soldiers, still in denial that one man could defeat his army. His was the last body to fall.

Hercules stood among the carnage as his father and a band of soldiers from Thebes arrived. They had seen the advance of the Orchomenos army and had come to investigate. With wide eyes, Amphitryon and his men surveyed the battlefield. One by one, they knelt before Hercules. A new hero had just been born.

Fitting to his new status, Hercules took Megara, princess of Thebes, as a wife. He counseled the king and led the army for several years. He and Megara had two young sons when Hera once again took notice of him. Hercules' fame had spread throughout the land, and the people had begun to revere and worship him. Hera's jealousy rekindled. She vowed that the people would shrink from their hero in revulsion and fear.

With venom in her heart, Hera cast madness down on Hercules in one of her most infamous deeds ever. Hercules' mind clouded with insanity, and he knew not friend from foe. In a frenzied mania, he built a fire in the hearth until the flames licked hungrily up the chimney. Without so much as a second thought, he fed his sons and wife to the inferno and burned the house down around them. He turned his attention to the city, and the people fled before his wrath, terrified by the crazed look in his eye. Athena, horrified by the spectacle, flung a stone from Mount Olympus and hit the out-of-control hero in the head to stop his rampage. As consciousness returned to him, Hera, with infinite cruelty, cleared to fog from Hercules mind and watched as the realization hit him.

Hercules stood in the smoldering remains of his house as the mists in his head gave way to clarity. A deluge of grief swept over the mighty warrior and brought him to his knees. He tore at his hair and wailed in despair. The people of Thebes shrank away from him, fearful and disgusted. With a heart heavy with remorse and lost in grief, Hercules left Thebes with no direction or purpose. As he wandered the road, he decided that his life should be forfeited in atonement for his actions. He drew the sword that Hermes had gifted him and laid the tip over his heart.

"Hold there," a strong voice called. Hercules looked up the road to see a powerfully built young man striding toward him. "You could hurt yourself that way," Theseus said, drawing the tip of the sword away from Hercules' chest.

"I deserve every bit of pain after what I have done," Hercules said miserably and told Theseus his tale.

"Poseidon, save us from meddlesome goddesses," Theseus murmured after hearing the story. "I understand the desire to put an end to your pain, but that is the easy way, the coward's way. You are the Hero of Thebes and a son of Zeus. I have heard your name revered all the way in Athens. You must face this wretched business and find a way to atone for your sins. Go to the Oracle at Delphi. In her divine knowledge, she will tell you what to do."

"You have spoken wisdom this day, and I thank you for it," Hercules said as he and Theseus parted ways. "Death would have been an all too easy escape."

And so, with new direction and purpose, Hercules struck out to Delphi. He set a grueling pace for himself, scarcely stopping for rest or refreshment. After days of travel, he knelt before the

Oracle. "I have come for my penance to pay for my hideous transgression. Tell me in your infinite knowledge how to scourge my soul and earn the forgiveness of my loved ones," Hercules asked humbly, all bravado gone.

The Oracle, having received instructions from Hera, set forth this punishment. "For the next ten years, you will serve the King of Mykenai. You will complete any request he makes for you. After ten labors set by the king, you can consider yourself absolved."

Hercules accepted his punishment and set out to Mykenai. He had no idea that Hera was up to her old tricks. King Eurystheus was a dedicated follower of the white-armed goddess since he owed his crown to her. Weak and inept, he danced to Hera's every tune.

Hercules duly reported to King Eurystheus. "Mighty king! I bow before you and present myself to you a servant and wretched man. I dedicate myself to you for the next ten years. Tell me what you would have me do."

Eurystheus looked down at the huge man at his feet. He had heard many rumors about the great Hercules, who despite his humble approach, was still intimidating. Eurystheus didn't want anything to do with the fallen hero, let alone be saddled with him for the next decade. However, he would not go against the instructions of his goddess. He followed the words Hera had sent to him on the wind.

"There is a beast terrorizing the plains of Nemea. It is a lion that has a taste for the flesh of man. Destroy it and bring me its pelt."

Hercules nodded and left the court. He traveled overland to the plains of Nemea. Just outside the village of Cleonae, he stopped and was offered hospitality by an old man named Molorchus. The old man didn't have much, but he shared it with Hercules. Over a meager spread of bread and fruit, Molorchus warned Hercules of the danger in the area.

"Heed my words, young man and do not tarry in this region. A beast prowls the lands and is no longer content with sheep and cattle. Only the flesh of man can stop his hunger."

"I have heard of this beast," Hercules told his host. "I have come to kill it and free the area of its menace."

The old man's eyes grew wide. "You have come to forfeit your life if that be the case. The beast, a lion, is the unholy offspring of the dreaded Typhon and the vile snake woman, Echidna. The Lady of the Night, Selene, gave it succor as a cub and presented it to Mother Hera as a plaything. When she tired of it, Hera cast it down from Olympus to range here on the plains. It has made its lair high in the hills in a cave with two mouths. Let us offer sacrifice to Father Zeus that he might aid you on this folly. For without his help, you have no hope of success." The man struggled to his feet, joints creaking in the effort. He began to shuffle around the hovel to gather his offering.

"Good Father," Hercules said as he got to his feet effortlessly. He guided the old man back to his seat. "Take your ease for now. Together, we will send an offering to Father Zeus in thirty days in gratitude of my success. If I am not here in thirty days, offer the sacrifice to Zeus and to me as a hero who has been struck down by the beast."

Hercules left old Molorchus and ventured out into the plains. He searched and searched for days but could find no sign of the beast. The fields and pastures were deserted as the villagers and farmers hid in their houses. The wild creatures stayed buried in their dens and warrens. No birds sang, and even the insects seemed to have fled. The abnormal silence rubbed against Hercules' nerves as he strained to hear any indication of the creature.

Finally, after weeks of searching, he found the monster's gruesome calling card. He could barely tell the grisly remains had ever been a human. Following the trail of gore, Hercules tracked the beast. He caught up with the creature when it rested in the sun to digest its meal. Hercules hid in some scrubby trees at the side of the clearing. His stomach churned with revulsion as the lion licked the blood from its paws and mane. In a smooth motion, he stood, nocked one of the arrows gifted to him by Apollo, and let it fly. The arrow flew straight and true, finding its mark. Instead of being the perfect kill shot through the lungs and heart, the arrow bounced off. It stung, nonetheless, and the lion roared its displeasure.

The giant beast sprang to its feet and charged at Hercules. Hercules rooted his feet and calmly shot two more arrows in rapid succession. Both struck their target but did not so much as scratch the lion. With ground-eating strides, the beast was upon him. He dropped the bow and drew his sword and club. The monster leapt, its great jaws open and ready to clamp down on tender flesh.

Hercules scrambled back and away from the gaping mouth, dodging the assault. As the lion went past, he struck with his sword, but as if it was as dull as a spoon, it slid uselessly off the impenetrable hide. Changing tactics, Hercules spun and brought down his club on the creature's head as it came back for another attack. The mighty club fell and broke over the thick skull. The animal staggered but did not fall. Instead, it glared at Hercules for a moment as if offended that he had dared fight back. Without warning, it turned and darted off across the clearing with its massive legs churning. Hercules gave chase and pursued it all the way back to its cave.

Remembering Molorchus' words, he found the second entrance to the cave and sealed it with a boulder. Quietly, he slipped into the darkness of the lion's lair. He heard the razor-sharp claws clicking on the stone floor. Silently, he followed it deeper and deeper into the cave. When at last the lion lay down to rest, Hercules pounced on its back. The lion roared and reared up, but Hercules held on with grim determination. The beast ran for the back exit of the cave but finding it blocked wheeled and ran for the front. Hercules wrapped his arms around its neck and his legs around its torso and began to squeeze. The lion's steps faltered, and it careened into the walls of the cave in an attempt to rid it of its passenger. With all his strength, Hercules clamped down on the beast until it finally fell dead to the ground.

From Olympus, Hera cried out in anguish when she saw her pet destroyed. The Queen of the Heavens cast the lion into the night sky as the constellation Leo so she would not lose the pleasure of seeing it. Of course, this only served to add more spite in her heart for Hercules.

In the cave, Hercules was pondering how to skin the lion. No knife or sword could cut the skin. Winged words from Athena reached his ears. "Use the claws of the beast."

Following this divine guidance, Hercules skinned the lion using one of its own claws. As before, he donned the pelt of the lion and descended out of the hills.

Molorchus scanned the horizon as had become his habit ever since the young hero, or fool as he had begun to think of him, had left. It was the thirtieth day, and Molorchus set about preparing for two sacrifices. He began the ritual with a heavy heart, for he had truly hoped that Hercules would be successful.

"Hold there, Good Father," a voice called, interrupting the opening of his prayer.

Joyfully, Molorchus turned to see Hercules striding down the sloping hillside. His heart almost stopped when he saw the pelt wrapped around the conqueror's shoulders. But he recovered by the time Hercules closed the distance between them.

"Zeus be praised," the old man whispered and together, he and Hercules performed the ritual of thanks to Father Zeus.

Hercules returned to Eurystheus' court. Without waiting to be announced, he strode into the hall wearing the pelt of the lion. The great beast's head sat atop his, and the skin flowed down over his shoulders and chest. Eurystheus cried out in horror and ran from the chamber. He hid in a wine jar in the cellar and ordered his herald to take a message to Hercules. Bearing his master's words, Copreus told Hercules his next assignment.

"You must travel south to the land of Argos. There you must vanquish the multi-headed hydra of Lerna. Good luck, Hercules. And may the white-armed goddess bless you," the herald dismissed him with the traditional blessing.

Hercules couldn't help but laugh as he left the court. Hera, the white-armed goddess, would sooner eat his liver than bless him.

The swamps of Lerna were many leagues away, so Hercules sought out his nephew, Iolaus, to be his charioteer for the long journey. As they traveled, Hercules told Iolaus what he knew about his next adventure.

"I have heard tales of this beast. Her breath is said to be so venomous that if she but breaths on the foot of a passing man, he will die in agony. The last accounting I heard numbered her heads at nine in total, but one is immortal. She will not be easy to kill," he mused as they traveled. "She nests near the Well of Amymone and is deep into lands dedicated to Queen Hera. I fear we will have no help from the people of the area, though they are likely eager to be rid of the beast. It is said that Hera raised the venomous creature after her parents, Typhon and Echidna, found her too difficult to tame."

Finally, Iolaus steered the chariot onto the flats that boarded the marshlands. "From here, we go on foot," Hercules said, strapping on his weapons and striding confidently into the swamp.

Finding the enormous nine-headed hydra wasn't as easy as the hero thought it would be. She shrank into the depths of the marsh and refused to engage Hercules in battle.

"She will come out if we nettle her enough," Hercules growled. He set his spears alight with fire and flung them into the marsh. After landing a couple of solid hits, the hydra did indeed come out.

With nine poisonous mouths snapping and spitting, the hydra launched herself out of the marsh at Hercules. He drew his sword and with a lightning-quick stroke, severed one the heads. To his horror, two more erupted in its place. He swung twice more and cut off two more heads but fell back when they too regenerated with more heads.

"This isn't going to work," Hercules said to Iolaus, falling back out of the range of the hydra's many snapping jaws. Changing tactics, he switched to his club. "Perhaps if I just bash in the heads, they'll stay dead."

Darting in amongst the weaving heads, Hercules began to lay about with his club. He bashed two heads so hard, they parted company from their necks, and of course, now he had four heads to deal with instead of two. He covered his head with his shield and searched the beast for any signs of weakness.

"Hercules, watch out," cried Iolaus. Hercules spun around, expecting a strike from the hydra's heads, but felt a mighty pain in his foot instead. Clamped around his foot was a massive claw of a giant crab. He brought his club without hesitation. The claw immediately released his foot, but before the crab could escape, he split its shell open with another blow from his club. The hero, frustrated and wounded, limped away from the hydra again.

Hercules' foot bled freely from a jagged cut. Iolaus stoked the fire high and thrust the point of Hercules' sword deep into the white-hot bed of embers. When it glowed red, he pressed it against the bleeding wound, and Hercules' howl of pain shook the trees.

Athena's voice came on winged words in the echoing silence of his cry. "You must stop the flow of immortal blood. As long as the blood flows freely, the heads will keep regenerating. Use your wits as well as your muscles, Hercules."

"Add more wood to the fire, Iolaus," Hercules commanded. "I have a plan."

Once the fire was burning hot, Hercules once again attacked the hydra. This time, as he cut off a head, Iolaus would burn the stump with a torch he kept blazing in the fire. Just like with Hercules' foot, the seared stumps stopped bleeding, and no heads regenerated. The last head Hercules lopped off was the immortal head. The carcass of the great beast slipped down into the marsh while he buried the immortal head deep in the earth and rolled a boulder over the spot. Before the hydra's body was swallowed by the swamp, Hercules coated the tips of his arrows in her venom.

These poisoned darts would kill anyone even with the smallest scratch.

Hera, from her heavenly perch, watched Hercules destroy yet another one of her pets. Like the Nemean Lion, she cast the hydra into the stars. With venom every bit as nasty as the hydra's, Hera plotted the next labor for the hero.

Hercules and Iolaus traveled back to the court of Eurystheus. They strode into the court, but the king was nowhere to be seen.

"I have slain the nine-headed beast," Hercules announced to the court and gave Copreus, the king's messenger, the bag full of the hydra's head. "Take that to your king as proof."

Copreus took the gruesome package to the king while Hercules and Iolaus entertained the court with the story of their adventure. Hidden in the shadows, too afraid to speak to Hercules directly, King Eurystheus watched as his courtiers soaked up the hero's every word. Jealousy burned in his breast as he listened and Hera, always on the lookout for ways to make Hercules' life difficult, fanned the fires.

"Hercules did not complete the quest on his own as was instructed. His charioteer helped him. Do not let him get away with taking shortcuts," Hera whispered to Eurystheus on the wind.

"Copreus," the king called, and his servant scurried to his side. "I declare this quest will not count toward the ten labors the hero owes me! Hercules was to complete the task on his own. Apparently, he was too weak to do so, but I will give him another opportunity to serve me. Go deliver this message and tell Hercules of his next task."

Copreus strode into the hall and called the assembly to attention. As he gave Hercules the news that the last quest would not count, the court erupted in whispers and calls in support for Hercules. Copreus help up his hands to quiet the crowd. "The noble King Eurystheus has granted Hercules another chance to serve him. Hercules, you will retrieve the Cerynitian Hind and deliver it alive to his majesty. His Majesty directs you to start immediately."

Hercules rose to his feet and swept a courtly bow to the corner shadows of the room where everyone knew the king was hiding. He embraced Iolaus and left the court amid cheers of support. In his corner, Eurystheus ground his teeth in irritation but reminded himself that this task would inevitably bring about the end of Hercules.

Hercules did indeed set out immediately. While the hind, a large stag-like animal, was not vicious like his last two opponents, she was faster than a flying arrow and more agile than a feather dancing on the breeze. Taygete, a mountain nymph, created the mythical animals with bronze hooves and golden antlers that adorned both the males and females of the species. She gifted Artemis, the goddess of the hunt, five of the creatures when Artemis saved her from the ravages of Zeus. The small herd pulled Artemis' chariot, but Hera caused one of them to become confused and wander alone in the wild hills. This was the creature Hercules sought, and even though the hind herself posed no threat to him, the goddess of the hunt would kill him on the spot for molesting her sacred animal. He had to hand it to Hera and Eurystheus. This was definitely the most dangerous and challenging quest yet.

Hercules traveled for many weeks before catching a glimpse of the creature. Finally, on a warm summer morning, as Helios pulled the sun into the sky, Hercules saw a glimmer of gold high on a ridge. He gave chase and thus began a year-long game of hide and seek. Over the hills of Greece to the very shores of the Black Sea and back again, Hercules chased the hind, never getting more than a glimpse of its golden horn or flash of a bronze hoof. Finally, both the hind and the hero grew weary of the game. The beast sought refuge high in the craggy peaks of Mount Artemision.

Hercules knew that the animal wanted nothing more than to rest. He withdrew his pursuit and let her bed down in the soft mountain moss. He worked feverishly to craft a net by unraveling the cloak Athena gave him. Without making a twig snap or a blade of grass rustle, Hercules approached the sleeping animal. He threw the net and launched himself right after it. Tangled in the net made of unbreakable thread, the hind struggled. Hercules landed on the flailing creature and fought to find a handhold. His fingers closed around a golden antler that was wrapped in the net. It snapped off in his hand, and the hind scrambled from beneath the edge of the trap.

She raced over the mountain rocks and ridges. Her feet scarcely touched the ground as she bounded away from her captor. Hercules knew he would never get another chance to capture the elusive creature. He shot an arrow between its front legs, tripping it and making it tumble head over hoof down the side of the mountain.

Bruised and battered, the hind didn't have any fight left in her when Hercules tied her legs together and slung her over his shoulders. She was alive and would heal. Hercules spoke soothingly to her as he began the journey back to Mykenai.

He traveled at a grueling pace, for the danger of his quest had reached its pinnacle. Artemis was sure to know that her beloved creature had been captured. He made it as far as Arcadia when Artemis and her twin, Apollo, appeared on the road in front of him. Hercules stopped in his tracks and bowed the best he could with the burden on his shoulders.

"What is this," Artemis demanded. "You dare to hunt my sacred animal. You will pay for your impertinence, Son of Zeus." She and Apollo both drew an arrow from their quivers.

"Wait! Most gracious Artemis, greatest hunter among gods and men! I beg you hear my story before you pass judgment," Hercules pleaded. Hastily, he added, "The hind is well, My Lady. See how she rests?"

Artemis peered at the animal, who did indeed look relaxed and unconcerned about the whole proceedings. "Very well. Tell me your tale but know that if it does not please me, your life is forfeit."

Hercules quickly told her about his crime, penance, and Hera's grudge against him. He told her that he had to bring the hind to King Eurystheus to complete his quest. By the end of his tale,

Artemis' eyes blazed with anger but not for Hercules. "We know what is like to have Hera's wrath focused upon you. Her jealousy warps her mind. But, I cannot allow you to give my animal to a mortal king."

Hercules hastily agreed, sensing that Artemis was sympathetic to his plight. "Perhaps I could borrow her. If I promise to return her to you, will you allow me to present her to King Eurystheus and complete my quest?"

"I think you make a promise you cannot keep," Apollo chimed in. "You have injured the creature. See her broken antler and scraped hide. Artemis, let us finish this now."

Artemis glared at her brother. "I decide what is best for the beast, and I believe our young hero has a plan. Besides, it will vex Hera to have another one of her plans thwarted." To Hercules, she declared, "You have until Selene shines the full radiance her face upon the earth to return her to me. If you do not, I will hunt you to the ends of the earth." With that grim promise, she and Apollo took their leave as abruptly as they had appeared.

Breathing a sigh of relief, Hercules hurried on. The full moon was only a week away, and he still had many leagues to travel.

On the afternoon of the full moon, Hercules burst into the hall of King Eurystheus. Sweating and covered in dust from the road, he led the hind, who had healed completely and regenerated her antler, by a rope around her neck. Surprised by this sudden appearance, the king had not had time to hide away in the shadows. Hercules pressed his advantage, for his plan hinged on Eurystheus' participation.

"King Eurystheus, behold the Cerynitian Hind, the sacred animal of the goddess Artemis," Hercules stopped and presented the animal without getting too close to the raised dais where the king sat.

King Eurystheus was so excited by the animal, he forgot his fear of Hercules. "Bring her to me," he demanded, bouncing in his seat eagerly. "What a beautiful addition to my menagerie!"

"You must come and get her, your majesty," Hercules lied smoothly. "Otherwise she will not stay willingly."

Eurystheus, greedily anticipating the envy of the other nobles at his newest treasure, didn't hesitate to hurry off the dais and across the hall. Just as he reached to take the rope, Hercules opened his hand, and the hind bolted. In the blink of an eye, she ran out of the hall into Artemis' waiting arms.

"You let her go," Eurystheus screamed at Hercules.

"I completed my quest to bring the animal alive to you. It's not my fault you were too slow to catch her," Hercules replied with a shrug and didn't bother to hide the smirking smile that tugged at his lips.

"You won't be smirking after your next quest, Hercules," Eurystheus spat at the hero. "Bring me the Hus Erymanthios, the great boar of Erymanthos, or die trying. If the boar doesn't kill you, the freezing temperatures probably will. Either way would suit me fine." The king turned on his heel and stalked from the hall.

Hercules once again left the kingdom of Mykenai and traveled for many weeks into the Erymanthos mountain range. Higher and higher, the hero climbed. The temperatures plummeted even though it was summer, and snow capped the twin peaks of Mount Erymanthos. Wrapped in his trademark lion pelt, Hercules stopped to see an old friend and find out some more information about the beast he sought.

Pholos, the centaur, led a solitary life in the caves of the Erymanthos. A philosopher by nature, he found the noise of cities and even of his centaur brothers distracting to his ponderings. He was nonetheless overjoyed to see Hercules coming up the path to his cave. He had not seen the hero for many years.

"Hercules! Be welcome here, my friend, and take your ease. Come in and dine with me. Tell me of your adventures and what brings you climbing up the unwelcoming face of Mount Erymanthos," Pholos called, cantering down to meet his friend.

Hercules gratefully accepted Pholos' hospitality and warmed himself next to the fire. Pholos bustled about laying out a meal of raw meat and bread. They ate together, but the raw meat did not sit well with Hercules' palate and began to choke him.

"Pholos, my friend, I must have wine to wash down this meat," Hercules exclaimed.

The centaur rose to his feet. "Of course! I forget that you are not accustomed to our eating habits. I only have one bottle of wine, though. Dionysus in his wisdom entrusted it to me many years ago and said I would know the time to open it. I do not think this is the time, Hercules. If you will wait, I will fetch you water from the stream." Pholos made to leave, but Hercules, gagging, and retching, brought him up short.

"I cannot wait for that. Give me the wine or watch your guest perish before your eyes," Hercules gasped, perhaps a bit more dramatically than necessary.

Pholos grabbed the dusty bottle down from a dark corner of the cave and hastily thrust it into his visitor's hands. Hercules pulled out the cork and drank down almost half the bottle. Instantly intoxicated, for the wine of Dionysus was not to be taken without mixing it with water, Hercules passed the bottle back to Pholos and encouraged him to take a drink. Pholos took a deep draft from the bottle and was immediately in the same state as Hercules. The smell of the wine wafted from the mouth of the cave and was carried off on the mountain breezes. Soon, a herd of centaurs crowded around Pholos' cave. The bottle was passed around, and there wasn't a sober centaur among them in the space of a few minutes.

It didn't take long for the party atmosphere to disintegrate into bickering over nonsense, and one of them finally spied Hercules in the cave. "What is a mortal doing here? He is not welcome in our land," cried one of the largest centaurs. "He is here to steal our secrets!"

The centaurs all turned on Hercules and began to attack him. Trapped in the cave, he had no choice but to use his weapons to save himself. He drew his bow and fired off a volley of arrows. The centaurs died one by one as they were struck by poisoned arrows. The few who had not been hit fled the cave.

Pholos, who was sobering rapidly, looked around at the carnage. "How can such a little thing bring about so much destruction," he mused as he pulled an arrow from the flank of one of his fallen brothers.

"Pholos, do not touch that," Hercules shouted as the centaur turned the arrow in his hands.

Alarmed, Pholos dropped the arrow, and it fell point first into his hoof. He crumpled to the ground, dead, as Hercules ran to his side. Grief welled in the hero's chest as he built a funeral pyre for his friend and the other centaurs. He lit it and held vigil until the spirits of the fallen centaurs were set free among the stars.

With his heart heavy in his chest, Hercules continued his journey, but he hadn't gotten far when he heard something wailing in pain. He hurried to the sound, thinking to put the poor creature out of its misery. He found Chiron, an immortal centaur, who had been struck by one of his arrows. Since he was immortal, he didn't die, but the poison ate away at him, causing him terrible pain.

"What can I do to help you, wise one," Hercules asked, falling to his knees next to the writhing beast.

Chiron, who was the wisest of all the centaurs, knew the ways of gods and man. He knew the secrets of the earth that many had long forgotten, and he knew he had an opportunity to set right an ancient wrong. "Take me to Mount Caucasus. There, the creator of man and beasts has suffered long enough."

Hercules didn't understand what the centaur was talking about, but he carried him all the way to the peak of Mount Caucasus.

They arrived in the early light of day and found Prometheus, still bound to the boulder and tormented by the eagle that tore out his liver every day. Countless years of torment had taken their toll on the Titan, and he wearily raised his head to see who approached his long-forgotten place of exile.

Gently, Hercules sat Chiron on his feet and supported him when he swayed in pain and weakness. "Prometheus, creator of the bronzed-skinned man, your penance is at an end. I will take your place, and you shall once again walk the earth among your creations," Chiron declared. "Father Zeus, see that I willingly take up his bonds as my own!"

With those words, Prometheus' shackles faded away and wrapped themselves around Chiron. Prometheus stared at his savior. "I thank you, noble Chiron, wisest of all the centaurs. I will ensure that your name is known forever among men and gods alike." Prometheus shuffled away on unsteady feet.

"Thank you, Hercules, for seeing this thing done. Go now, your work is done," the centaur said and closed his eyes. The faint screech of an eagle came to them on the wind. Hercules frowned and looked to the sky. His keen eyes picked out the black dot that slowly grew in size until they could see its razor-sharp talons glinting in the sun. Hercules drew an arrow back in his bow and sighted the bird along the shaft. The twang of string sounded a split second before the mighty eagle fell from the sky.

"You have suffered enough, Chiron. The whims of the gods will not plague you further," Hercules told him and followed Prometheus down the path.

Zeus had watched the entire drama unfold and decided that the centaur was too noble a creature to stay bound to boulder for eternity. He cast him with his brothers amongst the stars and thus ended the life of the noble Chiron.

Hercules easily caught up with the slow-moving Prometheus. "Wise one, I am on a quest to capture the Erymanthian Boar. Would you have any ideas on how I can achieve this?"

Prometheus thought for a moment before answering, "The winter snows will soon blanket Mount Erymanthos. Chase the beast into the snow, and he will soon spend his energy fighting through drifts."

Hercules thanked Prometheus and set off back to the Erymanthos Mountains. This time he went far around his erstwhile friend's cave and the site of so much tragedy. The boar, unlike the hind, was easy to find as it left a trail of churned up earth and half-eaten lambs and goat kids. Following Prometheus' advice, Hercules kept the boar climbing higher and higher into the snow. Finally, the boar's short legs couldn't keep him moving through the deep drifts of snow, and Hercules cast his net over the creature. He wrapped him snuggly in the unbreakable net and draped the boar over his shoulder as he began the long journey back to Mykenai.

Many days and dust-covered miles later, Hercules entered the hall without waiting to be announced. He was beyond weary. He just wanted to be done with this quest and all the misery it had caused. King Eurystheus sat in his high throne watching his courtiers mill about. Hercules marched up to the dais and cast the boar, squealing and squirming at the king's feet. Eurystheus screeched and screamed, sounding very much like the boar, and shot out of his throne, diving into the large wine jug in the corner.

"Get it out of here! Take it away," the king shrieked from his hiding place.

With a long sigh, Hercules picked the massive animal up and placed it back on his shoulders. He left the hall without any further conversation. He had no wish to retell this adventure that had cost so many so much. He carried the boar to a far off, desolate stretch of mountains and turned it loose to forage. Then, with a heart heavier than the mountains themselves, he returned to Mykenai for his next labor.

King Eurystheus didn't like the acclaim Hercules was gathering among his court, and Hera's frustration only continued to grow with every successful quest. His fame was spreading, and there was a growing sympathy among the people for his plight. King

Eurystheus complained bitterly about it as he prayed to his goddess, and Hera agreed that Hercules needed to be knocked down to size.

King Eurystheus summoned Hercules to court. Hercules reluctantly bowed to the king for whom he had no respect and an increasing loathing. "Hercules, for your next labor, you will travel to the kingdom of Elis. There King Augeas, son of the Radiant Helios, houses many divine herds of cattle in a stable. I have heard that the stable is in need of cleaning. Your task is to muck out the stable in less time than it takes Helios to make his cycle above and below the earth. Good luck, Hercules. This is work worthy of your station," Eurystheus said snidely and dismissed the hero with a wave of his hand.

Hercules gathered the reins on his temper and left on his quest immediately, journeying to the western region of the Peloponnesos. As he traveled, he wondered what the challenge would be. While it was work that was not worthy for a warrior, cleaning a stable wasn't difficult. There had to be more to it. Before he even saw the palace of King Augeas, he could hear the lowing of cattle followed closely by the overwhelming smell. He couldn't help but stop and stare at the herd of several thousand cattle all sharing a communal shed that stretched for acres and acres. Cleaning it in one day by hand was going to be impossible. It would take years to clean with a shovel and rake. Standing high above the enclosure, Hercules remembered Athena's words about being smart over being strong. He smiled to himself as a plan formed in his mind.

Hercules presented himself to King Augeas and swept a low, courtly bow. "My Lord, what a fine herd of cattle you have, but their stable is in a sorry state. I think I can help you with that."

King Augeas regarded the powerful stranger in front of him. He certainly didn't look or act like a transient laborer looking for work. "That stable has never been cleaned. Why would you take on a task like that," the king asked with one part suspicion and one part curiosity.

Hercules shrugged off the question and countered, "Your Highness, I can not only clean your stable, but I can clean it in a single day."

The king laughed at Hercules until he saw that the hero was serious. "That's impossible! You're a strong, broad-shouldered fellow to be sure, but you cannot hope to clear all that muck in a day. It simply cannot be done. Why would you even try?"

Again, Hercules dismissed the question. "I propose that if I accomplish this thing that you will give me ten percent of the herd in exchange for my efforts. What say you?"

King Augeas considered for a moment. It was an outrageous endeavor, and he was sure that there was something that the stranger was not telling him. Still, he was intrigued by the suggestion, and since it was physically impossible to accomplish, it couldn't hurt to let it play out. It might even prove amusing.

"Very well, sir. You are welcome to ten percent of my herd and grazing lands for them if you can clean the stable in a single day," the king agreed.

Hercules sketched another bow to the king and focused on the young man sitting at king's right side. "Prince of the realm, I ask you to meet me at the stable yard as Mighty Helios brightens the sky in the morning to bear witness to my accomplishment."

The young man nodded his agreement, and there it was left for the evening.

The next morning Hercules and the prince, Phyleus, stood surveying the mountains of dung in the building that stretched farther than their eyes could see. The cattle had all been driven out to pasture for the day to allow Hercules to perform his chore. Phyleus looked at Hercules in amazement. "Stranger, you look strong enough to lift an ox, but there is no way you can clean all of this in the space of a day," the prince exclaimed.

"Prince Phyleus, if you would take your place on the hill just over there, it will all be clear very soon," Hercules instructed, pointing out an outcropping of rock that would give the prince a view of the entire area.

Once the prince was in his position, Hercules ran to the far end of the stables and uprooted the foundations, so the end of the enclosure was open to the valley beyond it. Then, he ran back to the other end of the stables and pulled up the foundations there as well. The barn was now one long, open channel. Using the foundations, Hercules built a levee to divert the swiftly flowing waters of the rivers Alpheios and Peneios Rivers that ran on either side of the stables. A great torrent of water sluiced down the valley and through the channel of the shed, carrying away decades of muck and filth in a matter of minutes. Once the area was well rinsed, Hercules reestablished the foundations and the stables were clean. Helios was only halfway through his daily journey, and the business was done.

Phyleus ran down the hill to where Hercules stood proudly. "You must tell me your name, stranger! What an amazing feat!"

"I am Hercules come from the kingdom of Mykenai," the hero replied as the king, hearing of the miraculous deed, came hurrying up.

"Hercules of Mykenai? You have come here under false pretenses, sir," the king accused, looking with wide eyes at the clean stables. "You were ordered here by King Eurystheus and are bound in penance to do this labor. I owe you nothing for the job done here today." King Augeas turned and began to walk back toward his palace.

"Your Highness, we had a bargain," Hercules thundered so loudly that Augeas jumped and spun around to face him. "You will pay me as we agreed, or I will ask the justices convene to hear the matter."

The king wanted to refuse, but the look on Hercules' face made him reconsider. "Very well. We will seek arbitration."

The justices were called, and everyone gathered in the great hall. Each side presented their case. The judges appeared to be siding with Augeas until Hercules called Phyleus to bear witness. Not only did the prince tell of Hercules' unbelievable strength and cunning, but he also bore witness that his father had indeed struck a bargain with Hercules. After hearing all the evidence, the panel of judges decided in Hercules' favor and ordered the king to give him the promised land and cattle.

King Augeas' anger erupted, and he called his army forward to drive Hercules and his son from his kingdom.

Hercules fell back, though he was sorely tempted to stand and fight. He was not free to fight this battle at the moment. "Oath-breaker, Augeas, know you live on borrowed time. I will return and claim your throne for my own," Hercules vowed.

Hercules journeyed back to King Eurystheus' court in Mykenai. His story, however, preceded him. Eurystheus was waiting eagerly for him when he walked into the hall.

"Here is our hero turned stable boy," the king called from his throne as Hercules made his way to the dais.

"I have completed the quest that you set for me, Eurystheus," Hercules growled. "I have witnesses to prove it."

"I do not need your witnesses," Eurystheus snapped. "I have already heard about the water washing out the stables. However, you were supposed to clean the stables, not the water, and you were most certainly not to be paid for it. I declare this quest null.

It will need to be repeated," the king announced with smug satisfaction while the court let out a collective gasp. They had all been in awe of how Hercules had not only cleaned the stables but did it without having to stoop to manual labor that was beneath the son of a god.

Eurystheus watched with satisfaction as Hercules clenched his jaw in frustration. The king pressed on over the whispers of the courtiers, "You will leave immediately for your next quest to the land of Arcadia. There, on Lake Stymphalis, the flock of Stymphalian Birds is wreaking havoc on the people of the region. You will kill them and restore the peace."

Hercules, barely containing his fury, nodded once, turned on his heel, and left without another word.

He traveled again to Arcadia where the locals knew all too well about the vicious birds of Lake Stymphalis. They pointed Hercules on his way and wished him well, though they didn't expect him to have much luck. About the size of a crane, the birds had beaks made of bronze and metallic feathers that they could shoot like arrows. Their dung let off poisonous vapors and sickened anyone who breathed them in. They had claimed the lake as theirs and had slowly turned it into a dark, fetid swamp, unfit for any but them to inhabit.

Hercules went boldly forward into the swamp. The noxious fumes stung his eyes and made his guts churn. The birds chattered and called from the tops of the trees and systematically fell back deeper and deeper into the swamp as Hercules pushed forward. He didn't make it far before he was forced to retreat, lest he succumb to the fumes.

After he rested and recovered himself in the clear air on the edge of the swamp, Hercules shot arrow after arrow into the trees, but none found a target. The birds simply flew back out of range and waited, mocking him with their calls. Frustrated, Hercules drew in a huge lungful of air and ran full-tilt into the swamp. Instead of falling back, the birds let their dagger-like feathers fly. Hercules threw his shield over his head and took cover behind a tree. His air expended, he was once again forced to the edge of the swamp to breathe and regroup.

"I must get them to come out of the swamp," he mused to himself.

As if in answer, Athena appeared to him. She wrinkled her nose as she took in her surroundings. "These unholy creatures were made by my brother, Ares. He thrives on violence and vulgarity. I wish you to rid our land of the pests," the goddess said as she handed Hercules two large brass clappers. "Master of the forge, Hephaestus, made these for you. Clap them together in the trees, and the birds will scatter out of the swamp. Once again, cunning will win the day." In the blink of an eye, she was gone, and Hercules was once again alone in the dismal place.

He didn't waste any time in putting Athena's plan into action. With another deep breath, he plunged into the swamp and clanged the bronze noisemakers madly. As the goddess predicted, the birds took flight and Hercules sprinted back to the edge of the swamp. Taking up his bow and arrows, he felled as many birds as

Minos snorted an incredulous laugh. "Eurystheus is welcome to the beast, but it is on his head when it turns out poorly. Good luck catching it." The king dismissed Hercules with a wave of his hand.

Hercules took his leave and went to find the bull. It wasn't hard, for the path of destruction and ear-splitting bellowing led him straight to it. Hercules stood for a moment and took in the enormity of the beast. At least twice the size of a normal bull, its legs were as big as tree trunks, and its razor-sharp horns stood as tall as Hercules. The beast turned his malevolent stare at Hercules, and there they stood, sizing each other up, one brute to another.

With astounding speed, the bull lowered its head and charged at Hercules, throwing up huge divots of land with each stride. Hercules waited until the beast was almost upon him before vaulting himself onto its back. He hung on, clinging like a tick while the bull bucked and twisted. Hours passed before the bull ceased its efforts to throw Hercules off and wearily sank to its knees. Surprised that the creature had given in so easily, Hercules fashioned a halter from the unbreakable thread of Athena's cloak and led the animal toward the sea.

There was still the trouble of getting across the sea back to the mainland. No ship could hold the massive bull. Hercules stood on the shore surveying the harbor full of ships and wondering what to do next when he noticed the bull wandering into the surf. To his amazement, its hooves didn't break the surface of the water. As a creation of the sea, the bull, despite its bulk, could walk on water. Problem solved, Hercules hopped on the creature's back and urged it over the waves toward the Arcadian harbor.

He rode the bull all the way back to Mykenai where he presented it to King Eurystheus. The court exploded in cheers for the hero and cries of amazement at the size and strength of the beast. Of course, the massive animal terrified the king. "We will sacrifice it to Queen Hera in gratitude for her wisdom and blessings," Eurystheus declared, for he could not ever be comfortable with such an animal in his kingdom.

Hera, however, did not like this plan. In a dream, she told Eurystheus to sacrifice a bull from his own herd instead and make Hercules escort the Cretan Bull far away from Mykenai. If Eurystheus offered the mighty beast, the glory would be to Hercules' achievement, and Hera would not abide that.

While the city held a festival in Hera's honor, Hercules took the bull to the faraway land of Marathon and turned it loose to graze in the lush hills and valleys. Of course, this bull would later go on to terrorize the region and be killed by Theseus. Hercules still had several labors to perform, so he trudged back to Mykenai and reported back to King Eurystheus.

Buoyed by the recent celebrations, Eurystheus received Hercules with enthusiasm. He couldn't wait to see if the hero managed to complete his next task. Secretly, Eurystheus thought that it was the most likely to best Hercules. He tried not to sound overly eager when he informed Hercules of his next assignment. "For your next labor, you will bring me the Mares of Diomedes. I am sure the Thracians will make you feel most welcome," the king quipped and enjoyed the titters of his courtiers as they laughed at his joke. Everyone knew that inhabitants of Thrace were barbarians and possibly even cannibals. Descendants of the quarrelsome war god, Ares, they were as welcoming as the infertile obsidian waters of the Black Sea by which they lived.

Hercules showed no reaction as he left the hall, though his heart had sunk at the proclamation. Thracians didn't share well and would just as soon kill a man as speak to him. Hercules wasn't going to be able to just ask for the horses like he had the Cretan Bull. He would have to steal them right out from under the nose of Diomedes.

Hercules recruited his most trusted friend, Abderos, to accompany him. Recalling his adventure with the hydra, he swore Abderos to secrecy about any involvement in the scheme to capture the horses. The road was long, but the journey was more pleasant for Hercules with the company of his friend.

In the city of Pherae, they stopped in to see some old friends of Hercules', King Admetus and his wife, Alcestis. Their marriage had begun in an unconventional way. Alcestis' father deemed all her suitors too weak to marry his daughter and decreed that she would only marry a man who was able to harness a boar and a lion to a chariot. King Admetus convinced Apollo to help him in exchange for a sacrifice to the Archer Prince's sister, Artemis. Admetus won the lady's hand in marriage through the divine intervention of Apollo and Artemis. However, on his wedding night, Admetus was so distracted with the festivities and the beauty of his new bride, he forgot to offer the sacrifice to Artemis as agreed. King Admetus carried his new queen into the bridal chamber and found it full of snakes. He hastily made his sacrifice, begging the goddess' forgiveness. Artemis, feeling magnanimous, accepted the apology and banished the snakes. Even after such an inauspicious beginning, the couple fell in love and ruled for many years in harmony.

The king welcomed the travelers to his home, but it struck Hercules as odd that the court, typically so full of life, was subdued and melancholy. Queen Alcestis was nowhere to be seen. Finally, after a very strained meal, he finally asked if everything was alright.

King Admetus looked at his friend and could no longer hold back his distress. "Hercules, I don't know what to do. I have done something so foolish!"

The king told Hercules his sad story. When he and his wife were newly married, Admetus had sought out Apollo because he had heard a prophecy that his death would come while he was still a man in his prime. Apollo liked the young king, so he took some of Dionysus' wine to the Sisters of Fate and drank with them until they were drunk. While they were intoxicated, they granted Admetus an escape from death. They decreed that when Thanatos, the god of death who escorted souls to the Underworld, appeared to Admetus, he could ask if anyone else was willing to take his place. If he could find a volunteer, Thanatos would take that person instead. Admetus thought that one of his elderly parents would walk with Thanatos in his stead, but when the time came, they refused. The only person who was willing to take his place was his beloved Alcestis.

"Thanatos is here for her even now. It should be me making the dark journey, but now I shall live the rest of my days in darkness," the king cried bitterly into his wine.

Hercules left Abderos to console the king and went to the queen's tomb. He found Thanatos coaxing Alcestis' soul from her body. "Hold there, Dark One," Hercules cried as he threw back the door of the crypt. Puzzled, Thanatos looked up from his work. Hercules pushed into the small space and crowded Thanatos back and away from Alcestis. "Leave this woman. She has made a noble sacrifice, but it is not her time."

"The Fates have spoken, and I cannot disobey. I cannot return to the Underworld empty-handed." Thanatos tried to step around the hero to continue his task.

"I will take her place," Hercules declared, and when Thanatos looked at him in surprise, he continued, "I will walk into the darkness with you if you can beat me in wrestling. If I win, you leave this place empty-handed and will find your quota elsewhere. Agreed?"

Thanatos shrugged. One mortal soul was the same as another. Hercules didn't give him a chance to think about it further. He launched himself at his opponent. In the small space, they grappled with each other until Hercules was able to get his arms around Thanatos. In what was becoming his signature move, he squeezed until the god of death yielded. As agreed, Thanatos left the crypt alone, and Alcestis opened her eyes and sat up.

The king and queen were reunited, and they celebrated in Hercules' honor for several days. The travelers could not tarry long, and despite their hosts' protest, they left the joyful kingdom to continue their quest.

After many weeks of traveling east, they finally could hear the waves of the Black Sea and caught their first glimpses of the dark, inhospitable waters. Soon, they came to tribal lands of the Bistones. Hercules hid Abderos in a seaside cave while he presented himself to King Diomedes.

Hercules and Abderos had asked about the horses and Diomedes on the road. The gruesome stories that had been told about the king feeding guests and prisoners to the horses had chilled their blood. It was rumored that Diomedes had corrupted the horses, so they only ate the flesh of man and had to be tethered in a stable by chains. Others said that the steeds were demons escaped from the Underworld. Everyone they spoke to agreed, the kingdom of Thrace was a cursed and deadly place. And so, when Hercules stood before the king, he went straight on the offensive.

"King Diomedes, I have come to retrieve the four divine steeds from your stables," Hercules declared confidently, though he had to admit that Diomedes was a brute of a man whose massive arms looked like they could rip a person limb from limb.

The king looked mildly amused. "You are a stranger in our land, and yet you walk into my hall and tell me you plan to take my horses. Do you know what we do to strangers here," Diomedes asked casually.

Hercules, who had no intention of ending up horse-chow, answered swiftly, "Oh yes! Thracian hospitality is legendary." He sketched a mock bow and pressed on before the king could say anything more. "I beg your pardon, great king! I should have spoken more plainly. I will take your horses after I have beaten you in the game of your choosing."

Diomedes' eyes went wide at the bold statement, but a slow grin crept across his face. He was going to enjoy feeding this brawny would-be hero to his pets. "I should kill you where you stand, but you've piqued my interest. I challenge you to a wrestling match and to the victor go the horses!"

The crowd parted and formed a large opening in its center. Hercules cast off his sword, bow, and arrows and strode toward the center of the makeshift ring. King Diomedes met him in the center, and without further discussion, the match commenced. Hercules had been trained by the finest tutors on the techniques of combat, boxing, and wrestling, but he had his hands full with the King of the Bistones. As the son of Ares, Diomedes reveled in violence, and what he lacked in technique, he made up for in brute strength and savagery. The match was ruthless and bloody but mercifully short. Hercules was a fraction quicker and was able to gain the upper hand when he managed to get his arm around Diomedes' neck. He squeezed viciously until the king slapped the ground in surrender.

"The horses are mine," Hercules confirmed after loosening his grip slightly but not enough to let Diomedes free.

"Yes," the king rasped, his face reddish purple with exertion and rage.

Deciding it wasn't wise to tarry and test the hospitality of his host, Hercules went directly to the stables. His stomach heaved at the grisly sight. Blood covered the walls and bones littered the floor and mounded up the walls. The horses' manes and tails hung in tangled clumps flecked with blood and were so long they touched the ground. Their onyx coats that should have gleamed a glossy black were caked in filth and grime. At his approach, four sets of eyes rolled, full of madness and blood lust. Hooves bigger than his head shook the ground, demanding to be fed while their chains rattled with their impatience. Hercules could only stare for a few moments and concluded that these beasts had to have come from the deepest, foulest pit of Tartarus.

One by one, he muzzled their snapping jaws with their chains and led them out of the stables. The Bistonians stood in small groups and watched him lead the horses away while Diomedes glowered down at him from a high hill at the edge of town. The four mares danced on their tethers and tested Hercules' strength to keep them in order. Finally, they made it to the seaside cave where Abderos blanched at the sight of a battered Hercules leading the four hellish horses.

From the vicinity of the town, a large dust cloud was forming. Hercules sighed when he saw it. Time for a change in plans. He herded the four ill-tempered animals into the seaside cave and blocked the mouth with a large rock that left only a small crevasse open. "Watch them, Abderos, but do not try to touch them. They have a taste for the flesh of man, and they are hungry. We cannot outrun the army and keep those abominations in check. I must go back and defeat Diomedes before we can carry on."

Hercules disappeared back down the trail toward the growing clamor of the advancing troops.

The horses ran madly around in the cave. Abderos perched on a rock and peered into the cave. Their hooves sounded like thunder, and they threw themselves against the walls of their prison. One ran headlong into the boulder blocking the cave, shifting it slightly. Abderos, who had been watching through the crevice opening, toppled into the cave. His cries were drowned out by the unearthly shrieking of the horses as they devoured him.

Hercules, ignorant of his friend's death, engaged Diomedes and his army. His sword and club slashed and struck in a blur of motion. Bistonians fell before him like saplings under an ax until he got to Diomedes. Again, Diomedes proved to be a worthy foe, and their swords crashed over and over. Finally, Hercules wore the other man down until he was able to get under Diomedes' guard with a lethal thrust to the heart. At the fall of their leader, the rest of the army scattered.

Wearily, Hercules shouldered Diomedes' corpse and traced his path back to the sea cave. The unholy neighing and shrieking from the horses made him quicken his pace. When he saw the boulder ajar and no sign of Abderos, Hercules cried out in anguish. He rolled the stone aside and flung Diomedes' body deep into the cave. With blood-chilling zeal, the beasts ran after it, tossing their heads, so their chains added to their awful melody.

Hercules retrieved what was left of his friend's body and sealed the cave once more. In a fit of anger and sadness, he laid Adberos to rest and built an entire city overnight in his memory before he collapsed with fatigue and grief.

Helios was already most of the way across the sky when Hercules raised his head. He staggered to his feet and made his way back to the cave. Not a sound came from inside, and for a moment, he wondered if the insane creatures had killed each other. Then, he heard the low nicker of a horse, a normal everyday sound from a normal everyday horse. Curious, Hercules rolled the boulder from the mouth of the cave and stared in amazement as the four mares stood docilely with clear eyes apparently free from the madness that had gripped them. It seemed that by consuming their tormentor, they were cured of their insanity.

He led them from the cave and started the long journey home. As they traveled, he cut their manes and tails and cleaned their coats of the layers of blood and dirt. When he once again returned to Mykenai, he led four beautiful, well-mannered mares that made everyone stop and stare. Even King Eurystheus was taken aback by their beauty. "I give these noble beasts to the white-armed goddess, Hera, that she will continue to bless us with her good will," Eurystheus proclaimed and commanded Hercules to take the animals to graze at the base of Mount Olympus. It is said, the legendary mount of Alexander the Great, Bocepheus, could trace his bloodlines to these mares.

It didn't take long before Eurystheus dispatched Hercules on his next quest. "Bring me the sacred belt of the Amazons. I wish to give it to my daughter. I imagine these warrior women will know how to deal with one such as you."

Hercules said nothing. He was so accustomed to Eurystheus' insults that he didn't even hear them anymore. The land of the Amazons lay to the Far East, and the tribe of warrior women who lived there was rumored to be more savage than any group of men that ever banded together. Amazon meant "missing one breast" and had been bestowed on them because when they came of age to join the ranks of warriors, they cut off their right breasts since it hindered sword and spear movements. Despite their savageness, they were said to be some of the most beautiful women in the world.

Hercules journeyed eastward over the sea. His ship dropped anchor in the harbor while a band of warrior women stood waiting on the shore. He rowed a small boat to land and cautiously walked toward the group. The women dressed in armor and each carried a shield, spear, and sword. Hercules realized with amazement that they were as tall as he was, and their shapely forms were muscular and strong.

One of the women stepped forward. She wore a belt of fine craftsmanship that could have only been divinely made. From it swung her spear and sword as she walked toward Hercules. "I am Hippolyta, daughter of mighty Ares and Queen of the Amazons. Why are you on our land?"

Hercules bowed low to the queen with all the gallantry he possessed. "I am Hercules and have been sent by his majesty, King Eurystheus, to see if the legendary beauty of the Amazon women was the truth. It is unfortunate that I will have to tell him that is was a lie," he said, shaking his head sadly. The women hissed at the words and in unison, drew their swords. Hercules held up his hands to calm them. "I will tell him that beauty is far too simple a term to describe the wonder of the Amazon women. I will tell him that they are divinely made and rival even the most beautiful of the goddesses."

Queen Hippolyta made a motion with her hand, and the women all sheathed their weapons. "Hercules, your honeyed words do not trick me, but they do please me. Come with me as my guest." Hippolyta led the way back to her village and shared a meal with Hercules. She was utterly smitten with the hero by the time they were finished eating. Hercules sensed her affection and monopolized on it.

"My lady, I did not speak the whole truth earlier about my reason for coming here," he told her quietly as they lingered over fruit and wine. "My king has sent on a quest so I can atone for the death of my family. The only way I can satisfy his demands is to present him with your belt. He has heard of its magic and wants it for his daughter."

Hippolyta's eyes flared with indignation at the bold demand. "I earned this belt. Ares bestowed it upon me as a sign that I am the strongest and most cunning warrior among this tribe. Your king," Hippolyta scoffed and shook her head. "Your king is inept and weak. Go back to your ship and leave. You will not be welcomed on this shore again." Her heart broke as she left him sitting alone at the table.

Antiope, Hippolyta's sister, appeared to escort Hercules back to his ship. He followed her, and they walked in silence. Just before he got into the waiting boat, he grabbed Antiope and forced her into the vessel. As soon as they reached the main ship, they set to sail away, abducting Antiope.

Hippolyta mounted her defenses and pursued Hercules. She caught up with them as they arrived in Athens. King Theseus, his friend, and fellow hero, gave Hercules and his crew refuge and rallied his troops to defend against the oncoming Amazon army. In an effort to spare lives, Hercules sent word to Hippolyta that he would be willing to exchange Antiope for her belt. They met on the deck of his ship to discuss it.

While the leaders stood in discussion, Hera appeared disguised as an Amazon woman among the army of warrior women. Every eye was intently watching the exchange on the ship in anxious silence. They expected Hercules to double-cross their queen. Hera smiled as she laid a spark to the dry kindling of tension that was building amongst the ranks. "Do you see what he is doing? He is taking the belt! He means to steal our queen! He means to harm her!"

That was all it took. The Amazon women let loose their battle cry and launched themselves against the opposing troops. On the ship, chaos broke out as the leaders tried to get control of their forces. In the melee, Hercules and Hippolyta found themselves crossing blades. In a flurry of parries and strikes, their swords flashed and danced until they were both forced to concede that they were evenly matched. Hippolyta, still enamored with Hercules, was impressed by his swordsmanship and ability. She called a halt to their engagement and Hercules, bewildered, lowered his sword and waited. As the battle raged around them, she stripped off her belt and gave it to the hero.

"Go complete your quest, Hercules and may the young princess grow into a woman worthy of this belt." Hippolyta whirled around and disappeared into the fray.

Hercules called his troops to him, and they left Athens immediately, leaving Theseus and his army to deal with subduing the Amazons. Eventually, Theseus and Hippolyta would settle a truce between the two nations. Meanwhile, Hercules made his way back to Mykenai.

Hercules reluctantly presented Eurystheus with the belt and his ninth labor drew to a close. The king wasted no time sending him back out on his next challenge. "Your next task will take you to the farthest edge of the earth, well past the borders of civilized men. Bring me the Cattle of Geryon so I might sacrifice them to the glory of Hera." Eurystheus waved his hand to dismiss Hercules. Surely, this would be the trial that would bring the hero down. Eurystheus hoped that a sea monster would have him for a snack or at the very least, he would fall off the end of the earth. Either would suit him fine, just so long as Hercules never appeared in his court again.

Hercules simply left the court without any indication of hearing his instructions. His mind was already beginning to consider this task. The fabled land of the giants lay on the western edge of the world. On any map that Hercules had seen, Erytheia was an ill-defined island that was colored red since it was the last thing on earth cradled by Helios' setting rays. It would take him months to reach and involved crossing the open ocean. It was by far the most challenging task he had been given.

Hercules set out immediately, traveling westward. He was moving well until he came to the desert of Lybia. The heat bore down on him, and his feet moved slower and slower. Sweat rolled off his body in rivers, and he felt his strength sapping away. Irritated, he drew his bow and nocked an arrow. He pulled the string back as far as he could and sent an arrow soaring toward Helios in his chariot high above the earth.

Helios laughed at the pithy hero and decided that his bravery should be recognized. "Hercules," he called from his chariot, "your journey is long and tiring. I have a gift for you. You will find it waiting for you on the shore of the great open water. Good luck, Son of Zeus!"

Hercules shaded his eyes, looking into the blinding light that spoke to him. "Thank you, Bright One! If your rays do not turn me to dust before I get there, I will be sure to make good use of it," Hercules groused as he plodded on.

Helios laughed again and gathered clouds to shade the hero as he finished his trek across the brutal landscape. Finally, desert gave way to foothills and then to mountains. Hercules enjoyed the cooler temperatures as he traveled through the mountain passes and with relief reached the edge of the sea.

As promised, a golden vessel that looked more like a giant cup than a ship bobbing in the waves, waiting to take the hero on the next leg of his journey. Hercules climbed aboard, and the boat swept out to sea. He didn't get far. The water was blocked in the narrows between Lybia and Europe, or what in the modern day is known as the Straits of Gibraltar. Hercules climbed out of his boat and with his mighty strength, he widened the passage, building two massive rock formations on either side of the strait. He purposely left them only wide enough to allow vessels and water through lest the wild sea monsters from the deep ocean invade the civilized world.

"These pillars will mark the furthest west I have ever traveled and will serve as a monument to all explorers that they are passing into the realm of the unknown," Hercules decreed. He climbed back into his golden cup and sailed into the unknown.

The island of Erytheia beckoned from the western horizon. Hercules' vessel took him straight to the Red Island. His foot had barely touched the soil when a vicious cacophony of barking split the peaceful sounds of the ocean. He spun and raised his club just in time to defend himself against the snapping jaws of Orthos, the two-headed dog who guarded the island. Hercules fought the beast until he managed to club it to death. In the silence as he struggled to catch his breath from the sudden attack, he heard what sounded like an avalanche heading straight for him.

Out of the trees emerged a fearsome giant. Eurytion, the cowherd to Geryon, burst onto the shore, and his cry of dismay when he saw his dog lying dead on the sand shook the ground. Hercules barely had time to raise his shield before the giant was on him, raining down blow after blow with his club and his fists. Hercules ducked, dodged, and blocked until he was able to get an opening. With one mighty swing, his club connected with the giant's head, bashing in his skull. Eurytion fell as silent and still as his dog.

Hercules didn't have time to wonder what would be coming next, and even if he had, he could have never imagined what appeared from the trees. A hideous monster, Geryon, crashed onto the shore. Geryon, the grandson of Medusa, had three giant bodies joined together at the belly. Six arms and legs sprouted from him, and his three heads looked in all directions at once. He had massive leathery wings that he unfurled threateningly at Hercules.

The hero ducked out of range of the six arms. He scuttled back until he found a small crevice in the rocks. He wedged himself inside while the giant bellowed his frustration at not being able to reach him. Hercules thought furiously. He would never be able to defend against that many arms, legs, and wings. He had only one shot. In a smooth motion, Hercules drew his bow and arrow and let one of his poisoned arrows fly at the center head of the giant. It flew straight and true and struck the giant's forehead. Such was the force of his bow, the arrow penetrated the giant's skull, and he wilted like a flower in the cold grip of winter. The only sound to be heard was the waves rolling gently onto the beach.

With all the guardians slain, Hercules set about gathering the stunning red-coated cattle. However, the bull had other ideas and led Hercules on a merry chase all over the island. He could not leave without the bullm for Eurystheus would say that the herd was not complete without it. For weeks, Hercules chased the animal until finally capturing it. He loaded all the cattle on his golden vessel, and they sailed back across the ocean.

As he unloaded the cattle on the European side of his twin monuments, Hercules returned the boat to Helios with an offering of thanks. Then, he began his long trek back to Mykenai, which was slow going with such a large herd. One night, high in the hills of Italy, the fire-breathing giant, Cacus, stole half the herd of cattle while Hercules was sleeping. He made the animals walk backward so they would leave no trail, which was a trick first used by Hermes, who among other things was the god of thieves.

When Hercules awoke and found half of the herd gone, he was furious. He hunted everywhere but could find no trace of them. Frustrated, he sat on a boulder to think. While he was thinking, he saw a beautiful giantess coming toward him.

"My Lady," he called to her. "Have you seen a herd of cattle? They have coats of brilliant red, and I confess they seem to have disappeared overnight!"

The giantess smiled sweetly and looked at the handsome hero. "How did you manage to lose a whole herd of crimson cattle," she asked in a flirtatious tone. "I am Caca, and if you amuse me, I will help you find your cattle."

Hercules was no stranger to amusing women, even giant ones. Once Caca was properly amused, she said, "My brother, Cacus, has your cattle. They are hidden in the high cave to the north. But, be careful, Hercules. He will not let them go without a fight."

Hercules assured her he could take care of himself and went to find the rest of his herd. He heard them lowing before he could see the cave itself. Cacus sat at the entrance, guarding his ill-gotten treasure. Hercules didn't hesitate. He marched up to Cacus and drew his sword. The giant stood and towered over him with a cruel smile. "Come, little man. If you can best me, you can have your cattle back," the giant taunted.

Hercules didn't bother responding. He went on the offensive, and Cacus was soon too busy defending himself to say anything else. After a brief, furious battle, Cacus lay dead next to the cave. Hercules recovered his cattle and rejoined the other half of his herd.

Eastward, they traveled over mountains and through valleys. Hercules gratefully accepted the hospitality of King Bretannus and slept soundly in a comfortable bed for the first time in months. When he woke the next morning, eager to be on his way, the whole herd was gone. However, this time, he didn't have to look far to find out what had happened to them. Celtine, the king's daughter, came to him with a proposition.

"Forgive me, mighty Hercules, but I could not let you leave so quickly. I wish you to lay with me so I might show you my love and carry a part of you with me forever. Do this for me, and your herd will be returned to you."

Hercules had little choice but to comply. He took Celtine to bed and lay with her. True to her word, she gave him back his cattle, and he continued his journey.

Day after day, Hercules drew closer to Mykenai. When he drove the herd onto the soil of Greece, Hera once again took notice of him. She felt Hercules had had an entirely too easy of a time with his quest. With a malicious smile, Hera sent a swarm of gadfly among the herd. The biting insects tormented the cattle, driving them into a frenzy and scattering them across the countryside. It took Hercules an entire year to gather them all back together and resume his trek.

When he arrived at the mighty Alfios River, Hera summoned a flood, causing the river to rage with torrents of water. Unable to ford the river, Hercules had to build a bridge by piling boulders in the river. Ultimately, he was able to get the cattle to the other side, but Hera's meddling had delayed him by several more months.

Finally, almost three years after he left, Hercules returned to Mykenai with the Cattle of Geryon. Reluctantly, Eurystheus accepted the herd. He had been holding out hope with every passing month that Hercules had met his end. He dedicated the herd to Hera and ordered a sacrifice of the best animals in her name.

Hercules answered the king's summons to court shortly after he had delivered the cattle. Technically, he had completed his ten labors and his time of servitude was complete. However, since Eurystheus refused to acknowledge two of the labors, Hercules was still bound to serve him. He entered the hall and braced himself for his next set of instructions.

"Hercules, I wish you to fetch me the golden apples of Hesperus. Their taste is said to be as impressive as their magical properties. I wish to have this magic at my command," the king commanded.

"Zeus knows you need all the help you can get," Hercules muttered as he left the hall. As usual, he departed immediately on his quest. Now that his sentence was nearing an end, he was impatient to be free of it.

First, Hercules had to discover the location of the Garden of Hera where the apple tree had been planted when it had been presented as a wedding gift from Gaia to Hera and Zeus. The garden was Hera's domain, and she hid a multitude of treasures within its boundaries. Its whereabouts was a deeply guarded secret, and only a handful of divine creatures knew it.

Hercules had heard of a sea god who knew all the secrets of the world and would answer one question for anyone who could catch him. He could change forms which made him nearly impossible to capture. The sailors called him the Old Man of the Sea, but they steered well clear of the creature. He had a nasty reputation of enslaving anyone who tried to question him by making them carry him ceaselessly upon their back until they died of exhaustion. Hercules hired a small vessel and headed out into the deep sea.

It took days of drifting on the ocean before the sea god took any notice of Hercules. Finally, the Old Man of the Sea rose up to see what the hero was doing just floating around without any direction or purpose.

"You are a very poor sailor, indeed," the sea god said, manifesting off the bow of Hercules' boat. "You have no sail set, your rudder flops uselessly against the hull, and you are drunk! What are you doing   out   here?"
Hercules, who was only acting intoxicated, hiccupped and offered the sea god a bottle of Dionysus' best wine. "I am drowning my troubles before I decide if I should drown myself," Hercules slurred.

Intrigued, the Old Man of the Sea joined him in the boat and took the offered bottle of wine. Hercules shared his sorry tale while he plied the god with more and more wine. The sea god drank and listened and was soon very drunk. When he started to doze in a drunken stupor, Hercules struck with lightning quickness and bound the god's hands and feet.

The Old Man of the Sea struggled against his bonds but quickly gave up, sagging against the side of the boat. "What do you want," he grumbled.

"I have captured and bound you. I want an answer to my question," Hercules said and waited for the sea god to nod his agreement before continuing, "I am seeking the nymphs of Hesperus, the guardians of the sacred golden apples. My quest is to retrieve the apples. How do I do this?"

The Old Man of the Sea hated to give away secrets, but he had no choice. "You seek the daughters of the Evening Star and the mighty Titan, Atlas. You have a long journey ahead. Travel west on the straight road to the horizon. Follow the evening star past the Boreades. Be careful here that the hurricane does not pluck you from the earth and cast you into its abyss. You will cross vast deserts and come to the edge of the world. There, you will find Mighty Atlas with his burden on his shoulders. His daughters will let him take as many apples as he pleases. He can get the apples for you - if you're able to convince him. Otherwise, you'll have to slay Drakon, the hundred-headed serpent who Hera set to guard the tree. Either way, you will more likely die than succeed." With his obligation fulfilled, the Old Man of the Sea transformed into a fish, his bonds falling uselessly to the bottom of the boat. He flopped overboard and swam out of sight. Hercules set sail for the western shore.

The straight road was easy to find but long to walk. It stretched on and on, seemingly forever. Hercules traveled quickly until he came to the drought-stricken land of Aigyptos. For eight years, the sky had refused to rain, and King Bousiris had desperately sought advice from an oracle on how to end the drought. He interpreted the prophecy to say that travelers must be sacrificed to the gods in order to bring rains to the region. Ever since then, anyone who walked the straight road through the kingdom had been offered to the gods. Hercules, of course, was ignorant of this and walked right into the ambush the king had set to capture travelers. It took many men, but Hercules was finally subdued and bound before being taken to the king.

King Bousiris ordered Hercules to be offered in sacrifice to fulfill the prophecy. The soldiers took him to the altar and made their preparations. Hercules waited until they stepped forward to cut his throat before, in a fantastic show of strength, he broke free of his bonds and disarmed the advancing guards. The assembly watched as Hercules killed King Bousiris by running him through with a sword. A stunned silence stretched out as everyone stared at Hercules and then, a deafening cheer went up. The people had hated their king and his barbaric ways. They embraced Hercules as their hero before sending him westward.

The road continued straight and true, and Hercules dutifully followed it, though after being caught in an ambush he stayed more alert than before. Which is why he was prepared when Antaeus, a giant who terrorized a section of the road around Lybia, stepped onto the path and blocked his way. Antaeus didn't like travelers using what he thought of as his road. As a toll, he challenged travelers to a wrestling match in which the penalty for losing was death. Of course, since Antaeus was a giant, he always won. At least, until he met Hercules.

"Traveler, you must beat me in a wrestling match if you wish to pass," the giant declared and set his feet in preparation.

Hercules put aside his belongings and similarly set his feet. He wasn't afraid of giants. They came together with furious intensity, each seeking to gain an early advantage. The match wore on, and Hercules marveled that while his own strength was being sorely tested, the giant didn't seem to tire in the least.

He heard Athena's voice on the wind, "Antaeus is a son Gaia. As long as he is in contact with her, he draws power. Be clever as well as strong, my warrior."

Digging deep into his quickly ebbing strength, Hercules flipped the giant over and held him upside down so that no part of him was in contact with the earth. He wrapped his mighty arms around the giant's chest and began to squeeze. The giant flailed and kicked, but Hercules managed to keep him aloft while he squeezed the life out of him.

Continuing on, Hercules finally came to the hurricane of the North Wind. The power of the cyclone pulled at him, but he clawed his way past. On the other side of the storm, a peaceful, lush valley ringed by mountains opened before him. He didn't have to search very long before he found Atlas standing with the weight of the heavens balanced on his stooped shoulders.

"Mighty Atlas," Hercules called as he approached. "I am Hercules and am on a quest for my king. I am sent to gather the golden apples of Hesperus and have been told that you can help me."

Atlas glowered at the young man. "I could help you, but if you haven't noticed, I am rather tied up with holding the heavens on my shoulders. Besides, I don't want to help you. Go away and leave me be."

"It looks to be a tiresome business," Hercules said sympathetically. "What if I shouldered your burden for a while and in return, you bring me the golden apples? What say you to that?"

"I say that no mortal man could hope to shoulder my burden. Now be gone. You are as annoying as a buzzing insect inside my ear!"

"I am a son of Zeus and am strong enough to hold up my end of the bargain. Of course, if you cannot get the apples, I understand. I guess I will just have to get them myself since you are too weak and feeble to anything but stand there rooted in the earth."

"Very well, Son of Zeus. Let's see you shoulder my burden, and if you are not squashed like a bug under the weight, I'll get the apples you seek." Atlas groaned as he shifted the weight off his back and onto Hercules'. Hercules bent under the staggering weight, but with an effort, straightened his back and balanced the heavy load across his shoulders. As soon as he saw that Hercules was equal to the task, Atlas went about keeping his side of the bargain.

It wasn't long before the Titan returned with a bag of golden apples. Atlas looked at the young hero who was balancing the heavens and earth without any apparent difficulty. "I have been holding that burden for centuries. I have done my time. Your back is young, though after a few decades you will be stooped like me," Atlas observed, taking a golden apple out of the sack and biting into it.

Hercules smiled at the enormous Titan. "I'd be happy to! You have surely paid your dues. Before you go, would you mind terribly holding it for just a moment so I can pad my shoulders with my cloak? You know how badly the weight digs into your shoulders."

Atlas nodded sympathetically. "Indeed it does. Let's get you comfortable," he said amicably and took the weight of the heavens and earth back onto his shoulders, where it settled back into its accustomed position.

Hercules made a show of swirling his cloak around his shoulders before darting in to grab the bag of apples that hung off Atlas' belt. The Titan had his hands full balancing his load that he couldn't stop Hercules from snatching the sack of apples.

"I thank you, Mighty Atlas! I will give your respects to King Eurystheus," Hercules called as he dashed down the path back to the straight road that would take him home. For once, his travels to Mykenai were uneventful, and he presented the apples to the king without any fanfare. He tossed the sack at his feet and left the court.

Even though Hercules' task was complete, all was not well in the world. Atlas was furious about being tricked and had been shaking the heavens and earth in his ill temper. The Nymphs of Hesperus were out of sorts since their apples had been taken and were not tending Hera's garden as they ought to. The balance of the mortal and divine world had been upset. To restore the balance, Athena retrieved the Golden Apples from King Eurystheus. "These apples were not meant to be in the realm of man," she declared as she scooped them up from where Hercules had dropped them. The king didn't dare argue as she left the court as abruptly as she had appeared. Once the apples were returned, the nymphs once again took up their duties, and Atlas' temper cooled. The balance was once again restored.

Hera and Eurystheus had one last chance to bring an end to Hercules, and they pulled out all the stops on his twelfth and final labor. "Hercules, you will bring me the dreaded Cerberus, the guardian of the Underworld." Eurystheus couldn't suppress a nasty smile as he made his proclamation. No mortal could go to the Underworld and return. This would finally be the last chapter in the life of Hercules.

For his part, Hercules carefully kept his face blank, disguising the dread seeping through him. He could not go to the Underworld. He had not completed his penance and had more stains upon his soul for the deaths of the innocent Centaurs. His eternity would be miserable if he had to stay in the Underworld in such a state. He nodded to Eurystheus and left without a word.

Hercules immediately sought out the prophet, Eumolpus, to indoctrinate him in the Eleusinian Mysteries. The Eleusinian Mysteries were a series of doctrine that celebrated the myth of Demeter and Persephone and revealed the mysteries of the Underworld. By completing a study of them, Hercules ensured that he could dwell happily in the world of the dead - just in case his quest didn't end well. He was also granted absolution by Eumolpus for the deaths of the Centaurs.

With his immortal soul secured, Hercules made the arduous journey to Taenarum in Laconia. There, deep in the earth, was a crevice that joined the world above and the world below. He traveled deeper and deeper into the dark pit until he came to the River Styx.

On the rickety pier, Charon, the ferryman, waited for souls to present themselves for passage. Hercules strode over him and demanded, "Ferryman, I wish to cross the river. Take me to the other side." He made to step onto the boat but was sent staggering back when Charon's boat pole whipped out of the water and struck him upside the head.

"There are two requirements to get aboard the boat. First, you must pay for passage, and second, you must be dead. You haven't met either requirement, so off with you!" Charon glowered at Hercules in disapproval.

Hercules, recovered from the surprise blow, felt his temper rising and did nothing to check it. He glared back at Charon with such viciousness that the old man quaked in his boots.

"Very well," Charon conceded and allowed Hercules to board the ferry.

On the other side of the river, Hermes waited for the young hero. The Land of the Dead was fraught with danger, and he and Athena wanted Hercules to be successful on his last quest.

Hercules bowed to the Messenger of the Gods as soon as he stepped off the ferry, but he didn't get a chance to say anything because the shades of the dead swarmed all around him. Hermes grabbed ahold of his arm and pulled him through the Underworld's welcoming committee. Hercules cried out and hid his face in his hands when the shade of Medusa loomed before him.

"She is but an empty shell here and cannot harm anyone. Pay her no mind," Hermes told Hercules and waved his hand to banish the snake-haired shade.

A warrior approached, and Hercules recognized Meleager, who he had crossed paths with in his travels. "What is this? The mighty Hercules has fallen," Meleager asked, surprised.

"Nay, my friend. Zeus willing, I will once again walk in the land of the light."

"This is good to hear! The world needs a mighty warrior such as Hercules to protect it. I have a sister, Deianira, who needs a husband. If you return to the land of the living, promise me you will seek her out and marry her," the spirit of his departed friend begged.

"I will see it done if it is in my power," Hercules assured him, and he and Hermes traveled deeper into Hades' kingdom.

Souls rustled and shifted around Hercules, restless with a living man walking among them. To calm them and to gain their support, Hermes suggested Hercules make a sacrifice to them. The divine cattle of Hades were just ahead, and Hercules availed himself of one of the beasts as a sacrifice for the departed souls.

As soon as the blood spilled, the shades quieted, but Menoites, the cowherd, was furious that Hercules had killed one of his cattle. He launched himself at the hero in defense of his herd. The two wrestled, and Hercules quickly gained the upper hand. He wrapped his arms around the chest of his opponent and with a mighty squeeze, broke several of his ribs.

"Release him," a cool feminine voice commanded.

Hercules compiled at once, and Menoites fell in a heap at his feet. Hercules and Hermes bowed low to the Queen of the Underworld. Persephone smiled at Hercules and said, "I ask that you allow Menoites to go about his duties."

"Of course, my Lady Queen," Hercules replied, donning his best courtly manners and helping Menoites up from the ground. The cowherd shuffled off to look after his herd, grumbling under his breath. Hermes took his leave as well, saying Hercules was in good hands with Persephone.

"Why have you come," Persephone asked, linking her arm through the hero's and leading him deeper into the labyrinth of the Underworld.

"I must take the Hound of Hell to King Eurystheus to complete my penance," Hercules started to explain, but stopped before elaborating. A hand was sticking out from under a large boulder. Intrigued, he rolled the rock away to reveal Ascalaphus, a spirit of the Underworld who used to be Hades' gardener.

Persephone frowned at the demon. Her mother, Demeter, had trapped him under the rock when he confirmed that Persephone had eaten pomegranate seeds while in the Underworld, thereby cementing her fate to dwell there. With a wave of her hand, Persephone transformed Ascalaphus into a screech owl so he could serve as a harbinger of ill deeds and omens in the mortal world. He flew away screeching his indignation at his continued punishment. Persephone shrugged and continued to lead Hercules into the darkness.

"Hercules," a voice called from a shadowy corner. Hercules peered into the gloom and saw two faces he recognized.

"Theseus! Pirithous! What has happened that you are here in the Land of the Dead?" He looked closer, shocked to see the stones that the two men sat on had engulfed their arms and legs and were slowly turning them to stone. Without a second thought, Hercules grabbed Theseus and pulled until he separated him from the rock, though he left a good chunk of each buttock behind. While Theseus howled in pain, Hercules tried to do the same for Pirithous. The ground shook and groaned every time Hercules touched him. From deep within the endless dark came a blood-curdling screech. Hercules threw his arm over his head as a band of Furies descended from the air on their leathery wings. Fangs and talons bared, they swept past Hercules and Theseus and swarmed over Pirithous, whose screams were every bit as blood-curdling as his tormentors. They dug their claws into his stony flesh and bore him off into the dark. Persephone sent Theseus on his way with another wave of her hand.

"He shouldn't have tried to steal my wife," Hades said quietly from the shadows. "So, you want to take my hound to the worthless king of Mykenai?"

Hercules spun around to face the King of the Dead. "Yes, mighty Hades. It is my last quest in my penance for a dreadful deed I committed." The souls of the dead pressed in around them. Thanks to the sacrifice, they spoke to Hades in support of Hercules, urging him to honor the hero's request.

"I am well aware of Hera's persecution of you. I have no problem with you taking Cerberus to King Eurystheus. However, Cerberus might be of a different opinion. If you can convince him to go with you, without the use of your weapons, he is free to go. He must not be harmed, Hercules, or you will know my displeasure." Hades took his wife's arm and together they left a stunned Hercules staring after them.

Hercules found Cerberus without any difficulty by following the sounds of his barking. He looked up at the three massive heads and watched the serpent tail swaying back and forth menacingly. Hercules pulled his ever-present lion's skin tightly about him, so he was covered from head to foot. With a mighty leap, he landed on the beast's back. The serpent immediately tried to bite him but could not penetrate the impervious hide. Hercules gathered the heads together by looping his arms around the necks. In his signature move, he squeezed until the dog wilted in submission. Hercules released him, and the great hound lowered its heads to be leashed by a chain.

Athena appeared next to Hercules. He swept his patron a low bow.

"Well done, Hercules. You've used your cunning to win the day. Now, you must escape the world of darkness. Getting in is much easier than getting out."

"I will go back by ferry. The ferryman will give me no trouble," Hercules said, heading off in the direction of the river.

"Charon has been chained for a year and a day for bringing you across in the first place. You cannot take the ferry back out. Follow me," Athena commanded and set off in the opposite direction. They traveled many miles in the darkness until the goddess led them through a cave that opened into the light. Hercules stood with Cerberus taking in the rays of Helios on a barren mountainside in the Peloponnese. With a grin on his face, he and his three-headed companion made their way out of the mountains and to Mykenai.

Cerberus was too big to take into the great hall, so Hercules bellowed from the top of the city's wall. "King Eurystheus, I have brought you the mighty Hound of Hell. Come and behold the great Cerberus!"

The crowd parted, and King Eurystheus emerged. The color drained from his face when he beheld the demon dog with its slowly undulating serpent tail and three massive sets of fangs - all bared viciously at him. His courage failed him completely, and he unceremoniously ran back inside. From behind the closed and barred doors, Eurystheus yelled, "Very well, Hercules! I see the beast. I bid you return it to the bowels of the earth where it belongs!"

"I will return him once you release me from any further obligation to you or your court," Hercules countered.

"Yes! You are free from any further obligations from me or my court! Now, go! Take that dreadful beast and never return to Mykenai!"

And so, Hercules returned Cerberus unharmed to his post guarding the gates of the Underworld. Free from his long penance, he took up with Jason and the Argonauts on their famous adventure in pursuit of the Golden Fleece. Eventually, he traveled to the land of Oechalia where an archery tournament was being held to win the hand of the Lady Iole. Hercules entered the contest and won easily, even beating all the princes who were legendary archers. However, when he went to claim his prize, he found his way barred by Iole's brothers.

"Mighty Hercules! Hero of Mykenai! We are humbled by your presence here, but I am afraid I cannot let my only daughter be wed to you," King Eurytus told him regretfully. His sons, save one – Iphitus – nodded their agreement. "You cannot guarantee that you will not be afflicted by madness like you were before and kill my beloved daughter."

Hercules had learned during his labors that brute force was not always the way to settle a disagreement. So, he curbed his impulse to slay the king and his sons where they stood and left with a promise to return for his prize. Prince Iphitus pleaded with his father to reconsider, for he realized Hercules was not a man to make an enemy of. However, his father and brothers were adamant - Iole would not wed the Mad Hero of Mykenai.

That evening, King Eurytus' cattle were stolen. An infamous cattle rustler, Autolycus, had been seen in the area, but instead of drawing the obvious conclusion that he was responsible for the raid, the king and princes accused Hercules.

"I didn't steal your cattle, but I will be happy to return them to you," Hercules boasted and accepted Prince Iphitus' offer to help him. Together, they returned the cattle to the king, and the king began to soften his opinion of Hercules. This caught Hera's attention, and she again stirred madness in Hercules' mind. In his confusion, he flung Iphitus off the city wall and killed him.

Grief-stricken, Hercules once again sought out the oracle to assign him a penance for his ill deed. This time the oracle told him to become a slave for the space of three years. Hermes took Hercules to a slave auction and sold him to Queen Omphale of Lydia. She brought the great hero into her court and forced him to wear women's clothing and do women's work. His humiliation was complete when she wore his lion's pelt and carried his famed club. At the end of his servitude, she took him as her consort for a time before the call of adventure lured Hercules away from her.

Hercules went on several campaigns and sacked several kingdoms. While he was in Troy besieging the city (this was a long time before the famous Trojan War), the Titans, once banished to the depths of Tartarus, banded together and tried to rise up against the Olympians. The battles among the gods shook the earth and toppled mountains. The world slipped toward chaos as the gods quarreled amongst themselves. Zeus had received a prophecy many years before that when the Titans rose a second time the only way they would be defeated was through a mortal warrior. Zeus called to Hercules, "My son! We need you to join us if we are to save the world from devastation. You are the only one who can stop it." Hercules took up arms with the Olympians and together, they subdued the Titans.

And so, it went for Hercules, leading armies and living the life of adventure. Until one day, he was traveling through the kingdom of Calydonia, where they were gearing up for a wedding festival. Hercules learned that the princess Deianira was to be wed to the River God, Achelous. He remembered his promise to her brother, Meleager, and wondered if he should interfere with the wedding. After all, she was marrying a god, and surely her brother would see that as a good match. He decided to let it be. He led a soldier's life and did not need a wife. Then, he saw Deianira driving her chariot. The warrior princess stole his heart at first sight. When she rode past, he saw tears streaming down her face.

"What's amiss with the princess," he asked one of the courtiers.

"She does not wish to marry Achelous and live in his watery home."

As the most celebrated hero in the land, Hercules was invited to stay for the wedding as a guest of honor. At his first opportunity, he sought out the princess. "Lady Deianira, I hear whispers among the court that you are not happy with the match your father has made for you."

Her lovely face crumpled in distress. "No, I do not wish to become a wife to a fish! God or not, I want to live my life on dry land, but there is nothing that can be done. My father is set on it."

"If I save you from this fate, do you promise to marry me instead," Hercules asked boldly.

Deianira's eyes went wide at the suggestion. "I have heard of your mighty deeds, Hercules, but I do not believe that even you can save me. Achelous is shapeshifter and Prince of the Rivers. He commands all the water that flows through Greece," she sniffed and patted her eyes dry of their tears. With a determined air, she pulled herself together. "However, if you return from the water with your life, I will marry you."

With that assurance ringing in his ears, Hercules marched down to the river. "Achelous," he yelled across the water. "I have come to challenge you for the hand of Princess Deianira! Will you answer my challenge?"

The current flowed on unconcerned for a few moments before a half man, half fish with two large horns sprouting from his head rose from the water. "Who are you to challenge for my lady's hand? Her father has agreed to the match. Be gone, stranger!"

"I am Hercules, and I wish to have Deianira for my wife. I will not leave until you honor my challenge," Hercules replied stubbornly.

"The mighty hero has come! I may as well lay back down in my banks," Achelous taunted. "Bah! Wade in, hero! I will wash you away like the insignificant piece of flotsam you are!" With a roar, Achelous took on the form of a mighty bull and charged Hercules.

The hero stayed on the bank, knowing that he stood no chance if he went into the water. The bull thrust its vicious horns at Hercules. He dodged the lethal tips and twisted to wrap his arms around the creature's neck. He dug his heels into the soft bank of the river and began to squeeze. The bull thrashed and bucked, breaking Hercules' hold. The mighty beast tried to drag Hercules into the water, but the hero grabbed one of the massive horns and ripped it off of the bull's head. Achelous bellowed in pain and rage and shifted back into his merman form, clutching the ragged hole where his horn had been.

"You win, Hercules. I yield! Give me back my horn," the river god demanded.

"What will you give me in return? I must take something to the king to prove you have relinquished your claim on the princess."

Achelous glared at Hercules and from the water, produced a beautiful golden horn. "This is the Horn of Amaltheia, blessed by Zeus and magically endowed to produce whatever is needed. Take this, the Horn of Plenty, and return my horn to me."

Hercules made the trade, and the river god slipped back into his watery domain. Triumphant, Hercules returned to the palace, presented the treasure to the king, and promptly wed Princess

Deianira. Their married life started happily enough. They stayed in Calydonia with Deianira's father until Hercules accidentally killed King Oeneus' cupbearer. The king acknowledged it had been an accident and did not seek retribution, but the family ties became strained. Hercules decided it was time for him and his bride to move into a place of their own.

The couple settled on Tiryns. As they traveled, they came to the river Euenos which was wide and deep. An unusual ferryman waited to offer passage to travelers.

Nessus, a centaur whose name meant "the duck," met the couple on the banks of the river. "I will carry the lady across," he offered with a gallant bow.

Hercules eyed the river. He could not carry their belongings and his wife across in one trip. Eager to get the river crossing behind them, Hercules agreed and helped Deianira onto Nessus' back. He shouldered their packs and his weapons and waded into the swift current. He heard Nessus splash in behind him. As they climbed up the far shore, Nessus ran off through the woods, stealing Deianira away from Hercules. Deianira cried out for help. Hercules dropped the packs and in a practiced motion, drew his bow and arrow. His aim was true, and the arrow sunk deep into Nessus' chest.

The centaur collapsed, and Deianira scrambled away. Nessus had been struck by one of the poisoned arrows, and he felt the toxins spreading through his body. "Wait! My lady," Nessus cried as she started to run away. Deianira paused and came back to the dying creature. "Forgive me! I was overtaken with your beauty and sought to have you for my own. I wish to make amends. Take a few drops of my blood. It is enchanted and will ensure the love of anyone who comes in contact with it."

"I have no need for love potions," Deianira snapped and turned away.

"You might not now, but what happens when a younger and prettier woman comes along? The years are not always kind," Nessus called to Deianira's back.

Deianira paused. She had seen countless women watch helplessly as their husbands set them aside for a concubine. She did not want to join the ranks of discarded wives. She caught a few drops of blood flowing from Nessus' wound in a tiny vial. The centaur smiled weakly and closed his eyes. He died knowing he would have revenge on the one who killed him.

The couple finished their journey and settled down in Tiryns. The years slipped by and were overall happy and uneventful. Hercules, however, was not a domestic kind of man. He craved adventure, and ultimately, his restlessness won out. He set out on a campaign to settle an old score with King Eurytus, who had offended him by reneging on his promise of Iole's hand in marriage. He besieged the city of Oechalia until he breached the walls, conquering the city and killing King Eurytus. In her grief, Iole jumped off the remnants of the city wall. However, her gown billowed around her and acted like a parachute. Hercules caught her and took her to be his concubine.

Deianira watched in horror as Hercules settled his mistress in their home. It was a common enough practice, and she tolerated it as well as she could. However, as time went by, Deianira's insecurity began to build. She worried that it was only a matter of time before she was relegated to the tiny chambers on the edge of the house and Iole shared the marriage bed instead of her. In desperation, she took Hercules' famous lion pelt on the pretense of cleaning it. She anointed it with the blood of Nessus and anxiously gave it back to her husband.

The instant the tainted pelt touched his skin, Hercules' flesh began to burn in agony. Horrified, Deianira ripped the lion's skin off her husband, but it was too late. The poison had taken hold and was spreading. Hercules looked sadly at his wife through a haze of pain. "Wife, beloved, you have killed me," he groaned and stumbled out of their home. Deianira, realizing she had been tricked and unable to live with what she had done to her husband, hung herself in her bedchamber.

Since he was half divine, he knew he would not die quickly. To hasten his death, Hercules traveled to Mount Etna and built himself a funeral pyre of oak branches. He called to his friends to light up the pyre, but none of them had the stomach to do it while he still lived. Finally, Philoctetes, his faithful friend, climbed the mountain and sadly lit the pyre.

"Thank you, my friend," Hercules rasped through his pain. "My bow and arrows are yours. Use them well and may your aim be true." Hercules lay down among the flames to die.

Zeus and the other Olympians watched as Hercules lay dying. "Only the mortal part of Hercules dies today," Zeus proclaimed. "He has lived a noble life, and I am pleased that many of you have favored him. Once his mortal body is consumed, I will welcome his divine self to walk among us as a god. None of you can deny he deserves it, and I would have each of you make him welcome," Zeus gave a pointed look at Hera with these words.

Once Hercules' mortal coil had burned away, his divine being rose up from the ashes. Zeus lifted him to the heavenly court on Mount Olympus to start his life a god. He married Hebe, the goddess of eternal youth, and thus ends the story of the mighty hero Hercules.

Part 3   The Trojan War and Odysseus' Voyage

Home

The Trojan War

Historians have long debated whether the city of Troy actually ever existed. In the mid-1800s, a German archeologist claimed to have uncovered the ruins of the ancient city, but there was much skepticism about the find. Even after all these years, no one has unequivocally established that Troy existed, but there is a general consensus that to have inspired the epics of the *Iliad* and the *Odyssey*, a monumental event like the Trojan War probably occurred. As to the heroes, the gods, and the infamous horse, opinions still remain conflicted. Regardless of their veracity, the story of the war and its aftermath have become legend.

Late in the prehistoric bronze age of man, the mortal world had once again become crowded. Many of the mortals were demi-gods, thanks to the fraternization between gods and man. These partially divine mortals lived extended lives, had lots of offspring, and therefore, the population of man exploded. Unhappy with the overpopulation, Zeus pondered ways to decrease the mortal's numbers. He considered sending a plague or storms and sought out the advice of Themis, the ancient Titan goddess of justice and wisdom. She suggested a war would be effective at reducing the numbers and would leave the earth mostly intact. While he retired to his heavenly throne to consider his choices, he forbade any more relations between gods and mortals.

While he pondered the situation, an old prophecy was brought back to light, and Zeus was reminded that it was foretold that he would be overthrown by one of his sons. Furthermore, Prometheus, who had held his silence for eons, finally told him that his downfall would be through his son born of Thetis, the goddess of the sea. Zeus had long been enamored with Thetis but had not yet seduced her. This distracted Zeus from his troubles with the mortals, and he focused instead on preventing the prophecy from being fulfilled. Based on Prometheus' information, Zeus arranged for Thetis to marry an elderly mortal man, Peleus, but she flatly refused.

Peleus sought out the Old Man of the Sea and asked him how he could win the heart of the beautiful Thetis. The old sea god advised him to wait until she was sleeping, bind her securely, and hold on to her while she shifted from shape to shape. If he was strong enough to keep her bound through her transformations, she would marry him.

Peleus went to the edge of the sea and concealed himself in a cave. He waited until he saw Thetis fall asleep in the surf and quickly bound her. Outraged, Thetis shifted to a flame and then to water, but Peleus held fast. She became a serpent and a ferocious lioness, but Peleus held doggedly on. Exhausted, Thetis surrendered herself to Peleus and agreed to marry him.

The wedding of a goddess was always a grand affair, and even though Thetis was a reluctant bride marrying an old mortal man, that didn't stop the Olympians from throwing the newlyweds a huge party. On Mount Pelion, the wedding guests gathered in celebration. Zeus oversaw the proceedings and posted Hermes at the door to keep out troublemakers.

"Do not allow Eris to cross this threshold. She'll have the guests at each other's throats!"

Eris, the goddess of discord and strife, stirred up ill will and negativity wherever she went. Hermes nodded his understanding and took up his post.

The tables groaned under the massive spread of food, and the feasting stretched on most of the night. Apollo and the muses entertained the assembly. As was the custom, gifts were presented to the bride and groom. The newlyweds humbly accepted a spear made by Athena and Hephaestus, an embossed bowl from Aphrodite, and a beautiful cloak from Hera. Athena also bestowed a flute and Nereus, Thetis' father, gave the couple a basket of divine salt that when sprinkled on food made everything taste so good that people couldn't stop eating. Poseidon made a gift of two immortal horses, and Zeus gave them the Wings of Acre, which had been taken from the goddess Acre when she had sided with the Titans and been cast into Tartarus upon their defeat.

Properly gifted and fed, the newlyweds offered their sincere gratitude and made to retire. So distracted were the guests by the newlywed's speeches, they did not notice the scuffle at the door.

"You are not welcome," Hermes insisted and repelled an indignant Eris back from the door for a second time.

"Zeus has no right to keep me out," Eris hissed, but Hermes didn't budge. "Fine, I'll just give my gift from here." She lobbed one of the golden apples of Hesperus with a tag reading "For the Fairest" into the middle of the crowd. It had been meant for Thetis, but it landed at the feet of Athena where she stood talking to Hera and Aphrodite.

Intrigued, the goddess of war picked it up and read the inscription on the tag. She laughed with delight and showed her companions. "How appropriate this would come to me," Athena exclaimed.

"I am afraid you are mistaken, sister," Aphrodite cooed. "That could only be meant for me."

"You're both wrong," Hera snapped. "It is obviously a gift for me."

The bickering erupted into a full-on argument in moments, and the three goddesses were at each other's throats, scratching and fighting over the golden apple.

Zeus waded into the middle of them, glaring at Hermes, who merely shrugged. He hadn't allowed Eris to enter. The Father of All wearily took the apple and separated the goddesses like a parent would squabbling siblings. Immediately, the goddesses demanded that he chose among them who was the fairest and therefore, should receive the apple. Zeus was far too wise to make a comment on that score. He knew that no matter his choice, he would have two very powerful goddesses angry with him. He thought for a moment, and inspiration struck him.

Zeus had heard a prophecy stating the city Troy would be destroyed if Paris, the mortal prince of Troy, was allowed to become a man. On the day of his birth, the king and queen were supposed to kill him to prevent the prophecy. However, they could not execute their baby, so they took him to a shepherd and ordered him to do the deed. The shepherd could not kill the child either, so he abandoned it in the wilderness for nine days. When he returned, he found the babe healthy and unharmed, having been nurtured by a bear. So, the shepherd took the child and raised him as his own. No mortal knew that the young shepherd boy watching the flocks on Mount Ida was really a prince of Troy. However, Zeus, in his omnipotence, remembered, and he saw a way to solve two problems at once.

Paris also had credibility as a fair and astute judge of character and divinity. For entertainment during long hours in the fields, he often ran a bullfighting circuit in which his prize bull fought any takers. He even offered a golden crown for anyone who beat his bull. Local farmers brought their bulls to be tested, and they all lost. Ares, lover of violence and aggression, decided to teach the young shepherd a lesson. He transformed into a bull and challenged Paris' bull. Paris saw at once that he was of the divine and crowned him immediately. Thus, Paris' discriminating eye and honesty were established.

"Aphrodite, Hera, and Athena," Zeus interrupted their continued bickering, "You are all beyond beautiful in my eyes. I cannot choose between you. However, there is a young man, a shepherd on Mount Ida, whose eyes are most discerning. Go to him and let him judge between you!" Hermes escorted the goddesses to

Mount Ida, and Zeus sat back in his throne with satisfaction. There was no way that peace would continue on the mortal plane once the luckless Paris made his choice.

Before being judged, Hermes took the goddesses to the Spring of Ida, where they bathed and prepared themselves. Young Paris was more than a little surprised when three stunningly beautiful goddesses were suddenly presented to him by Hermes. He stood slack-jawed in awe of their radiance.

"Paris, you have been tasked with the responsibility to settle the dispute among these goddesses. They are each laying claim to the title of most beautiful, and it is your job to pick who is telling the truth," Hermes instructed.

Paris stared for a while longer and was utterly at a loss. It was as if he had been asked to pick the most beautiful star in the night sky. "I cannot choose the fairest from among the perfection that stands before me. Let each one reveal their body to me that I might ensure they do not hide a blemish under their clothing."

The goddesses quickly disrobed and turned this way and that before their judge. Paris shook his head sadly. "I simply cannot place one above the rest. You are all equally beautiful!" He made his pronouncement and retired to his home, eager to be away from the unhappy glares of the goddesses.

That night, each goddess visited Paris. First, the cunning Athena slipped into Paris' bedchamber.

"I will make you the greatest of all warriors. Your battle skills will become legend, and no man will be able to match your blade. Simply choose me, and it will all be yours," Athena promised.

Paris assured her he would think about. A while later, the manipulative Hera stole into the room, creeping quietly. "What a clever young man you are," she cooed and flattered. "You are destined for something far greater than herding sheep. I can make you a king among men. All of Asia Minor, including the great city of Troy, shall all be yours. Just name me the fairest."

Again, Paris agreed to consider it. He was unsurprised when Aphrodite crept in and whispered, "I have the power to give you the greatest gift any man could want - the love of a beautiful woman. I offer you not the love of just any pretty girl. I will make the most beautiful woman in the world fall madly in love with you and only you. She will never look at another man as long as you walk the earth."

Pairs, overwhelmed and excited by the offers, gave Aphrodite the same assurance that he would think about what she said. The next morning, the goddesses met Paris as he emerged from his home. They waited impatiently, each sure that her bribe would be enough to tip the scales in her favor.

Paris had made his decision, but now, staring at three gorgeous, very powerful goddesses, he was less sure. However, they would not be put off any longer. "How lovely you all look in the light of a new day. I considered the problem long into the night, and I stand by what I said yesterday. You are all perfection." He held up his hands to forestall the outburst that threatened. "But, you insist that I choose among you, and since you force my hand, I choose Aphrodite to be the fairest of all."

Athena and Hera let out angry hisses of disappointment and glared at Paris before making an ungraceful exit. Aphrodite lingered, beaming a beatific smile at the young man. "You have chosen well. Now, I am a goddess of my word, and you shall have the most beautiful woman, the lovely Helen of Sparta. But first, you have to take your rightful seat in the royal house of Troy."

Paris looked at her dumbfounded as she told him about his parentage. He followed her instructions and left his fields, sheep, and lover, the nymph Oenone, to journey to Troy. His parents were surprised and delighted to be reunited with their son. The prophecy apparently forgotten, they welcomed him back into the family. He accepted his birthright and became an official Prince of Troy. As a member of the royal family, he was given official duties to perform. With a little manipulation from Aphrodite, Paris was assigned a diplomatic visit to the kingdom of Sparta.

About the time Paris was reclaiming his family, Thetis and Peleus were blessed with a child, Achilles. Thetis was concerned that her child was part mortal and wanted him to have immortality. She secreted her baby away from her husband and traveled down to the Underworld. There, holding him by one heel, she dipped the baby in the River Styx, washing away his mortal body. She was discovered by the ferryman before she could finish the job, and he chased her away. Thus, the back of Achilles' heel remained mortal and vulnerable. When Peleus heard what his wife had done, he was furious. He confronted Thetis, and they argued bitterly. Thetis was so enraged by her husband's attitude that she jumped back into the sea and left him. After Thetis' departure, Peleus gave Achilles to Chiron, the wise and noble centaur, to raise. He grew quickly and soon became a renowned warrior under the guidance of Chiron.

Paris made the long journey over the sea to Sparta. His royal status entitled him a warm welcome, and there was a feast held in his honor. King Menelaus received the young prince with much pomp and circumstance. When he introduced his wife, Helen, Paris could only stare at her beauty. Aphrodite had neglected to mention that she was not only the most beautiful woman in the world, but she was the Queen of Sparta.

Paris also didn't know Helen's story or the story of her marriage to Menelaus. Helen's mother, Leda, like many other beautiful Greek princesses, caught the eye of Zeus. He seduced her in the form of a swan on the same night she lay with her husband, King Tyndareus. From this liaison, two eggs were produced and hatched two sets of twins. From one egg, Castor and Clytemnestra emerged and were the mortal offspring of the king. From the other, Helen and Pollux were born and were the children of Zeus, thus potentially immortal demigods.

Helen grew into a stunningly beautiful woman, and King Tyndareus was faced with the difficult decision of choosing a husband for her. Dozens of men sought her hand, and they were all very powerful. Tyndareus felt he couldn't pick one among them without risking the wrath of the others. Clever Odysseus, who was at court to woo Helen's lovely cousin, Penelope, offered a proposal. Odysseus proposed that all suitors vying for Helen must swear an oath that they would support the King's decision and would seek no vengeance if they were not chosen. Tyndareus made the decree, and despite much complaining among the suitors, they all took the oath over a sacrificed horse. Thus, no war ensued when King Tyndareus chose Menelaus as Helen's husband. His choice had been based on the fact that Menelaus was incredibly powerful and wealthy and that he had not come to seek favor himself. Agamemnon, Menelaus' brother, had acted in his stead. Menelaus had also petitioned Aphrodite for help in the matter, promising her the sacrifice of one hundred oxen. However, he neglected to follow through on his promise, thus earning her displeasure.

As Paris tarried in the Spartan court getting to know the lovely Helen, Menelaus was called away to Crete to attend the funeral of Crateus, his uncle. He left his many guests, the duplicitous Paris included, to Helen to be entertained. Shortly after the king's departure, Castor and Pollux, Helen's twin brothers who were at court, saw an opportunity to settle an old score.

Many years before, Castor and Pollux had gone on a cattle raid with their cousins, Lynceus and his giant brother Idas. The raid was a success, and the cousins celebrated their fine new herd by roasting a calf. Idas proposed that instead of dividing the cattle equally between them, whichever pair of cousins ate the most meat got the entire herd. Castor and Pollux agreed and were astounded when Idas quickly gobbled up all the meat before anyone else got a mouthful. Thus, he duped the brothers out of their cattle and set up years of resentment.

Idas and Lynceus happened to be at court when Menelaus left. Since the king was gone, Castor and Pollux were able to sneak away from court by making the excuse that they needed to follow up on some of the king's business in his absence. While everyone was generally engaged with having a good time, the twins looted the cattle herd of their cousins. Castor kept a lookout from a tree while Pollux opened the corral gates to liberate the cattle. Idas and Lynceus discovered their cattle being driven out of their pen, and Lynceus, who could see in the dark, spied Castor in the tree. The brothers immediately understood what was happening, and Idas angrily threw his spear at Castor, striking him through the chest. Castor just managed to shout his warning before the spear killed him. Pollux cried out in anguish as his twin fell dead from the tree and wasted no time in engaging Lynceus in combat. Pollux, fueled by his anger and grief, made short work of Lynceus. Idas, now equally enraged, picked up the fight. Swords flashed and danced in the moonlight and Idas, with his giant strength and size, gained the upper hand on Pollux. Zeus, who was watching his son from his heavenly perch, intervened and struck Idas dead with a thunderbolt.

Pollux immediately ran to his brother and cradled him in his arms. Zeus was moved at his son's grief and offered him a choice. "Pollux, your brother cannot walk the mortal plane anymore. You may choose to take your place here among us on Mount Olympus and walk with the gods as is your birthright. However, I will allow you to share your immortality with your brother on one condition. You will only be able to walk half the year on Olympus, and the other half must be spent in Hades to maintain the balance of life and death."

Pollux didn't hesitate. "I choose to have my brother with me for all eternity - regardless of where we must spend it." And, thus, Castor and Pollux left the world of man.

In the general melee that ensued at the disappearance of the Princes of Sparta and the death of Idas and Lynceus, Aphrodite saw the opportunity she had been waiting for. She whispered to Cupid, and he used one of his famous arrows to shoot Helen, causing her to fall madly in love with Paris. Helen, possessed by a passion and desire that derailed all other thought, abandoned her responsibilities to her brothers, her guests, and her kingdom. She and Paris stole away in the night and set sail across the Aegean Sea.

Vengeful Hera watched as the lovers crossed the sea. Her ire had not yet cooled toward Paris. She stirred the winds against him and blew him off course. They made landfall in the port city of Sidon, and Paris, who was beginning to realize the enormity of what he had done, decided to stay a while in the city, hoping that no one would come looking for them there.

Menelaus returned from Crete to find his kingdom in an uproar. The princes had vanished, and his wife had run away with the Prince of Troy. Menelaus counseled with his brother, Agamemnon, who was the overlord of much of Greece.

"We cannot allow Troy to steal the queen! Every man who sought my lady's hand swore to protect and uphold our marriage. It is time to make good on that oath," Menelaus urged his brother.

Agamemnon saw the wisdom in these words and sent emissaries to gather the warriors, kings, and princes from across Greece.

Thus, messengers scattered across the country. Palamedes was sent to fetch the cunning warrior, Odysseus. As promised for his assistance with solving the issue of Helen's suitors, Odysseus had won the hand of Penelope. He ruled as the King of Ithaca, and he and Penelope had an infant son, Telemachus. Word spread quickly from Sparta of the gathering forces. Odysseus did not want to leave his wife and baby, for he had been told by an oracle that his journey would be extensive and stretch over many years if he went to war.

When Palamedes arrived, he found Odysseus gibbering nonsense, and Penelope told him that her husband had gone mad just after the birth of their son. To convince the messenger of his madness, Odysseus sowed his field with salt and hitched up an ox and a donkey to the plow. Palamedes watched in horror as one of the greatest soldiers Greece had ever seen talked to air and drove his mismatched team in erratic circles in the field. However, something about the whole scene just didn't feel right to Palamedes.

"My lady, may I hold your son," Palamedes asked and accepted the squirming infant from Penelope, who stood with anxious eyes darting from her husband to her son.

Odysseus sang an incomprehensible tune, but his eyes tracked every movement Palamedes made with the baby. Acting on intuition, Palamedes laid the baby in the path of the plow and stood back. He caught Penelope's arm when she lunged to retrieve the child.

"Hold one moment, my lady. I'll let no harm come to him," Palamedes murmured in her ear.

Odysseus drove the team in a drunken line straight toward them, but at the last moment, he steered the plow around his son.

"I knew it," Palamedes cried as Penelope snatched up her child. "You are no more mad than I am. I don't blame you. I wouldn't want to leave my beautiful wife and new baby, but the call has come from your king to defend your county's honor. You cannot turn a deaf ear."

Odysseus, realizing the ruse was up, sadly packed his gear. He said goodbye to a tearful Penelope who promised to always be faithful and kissed his son's downy soft head. Then, he took to the road to gather more support to reclaim Sparta's queen.

King Nestor of Pylos prophesied that the Trojans could not be defeated without the young warrior Achilles. Thus, Odysseus and a fellow soldier, Ajax, were dispatched to retrieve him. Thetis heard of the brewing conflict and remembered a prophecy that had been whispered about her son. The oracle had said that Achilles would either live a long boring life or a short, glorious one. Putting the two prophecies together, she feared for her son. Hoping to ensure his long boring life, Thetis sent Achilles to the kingdom of Skyros.

"Achilles, you must not reveal your identity. Dress in women's garb and engage in women's work. Keep your face veiled and wait until I come to fetch you," Thetis instructed as she secreted him away.

Odysseus and Ajax searched and searched for the renowned warrior. They enlisted the help of Phoenix, Achilles' tutor, and finally followed the trail to Skyros. However, there was no sign of the warrior. There was only a multitude of ladies about their work. Odysseus, clever as always, thought it would be the perfect place to hide a warrior and devised a way to flush him out.

Odysseus and his comrades disguised themselves as merchants and joined the other vendors selling lovely silks and jewels. The ladies of the court filed in and flocked to the fake merchants with their bright, feminine wares. That is, all but one woman. A rather burly lass wandered over to the stall selling armor and swords. When she hefted one and gave a practiced swing, Odysseus laughed and vaulted out from behind the counter, scattering courtiers.

"Achilles, you cannot disguise your talent with blade behind silken skirts and veils," Odysseus cried, tearing away the scrap of fabric that hid the warrior's face. "Come! Your queen has need of your sword arm. We are gathering a force to take her back from those Trojan thieves."

Achilles was more than happy to don his armor and march off with Odysseus and his comrades. Being a woman had not suited the warrior's pride, and he had grown restless for action. Together, the small group traveled to muster point at Aulis.

Tens of thousands of troops gathered from across the region. Corinth, Sparta, Athens, Arcadia, Mykenai, and others were represented. Each army jockeyed for favor and power in the hierarchy of command. Idomeneus of Crete flat out refused to commit his army unless he was made co-commander in the ranks. The position was grudgingly given. The kingdom of Cyprus did not supply troops but sent their promised shipment of breastplates and 50 vessels. However, only one large ship appeared from Cyprus. When asked where the rest of the boats were, 49 clay ships were produced from the hold. There wasn't enough time to follow up on the insult, for the call to action had been sounded.

The troops gathered and offered a sacrifice to Apollo. They prayed for his protection and guidance. At the close of the ceremony, a great serpent appeared on the altar and slithered out of the temple. It coiled itself around a tree and devoured a bird and her nine chicks before it turned to stone. The prophet Calchas declared it a sign that Greece would prevail after ten years of war.

The great fleet sailed the next day. The only problem was, the Greeks didn't know how to get to Troy. They set out in the general direction without much more to go on than it was to the northeast. After sailing for many weeks, they made landfall on the western shore of the Aegean Sea. Unfortunately, they were too far south and landed in Mysia.

The king of the realm was Telephus, son of Hercules, and he did not take kindly to a large fleet of armed Greeks landing on his shores. The armies skirmished, and Telephus was wounded in the foot by Achilles. Realizing they were in the wrong place, the Greeks fell back to regroup at Aulis.

After the Greeks left, Telephus' wound refused to heal. All the surgeons and priests failed to cure him, and in desperation, Telephus sought out an oracle for advice. He was told the one who wounded him must heal him. There was nothing for it, but to seek out Achilles and ask him to heal his foot. So, Telephus sailed after the fleet to Aulis. However, when he asked Achilles to help him, the warrior refused.

"I am no man of medicine! I know how to inflict wounds, not heal them," Achilles argued and rudely left Telephus standing awkwardly in the street.

Changing his tactics, Telephus donned the rags of a beggar and waited until King Agamemnon passed by.

"My Lord," Telephus called and hobbled up to Agamemnon. "Please help me! One among your warriors can heal me, but he will not do it from the goodness of his heart. Will you persuade him?"

Odysseus was close at hand and heard the strange request. He had also heard Achilles talking about the strange man who asked him to heal his foot. Cunning as always, Odysseus put the puzzle together and intervened, answering for the bewildered Agamemnon.

"Come with me, sir," he said, sweeping Telephus away from the king and off to the side of the street. He called Achilles over, who made a sour face when he saw Telephus leaning on Odysseus' arm. Achilles started to protest, but Odysseus held up his hand to forestall the argument. "I only need your spear, Achilles," he said mildly, holding out his hand for the weapon.

Carefully, Odysseus unwrapped the foul wound on Telephus' foot and scraped shavings from the head of the spear into the bloody gash. The wound sealed itself in front of their eyes, and they all stared in wonder.

"Thank you, friend," Telephus exclaimed. "How can I ever repay you?" He bowed low to Odysseus and ignored the slack-jawed Achilles, who was staring at the tip of his sword.

Odysseus clapped his new friend on the shoulder and said, "I know just the thing, come with me." He led Telephus to King Agamemnon, and after a bit of negotiating, Telephus agreed to lead the Greeks across the Aegean Sea to Troy.

It took eight years to recover the fleet which had been scattered throughout the sea after a mighty tempest blew on their crossing back from Mysia. Finally, Agamemnon was ready to sail with his full complement of ships carrying thousands of troops. They loaded the cargo and men and prepared to leave the harbor.

On the morning they were to depart, the wind died. Not a breath of breeze stirred the slack sails. Agamemnon stood on the deck of the ship and looked morosely over his beautiful fleet that was going nowhere fast. Wise Calchas counseled his king, "My lord, this is surely the Goddess Artemis' work. She was most displeased when you shot her favored deer."

Agamemnon glowered at his advisor but didn't contradict him. He had not meant to offend the goddess, but that didn't matter. "What can be done to fix it? We must sail before the food and water spoil, and the men start to grow restless."

"I am most sorry to tell you, but the only thing that will appease the goddess of the hunt is the sacrifice of your daughter, Iphigenia."

Agamemnon, of course, flatly refused to sacrifice his beloved daughter. The situation grew dire. There was dissension among the ranks, and the sun beat down relentlessly on the deck, baking both the men and their supplies with its heat.

With no other choice, Agamemnon sent Odysseus to fetch Iphigenia. Her mother, Clytemnestra, was not keen for her daughter to join her father amid thousands of unruly soldiers. She knew all too well the ways of men.

Odysseus knew the way to soften a mother's will was to promise an advantageous marriage. "My Lady, your daughter is to be wed to the mighty Achilles," Odysseus lied. "This is why I have been sent to fetch her. However, we must make haste as her father desires the union before the fleet sails, and they are impatient to be under way."

As Odysseus had predicted, the promise of marriage to a prestigious warrior was all that was needed for Clytemnestra to pack her daughter off to Aulis with her blessings. Agamemnon met them at the docks and immediately led his daughter to the sacrificial altar of the goddess Artemis. He kissed her on the forehead and without a word of explanation, he swung his blade at her neck. A split second before his sword touched her soft skin, Artemis spirited her away, leaving a deer in their wake. Agamemnon wept with relief as the blood of the deer washed over the altar. Artemis took Iphigenia to her heavenly court to be one of her handmaidens. As soon as the sacrifice was complete, the wind stirred, and the sails filled. Finally, the fleet could set sail.

With Telephus to guide the way, the fleet made good time across the Aegean Sea. They put in on Isle of Tenedos to refresh their water supplies. Many of the men took the opportunity to explore the island. Philoctetes, Hercules' friend who had lit his funeral pyre and received his divine bow and arrows, was in charge of a contingent of seven ships full of men. While he and his men were exploring the island, a snake struck Philoctetes on the foot.

Philoctetes' foot grew infected and putrid as the venom did its work. His men made him comfortable, and Odysseus was called to evaluate the situation.

"Philoctetes, you cannot go on with a foot like that. You must stay and heal. Some of the island people know how to heal the snake's bite. I will take your men forth into battle. Remain here until I return for you."

In a fog of pain, Philoctetes agreed, and his men went to find islanders to care for their stricken leader.

On another section of the island, Achilles was having his own adventure. As he was exploring, he encountered a man and woman walking together. When they saw Achilles, they stopped and stared for a moment before the woman rushed forward. "Forgive us! We do not see many new faces on our tiny island! This is my brother and king of the island, Lord Tenes, and I am Hemithea." They each gave Achilles a small bow which he returned politely. However, after several months at sea, he had a hard time concentrating on anything except for the lovely Hemithea. He introduced himself and asked how the siblings had come to be on the island.

"It is a sorry tale," Tenes explained as he led them back to their dwelling. "Our father married a woman after our mother died. She was a cunning and evil creature, and after I spurned her advances, she convinced my father I had defiled her. Her traitorous flutist even corroborated her falsehood. My father believed her lies and put Hemithea and me in a chest and set us adrift in the sea. We washed up here, and the natives made me their king. We've been here ever since, even though my father learned the truth and tried to reconcile." Tenes made a bitter face and spat on the ground. "I cut his moorings to show him how interested I was in that!"

Achilles told the pair about the abduction of Helen and their mission to retrieve her. He was invited to stay as a guest for the evening meal. While his hosts were giving instructions to their household on dinner preparations, Thetis appeared to her son.

"Tread carefully here my son. I have seen that if you do ill to the king of this land, you will anger Apollo, who is the king's real father. Manage your impulses," Thetis warned and disappeared.

Dinner was a lively affair, and after several hours of merrymaking, the king excused himself for the evening. Finding himself alone with the beautiful Hemithea, Achilles could no longer contain his burning lust for her. Unfortunately, Hemithea didn't feel the same and did not welcome his advances. When he attempted to force her, she cried out for her brother, who came running to defend her.

Achilles crossed blades with King Tenes. The king may have been the son of Apollo but was no swordsman. After a brief engagement, Achilles plunged his sword through Tenes' heart and fled back to his ship, his mother's warning ringing in his ears. He had just gained the enmity of the Archer Prince and sealed his own fate.

The fleet sailed on until finally the shores of Troy were sighted. A cheer went up from the decks of the ships as the men clamored to see their destination. Wise Calchas received a revelation and spoke above the din so all could hear him clearly, "Behold, the land we shall conquer! The first man to step foot on the shore shall fall in battle but will gain glory in the Underworld and be welcomed as a hero!"

Suddenly, no one wanted to be the first off the boat. Glory in the Underworld was great but living in the moment was even better. A stalemate developed until clever Odysseus devised a plan. "Here now! Are we warriors of Greece or sheep? Since when is a warrior afraid of death? Let us storm the beach and inflict the first sting on these Trojan dogs!" He leapt from the boat with a roar that was echoed across the fleet. Soldiers began to overflow out of the ships. Odysseus stood on the shield he had cast down before him to keep his feet from touching the ground. He looked over his shoulder to see Protesilaus, the commander of the Phylaceans, step onto the shore. Protesilaus stared at Odysseus as he realized he had been tricked, but there was no time to argue about it. The first wave of Trojans was breaking from the trees and spilling onto the beach.

The still afternoon heat was shattered by battle cries and the crash of sword on sword. The first wave of battle erupted as the Greeks were given their long-awaited opportunity at vengeance. Furious hand to hand combat raged across the beach, and soon, the sand was sticky with blood. The Greeks came in wave after wave from the boats, pushing the Trojans back into the trees. As they fell back, the mighty Hector, a Trojan Prince and favorite of Apollo and Zeus, joined combat with Protesilaus. Their blades whirled and crashed again and again, but Hector, as the last of the Trojans left the beach, struck down the unfortunate Protesilaus, thus fulfilling the prophecy of Calchas.

The Trojans conceded the beach but made a second stand in clearing outside the city gates. Again, the combatants crossed blades under a volley of arrows and spears being rained down from both sides. In the melee, Achilles found himself face to face with Cycnus, son of Poseidon. The sounds of their blades clashing drown out everything else. The fierce battle became the focal point, and the rest of the field seemed to rotate around it. So evenly matched were the warriors, that the sun was dropping low in the horizon before Achilles was finally able to tip the scales and cut down Cycnus. The Trojans had barely been maintaining their position, but at the fall of Cycnus, their ranks broke. In complete disarray, the Trojan forces fled the field and fell back behind their massive city walls.

Thus, began the nine long years of siege. The walls of Troy had been built years before by Apollo and Poseidon in penance for plotting with Hera to overthrow Zeus. Having been created by two gods, the walls were thicker, taller, and stronger than any other city's walls.

Like many sieges, the long, drawn-out process took its toll on both sides. The Greeks soon found out what all armies who attempt a campaign of foreign shores discover, keeping the army fed, funded, and supplied became the full-time job of over half the troops. They infiltrated the Thracian Peninsula to the north and set up farms and supply depots.

The Trojans, on the other hand, were confined to the city. However, the Greek forces were never quite able to establish a stranglehold on the city. They simply didn't have the troops to completely cut off every access point into the massive city, so communication and supplies continued to flow.

It didn't take long for the soldiers to become restless. They saw minimal action and began to murmur of deserting and returning to their homes. Achilles heard these rumors and knew that he must keep them busy. He began by raiding the surrounding countryside. The soldiers, anxious to be active, threw themselves into the campaigns with gusto. They sacked city after city and left them looted and devastated in their wake. Achilles led troops to over ten different island nations and conquered them as well.

Early on in the siege, Athena whispered to Achilles a prophecy she had heard. "Achilles, hear my words and heed them well. The fate of Troilus, son of Apollo and a Trojan Prince, has been linked to the fate of the city of Troy. He must fall before his 20th year, or Troy will stand forever. He likes to ride to the Archer's temple in Thymbra outside the walls of the city. Lay in wait for him there."

Achilles scouted the area and found the perfect place to ambush the unsuspecting prince. As promised, the prince and his sister traveled the road toward Apollo's temple. As they dismounted, Achilles pounced. Troilus and his sister ran for their horses. They mounted like the skilled riders they were and raced in opposite directions. Achilles, as swift as a deer, caught up with Troilus as he gained the steps of Apollo's temple.

Grabbing him by the hair, Achilles dragged him inside. On the altar of his father, Achilles let his blade fall and cut off Troilus' head. Apollo's rage at Achilles built ten-fold as he watched his son's blood stain the altar.

Achilles led more campaigns and harried the surrounding villages, stealing cattle, sheep, and looting whatever he could find. He traveled south to the city of Lyrnessus and sacked it. It was a bloody battle, and Achilles and his men slaughtered the entire royal family, except for Briseis, whose beauty stole his heart. The city had been full of visitors to observe the festival of Artemis, so the booty taken by the warriors was far more than usual. Along with the princess, many other women were taken as slaves and concubines. When Achilles and his men returned to Troy, the women were divided amongst the officers. Achilles kept the lovely Briseis with her dark curls and bright smile as his own. King Agamemnon took his pick, choosing Astynome, whose golden blond hair and virginal status caught his eye.

Achilles wasn't the only warrior out wreaking havoc across the Trojan countryside. Ajax the Great was the son of King Telamon. He and his brother, Teucer, commanded a legion of troops and did their share of pillaging. Ajax the Great was named for his enormous size and strength. He carried a huge shield made of seven ox hides and a layer of bronze that was big enough to protect both him and Teucer, who was a famed archer, on the battlefield. They led their men to ravage the Thracian kingdom, and they captured Polydorus, the youngest of the Trojan princes who had been sent away from Troy to avoid the fighting.

The days moved slowly for most of the warriors and their commanders. Ajax and Achilles sought to pass an afternoon in a game of petteia, a board game that may have resembled checkers or chess. The warriors pitted their skill in strategy against each other. Every move was calculated and considered. They eyed their choices shrewdly and slowly and became so engrossed in the game that they did not even notice a Trojan battle party had invaded the camp. The Trojan warriors spied the two famed generals of the Greeks and saw an opportunity to tip the scales in their favor. Quietly, they approached the warriors with their blades drawn. Just as they swung the death blow, Athena flipped over the board with such violence that the warriors were blown backward, out of harm's way. Ajax and Achilles, surrounded by Trojan warriors, leapt to their feet, stunned and surprised. However, such was their skill that soon the ground turned crimson with Trojan blood.

There were many such encounters, but not all threats came from the enemy. As with any hierarchy, men sought to improve their standing, often at the expense of someone else. Close quarters of the field camp also led to bickering, and smoldering old grudges quickly ignited into fiery disputes. Odysseus had never forgiven Palamedes from rousting him from his family and putting his baby in danger. For many years, he nursed his resentment as Palamedes rose higher and higher in the ranks of the Greek army. He was one of their most skilled strategists and created eleven letters of the alphabet. He taught many of his comrades to count and do figures. As respect and admiration for Palamedes grew among the troops, so did Odysseus' hatred.

Odysseus was sent on an errand to Thrace to retrieve a boatload of grain to feed the troops. The journey seemed to be doomed from the start and everything that could go wrong did. Odysseus returned with an empty ship and a heavy heart. Palamedes mocked him openly among the other commanders.

"Come now, clever Odysseus! You couldn't even gather one kernel of grain to feed our hungry troops? What are the men to eat? Shall they graze on grass like cattle? This is why we should forego this folly and return to our home shores. It has been almost nineteen years since the queen was stolen. Let it rest, and let us get back to our families," Palamedes urged Agamemnon. There was a growing resistance among the soldiers led by Palamedes that felt it was time to accept defeat and return to Greece. It was a movement that was gaining support at an alarming rate and causing great concern among the leadership of the army.

Odysseus, nettled by the comments and eager to get rid of Palamedes if only temporarily, challenged, "If you think you can do better, great and wise Palamedes, go forth and do it. At least it will quiet your traitorous tongue for a moment!"

Agamemnon, who also struggled with Palamedes' arrogance, supported Odysseus' challenge and sent him to Thrace to gather grain. To Odysseus' intense embarrassment, Palamedes returned in half the time with a boat stuffed with grain.

Triumphant, Palamedes walked about crowing over his accomplishments, and Odysseus couldn't stand it anymore. He had to get rid of Palamedes.

Odysseus visited the prison camp where they housed their Trojan prisoners. He found a steward of King Priam, Paris' father, and forced him to write a letter insinuating that Palamedes was accepting gold from the Trojans in return for information about the Greek's plans.

The next day he spoke to Agamemnon. "My king, the camp is filthy. We must pick up all the tents to level the ground and reroute the ditches."

Agamemnon supported the suggestion, and the entire camp was packed up. While the men were busy digging new ditches and releveling tent sites, Odysseus buried a cache of gold under the site of Palamedes' tent. As he supervised the raising of Palamedes' tent, he stashed the letter under Palamedes' bunk. In the tumult of the day, none of his actions looked the least bit suspicious. By sunset, the camp was re-established, and Odysseus' trap was set.

Odysseus wasted no time. He went to Agamemnon with the first rays of sun in the morning. "Agamemnon, I have just received the most disturbing intelligence. Palamedes, your trusted strategist, has been undermining your cause. He has been giving information to the Trojans in exchange for gold," Odysseus told him in urgent tones, feigning distress and concern.

Agamemnon's brows lifted in surprise. "Those are heavy accusations, Odysseus. You have long been my trusted counselor, and I know Palamedes' arrogance is difficult to tolerate, but I cannot just take your word on this. What proof do you have?"

Odysseus told him all about the letter and gold that had been discovered in Palamedes' tent during the clean up the day before.

He urged Agamemnon to go see for himself. So, Agamemnon ordered Palamedes' quarters searched, and sure enough, the letter and the gold were discovered. A dumbfounded Palamedes protested and claimed his innocence, but the incriminating evidence was damning.

"At least allow me to present a prepared defense. The laws of justice permit me that," Palamedes insisted. Agamemnon agreed and set the time for his hearing.

Palamedes addressed the officers of the army and his king later that afternoon. "My lords, I know that the evidence points to my guilt, and I cannot explain how those items got into my tent," he said with a sideways glare at Odysseus. Though he could not prove it, Palamedes felt that Odysseus was responsible for his current predicament. "I can, however, offer some doubt to the validity of these claims. First of all, the amount of gold that I supposedly accepted in exchange for information is a pittance. I have many times that amount already. Why would I take such a risk for such a small amount? If I had only buried part of the payment and the entire sum was much larger, it would have required many men to move such an amount. How could a contingent of men moving a large sum of gold go unnoticed in the camp or sneak past our guards at night? It's implausible! Of course, then there are the supposed men themselves. A secret such as this would not stay secret for long in this camp. These men gossip more than women at the well! There is no way that this is anything other than planted evidence to taint my reputation." Palamedes made his case and waited while the officers discussed his fate.

In the end, the physical evidence could not be overlooked. Agamemnon sentenced Palamedes to death by stoning. Thus, ended the life of Palamedes, and Odysseus gained his revenge.

However, Palamedes' death did not go unavenged. His father, Nauplius, one of the best captains in the fleet, protested and demanded justice for his son. His grievances fell on deaf ears, and Agamemnon dismissed him. Nauplius sailed back to Greece and spent the remaining years of the war sowing discord among the wives of the officers. He spread the rumor that all the officers were bringing home Trojan mistresses and planned to set their Greek wives aside for them. He encouraged the wives to take a lover who could protect them once their husbands returned home.

Unrest continued among the troops after Palamedes' death. Lack of supplies made the men insolent and short tempered. Rumors of mutiny spread and gained momentum. The men began to organize a revolt. Achilles heard the whispers and sought out Agamemnon to discuss it.

"Mighty king, the men grow restless. They long for comfort and their homes. We must fill their bellies and slake their thirst if we hope to keep them in their camps," Achilles warned.

Agamemnon was well aware of the supply issues and the trouble they were causing. The Trojans had been very efficient at disrupting their supply lines. He had come up with a solution, if only it arrived in time. "I hear your wise words, Achilles. I count on you to hold the men in check. Relief is coming. I dispatched

Menelaus and Odysseus to retrieve the Winegrowers from Delos," the king reassured Achilles.

For weeks, Achilles worked to distract and soothe the increasingly discontent soldiers. Agamemnon kept his eyes to the sea, watching for sails that would signal salvation. The situation grew desperate, and Achilles had stationed himself on the docks, barring the passage of anyone trying to sneak away. Just when it appeared that he would be overwhelmed by sheer numbers, "Sail Ho!" sounded across the bay.

Everyone watched the ship glide slowly into the harbor and held their breath as Odysseus led three beautiful women down the gangway. Oeno, Spermo, and Elais accompanied him through the throng of men, who quickly stepped aside as they stared. The men followed in one great mass back to the camp where Agamemnon joyfully welcomed the three women.

"Daughters of Anius, welcome and thank you for coming in our time of need. Your father offered your services many years ago, and I am relieved to see he has not forgotten! Will you, with your divine gifts, feed my army and provide them the nourishment they lack?"

Oeno stepped forward and from the earth, drew forth wine which was distributed throughout the ranks. Spermo produced corn which was taken to the kitchens to be prepared while Elais tapped the earth for olive oil that filled cask after cask. The men rejoiced, and there was much celebration among the camp.

The Winegrowers performed this service time and time again until they grew weary with the constant demand. They petitioned Agamemnon to return them to Delos. They had made enough stores to see the Greeks through the prophesied tenth year of the war. However, Agamemnon was not keen to lose his army's meal ticket. He put them off and promised that he would send them home soon. Finally, they figured out he had no intention of sending them home, so they petitioned Dionysus for help. The God of Wine, who had blessed them with their gifts, turned them into doves so they could return on their own.

Agamemnon had bigger things to worry about than the Winegrowers. The father of Astynome, his mistress stolen in the sac of Lyrnessus, had sailed into the harbor with several ships. Chryses was demanding that his daughter be returned to him. He offered Agamemnon a large sum of gold and silver in exchange for her freedom.

"Be gone from here! Your daughter pleases me more than my own wife, and I will not be giving her back, now or ever! Now leave this port and never return or you will feel my wrath."

Chryses knew he couldn't stand up to Agamemnon with all his soldiers and weapons. So, he took his leave and went back to his temple. There he called to his god, Apollo, "God of the Silver Bow, I beseech thee! I have been faithful to you. See your temple decked in garlands and finery! I ask you to hear my prayer. My daughter has been stolen by the king of Mykenai, Agamemnon. He refuses to return her though I offered him a fair exchange. Return my daughter to me!"

Apollo heard faithful Chryses' pleas. His wrath had already been stirred by several of the acts of war made by the Greeks, so he was only too happy to exact revenge on them. He slung his bow and quiver over his shoulder and set up just outside the Greek camps. He shot a volley of arrows down on them, striking their animals and causing sickness to spread among the cattle, oxen, and horses. Even the dogs sickened. The next round fell on the soldiers. For nine days, Apollo mercilessly let arrow after arrow fly. Each one spread pestilence among the Greeks.

Agamemnon called his officers together. Achilles spoke first, "What has caused the wrath of Apollo to rain down on us? Did we omit a sacrifice or overlook some holy rites? Wise Calchas, prophet, speak plainly that we might rid ourselves of this plague!"

Calchas glanced warily at Agamemnon. "Achilles, I have answers for your questions, but do you promise to protect me if my answers offend powerful men? I am old and cannot wield a sword myself."

Achilles didn't hesitate. "You have the protection of my blade. If you name Zeus himself at fault, he will have to come through me to get to you."

Satisfied with this promise, Calchas told the assembly, "The Archer Prince shoots his silver bow not out of dissatisfaction with the rituals paid to him. He brings death and disease among us to avenge his priest, Chryses, and his daughter, who Agamemnon refused to return to him. It will not cease until she is given over to her father without payment or ransom."

Agamemnon, as Calchas predicted, jumped angrily to his feet. "Why should I have to give up my mistress? She pleases me, and it is not seemly that the king should be left womanless while all the rest of his officers enjoy womanly comforts. If you can replace her, then you can take her!"

"Where are we supposed to get you a replacement? Women do not grow on trees. We do not keep them in the common store. Men are dying by the dozen! Stop your moaning and do what needs to be done," Achilles countered angrily.

"Fine, Achilles. I will take your Briseis instead. Take my lovely Astynome, Odysseus, and return her to her father with compensation. That should still the Archer's bow." Odysseus didn't even get out of the room before Achilles shot to his feet, his hand on his sword.

"You dog-faced coward! I am here to right a wrong done to your house. I have no quarrel with the Trojans, but we answered your call. Here you moan about an empty bed when these men haven't seen their families in over a decade because of you!" His grip tightened on his sword, but before he could follow his intention and draw it to engage Agamemnon, Athena appeared to him, though no one else could see her.

"Mighty Achilles, I have come from Zeus, who loves both you and Agamemnon. He bids you stay your hand. Heed my words, and your insult here today will be paid back three-fold," the goddess of war whispered to him.

Achilles dropped his hand from the hilt of his sword and nodded to Athena. "However hot my temper burns, I will always heed the instructions of the gods." He stormed out of the assembly, leaving Agamemnon and the others standing in bewilderment at his abrupt departure.

Agamemnon sent men to retrieve Briseis from Achilles. They tentatively stood outside his tent. "Fear not, my quarrel is not with you," he told them. "Patroclus, give Briseis to these men and bear witness that if the greedy king Agamemnon looks for help from Achilles in the future, he will not find it!" With that proclamation, Achilles quitted the field.

As Achilles and his men took up residence in their ships, he called his mother, Thetis, up from her watery abode. "Mother, go forth to Father Zeus and petition him for me. Tell him of the wrongs done to me and ask him to bring the Greeks to their knees so they will know just how sorely they need me," Achilles instructed Thetis. She carried the message to Olympus and with much coercion, got Zeus to agree he would turn the tide against the Greeks until they begged Achilles to help them.

In the wake of Achilles desertion, Zeus visited Agamemnon in a dream. Zeus told the Greek king to rally his troops. The gods were aligned on the side of the Greeks, and if they struck quickly, victory was assured. Agamemnon sat bolt upright in bed and immediately called his officers to attend him. When he shared his dream, they rejoiced at the prospect of ending the long siege.

Before they went into battle, Agamemnon wanted to test the troop's loyalty. He put about the rumor that they were leaving off with the siege and returning to Greece. He never anticipated the desire of the soldiers to go home. Like waves on the ocean, the men swarmed to the harbor. They left their arms and treasures behind in their haste to launch the boats. Agamemnon stood gaping as the men deserted the field.

From the heavens Hera looked down, distraught. "What is this? Why do they leave without sacking the city and retrieving Helen? I was promised that Troy would fall! Athena, go amongst them and calm their flight. This is Zeus' mischief at the request of that fish-wife, Thetis."

Athena went forth and found Odysseus, who had been caught up in the mob. "King of Ithaca, where are you going? Are you fleeing and leaving the fair Helen behind? Since when did a warrior of Greece flee like a deer before a lion?"

Odysseus knew the voice of the goddess and heard her words. He fought his way to Agamemnon and took his ancestral staff as a symbol to rally the troops. He spoke to the other kings and chief warriors. "We must stop this flight. We have the heart of lions, not the weak, frightened hearts of deer. We do not flee because the path is long. We must stay and see this through. Besides, we are within a year of the prophesied ten years. We must see if old Calchas was right or wrong!" The men saw the staff and heard Athena murmuring in their ears encouragement to stand their ground. Their momentum shifted. Soon, they were piling back into the camp, uttering their battle cries, and taking up their weapons.

From the walls of Troy, King Priam, Paris, and their officers watched the Greek troop movement and mustered their own armies once it became clear that the Greeks meant to engage them that day. The Trojan army fell in quickly and spilled from the gates of Troy like ants from their mound. Their unnerving battle cry echoed over the field like the screech of angry hawks. The Greeks advanced in utter silence.

Paris marched in the front of the Trojan soldiers as was fitting a Prince of Troy. Garbed in a panther's skin with a sword, two spears, and a bow, he strode forward confidently until he saw Menelaus coming straight for him.

Menelaus smiled when he saw the Prince of Troy. The Greek king looked like a lion stalking a sheep as he dismounted from his chariot and began to close the distance between him and Paris. Clad in armor with a mighty sword and shield, his battle prowess radiated across the plain. His mighty battle cry cut across the Trojan's screeching and Paris suddenly lost his nerve. He scurried back into the ranks.

His brother, Hector, caught his arm as he ran by, "Where are you going, coward? You are the reason for this miserable war. Stand and fight! Show the Greeks what a Trojan Prince is made of!"

Paris accepted the rebuke, for he knew he deserved it. He squared his shoulders and announced, "I shall fight Menelaus of Sparta!

Let us end this conflict here and now. To the victor goes the lovely Helen and thus will end this struggle!"

Hector bade the men stand down. When the Greeks saw this, they thought to take advantage of their enemies' lowered defenses, but Agamemnon stilled their bows. "Wait! See, the mighty Hector steps forward to speak."

Hector proposed a truce and said that Paris wanted to fight Menelaus in single combat for the hand of Helen and end the war. Menelaus was more than happy to comply, and the Greek army similarly lowered their weapons. The men took off their armor and sat on their shields as the preparations were made.

The Trojan king, Priam, came to the field to sanctify the battle with a sacrifice to Zeus. Menelaus and Paris donned their armor and drew lots to see who would throw their spear first. Paris won, and the two warriors took up their positions.

A hush fell over the field as the soldiers watched their leaders square off. High from the walls of Troy, Helen looked down on the scene. Her heart squeezed as she saw Menelaus from whom she had been stolen all those years ago. She held her breath as she watched her two husbands face off.

Paris threw his spear. Its aim was true, but Menelaus blocked it easily with his shield. Then, the Greek king set his feet and drew back his arm. "Zeus guide my hand and let me prevail over he who wronged me and took what was mine," he prayed to the Father of All.

His spear rocketed through the air and passed straight through Paris' shield. Paris jerked in shock, and that small movement saved his life. The spear passed over his shoulder, harmlessly cutting his arm. Menelaus bellowed an earthshaking battle cry in frustration and drew his sword. With a stroke that would have beheaded an ox, he struck Paris' helmet, but instead of cutting through, the sword shattered in his hand.

"Zeus! You are the most spiteful of gods! My revenge was assured, but you have stopped it," Menelaus shouted to the heavens. In exasperation, he grabbed Paris by the plume on his helmet and began to drag him toward the Greek lines. The strap of the helmet cut into Paris' throat, choking him. The prince clawed at the leather strap but couldn't get his fingers under it. He thrashed about like a fish on the end of a line, but Menelaus took no notice and marched grimly forward.

Aphrodite, seeing her favorite about to die a most ignominious death, surrounded Paris in a fog and cut the helmet strap. She stole him away, cloaked in mist, to his bedchamber and sought out Helen to tend to him. Disguised as an old woman, Aphrodite pulled at the Queen's robes to get her attention. Helen saw her at once for what she was, for no disguise could completely conceal the beauty of Aphrodite.

"Goddess, what do you want with me? Haven't you caused enough trouble when you clouded my heart and my eyes and made me run away with Paris? My true husband stands on the field of battle, robbed of victory by you!"

Aphrodite's eyes flashed with anger. "You'll go to your husband who lies in his bedchamber in need of your attention. You will go as a happy and willing wife, or I will stir trouble between the Greeks and Trojans that will never be settled!"

Helen bit her tongue and did as she was bid. She tended Paris in his bed, but her heart yearned for Menelaus and her Greek homeland.

From the battlefield, a cry went up as Menelaus was announced the victor of the day. The truce still stood, and the troops retired for the evening. They all wondered what the next day would bring.

High in the heavens, the gods gathered in assembly. Zeus, though it was akin to poking a hornet's nest with a stick, teased Hera and Athena, "Poor Menelaus! Such friends, he has in his two patrons, Hera and Athena. They let his victory slip away. Aphrodite was not afraid to get her hands dirty. Her champion is safe in his bed."

Hera, seething with anger after the battle, was all too happy to rise to Zeus' baiting. "Son of Cronos, your hand is in this! I worked so hard to arrange this and watch the fall of Troy. Yet, it still stands! You've ruined everything!"

Zeus' anger flashed. "Wife, you are a vengeful creature. What did the Trojans ever do to you? They are my most esteemed people, and it is against my will that I let you sack the city. If I do this, I will have your assurance that if I ever turn my wrath on your favorites, you will not stay my hand."

"My three favorite cities are Sparta, Mykenai, and Argos. You may level them to dust, and I will not stir to defend them," Hera vowed. "Now, send our cunning Athena into the midst of the Trojans that they may break the truce."

Thus, Zeus gave his instructions to Athena. Like a comet, she streaked across the night's sky and stole into the Trojan camp. Taking the form of the Trojan commander, Laodocus, she whispered in the ear of the famed archer, Pandarus. "Do you dare to send an arrow into the Greek camp? Can you hit Menelaus? Think of the glory that will be to you if you strike down the Greek king who has caused all this mayhem!"

Pandarus did as he was commanded. He knocked his arrow and sent a prayer to Apollo that it would fly true. With a twang of the bowstring, the arrow shot in a high arc over the fields and down into the Greek camp.

Athena was already there. She brushed it aside so that it merely grazed Menelaus. At first, both Menelaus and Agamemnon just stared at the wound that appeared to come out of nowhere until they spied the arrow. "The Trojans have broken their oath," exclaimed Agamemnon. "Get your wound tended to, my brother. We shall not let this go unanswered!"

As the first rays of morning lit the sky, the Greek troops formed ranks and marched in silence to the battlefield. The Trojan army called their battle cries and joined them. The truce was over.

Swords clattered across shields. Men cried out in agony and victory. Spears and arrows whizzed through the air. Athena bolstered the courage of the Greeks. Ares, the god of war, took the side of the Trojans and made their hearts courageous. Apollo reminded the Trojans that Achilles was not in the field, and it was their chance for victory. The Trojans surged forward. Strife, Panic, and Rout were set free on the battlefield and left chaos in their wake. Trojan and Greek blood stained the ground red.

With Achilles out of the action, Athena chose a new champion. Diomedes gained her favor, and she blessed him. "Brave Diomedes! I strengthen your heart full of courage. Your limbs will feel no fatigue. Your sword will strike true, and I raise the veil from your eyes so you can tell god from man. Hear my words, my warrior, should you see the fair one, Aphrodite, mark her with a wound from your sword."

Diomedes, filled with the grace and might of Athena, waded into the battle. Trojans fell before him like trees before an ax. Athena sought to help her champion further. Speaking to Ares, "Come, Master Ares, this is a war for the mortals to fight. We must go away lest we anger Zeus with our interference." Ares, wary of Zeus' wrath, left with her.

The battle wore on, and both sides lost soldiers and officers. Diomedes, however, fought like a machine, and the Trojans fell back from his onslaught. Two of the Trojan princes fell to his sword. Without Ares to stiffen their resolve, Panic and Rout stirred their blood, and they began to break their ranks to retreat. Pandarus took aim and shot Diomedes in an effort to take down their champion. The arrow lodged in his shoulder, but Diomedes, with the help of Athena, pulled the arrow free and continued fighting.

Aeneas, a Trojan warrior, and son of Aphrodite, surmised that Diomedes had a god at his side and found Pandarus. "Take down their champion with one of your bolts," he commanded from his chariot.

"I already tried, but he has the protection of Athena. Naught we try will affect him," Pandarus groused.

"Bah! A spear to the guts will drop any warrior, god or not! Come, let us end this and rally our men," Aeneas called and pulled Pandarus into his chariot. Together they raced across the battlefield. Pandarus flung his spear as they closed the distance. Diomedes, warned by his second in command, caught it with his shield. It penetrated through and lodged in his breastplate, not even scratching his skin. Pandarus whooped in triumph, thinking it had sunk home in his belly, but Diomedes cast it aside and answered with his own spear. Pandarus fell as the spear hit him through the eye. Aeneas cried out and stopped the chariot to protect Pandarus' body. Diomedes, infused with the strength of Athena, threw an enormous boulder at Aeneas and shattered his hip. The warrior fell, unconscious with pain.

From her vantage point, Aphrodite saw her son fall, and she immediately flew to his side. Tenderly, she gathered Aeneas to her, but before she could spirit him away, Diomedes, who could see her, struck her with his spear, cutting her wrist. Ichor, the god's version of blood, spilled from Aphrodite's wrist as she dropped her son. Swift Apollo caught Aeneas and concealed him in a cloak of darkness. Crying in pain, Aphrodite withdrew. Iris, the goddess of the winds, led her back to Olympus where she moaned in pain. Dione, one of the Ocean Titans and the closest thing to a mother Aphrodite had, comforted her and healed her wound.

Athena laughed and mocked the goddess of love. "Poor, pretty Aphrodite! She cut herself on the gold pin of her brooch. Leave the fighting to warriors and stick to your lady's work!"

Zeus laughed and patted Aphrodite's hand. "Daughter, you are suited to love, not war. Leave off in this conflict and let Athena and Ares sort it out."

On the battlefield, Diomedes, emboldened by his easy victory over Aphrodite, charged Apollo to challenge him for the fallen hero, Aeneas. Three times in a row, Apollo tossed Diomedes back like he weighed nothing and on the fourth time, Apollo thundered, "Do not try again Diomedes! For those who walk the mortal plane cannot contest with gods!" So fierce was the resolve on Apollo's face that Diomedes' courage failed him. He left off trying to steal Aeneas and fell back. Apollo carried Aeneas away to his mother and sister, Leto and Artemis, to heal. In his absence, he cast a phantom of Aeneas amid the armies. Bitter fighting broke out around the false image as the Trojans tried to protect their fallen comrade, and the Greeks sought to steal him away as a captive.

In the heavens, Apollo spoke to Ares, "Diomedes dared challenge me as if I were his equal. Can you not go down and take him from the field? He is doing much damage to our Trojan favorites."

Ares, restless and tired of watching from the sidelines, went back down to the battle and took Eris, goddess of strife, in hand. Together they inspired a battle frenzy in the Trojans. Apollo returned a newly healed and reinvigorated Aeneas to the field. This further fueled the Trojans, and they began to push the Greeks back toward their ships.

Seeing the Trojans rallying, Hera and Athena decided that they needed to help the Greeks to even the odds. They donned their armor and mounted their chariots, and into the fray, they rode.

Athena pulled Diomedes into her chariot and healed his wounds. Together, they made straight for Ares whose sword flashed too fast for the eye to see. Corpses littered the ground around him in heaps. Athena strapped on Hades' Helm of Darkness so Ares could not see her. When Ares saw the chariot with only Diomedes heading toward him, he hurled his spear at the Greek warrior. Athena turned the spear away. Diomedes answered with his own throw as the chariot bore down on Ares. Athena guided the tip of the spear, so it slipped under Ares' under-girdle and drove into his belly. Ares roared in pain and anger, and the ground shook in his fury. Greeks and Trojans alike cowered at the sound.

Ares fled to Olympus where he complained bitterly to Zeus, who had no patience for it. "Ares, least loved of the gods, stop your whining! You cause enough trouble everywhere you go. It's about time someone gave some back to you," Zeus snapped, but healed Ares' wound despite his sharp words.

Having equaled the odds again, Athena and Hera retired back to Mount Olympus, and it was the Greek's turn to put the Trojans on their heels. Hector and Aeneas tried to reestablish organization among their ranks. Hellenus, a famed seer and Trojan Prince, urged Hector to go within the walls of Troy and rally support there.

"I cannot leave! The battle is engaged! My sword is needed here," Hector protested.

"Nay, brother. Fly now to our mother and tell her to set the women to offering a sacrifice to Pallas Athena. We must beg the goddess of war to take pity upon us! Until her will is changed, we cannot win. You must do this!"

So, Hector reluctantly quitted the field and rushed inside the walls. "Mother," he said urgently to the Queen of Troy, "rally the women. Pallas Athena has set her will against us. Make offerings to her to soften her heart to our Trojan warriors. Without her, we cannot win the day!" His mother assured him she would make it so.

Hector went to rouse Paris. He found him lying in bed, with Helen and her ladies fussing over him. "Rise from your bed! Men are dying defending your choice. Get up before the city is burned around your ears," Hector berated younger brother.

Paris, accepting the rebuke as just, pushed from his bed and donned his armor. "I will meet you on the field of battle, brother. Go and inspire the men to hold their ground!"

Hector sought out his wife on the way out of the city. "Cry not for me, my wife. I am proud to protect you and my city. If I fall, you can hold your chin high. I died a warrior's death and will be welcomed in the Underworld."

His lovely wife, Andromache, raised her tear-stained face to his and said, "I don't want to be an honored widow. I want to be a wife to my husband and him to be a father to our child," she said, weeping over her baby's downy hair. She straightened her spine and dried her tears, determined to see him back into battle with a smile. "Come back to me, husband, and fight well," she murmured in his ear before she kissed him. Hector, his heart buoyed by seeing his wife and child, kissed her soundly and left them once more to join the battle.

The women of Troy laid out a lavish sacrifice for Athena. They sent up their prayers and beseeched the warrior goddess to have mercy on their men and their city. Athena turned a deaf ear to them, and the Trojans continued to fall back toward the city.

Hector met Paris at the gates of Troy, and together they re-entered the battle. Rejuvenated by seeing their leaders once again standing together and fighting, the Trojans found a toe-hold and held fast. Athena noticed her Greeks beginning to lose precious ground again and made her way back to the battlefield. However, before she could do anything, Apollo intercepted her.

"Daughter of Zeus! Have you no room in your heart to show mercy to the Trojans? So sweetly they beseeched you! Come now, let us find a way to end the bloodshed for the day," Apollo implored her.

Athena had softened ever so slightly toward the Trojans after their prayers and all warriors, regardless of their allegiance, were dear to her. The loss of so many proud fighters was devastating, so she listened to Apollo's plan.

"Let us go each to our troops and convince them to appoint a champion from each side to settle this business," Apollo proposed and when Athena agreed, they went their separate ways.

Apollo whispered to Helenus, who went directly to Hector. "Brother heed me now! I have heard divine counsel. Bid your troops to sit and lower their weapons. Offer to settle this thing on your honor. You will fight any warrior they will send to settle this struggle."

Hector, who trusted his brother in these matters, bade his troops lower their weapons and fall back. Agamemnon, seeing Hector marching to the front lines, ordered his men to stand down. Hector yelled that all men might hear him, "Greeks and Trojans, hear my words! I stand here before you to fight for Troy. With my life or with my death, so shall it be for Troy! Send any among you to face me, here and now. If I should fall, strip away my armor, but let my body be sent back to my wife that I may be prepared to meet the Lord of Darkness properly! If Apollo grants my victory, I shall show the same respect to your champion!"

Hector drew his sword and made himself ready. However, no one came forward from the Greek contingent. Not a soul said anything, until, in disgust, Menelaus stepped forward, strapping up his breastplate. "Cowardly dogs! I will go and fight the mighty Hector! He is but a man!" Agamemnon, knowing that Menelaus was not equal to the challenge, held him back, while King Nestor rallied the troops with a rousing tale of his adventures as a young warrior. Inspired, nine Greek warriors, including Odysseus, Ajax the Great, Ajax the Lesser, and Agamemnon himself, stepped forward and cast their lots.

Ajax the Great won the casting of the lots. His squires adjusted his armor, and the great man took up his massive shield and spear. Hector's heart skipped in his chest as the grim-faced warrior approached. "Noble Hector, let us face off man to man that you will know the heart of a Greek warrior. Let the fight begin!"

Hector threw his spear with all his might. Ajax caught it in the gigantic shield. It penetrated through six layers of hide, but no further. Ajax threw his spear like a dart at Hector. It sliced through Hector's shield, and he barely twisted away from the lethal point, sustaining only a cut along his chest. Each warrior took up the spears and fell on each other in hand-to-hand combat. Ajax, bigger and stronger, soon had Hector back on his heels, bleeding from multiple wounds. The Trojan's hand closed on a large rock as he pushed himself up from the ground after a particularly brutal onslaught by Ajax. He flung the rock with all his strength, and it scored a solid hit on the enormous bronze-plated shield. Ajax laughed as the rock bounced off and hurled a colossal stone at Hector that caved in his shield and sent him flying backward.

Apollo picked up his champion and infused his limbs with strength before he went back to face his foe. Just as the pair were about to cross swords, the noble heralds of both armies stepped between them.

"Behold, the light of day is fading! Night is nigh! As decreed by the gods, we will break for the night. You have both fought valiantly," the Greek herald, Idaeus, proclaimed.

Both the champions agreed as it was the custom of the day. Before quitting the field for the night, Hector presented Ajax with silver studded sword and scabbard. In return, Ajax gave the Trojan warrior a lavish purple girdle. They parted as friends, and both sides felt honored and fairly treated.

As the night wore on, both camps held councils. The Greeks sacrificed to Zeus, mourned their dead, and celebrated their courage and victories. However, there was a very different tone in the Trojan war council. "We should return Lady Helen and the treasure. How many more Trojan sons must die for this woman," Antenor, a wise and respected warrior, argued angrily. He had lost many troops on the field, and it weighed heavy on his heart.

"I will not simply return my wife," Paris snapped, frustrated and scared. He, too, had been appalled at the loss of life and was, in truth, quite worried about his own. "However," he continued over the fierce debate that raged around the table, "I will relinquish the treasure I took when I brought Helen to Troy. Perhaps they will be appeased with that and leave well enough alone. We are not the only ones who lost brothers on the battlefield today."

Thus, it was agreed, and a Trojan envoy was sent with a proposal to the Greeks. Of course, the Greeks hadn't spent the last two decades away from their home only to return with half of what they came for. They turned down the offer but agreed to take the next day off fighting so both sides could tend to their dead and wounded.

The next day, half the Greek army pulled carts through the field picking up their fallen comrades while the other half dug a ditch and erected a wall as a fortification to their camp. The Trojans were similarly engaged with retrieving their friends, brothers, and sons from where they lay. Great funeral pyres were lit, and the fallen warriors in the first great battle of the Trojan War were sent to the Kingdom of Darkness. Both sides feasted and toasted in honor of their dead as the Nyx drew her veil of darkness over the earth once more.

As Helios began his journey the next morning, Zeus called the gods together in assembly. "Hear me now, none of you shall meddle in the mortal war this day! I have decreed it and am more powerful than all of you put together. You will incur my wrath if you disobey," he added with a meaningful glance at Hera and Athena. With that final warning, he left them and took up a post on Mount Ida, setting up the scales of fate and waiting for the day's battle to begin.

The fighting commenced for the day. It was midday before Zeus stirred to action. Placing death on either side of the scale, he weighted the Greek side down until it sat on the earth. The tide on the battlefield turned, and the Greeks began to lose ground. Zeus hurled down thunder and lightning upon the unfortunate Greeks. With the might of Zeus against them, they fell back behind their newly constructed fortifications. The Greek losses were heavy, and their hearts were bleak as they dug in behind their last line of defense.

Hera, on Mount Olympus, raged and pulled at her hair. "How dare he forbid me from helping my champions while he plays with the balance of fate for his own side! He did not say I could not advise my brave warriors." Hera spoke words on the wind. She counseled Agamemnon to hold his ground behind his fortifications and to offer a sacrifice to appease the ill-tempered Zeus.

Agamemnon heeded her guidance and offered prayers and roasted meat to the Father of All. Zeus' heart was moved by the offering and to reassure the Greeks that he had not forgotten them, he sent an eagle to soar over them. When the Greeks saw the majestic bird, their hearts lifted, and they rallied. Diomedes and Agamemnon led their defensive charge while Ajax the Great and his brother, Teucer the archer, dropped soldier after soldier with a volley of arrows that all met their marks, except the one meant for Hector. Apollo deflected that one, breaking Zeus' no interference rule.

The Trojans gave ground under the renewed onslaught, but Zeus again tipped the scales in their favor, causing them to rally. Hera and Athena couldn't stand by and watch their Greeks be routed. They hitched up their chariots and began to pull on their armor. From Mount Ida, Zeus saw this and grew angry. He sent Iris to remind them of his decree. "I expect this disrespect from Hera.

She never does what I tell her without a fight, but not Athena. You tell my gray-eyed daughter that if she disobeys me in this, I will lame her horses, destroy her chariots, and burn her with my lightning so severely that she will not recover for 10 years!"

Thus, Iris flew to Olympus with her message. Upon hearing it, both Hera and Athena ceased their preparations and cursed Hector and Zeus bitterly as they watched their warriors be driven back. They cried and tore their hair when the Greek fortifications broke, their gates burned, and the soldiers fled to their boats. "Have mercy, Zeus! You are killing the ones dear to me. We all well acknowledge your might and supremacy," Hera called to her husband. "Leave off your torment of my Greeks!"

"The Fates have spoken, and your Greeks will suffer until Achilles stops sulking in his ships and joins the battle. Now, cease your squalling," Zeus retorted.

Night fell on the field, and the fighting wound down for the day. The Trojans did not retire to their homes inside the walls but camped on the battlefield to keep the pressure on their opponents. Hector, inspired by the day's accomplishments, called for campfires to burn brightly and ordered all the fires inside the walls lit as well. The Trojans showed their pride by lighting the night sky.

On the Greek side of the field, the story was very different. Panic and Strife wove through the troops, sapping their fighting spirit. In the assembly of officers, Agamemnon announced that he was ready to call it quits and sail for home.

"You forget, my king, Troy is fated to fall. I will not return home and let the deaths of my brothers in arms be for naught because you haven't the stomach for battle. We must see this through," Diomedes demanded, and his comrades roared in support.

Wise Nestor stood, and the men quieted. Nestor's counsel was always to be heeded. "Agamemnon, you know what you must do. You must unstiffen your neck and make peace with Achilles. Only he and his troops can turn the tide for us."

Agamemnon nodded, for he knew the truth and wisdom in the words. He sent Odysseus, Ajax the Great, and Phoenix to convince Achilles to rejoin the battle. He sweetened the offer by saying if Achilles took up his arms, he would give Briseis back in addition to a large treasure and one of his daughters in marriage once they returned home.

The trio made their way to Achilles' ship and received a warm welcome with food and wine. The great warrior himself sang to them and played for them on the lyre. Finally, Odysseus made the king's request.

"Nay, Odysseus," Achilles answered, "I will not draw my sword on this field again. My mother said I could live a long boring life or a short and glorious one. Zeus has set himself against us. We cannot win, and it is folly to keep fighting. There is no treasure worth my life. I choose a long boring life. Me and mine will sail in the morning."

Odysseus and Ajax cajoled and begged, but failed to persuade Achilles. They left empty-handed, but old Phoenix remained behind, intending to return home with Achilles and his men.

Agamemnon and the rest of the officers read the bad news on their faces as soon as they entered the tent. A groan of despair rose from their lips, but Diomedes stood and quieted them. "Achilles' neck is stiff, but he will come in his own time. Until then, we must not lose heart. Let us each go to our beds and rest. Another day lies ahead with its own trials."

That night, Agamemnon could not rest. The light from the Trojan fires kept him awake, and he finally decided to go discuss strategy with Nestor. On his way to Nestor's tent, he met Menelaus, who was having similar trouble sleeping. Together, they roused the highest officers and counseled with Nestor to come up with a plan to save the situation.

After much discussion, Nestor rose and spoke, "We need information on the Trojan strategy for the morrow. Is there any among us who feels equal to the task of infiltrating their camp and investigating their plans?"

Diomedes immediately volunteered, and out of the many other men willing to accompany him, he chose Odysseus. Together, they prayed to Athena for guidance and support. The goddess of war sent a great heron as a sign that she approved of their mission.

Like shadows, the two soldiers crossed the battlefield, picking their way through corpses and debris. In the dark, they saw a shadow, similar to their own, who was making its way toward the Greek camp. Silently, Odysseus and Diomedes flanked their quarry and sprang upon him. They made short work of subduing the Trojan, Dolon, who revealed he was on the same mission they were. With a bit of persuasion, Dolon told them the layout of the Trojan encampment. The terrified soldier spilled all the information he knew and begged to be taken alive and kept as a prisoner. Diomedes answered his pleas by severing his head from his body and offering his armor and weapons to Athena.

With the information from Dolon, Odysseus and Diomedes made their way to the edge of the Trojan camp where a group of Thracian warriors gathered.

"Let us steal their horses as an inspiration to our men," Odysseus whispered. "I'll get the horses, and you take care of those soldiers there. But, Diomedes, do not tarry and do not think of building your stores of gold or armor. We must be quick and have no time for that tonight." With that warning, they went about their business.

Diomedes cut down the guards before they could raise the alarm, and Athena infused him with courage and strength. He fought with the power of ten men and soon had killed thirteen of the Thracians, including the king. He heard Odysseus gathering the horses and saw the king's chariot with his armor. Diomedes wanted it and was considering how to get it back to camp when Athena whispered in his ear.

"Make haste, my warrior. You must make the safety of the ships, and Apollo is rousing the Trojans!"

Diomedes heard her words, and he caught up with Odysseus and the horses. They each mounted a horse and rode flat out as the Trojans came screeching out of their tents in pursuit. Odysseus and Diomedes made it back to their fortifications well ahead of the Trojans, who gave up the chase once they saw they had no hope of catching them. The Greek soldiers celebrated their victory and as hoped, rallied around their heroes, Diomedes and Odysseus.

The next day dawned, and Zeus sent Eris, goddess of strife and war, to stir valor in the breasts of the Greeks. They awoke full of courage, strength, and hope for the day ahead. Eagerly they donned their armor, but as they took the field, the sky began to rain blood. Panic spread throughout their lines, but Agamemnon steadied them. They met the Trojans in the day's fighting. Zeus and Eris stood apart, taking no hand in the combat. Soldiers fought and fell on both sides of the battle.

Agamemnon, inspired by Athena and Hera, fought like a dozen men. Under his onslaught, the Trojans fell back, and the Greeks, rallied by their leader's ferocious fighting, pressed them back to the gates of the city. Hector was about to sound the retreat when Iris, sent by Zeus, appeared to him and told him to hold fast. "Wait until you see the mighty Agamemnon leave the field wounded. Press your advantage, and you shall win the day," so said the Father of All.

Hector heeded the counsel, and he stayed aloft on the walls, urging his troops to hold their ground. Trojan soldiers were still falling at an alarming rate to the sword of Agamemnon, who showed no signs of fatigue until a spear lodged in his arm. Roaring with pain, he pulled the spear free and sent it right back at who had thrown it, striking down the brave Trojan warrior, Coon. Blood flowed freely from Agamemnon's ragged wound, and he was forced back to the ships to have it mended. Hector took his cue when Agamemnon left the field and came down from the wall.

Now Hector, infused with the strength and purpose of Zeus, pressed forward into the Greek lines, leading a resurgence of Trojan forces. Without Agamemnon's leadership, the Greeks were pushed back, though the other officers tried to hold their positions. Diomedes and Odysseus stood their ground. Diomedes took aim and hit Hector in the helmet with a spear, dazing him and causing him to pull back from the front. Side by side, Diomedes and Odysseus led their troops forward, inching back over the ground they had lost.

Paris, from his protected position on the wall, saw the pair and took aim at Diomedes. His arrow missed the mark of a lethal strike but sunk into the foot of Diomedes. Though it didn't kill the mighty warrior, it did take him out of the action. As he retreated to have his wound tended, he yelled at Paris, "You are too afraid of getting your pretty face scarred to fight like a real man. A woman could have wounded me as lightly as you have this day. You have done nothing but anger me, and I will be back to vent my anger. I will find you then!"

Odysseus alone tried to hold the line. He fought valiantly until a spear crashed through his shield. Athena turned the deadly tip away, so it cut his flesh instead of killing him. Still, the wound bled and pained Odysseus mightily. He fought on until Ajax the Great came to his side. Ajax, with his mighty shield and the blessing of Athena, held the line while Menelaus helped Odysseus back to the ships. On a distant part of the battlefield, Machon, the great healer, and seer, was wounded by an arrow to the shoulder, and Nestor was forced to leave the battle to escort him to safety. With so many of their champions out of the fight, the Greeks began to lose ground. Ajax fell back strategically, allowing the Greeks to settle into the fortifications around the ships and ready themselves for the Trojan onslaught.

Achilles watched the battle from his ship and shook his head. "They are certainly missing my sword today. Patroclus, go down and find out how things fare. Discover who is wounded and who has fallen." Patroclus took his instructions and hurried to where the injured were being tended to. Nestor saw him there and implored him to convince Achilles to rejoin the fight.

"I have no power to move the mind of Achilles," Patroclus said sadly. He hated watching his comrades fighting and dying while he sat on the ship doing nothing.

"What if you donned the armor of Achilles and appeared on the battlefield," Nestor suggested. "Such a sight would fill every Greek soldier with hope."

"Cunning and wise Nestor, I will bring this plan to him and see what he says," Patroclus promised and hurried back to his ship.

The Trojans came hard up against the fortifications of the Greeks. They could not drive their chariots through the trenches, and the Greeks rained down rocks from their walls like hail from a thunder cloud. Overhead, an eagle soared over the battlefield, carrying a serpent in its talons. As they flew, the snake bit the eagle on the breast and neck until the eagle dropped it from its grip and flew off shrieking. The Trojans worried that it was an omen that they would lose the battle, but Hector rallied his men. "Fear not a bird in the sky! We are the blessed sons of Zeus, and he will see us through. Fight for your country - that is the only omen you need to concern yourselves with!"

Following their brave leader, they slogged across the fortifications of the Greeks and stormed the walls on foot. The Greeks met them, and the most furious fighting thus far broke out. Hector, sensing the momentum was with him, hurled a massive boulder at the gates and shattered them. With a powerful surge, the Trojans trampled through the last lines of Greek defense and swarmed over the walls into the Greek encampment.

Zeus, thinking the Trojans had things well in hand, took his mind and eyes off the battle. Poseidon noticed his inattention and sought to help his favorites. He united both Ajax the Greater and Lesser along with Teucer and infused with them his strength and vigor. They stood firm against the Trojan forces and began to beat them back. Poseidon spoke to the entire army and encouraged them to stand fast. The Greeks made small advances, and when

Amphimachus, Poseidon's grandson, fell, he urged all the Greeks from their tents where some were resting and tending to the wounded. Thus, the full force of the Greeks fell upon the Trojans with the passion of Poseidon goading them forward. Hector and the Trojans fought valiantly, but they began to lose ground.

Hera, from her vantage point on Mount Olympus, saw Poseidon's efforts and was pleased. She devised a plan to keep Zeus' attention turned for a while longer. She bathed in sweet waters and put on her finest robes and jewels. Then, she summoned Aphrodite. "I wish to reconcile the great Titans Tethys and Oceanus. They are dear to me, as they sheltered and cared for me when I was young. They have been quarreling for ages. Will you give me one of your charms that will make it so they cannot resist each other? I would see them happy once more," Hera lied to the goddess of beauty and love.

"How can I refuse you, wife of Zeus? Take my girdle. When you wear it, whatever you desire will come to pass," Aphrodite replied and handed over her richly embroidered belt that held all of her womanly charms.

Hera put on the girdle, but instead of heading to Tartarus to see the Titans, she went to the city of Thaos to find Hypnos, the god of Sleep. "Come with me," Hera commanded Sleep. "I need you to lull Zeus into slumber, so my Greeks might prevail in Troy."

Sleep shook his head. "Nay, Lady Hera. Last time I helped you, Zeus was so furious that he threw thunderbolts all over the court, and the gods fled before his wrath. He would have cast me into the depths of Tartarus had he found me, but Lady Nix, the goddess of night, hid me from his sight. I have no desire to provoke mighty Zeus ever again."

"Come now, Hypnos. Zeus need not know of your involvement, but to sweeten your disposition, I promise you can marry Pasithea. You've had your eye on her for a long time. If you help me, she is yours, I swear on the dark waters of the Styx."

Sleep, hearing the solemn oath, relented and went with Hera to Mount Ida. He concealed himself as a bird in the branches of a tree and waited. Hera went to her husband, who was surprised at her sudden appearance.

"What brings you here, wife? You look lovely and smell so very sweet," Zeus told her as he pulled her into his lap.

Hera pushed away from him and told him the same tale she had told Aphrodite. "They have been fighting for ages and can wait for a while longer. Stay here with me and lay with me as my wife. You cannot come and go so quickly from me," Zeus said, catching her wrist and pulling her back to him.

"Zeus! Would you have me lay with you on top of Mount Ida, clear for all the gods and man to see? I would never be able to show my face in court again," Hera protested.

Zeus laughed and enveloped them in a dense fog, concealing them from the eyes of any other living being in heaven and earth. They lay together, and Hypnos sent the Father of All into a deep slumber.

Once Zeus was fast asleep, Hypnos went to Poseidon. "Zeus sleeps. Now is the time to rally the Greeks! He will not sleep for long, so make haste!"

Poseidon wasted no time. With no fear that Zeus would see him, he led the Greeks himself, and they pushed the Trojans back. Hector finally sounded the retreat. The Trojans worked their way back over the fortifications they had fought so hard to cross earlier that day. Great Ajax saw a clear shot at Hector and threw a massive rock. It rolled over the top of the Trojan general and knocked him senseless. His comrades caught him up and carried him from the field. The Trojans' ranks broke, and they ran pell-mell for their lives in front of Poseidon and the Greeks.

High on Mount Ida, Zeus woke from his slumber. He turned his eyes to the battle and saw the Trojans being routed. Thunder rolled as his anger built and lightning flashed in the sky when he saw Poseidon leading the Greeks.

"Hera, you mischief-making vixen, I see your hand in this! Do you not remember how I hung you in the heavens before for defying me? Perhaps you need to be reminded of your place," Zeus thundered at his wife.

Hera trembled at his words, and she spoke sweetly to soften his temper. "Husband, I swear this was no intrigue of mine! The Earth Shaker acts of his own will. I swear by the rushing waters of the Styx that I had no hand in this."

"We had a bargain. If you and the rest of the lot would leave off interfering in my plans, all will come to pass that has been promised. I must induce the stiff-necked Achilles to join in the battle. Once that happens, your Greeks will be unstoppable, and Troy will fall. Now, show me how you can obey me and bid Iris and Apollo come to me."

Hera, wisely choosing to hold her tongue, returned to Olympus, and dispatched Iris and Apollo to Zeus. "Iris, be swift as the wind and tell my brother to leave off his fighting. He must return to Olympus or down to seas, but he will not have anything more to do with the conflict below." Swift-footed Iris left with the message as Zeus turned his attention to Apollo. "Hector has been laid low, but he must return to the fighting. Go and revive him and rally the Trojans!" Apollo was right on Iris' heels as he made his way to battle.

Poseidon did not welcome the decree from Zeus but ultimately left the field after Iris reminded him of the repercussions of defying the Father of All. Apollo found Hector close to death but healed his wounds and revitalized his limbs. With the strength of ten men, Hector made his way through the lines. The Trojans sent up a mighty battle cry when they saw their champion retake the field. With renewed vigor, they fought and soon turned the tide back against the Greeks.

Apollo helped them further by filling in the trenches around the Greek fortifications. The Trojans were then able to drive their chariots straight into the Greek camp. Utter chaos reigned as the Greeks scattered to their ships. Great Ajax defended one of the ships singlehandedly and held the Trojans at bay with a twelve-foot-long pike. Great though he was, he was one against many, and the Trojans succeeded in firing the ship. At which time, even the mighty Ajax was forced to fall back.

Patroclus watched in horror as the Greeks fell apart, and the ship burned. He hurried to Achilles. "Come Achilles! Surely now is the time to put aside your differences and aid our comrades. They are hard back on their heels and need your strength." When Achilles refused, Patroclus pressed on, "Let me don your armor then. The Trojans will know fear when they see it, and the Greeks will find their pride again."

Achilles reluctantly agreed. "However," he cautioned his friend, "do not pursue them. Once they are driven back beyond the fortifications, come back lest you gain the glory that should be mine or be injured."

Patroclus wasted no time gearing up and with Achilles' men behind him, took to the field. The Trojans all shouted and pointed at the brilliantly clad warrior. Fearing Achilles' had finally rejoined the battle, they lost their courage and broke their ranks. They fled in terror as Patroclus and his men mowed down several lines of Trojan soldiers. In the panicked retreat, large numbers of Trojans fell into the trenches that hadn't been filled in, and the Greeks fell on them without mercy.

Great Ajax and Hector squared off again, but Hector disengaged from the fight to lead his men to safety. Patroclus cut down anything in front of him. He crossed blades with a Trojan and son of Zeus, Sarpedon, and after a brief, but fierce battle, Patroclus stood victorious over Sarpedon's body.

A general cry of lament ripped through the Trojan lines. Sarpedon had been one of their most beloved champions. An intense battle broke out around the fallen Trojan's body with both sides sustaining heavy losses. Zeus decided to allow Patroclus to earn more glory and respect and cast fear into the heart of Hector, who fell back immediately. However, he did not want the Greeks to mutilate Sarpedon's body, so he sent Apollo to retrieve his son's corpse and see it safely tended to. With that business handled, the Father of All sat back and watched the battle play out.

With no body to squabble over and the Trojans giving ground, Patroclus pursued them right up to the gates of the city. Three times he tried to breach the gates, but each time Apollo flung him back. On his fourth attempt, Apollo faced him in all his glory and thundered with a dreadful voice, "It is not your destiny to sack this city, Patroclus. Cease your attempts and turn your attention elsewhere."

Patroclus had little choice but to heed the Archer's words, for it was utter folly to challenge him outright. With Patroclus turned away, Apollo went to Hector in the guise of one of his warriors, "Why do you cringe here, noble Hector? It is not worthy of you. Have heart and should Apollo will it, you shall triumph over Patroclus!"

Hector, with renewed purpose, heeded the words and instructed his driver to head straight for the Greek warrior. Patroclus saw them coming and flung a rock at the charioteer, killing him. Hector sprang from the chariot to protect the body of his fallen comrade. Patroclus grasped the feet of the corpse, but Hector held firmly onto the shoulders. They fell into a macabre tug-of-war until others joined in, and they were forced to abandon their hold to defend themselves with their shield and blades. Patroclus fought like a lion and killed all who approached. However, Zeus decreed his time had come and Apollo, cloaked in a cloud of darkness, knocked him on the head from behind, scattering his senses. He cut the straps holding Patroclus' breastplate in place just before Euphorbus thrust his ashen spear at the hero's heart. Patroclus twisted to avoid the killing blow but was still grievously wounded. Hector saw him fall to his knees and hurried to deliver the fatal blow.

"Hector," Patroclus rasped, "you may deliver the final stroke, but it was Zeus and Apollo that has laid me low. I could have fought off 20 of you without their interference. You will get yours, Hector. The blade of Achilles will find you before it is all done!" Hector thrust his spear through Patroclus' heart before he could say more, and thus ended the life of the noble Patroclus.

The two armies vied for possession of the fallen hero's body. Menelaus and Ajax the Great confronted Hector as he tried to take the body so he could feed it to the dogs of Troy. Hector abandoned his plan in the face of Ajax's strength and settled for donning the armor of Achilles.

Zeus shook his head while he watched and murmured, "You wear the armor of a hero, and I give you strength, but you will not live to present your trophy to your lovely wife."

Hector, clad in Achilles' armor, gave new hope to the Trojans, and they once again rallied. The Greeks, devastated at the loss of Patroclus, fell back and soon were in full retreat to the ships. Achilles saw the change in tides and his heart sunk. If Patroclus still prevailed, the Trojans would be the ones retreating. When the messenger arrived with the news, Achilles let out a cry that shook both Trojans and Greeks alike. He wept and tore at his hair in grief and lamented his inaction. Thetis heard his distress and rushed to his side. "I would die now, Mother, save for the fact that I must see Hector dead at my feet," Achilles raved.

"You have no armor, my son. Stay away from the battle until tomorrow's dawn. I will have a new set for you by then." Thetis disappeared back into the ocean, hurrying to Mount Olympus to commission a new set of armor from Hephaestus.

Hector had given chase, pursuing Menelaus and Ajax to recapture Patroclus' body. He was close on their heels with the entire Trojan army right behind him. Iris, sent from Zeus, appeared to Achilles. "You must help your brothers in arms lest Patroclus be denied a proper burial," she urged the distraught warrior. When he protested that he had no arms or armor, she replied, "You need not take up arms. Let them see you in your glory. That will be enough to dissuade the Trojan pursuit."

Achilles ran to the highest point of the Greek fortifications. There, he yelled a terrible battle cry, and everyone stopped to look up at him. Athena shone a golden aura around him. Panic settled in the hearts of the Trojans at the dreaded sight. As predicted, it was all that was needed to allow Menelaus and Ajax to slip away with Patroclus' body. Night fell on the battle, and the day drew to a close.

That night, Hector, influenced by Zeus, commanded the Trojans to camp on the field instead of retiring inside the walls of the city. The Greeks mourned their fallen hero. Achilles decreed that Patroclus would not be laid to rest until Hector was slain. Thetis promised she would preserve the body from rot.

"I shall never again sail home," Achilles lamented and tore at his hair in his grief. "It is as you said, Mother. I shall not live to see my hair turn gray with age, and now, I do not want to! Without my friend, my life is not worth living." Thetis could say nothing to comfort her son, for what he said was true. He would enter the fighting the next day and would die all the sooner for it. She left him to retrieve his armor from Hephaestus.

Dawn settled herself across the sky, and the troops began to gather for the day. Achilles put on his new armor, and everyone stared at the magnificent sight.

Agamemnon approached him warily and said, "Before we go into battle this day, let us go as friends. I have seen the Lady Briseis returned to your ships as well as the treasure I promised."

Achilles shrugged his shoulders. "It doesn't matter anymore, but the gesture is appreciated. Come, let us get an early start on the day. The sooner we fight, the sooner we can end this miserable war."

"The men must eat first, and so should you," Odysseus put in, but Achilles had no appetite.

"Let the men fill their bellies and offer their sacrifices. I will wait here with my friend," Achilles said despondently and sank down next to Patroclus' body.

Zeus, whose heart was softened by Achilles' grief, sent Athena to nurture him with ambrosia, lest he faints during the fighting. Invisible, she let drops of the magical nectar drip on Achilles through the chinks in his armor. Invigorated, Achilles called his troops to line up and stepped into his chariot. His horses, the immortal steeds that had been gifted to his parents at their wedding, stamped impatiently. "Yes, Xanthus and Balius, we fight again today. Do not let me die on the field like you did poor Patroclus!"

Xanthus, given voice by Hera, answered him, "Dread Achilles, we will save your life today on the field, and it was through no inattention of ours that Patroclus met his doom. Your fate will go the same, but it will not be as a result of our actions. Your fate is controlled by the hand of Zeus, and it draws near."

"I do not need my horse to remind that my time is short," Achilles snapped. Tired of talk and ready for action, he let loose his bone-rattling battle cry, and his chariot lurched forward as Xanthus and Balius leapt into action.

Zeus called an assembly on Mount Olympus as the day's fighting began. "I know many of you wish to join the fray. Today, Achilles rejoins the battle and shall win glory as I promised. He will be unstoppable today and will sack the city if left unchecked. However, the time is not yet right for Troy to fall, so I give you leave to join the battle as you are clearly want to do."

Athena, Hera, Hermes, Poseidon, and the lame-legged Hephaestus wasted no time donning their armor. They joined the Greeks, and Athena's battle cry echoed across the field. The Greeks cheered as they saw their gods standing beside them.

Ares and Apollo stood beside the Trojans and were joined by Artemis, Leto, and the river god, Xanthus. The Trojans took heart as Ares bellowed back across the plain in answer to Athena.

The two fronts came together - man against man and god against god. Such was the uproar that on his dark throne in the depths of Tartarus, Hades cringed and worried that the earth would be split open and reveal his dismal kingdom to the light of day.

Apollo instructed Aeneas, Aphrodite's son, to fight Achilles, telling him he was born of a higher goddess than Achilles and therefore, would be stronger and better loved among the gods. Aeneas didn't really want to fight the Greek, for his sword and spear were unstoppable, but Apollo infused him with courage. Aeneas aimed his chariot for Achilles and urged his charioteer to lay his whip to the horses.

Hera saw the impending attack and called to Poseidon and Athena to stand next to Achilles. Poseidon refused, saying, "This is a fight for the mortals. We shall not intervene unless Apollo or Ares hinder Achilles in some way. Come, let us sit back and watch the battle." He drew a reluctant Hera, Athena, and the other Olympians to the sidelines. Apollo and his contingent did likewise.

Achilles and Aeneas came together in a flurry of spear thrusts. Achilles penetrated Aeneas' shield and was about to finish him with his sword when Poseidon intervened. Though he supported the Greeks, he did not want to see a divine son cut down before his time. He whisked Aeneas away from the battle and told him to stay clear until Achilles fell. Once that happened, no Greek would be able to slay Aeneas.

Once free of Aeneas, Achilles went on the warpath, dropping any Trojan who was unfortunate enough to cross his path. He was on the hunt for Hector, who was evading him on the instructions of Apollo. The Trojans fled from in front of the maddened Greek warrior. He divided their force in half. One half fled the field for the safety of the city walls, and the other plunged headlong into the river Xanthos. Achilles pursued the Trojans into the river, slaying so many Xanthos bid him stop.

"Leave off with this slaughter, son of Peleus! You are choking my outlets with corpses, and my waters are befouled with blood!"

Achilles paid him no heed and continued to kill Trojan soldiers, both in and out of the river. Xanthos raised up a mighty wave and trapped Achilles under its watery depths. Achilles kicked and swam but could make no headway against the water. "I am destined to die in glory, as a soldier ought, but here I am drowning and will be washed out to sea like a dead fish," Achilles moaned as he thrashed about.

Poseidon spoke to Achilles in his mind, "Fear not, you will not perish in these waters. You are destined for greater things. Gain your feet. Seek out and kill Hector. Then, return to your ships, and I promise you will be safe."

Achilles' feet found purchase on the muddy bank, and he scrambled to safety. However, everywhere he ran, Xanthos chased him with floodwaters. Soon, the whole plain was flooded. Corpses floated about like ghoulish bobbers. Achilles could find no place to stand, let alone seek out Hector to kill him.

Hera called to Hephaestus, "My crooked-legged son, come with your fire and beat back Xanthos. Burn the trees from his banks and scald the waters until they hiss and boil. Do not leave off when he speaks pretty words to you. Wait for my signal!"

Hephaestus hurried to obey and kindled a hot fire that he sent down the banks of the river. He cast flames over the floodwaters until they evaporated in a cloud of steam. Xanthos begged him to stop, but the god of the forge kept his fire pouring forth. Finally, once he was reduced to a trickling stream, Xanthos cried out to Hera, "Lady Hera, have your son leave off his torment. I will not rise again to help the Trojans!" With that promise, Hera told Hephaestus to stand down, and the gods turned their attention to fighting amongst themselves. In the end, Artemis and Leto abandoned the fight after Hera boxed Artemis' ears for taunting her. Athena knocked Ares and Aphrodite senseless, and they fled back to Olympus to lick their wounds.

Achilles was back on the rampage and pursued the other half of the Trojan army toward the city. The Trojan king, Priam, ordered the gates be opened to let the soldiers inside the walls. Apollo inspired the Trojan warrior, Agenor, and concealed him in a mist. As Achilles ran past, Agenor threw his spear, hitting his god-made armor. The spear bounced off harmlessly, but Achilles spun around to see who had thrown the spear. Apollo whisked Agenor away from the battle and assumed his appearance. He taunted Achilles and led him on a chase while the Trojans poured into their walled city to safety.

In time, Apollo let the illusion slip away and rounded to face Achilles, "Dread Achilles, why are you chasing me thus? Do you dare cross swords with me, a god and immortal?"

Achilles' roared in anger as he realized he had been duped. He spun on his heel and raced back toward the Trojan gates. There Hector waited for him, despite the pleas from his parents to come safely within the walls. Hector knew that it was time for him to face the mighty Achilles, and he resolved to do it bravely. However, when he saw Achilles bearing down on him like a madman, his courage faltered, and he ran for his life. Three times around the city the warriors ran. Achilles could gain no ground on the fleet-footed Hector.

Athena whispered to Achilles to keep chasing him and that she would see to it that on the next lap, he would stand to fight. Taking the form of Hector's brother, Deiphobus, she met him at the gate as he ran away from Achilles. Gladdened by the sight of his brother, Hector stopped his flight. "You have come to face Achilles with me, brother? Together we can best him," Hector cried as he turned to set his feet for battle.

As Achilles closed the distance between them, Hera and Zeus looked on from their heavenly perch. Zeus felt sorry for Hector and was tempted to save him from his fate. "Nay, Husband," Hera chided, "you cannot change what has been long decreed. Hector will fall this day." Thus, Zeus tipped the scales down against the Trojan prince.

Hector stood bravely in front of Achilles. "I will run no further. Here I will stand to fight. But let us promise each other that whoever wins will respect the body of the other and send it back for proper burial."

'Bah! I will not stand here making promises like a woman. You will stand, and you will die," Achilles challenged, and then spoke no more. Taking aim, he sent his spear at the heart of the Trojan champion. Hector, who was ready for the throw, ducked it easily. Athena plucked it from the ground and shuttled it back to Achilles, concealed in a cloud of mist.

Hector answered with his throw. Achilles raised his divine shield that bore the whole world on its face, and the spear bounced off without even scratching the surface. Hector called to Deiphobus to give him another spear, but when he turned, his brother was not there. Realizing he had been tricked, Hector drew his sword and let loose his battle cry. He would not go down without a fight.

Achilles watched Hector launch himself toward him and drew his sword. He did not stand to wait for the fight to come to him but ran forward headlong to meet it. The crash of armor and shields was terrible to hear, but the battle was brief. Hector was not able to penetrate Achilles' armor. Achilles knew precisely where the weak point was in Hector's armor since it used to be his own. Ruthlessly, he drove the tip of his sword into the flesh of Hector's neck, just below the edge of his helmet.

As Hector lay on the ground, gasping his final breaths, he again beseeched Achilles to send his body back for a proper burial. Achilles' heart was stone with his grief for Patroclus, and he turned a deaf ear to Hector's pleas. "The dogs will feast on your corpse before the day is done," Achilles told Hector as his spirit left his body. Thus, ended the noble life of Hector.

The Trojans wailed from within their walls at the sight of their fallen hero, but none dared to go out to challenge Achilles for his body. The Greeks surged forward, and Hector was stripped of his armor. They took turns stabbing his corpse, and in the ultimate act of desecration, Achilles tied it to the back of his chariot and dragged it around and around the city. Finally, he remembered that he needed to see to the funeral of Patroclus, and he left off tormenting Hector's body, discarding it in the dust beside the Greek ships.

As soon as Achilles stepped from his chariot, the Greek soldiers engulfed their hero and bore him off for a night of feasting. Eventually, Achilles collapsed in exhaustion. In his dreams that night, he walked with Patroclus' ghost. "You have forgotten me," Patroclus chided. "I am dead and unburied. I wander the no-man's land, unable to cross the dark river Styx until you lay me to rest." Achilles attempted to protest, but Patroclus brushed away his words. "I must ask one last favor of you, my faithful friend. See that our bones rest together so that we will never be parted in the hereafter!" Achilles promised to see it done and as soon as his eyes opened with the light of morning, he began work on his friend's funeral pyre.

Soon it was built, and Patroclus' body laid on top of it. However, it would not burn. Achilles offered a sacrifice to North and West winds. Iris, who saw his piteous state of mourning, urged the winds to fly to his aid. Finally, the pyre burned and consumed the mortal coil of Patroclus. Painstakingly, Achilles gathered his friend's bones and sealed them in an urn. He proclaimed that upon his death he was to be similarly burned and buried with Patroclus. In final memorial to his friend, Achilles hosted elaborate funeral games that lasted the rest of the day.

That night, Achilles could not rest. He was tormented by grief and angered at the turn of events. To vent his fury, he once again tied the corpse of Hector to the back of his chariot. With a hateful heart, he rode like a lunatic around and around Patroclus' tomb, dragging the corpse behind him. Apollo shielded the fallen hero's body from decay and desecration, and eventually, after eleven days of this, the gods had had enough of Achilles' treatment of Hector's remains. Zeus dispatched Thetis to her son with instructions to make him hand over Hector's body to his parents. Zeus also sent Iris to King Priam to tell him that he must travel alone into the Greek encampment to fetch back his son's body.

Priam, though his heart was full of fear to go into the enemy's camp alone, hitched up his wagon and filled it with gold as ransom for Hector's body. He and his elderly man-servant made the slow trek across the battlefield and came upon a man standing alone in the field. Though they were afraid, they pulled up when the man hailed them.

"What business have you sneaking across the field under the cloak of night? You are too old to think to cause mischief for the Greeks. Are you bound to collect the remains of the fallen Hector," the man asked.

"How do you know of my son," the king demanded, still wary of a Greek ambush.

"I am a squire to the Dread Achilles and have been sent to escort you to him. Fear not. Your son's body remains unblemished and lays next to the tomb of the mighty Patroclus," the man, who was actually Hermes in disguise, assured him as he climbed aboard the wagon. "Drive on, and I will see us safely through."

Hermes caused the guards at the gates to sleep and concealed the wagon as it rolled through the Greek encampment. Once they reached Achilles' ship, Hermes unloaded the treasure for the old men and brushed away their thanks. He revealed his identity to them, saying, "It is I, Hermes, who has guided you tonight and will see you safely out again. Let your heart be easy, for Zeus has decreed that you shall not be harmed. I leave you now, lest Achilles be angered by my presence. Go on bended knee and beseech him to return your son."

Priam followed his instructions. In front of Achilles, the Trojan king fell to his knees and kissed the warrior's hand. Achilles welcomed him and offered hospitality. Priam declined and requested that they just get on with it.

"Do not anger me, old man," Achilles growled. "Hector's body will hold until I say it is time to return it to you. Now, we shall share a meal, you and I, and commiserate our fallen comrades."

Priam, not wanting to anger Achilles, agreed to sit and eat with him. Morosely, they shared their sorrows as they ate and drank together. They wept together over their losses, and once the meal was finished and their stories were told, old King Priam could hardly hold his head up.

"Noble king," Achilles said, standing and stretching. "I shall make you a bed in the gatehouse, lest you be stumbled on here by one of my lieutenants bringing me messages in the night." Achilles brought Hector's body and laid it in the king's wagon while his servants made up a bed for Priam. Once he saw his guest was resting, Achilles too found his bed for the night.

Before Dawn began to light the sky, Hermes woke King Priam from his slumber. "Tarry not here any longer, for, under the rays of Helios, you cannot hope to escape from here. Up now and to the wagon!"

Priam jumped to his feet and with the speed of a man many years younger, roused his servant and took up the reins of the wagon. Just as Dawn crept over the horizon, they slipped out through the gates where the Greek sentries still slept and raced across the battlefield. As the citizens of Troy opened their eyes on a new day, King Priam brought their celebrated son home to them. Trojans spilled into the street and wailed their grief. For the next eleven days, Priam and his city mourned the loss of Hector and saw him properly buried.

After these intense days of fighting and the death of Hector, the war settled back into its old routine of minor skirmishes and raids. Both sides had sustained heavy losses and struggled with low morale. The Trojans got two fresh infusions of troops when the Amazons, led by Penthesilea, and Memnon, King Priam's step-brother from Ethiopia, arrived. Fresh fighting broke out with the Greeks. Achilles met Memnon, who was the son of the Titan Eos, on the field of battle. As a soldier, Memnon was a true rival to Achilles and also wore armor made by Hephaestus. The epic battle between the two ferocious warriors was watched by all the gods. Zeus made them equal in strength, size, and speed, and the fight raged on and on. Finally, Achilles was able to find a tiny crack in

Memnon's armor and slipped his sword through it, piercing his heart. Memnon fell dead to the ground, and his troops bore him off immediately for a proper burial.

Buoyed by his triumph over Memnon and the exit of the Ethiopians, Achilles stormed the gate and managed to break through into the city. However, his time had run out. Zeus decided that he had attained sufficient glory to satisfy his vow to Thetis and if left unchecked, Achilles would kill many more of his favorites. With great solemnity, Zeus lowered Achilles' side of the scales, sealing his fate.

Paris watched Achilles break through the gate in horror and feared for his life. Apollo raced to his side and infused him with courage. He steadied the prince's shaking hands as he drew his bow and guided the arrow that he shot. It struck home on the back of Achilles' heel, the only mortal part of him. The great Greek warrior dropped dead to the ground.

Immediately, both sides sought to claim Achilles' body, but Ajax the Great was there with Odysseus to bear the fallen hero's remains away. Back in the Greek camp, mourning wails sounded as they gathered around their fallen champion. His armor stripped away, Achilles was burned, and his bones were interred with Patroclus' remains, as was his request.

Agamemnon was faced with the difficult decision of who to give Achilles' armor to. Both Odysseus and Ajax the Great laid claim to it, and it was to go to the best warrior in the army. Agamemnon couldn't decide so he sent spies among the Trojan prisoners to hear which one they feared the most. Athena, taking on the appearance of a Trojan soldier, spoke up for Odysseus and ultimately swayed opinion in his favor. The armor went to the King of Ithaca, and Ajax went wild with grief and jealousy. Bloodlust crazed his mind, and he wanted to kill his friends. Athena, not wanting him to tarnish his reputation, bewitched him to think that a group of cattle were Agamemnon and Menelaus. He butchered them where they stood before he came to his senses. Distraught that he could kill his brethren over armor, he committed suicide by impaling himself on the sword that Hector had gifted him after their duel. Thus, ended the life of Ajax the Great.

The war stretched on into the fabled tenth year, and the Greeks began to look for signs of what needed to be done to finally sack the city and retrieve their queen. Calchas, the prophet, and seer of the Greeks, saw that the city would not fall without the famous bow of Hercules. Ten long years ago that bow had been left with Philoctetes, who was now residing on the Isle of Lemnos. Odysseus and Diomedes were sent to fetch him and the magical weapon.

Upon their return, Philoctetes joined his brothers in battle. In a skirmish near the Trojan gate, Philoctetes hit Paris with one of Hercules' poisoned arrows. In agony, he was rushed inside the gates. Helen went to Oenone, the nymph who had been Paris' lover when he was a shepherd. She had once sworn she would heal him of any wounds. However, for over two decades Paris had ignored her, and she would not be moved by Helen's pleas to help the fallen Trojan prince. Paris died of his wound, and one more piece of the puzzle fell into place for the Greeks.

However, Troy refused to fall. Searching for further answers as to what needed to happen to finally sack the city, Odysseus waylaid Helenus, the renowned Trojan seer, and prince, as he tried to escape the city to seek haven on Mount Ida. With a bit of persuasion, Odysseus learned that Troy would not fall unless the Greeks retrieved the bones of Pelops, Achilles' son, Neoptolemus, joined their cause, and they stole the Palladium from within the Trojan palace. With this new intelligence, Odysseus and the other Greek officers constructed their strategy.

A crew was dispatched to Pisa to gather the bones of Pelops, Agamemnon's cursed great-grandfather. Odysseus and Diomedes made haste to the Island of Skyros where Achilles' son lived. They convinced him to join their cause, and upon arriving back at the front, Odysseus gave Neoptolemus his father's armor. Battles broke out regularly, and Neoptolemus acquitted himself well, killing many Trojans soldiers and living up to his family name.

There was only one thing left to secure the fall of Troy - the Palladium. This wooden effigy of Athena was sacred to the city and provided divine protection. Once again, it was Diomedes and Odysseus who were tasked with retrieving the relic. Odysseus disguised himself as a beggar and snuck into the city. Helen was tending to the poor and injured, and she recognized the king.

Pulling him to the side, she asked, "Odysseus, noble king of Ithaca, why are you here as a beggar in my streets? This cursed war drags on, and I want nothing more than to see my homeland again."

"Lady Helen, you can help speed your return home. I am sent to bring back the Palladium as the last piece of resistance protecting the city. Do you know where it is," Odysseus asked as he bowed and scraped as if he were a peasant in front of royalty.

Helen leaned in as if to press alms into his hand and whispered, "By the city gate, there is a secret opening that brings you into the main citadel. You will find the Palladium in the sacred temple of Athena."

Odysseus hastily left the city and relayed the news to Diomedes. Together, they made their way through the cramped confines of the secret passage and into the heart of the Trojan palace. They crept into the temple and stole the wooden statue. Diomedes presented it to King Agamemnon, and the final planning stage began.

It was clear after a decade of fighting that the walls of Troy were not going to fall, so the Greeks had to get inside the walls. There were too few gates to allow them to simply force their way in. The bottleneck would allow the Trojans to mount their defense. Finally, Odysseus devised a plan. Master builder, Epeius, was pressed into service to create an enormous wooden horse. The horse was a sacred animal to the Trojans which made it the perfect decoy. Athena oversaw the project and offered guidance for strategic openings in the hollow body. Once it was completed, the most famous ruse in history took place.

In the dead of night, the Greeks filled the hollow belly of the wooden horse with as many soldiers as they could. The rest of them fired the camp and took the boats out of the harbor. When the Trojans looked out on the field the next day, they couldn't believe their eyes. The entire Greek army had apparently turned tail and went home, leaving only a giant wooden horse inscribed with a prayer to Athena. Joyfully, the Trojans began to celebrate their victory and pulled the massive horse inside the walls. A debate broke out as to what to do with the monstrosity, but ultimately, the celebration swept away the issue. Cassandra, a powerful seer and Trojan princess who had been cursed never to be believed, tried to convince anyone who would listen that the horse was to be their downfall. Nobody paid her any mind. The horse issue could surely wait for another day to decide. After a decade of war, it was time to celebrate. The party raged into the night.

Unseen by the drunken Trojan guards, a Greek soldier, Sinon, signaled the fleet to return and gave the cue to the army in the horse that the time for attack was upon them.

Like shadows, the soldiers slid from the belly of the horse. They spread silently through the streets, leaving a trail of corpses behind them. Soon, the streets ran with blood, and the alarm was finally raised. The Trojans, caught with their defenses down, did their best, but the Greeks looted, raped, and pillaged their way through the city. Menelaus fought his way to find his Queen. He thought briefly of killing her for her perfidy, but her beauty stayed his hand. He stole Helen back to the boats while Neoptolemus wreaked havoc by killing King Priam and the other Trojan princes. Hector's infant son was thrown from the wall to prevent the royal line of Troy from continuing. Ajax the Lesser raped Cassandra on Athena's altar. The city was burned, and the inhabitants were enslaved. The women were distributed among the higher-ranking Greek officers. The Greeks finally succeeded in sacking Troy, ten years after they began.

Victorious, the Greeks set sail for home. However, their pillaging of Troy and desecration of the temples had angered the gods. They decreed that the Greeks would not return straight home and stirred storms that scattered the fleet across the Aegean Sea. Nestor was the only Greek officer to have a safe and straightforward trip home because he had not participated in the pillaging and looting. Agamemnon returned to his court many years later with Cassandra by his side, disregarding Cassandra's warnings that they would meet a bad end if they returned to Mykenai. As was her curse, Cassandra's prophecy turned out to be correct. Both she and Agamemnon were killed upon arriving home by Agamemnon's wife, Clytemnestra, and her lover. Nauplius, the father of Palamedes who Odysseus framed for treason, exacted further revenge on many of the Greek vessels trying to find their way home. He set up false lighthouses and lured them onto the rocks, causing them to wreck and perish in the sea. None of the other Greek officers ever returned home, save Menelaus and Helen, who eventually returned to Sparta after being delayed for eight years in Egypt.

Odysseus' Voyage Home

Of course, the most famous adventures home after the Trojan War was that of Odysseus. The king of Ithaca and his men were blown off course along with the rest of the Greeks. In need of food and water, Odysseus and his men put in at the Island of Ismarus. There, they found the Ciconians and conquered them. They pillaged their city, taking everything of value. Odysseus urged his men to head back to the boats and be underway, but the men had found vast stores of wine and food. They were in no hurry to leave. Ciconian reinforcements arrived, too late to help their fellow islanders, but in time to catch the Ithacan soldiers half in their cups and lazing about after their huge feast. The Ciconians drove them back to their ships, and Odysseus and his men were forced to tuck tail and retreat from the island.

Zeus was displeased with the conduct of the Ithacans. He sent more storms and winds to blow them about on the sea. The next opportunity they had to make landfall found them on the Isle of the Lotophagi or Lotus Eaters. They went ashore to refill their water and food stores. While they were there, Odysseus dispatched three of his most trusted men to investigate the inhabitants of the island. They were gone for many hours and finally, Odysseus went in search for them. He found his soldiers among the natives, eating the fruit of the Lotus plant. The natives were overjoyed to see another new face and plied Odysseus with fruit and drink. He declined and spoke sharply to his men. "It is time to make for the ships! Why are you here, lazing about, drunk on the fruit of the isle?"

The men simply shrugged their shoulders. They had no ambition to return home or do much of anything after eating the fruit. Exasperated, Odysseus forced them to their feet and tied them in the boat to keep them from jumping overboard in an effort to get back to the island for more fruit. Odysseus urged his men to make haste away from the isle lest they all succumbed to the temptation of the fruit.

Without any idea of where they were, Odysseus sailed generally westward, hoping they were heading toward their homeland. The next piece of land they happened on was a small archipelago. The first island they investigated was lush with forests and teeming with wild goats and other game. The men replenished their supplies and rested. Odysseus noticed smoke rising from a nearby island and in the quiet of the evening could hear voices and the bleating of sheep and goats. When the sun rose the next morning, he and his crew took a rowboat and crossed the small strip of sea that separated the islands.

Odysseus and his men explored the wild island and found a vast cave full of cheese and pens full of young lambs. The men began helping themselves and made a sacrifice to the gods in thanks for their apparent boon. They were in the middle of a celebratory feast when the owner of the cave came home. Polyphemus, a giant cyclops, strode into his cave, driving his flock of sheep and goats before him. With a flick of his wrist, he rolled a boulder across the mouth of the cave, sealing the sheep and Odysseus and his men inside. The cyclops set to work, milking his ewes and straining the milk. As he was storing the day's curds, he noticed Odysseus and his men hiding in the recesses of the cave.

"Who are you," the giant thundered. "Are you strangers, travelers from distant lands or lawless, wandering pirates with no place to call home?"

Odysseus and his men cowered in terror as the fearsome voice reverberated in the cave. Odysseus found his courage and answered, "We are sons of Greece and part of the mighty Agamemnon's group. Ill winds have scattered the fleet, but we are making for our home shores. Will you show us hospitality, my lord? Will you hold with the words of the gods and shelter the traveler in your midst?"

Polyphemus laughed a terrible sound that made Odysseus' blood run cold and said, "I care nothing for Zeus and his ilk. We Cyclops are greater than all of them put together. I will show you hospitality if I so choose. Tell me now, and tell me true, are you and yours alone or are there more waiting on my shores?"

"We are a sorry lot. Our vessel was tossed about by the mighty Earth Shaker and dashed upon the rocks. We alone survived," Odysseus lied.

The monster said nothing more. He simply reached out with a lightning-quick move and snatched two of the men from their hiding place. Before Odysseus' cry of protest even left his lips, the cyclops caved in the men's skulls and ripped them apart. He ate them raw as Odysseus and his fellows watched in horror. Full of his gruesome repast, the cyclops laid down in his bed and slipped into a deep, sated sleep.

The whole of that long night, Odysseus thought of a hundred ways to kill Polyphemus, but reason stayed his hand. The cyclops was the only one who could roll the stone away from the mouth of the cave. Thus, in the morning, he was forced to watch as two of their comrades became breakfast for the giant before he shepherded his sheep out of the cave for the day and rolled the stone firmly back in place.

While they were alone that day, the Ithacans devised a plan. They sharpened a long pole of olive wood to a lethal spike and hardened it in the fire. They hid it in the manure pile and waited for the monster to return home. When the milking was done, Polyphemus helped himself to two more of Odysseus' crew before relaxing against the cave wall. Odysseus cautiously approached him.

"Here now, Cyclops, I have wine for you, if you'd like to try it," Odysseus offered. They had taken the wine during their conquest on Ismarus, and the Ciconian vintage was 20 times more potent than regular wine. The cyclops took the offering and found it to his liking.

"Tell me, stranger, what is your name," the giant asked as he quickly drained another cup.

"Me? Oh, I am Nobody," answered the cunning Odysseus. "I would ask a favor of you since I am sharing my wine with you," the hero pressed.

The cyclops laughed his cruel laugh. "Nobody, I will give you a favor. The favor I give you is that you will be the last one I eat!"

The giant snatched the wineskin away from Odysseus and drained it in one long swallow. Unaccustomed to alcohol, his single eye refused to stay open as the drug worked its way through his system. With a thunderous crash, the giant passed out drunk to the floor of the cave.

Odysseus and his men wasted no time. They heated the sharp end of their lance in the fire until it was glowing red. They lined up on either side of the pike like a battering ram. With a running start, they drove the sharpened stick straight into the eye of Polyphemus. The hot wood burned the flesh and boiled the humors of the eye. Polyphemus sat up with a roar of pain and called for his brethren to help him.

From outside the cave, the other cyclops asked what was amiss. "Nobody is killing me," cried Polyphemus.

"If no man troubles you, be quiet so we can go back to sleep. If you are sick, take it up with the gods, and they will decide if you live or die. Now stop your caterwauling," the other cyclops yelled and stomped off.

The cyclops thrashed around blindly and finally rolled back the enormous stone from the entrance. He took up a post just inside the door and waiting, clearly hoping the men would try to make a run for freedom. Odysseus was far too smart to fall for that. During the night, he lashed the sheep together in groups of three and each of his men hid under the belly of the middle sheep. When the giant let his herd out the next morning, he ran his hands over the backs and under the bellies of each of the groups of sheep, not realizing there were three together. Odysseus hid under the belly of the great ram which was the last from the cave.

"Well now, dear ram, why are you last this morning? You are usually leading the pack! Do you feel sorry for your master," the giant murmured to the ram as he ran his hands over the soft fleece of the ram's back. "Oh, that you could talk. You could tell me where that base-born Nobody is hiding!" He let the ram follow the rest of the flock and kept his post by the door.

Odysseus and his crew drove the sheep onboard their little vessel and began to row furiously for the far shore. The king of Ithaca couldn't resist taunting Polyphemus as he stood high on his mountain peak, staring blindly all around him.

"Cyclops! Know that when you harmed my men, you provoked my anger. You broke hospitality, and for that, the gods shall punish you," Odysseus yelled.

The Cyclops roared in defiance and tore off the top of the mountain peak. He hurled it at the Ithacans. It hit just in front of their small boat, causing a huge wave that washed them back to the shore they were so desperately trying to get away from. Frantically, Odysseus and his men plied the oars. As soon as they were most of the way across, Odysseus yelled, much to the dismay of his crew, "Cyclops! When they ask who stole your sight, you will tell them - Odysseus, son of Laertes and king of Ithaca!"

The giant flung another boulder in the direction of the vessel. This time, it fell just to the stern of the boat, and the resulting wave carried them all the way to the far shore. There, they regrouped with the rest of the Ithacans and made ready to sail as quickly as they could.

The next landfall the wayward soldiers made was on the Aeolian Isle where Aeolus, god of the wind, resided. He made them welcome, and Odysseus and his men stayed a month in his court, entertaining them with tales from the war and their adventures. Odysseus was anxious to be home and begged leave of Aeolus, which was granted with joy.

"King Odysseus, much entertainment have you provided us, and for that I am grateful. I give you a gift that will speed your way home," Aeolus told Odysseus in private and gave him a bag that was tied with a silver rope. "Within this bag are all the winds, save the west wind. I will lose it to fill your sails and blow you directly to your homeland of Ithaca. Keep the bag closed until your feet are firmly on the soil of your native isle."

Odysseus thanked him profusely and eagerly set sail west. They had nothing but westerly wind, heading them straight for home. Over nine days, the small fleet sailed steady and true. Odysseus kept the bag with him at all times and handled the helm himself. He did not sleep. He did not eat. Finally, he saw the blessed shores of his home, and in his relief, exhaustion overcame him. Odysseus slumped at the wheel, and his crew muttered about him. They were convinced that he had been given a treasure but was withholding it from them. While he slept, the crew stole the bag and untied the silver rope just as they were entering the Ithacan harbor.

Great gusts of wind burst forth and loosed a storm that blew them directly back to Aeolus' island. Odysseus cried in dismay and tore at his hair as he berated his unfaithful crew. Hat in hand, Odysseus walked back into Aeolus' court.

"Odysseus! What is this? Why have you returned to these shores," the god of the winds asked.

When Odysseus told him the story, Aeolus grew angry. "Go forth from this court and never return. You are a wretch and unworthy of my help! No wonder you have fallen out of favor with the other gods, for you squander the gifts given to you!"

So, Odysseus and his crew had no choice but to pull their anchors and set out again. Of course, no winds blew, and the sea pitched them this way and that. After six days of drifting, they came to another island, Laestrygonia, where they moored their ships to the rocks and went ashore in search of provisions. Three men went to explore the city that was visible from the harbor. They came across a young maiden, who was every bit as large as the biggest man in their party. She took them to her mother, the queen of the island. The men trembled in fear as they stared up at the enormous woman. She was as big as a mountain and had a face that looked as if it has been carved from stone. She let out an earth-shaking guttural call that was echoed throughout the city. The king of the island, even bigger than his wife, arrived and without a moment's hesitation, snatched up one of the soldiers and devoured him in two bites. The other two soldiers fled as quickly as their feet would carry them, and the Laestrygonians gave chase.

Odysseus and the rest of his men heard the rumble of the giant's steps and saw their comrades running pell-mell toward them, screaming at them to get back to the ships. In a mad scramble, the entire contingent made for the ships and began to cast off, but they were too slow. The giants rained boulders down on the small fleet as they tried to loosen their mooring ropes and unfurl their sails. Odysseus hacked through the hawser of his ship, freeing it from the rock where it was tethered. Giants were wading into the sea and plucking Greeks from the water and wreckage. They gobbled them down like they were the sweetest of fruits. Odysseus and his crew were the only boat to escape.

Odysseus and his crew sailed blindly, lost in grief and despair. For six days they roamed the sea, no one having the heart to make an attempt at heading in any particular direction. They eventually washed up on the sandy beaches of Aeaea. Odysseus, leaving the men to make camp on the beach, climbed the highest peak to get the lay of the land. In the distance, he saw smoke from a chimney. The island was inhabited, but after their last several encounters, they decided to only send part of the crew to investigate.

Chosen by lots, the selected crew members made their way across the island to what turned out to be a palace. They watched in wonder as wolves and lions patrolled the grounds. Cautiously, they advanced and were astounded when the wolves fawned at their feet, and the lions rubbed against them like kittens. From within the palace came a sweet voice and beckoned them to enter. All save Eurylochus, who smelled a trap, went in and were made welcome by a beautiful red-haired woman. She gave them food and sweet drink and bade them welcome. In front of Eurylochus' unbelieving eyes, she waved her wand and changed the men into pigs as they ate and shut them up in a pen.

Terrified, Eurylochus ran back to Odysseus, who strapped on his sword and hurried back to save his crew. Hermes blocked his path and Odysseus listened to his wise counsel.

"You must not eat the food of the witch without first eating this herb, lest you end up with a tail and ears like your friends." The messenger god said and gave Odysseus a sprig of Moly to eat for protection. "Wait for her to draw forth her wand. Then, you must overpower her with your sword. Make her swear an oath to restore your friends and see you safely on your way. After that, you will have nothing more to fear from Circe."

Odysseus heeded the advice and ate the plant. Circe made him welcome and gave him food and drink. When she picked up her wand, intent on making him a pig, Odysseus drew his sword and held it to her throat.

"I swear on the river Styx that I will harm you no further, Mighty Odysseus and that your friends will be as they once were. Come, I would have you stay with me and be my friend and lover."

Odysseus agreed, and once his men had been restored to their original form, he and his crew spent several idle months with Circe, enjoying her charms and comforts. True to her word, she made no more mischief against any of the Greeks, but after a year, the soldiers reminded Odysseus that they needed to be on their way.

"I will be sad to see you go," the sorceress pouted when Odysseus told her they were leaving. "However, you must know that you will never find your way home by sailing straight for it. Your path is hidden but can be seen by the seer Tiresias. You must seek him in the Kingdom of Darkness. Only then will you be able to chart your course." Circe gave him detailed instructions on exactly how to find the entrance to the Underworld and what to do once they got there. She sent the Ithacans on their way with her blessings.

Odysseus wasted no time in putting Circe's instructions into action. Sails filled with a sweet northerly breeze from Circe, the ship went smoothly forth to the very edge of the world-encircling ocean. They dropped anchor and found the spring from which the river Styx flowed.

Following Circe's directions, Odysseus dug a deep trench with his sword and filled it with milk, honey, and wine. He sacrificed a ewe and a lamb and let their blood flow into the trench. It didn't take long for shades to be drawn to the offering. The first apparition to appear was Elpenor, one of Odysseus' crew who had fallen to his death on Circe's island just before their departure.

"You must go back to bury me! I cannot cross the river until you do and am miserable here wandering and waiting," the ghost wailed.

Shamed that he had not taken the time to see the youth properly buried, Odysseus promised to return and see to it.

Other shades appeared, but Odysseus was looking for one ghost in particular. He held the others at bay with his sword, even his own mother, though it pained him to do so. Finally, Tiresias appeared, and Odysseus let him drink his fill before sitting down to speak with him.

"Odysseus, king of Ithaca, you wish to return home, but I fear that your journey will be a difficult one," the seer said in solemn tones. Odysseus' heart sank. Their journey had been far from easy, and now it sounded as if it was only going to get worse. "Do not despair, son of Laertes. Poseidon bears you ill because of the injury you inflicted on his son the Cyclops, but you will once again see your homeland. The fate of your men, however, is less clear. You must travel to the Isle of Helios. If you and your crew control your appetites and touch not the cattle that dwell there, you will all return home. If you do not, then you alone will see Ithaca, but your journey will be long and difficult. Your wife awaits you, though she is surrounded by suitors who would take your place as king. She will remain faithful to you. Once you return home, you must not forget to appease the Earth Shaker with proper offerings or your homecoming will be brief and sorrowful." The prophet fell silent, and Odysseus thanked him for his counsel.

"I see my mother waiting, but I know not how to speak to her," Odysseus asked Tiresias as the shade began to drift away.

"Let any phantom here drink of the blood if you wish to converse with them but be wary. They will overrun you in their thirst."

Odysseus coaxed his mother's ghost to the trench, and once she had slaked her thirst, she sat and spoke with her son. She told him of Ithaca where Penelope was besieged with suitors but doing her best to fend them off. "Telemachus stands ever sturdy by her side, but your father is wasting away in grief for you. Of course, here I am, dead in my distress over losing you!" His mother wept. Odysseus tried to embrace her, but his arms passed right through her.

The ghost of Agamemnon approached and drank from the trench. Odysseus was dismayed to see his king in the Underworld and was disturbed by the tale of his murder. Achilles joined them and bemoaned the discomforts of the Kingdom of Darkness. However, once Odysseus told the hero of his son's triumphs, he drifted away a much happier ghost. The other shades grew restless as their thirst tormented them, and they began to crowd around Odysseus. He left them to their repast and hurried back to his ship and crew.

They sailed back to Circe's island to tend to poor Elpenor. Once his burial rites had been observed, Circe gave Odysseus a final bit of advice.

"Sail forth, my brave warrior, and pass by the Isle of the Sirens. Close the ears of your men with beeswax, so they do not hear their enchanting song. It lures all who hear it to their death. If you would hear it, have your men tie you securely to the mast of the ship, or you will dive into their watery trap. Once the Sirens are behind you, you must face two terrible monsters. On one side of a narrow passage, you face the dread daughter of Poseidon. Charybdis, with her unquenchable thirst, waits on the banks in her hideous form and tries to drink the ocean dry. You must avoid the sucking whirlpool of her gigantic maw. But on the other side lies Scylla with her six monstrous heads. Once each head has sated its hunger, she will let you pass," the witch told Odysseus, whose mind was already plotting how to survive the narrows. Circe shook her head. "I see what you are thinking! You cannot survive Charybdis or slay Scylla. Syclla is immortal, you fool! It is best to lose six men than the entire crew - heed my words!"

Odysseus and his crew once again took to the ship. Circe conjured a fair wind, and they were on their way. As they neared the Sirens, Odysseus made sure the men's ears were filled securely with wax, and in turn, the crew tied their captain to the mast. Bravely, the crew churned the sea with long strokes of their oars, and the vessel sped through the water. Odysseus wept with the beauty of the song and strained fiercely at his bonds in his desire to stay in the presence of the beguiling melody. Once the ship was out of range of the Siren's song, Odysseus' reason returned, and he commanded the men to unstop their ears and untie him from the mast. It was time to face the most dreaded part of the journey.

Odysseus didn't tell his crew about the dangers that were waiting for them. He was worried they would hide below decks in terror. Instead, he gave them instructions to watch for rocks and stay well away from the jagged cliffs ahead. Disregarding Circe's advice, Odysseus donned his armor and took up his spear and sword. He stationed himself on the bow of the boat. While all the crew kept their eyes trained on the rugged coastline that was the home to Charybdis, Odysseus stared through the sea spray and into the fog of the far shore for any sign of Scylla. He saw nothing.

Behind him, his crew let out a cry of alarm. Odysseus turned and watched in fascinated horror as Charybdis sucked down the sea in a vast draining whirlpool. They could see down into the grey depths of her gullet as the waves crashed, and the helmsmen fought to keep the boat from being drawn down into the cavernous mouth.

Another cry sounded, followed by several more. Odysseus spun about in time to see six of his crew being devoured by Scylla's six mouths. Their agonized screams were cut short as the men disappeared below the sea.

Finally, the sea spat the vessel out the other side of the narrow straits and before them lay the beautiful Isle of Helios. Green pastures and rolling hills covered the idyllic island. From the ship, the lowing of cattle could be heard. The sheer loveliness beguiled the hearts of the crew, and they sorely wanted to stop to explore the island and rest.

"Nay," cried Odysseus. "The seer foretold that this Isle would be a curse for us. Let us pass it by, friends, for nothing but trouble waits for us here."

The crew argued and complained bitterly until Odysseus relented. "We will stop, but each man will give me his solemn oath that he will not touch the sheep, cattle, or ox on this island. We must be content with the stores given to us by Circe." The men all agreed, and they made landfall on the Isle of the Sun.

For several days, the men mourned their lost comrades and rested their weary bodies. As they were preparing to leave the island, the south wind began to blow, banning their passage out of the small harbor. Steadily the wind blew, keeping Odysseus and his crew pinned on the island. Their food stores dwindled, but Odysseus kept the men in check, reminding them of their oaths. They fished and snared small animals to eat, but soon it wasn't enough. In desperation, Odysseus wandered all over the island in search of food and a way to find favor with the gods.

While he was away, Eurylochus gathered the men around him. "I say we kill one of those cattle and fill our bellies! We will offer proper sacrifice to Zeus and Helios. Surely that will appease them. I think it is better to take our chances and maybe die at sea than slowly starve to death here!"

The other men agreed, and they killed the best of the sacred cattle. Odysseus returned to find them feasting on the meat and cried out to Zeus in remorse. It was too late, unfortunately. Helios was furious that his cattle had been slaughtered and demanded justice, saying he would follow the men's shades to the Underworld and burn them with his light.

"Hold your temper, Helios," Zeus chided. "Shine your light on the mortal realm as is your duty. I will see these mortals for you."

After six more days which the men, save Odysseus, spent feasting, the southerly winds finally abated, and the crew scrambled to leave the island while they could. As soon as the ship reached the open seas, Zeus stirred up a vicious storm. Winds shrieked, and the mast broke. The hull cracked as the God of Thunder hurled down bolt after bolt of lightning. Odysseus was powerless to save his crew. He was the only one spared as the ship broke to pieces and his men were swallowed by the sea. He clung to a chunk of the mast that bobbed in the water, and the winds cruelly drove him back toward the deadly force of Charybdis.

The creature opened her mouth and sucked down the sea. Caught in the current, Odysseus has swept away with the rest of the wreck and water. Just as the whirlpool caught him in its grip, he saw a fig tree hanging over the abyss where it clung to the edge of a sea cliff. He lunged for it and just managed to grasp it as his makeshift raft was sucked down with the rest of the sea. There, he hung as the creature filled her belly. Finally, the cavernous jaws shut, and the sea ceased to swirl below him. Odysseus clutched to his lifeline and waited. With a mighty groan, Charybdis belched forth the sea she had just swallowed in a mighty geyser. Odysseus let go of the tree and was swept back out to the open sea. He clung to a bit of wreckage and drifted in vast waters of the ocean for nine days.

On the tenth day, Odysseus washed up on the sandy shore of Ogygia, home to Calypso the sea nymph. Calypso found poor Odysseus, half-drowned and exhausted on her beach. She revived him with ambrosia and nursed him back to health. She was the sweetest of companions and gave him anything he desired - except a way to leave the island. Odysseus begged and begged her over seven long years to set him free. A prisoner in a gilded cage, he was depressed, heartbroken, and homesick. Calypso even offered Odysseus immortality if he would stay with her on her island, but

Odysseus refused time and time again. All he wanted was to go home.

Athena's heart was moved by Odysseus' plight. He had always been one of her favorites, and she felt he had paid for his transgressions.

"Mighty Zeus, see how the son of Laertes suffers! Has he not served his penance? Can he not return to his homeland and the bosom of his ever-faithful wife," Athena implored her father.

Zeus regarded Odysseus and weighed his actions. It had been fated that Odysseus was to return to Ithaca. It was time to allow that to play out. "Hermes," Zeus beckoned his messenger. "Go to the red-headed nymph Calypso and tell her that it is time for Odysseus to find his way home. Tell her to provide him with clothes, supplies, and a sound ship. He is to go to Phaeacians, and they will see him to his home shores." Hermes departed with the message and Zeus turned his attention to Athena.

The goddess of war had been busy assisting Odysseus' son, Telemachus. With Odysseus' protracted absence, people thought that he had been lost at war. Penelope was besieged with dozens of suitors vying for her hand and the crown of Ithaca. For decades, she kept them at bay, faithful to her husband. Penelope put them off saying she would decide among them when she finished her weaving, but every night she unraveled what she wove during the day. Thus, she never finished her project and never made a choice. As the years drew out, the suitors made themselves at home in the

Ithacan court. They drained the stores of food and wine and undermined Penelope and Telemachus' authority in the court.

Telemachus wanted nothing more than to oust the suitors from his home and spent most of his time dreaming about how he would do it. One day, during his daydreams, Athena came to him in the guise of his grandfather's friend, Mentes.

"You must rid your house of these pests. Your father is alive. He is being held on a remote island, but I know he will be returning soon. Agamemnon's son, Orestes, avenged his father's death. You need to follow his example and clean out your father's court before he returns!"

"I would like nothing more, but no one will listen to me. I am still just a child in their eyes," Telemachus said morosely. "I have no proof that my father lives."

"Go to Nestor in Pylos, and then seek Menelaus in Sparta. They will give you news of the great Odysseus. Have patience, young one, as it will still be more than a year before he returns. Before you leave, you must take back your birthright and order the suitors to leave. Shore up your mother's spirit with your courage," Athena instructed and infused him with bravery, strength, and vivid memory of his father.

Telemachus thanked the old man for his wisdom and bid him to relax and refresh himself. To his amazement, the old man simply vanished. Telemachus stood for a moment, realizing that he had been in the presence of a god. The more he considered, he decided it must have been Athena and resolved to follow her instructions immediately.

Without hesitation, Telemachus strode into the hall and called for everyone's attention. "I give you notice here and now that I am the lord of this house as is my right. Tomorrow, I shall publicly denounce your presence in my court. Leave my house and do not bother my mother anymore!"

The assembly stared in wonder at the young prince and his new found confidence. Whispers broke out about the stranger they had seen the prince in conference with. It had to have been a god to inspire such a rapid change in the young man.

One of the most persistent suitors, Eurymachus, stood and spoke for the group, "No one challenges your right to your own house, Telemachus, but only the gods will choose the king of Ithaca."

The court dispersed for the night, each to their own bedchamber. The next day, as promised, Telemachus called a public assembly. It was the first since his father had left. All of the men of the realm gathered, and Telemachus eloquently spoke in front of the council, requesting that all the suitors leave his house. The suitors complained that the only reason they had stayed so long was that Penelope kept putting off her decision.

Telemachus stood once more and declared, "I will travel to the lands of Pylos and Sparta in search of news of my father. If I find evidence that he still lives, we shall wait one year. If by the end of that year, he has not returned home, then we shall observe his funeral rites, and my mother will pick her new husband. In the meantime, go back to your homes and live off your own food and wine!" At the end of this speech, two eagles swooped down over the assembly. Many of the men read them as a sign from Zeus that he supported Telemachus.

Eurymachus, however, dismissed them. "There are many birds in the rafters here," he scoffed and continued saying, "We're not going anywhere until Penelope chooses among us!"

Telemachus left the assembly and immediately prepared for his journey. Athena, this time in the guise of Mentor, facilitated in hiring the vessel and gathering a trusted crew. That very night, Telemachus sailed with Athena to the mainland.

The goddess of war guided him to Nestor who told the young prince about his father's heroic actions during the war. Then, they traveled on to Sparta where Menelaus confirmed that Odysseus lived but was being held by Calypso on her island. He had been told about Odysseus' fate when he had captured the Old Man of the Sea. Joyful of the news, Telemachus began to make his preparations for the journey home.

Telemachus had no idea that in his absence his mother's suitors had been plotting his assassination. They were waiting for him offshore to make sure he never returned to Ithaca alive. Zeus, of course, knew about their nefarious plans. After he sent Hermes to Calypso, he dispatched Athena to ensure Telemachus' safe return.

"Go now, daughter and see both father and son safely home to their native shores. It is time to set the House of Ithaca in order," Zeus commanded, and Athena left straight away. While Athena began to put her plans in action, Hermes informed Calypso of Zeus' decree.

Calypso's beautiful face filled with sorrow at the proclamation. "Oh, you vengeful gods! If we goddesses take a mortal man into our arms, you cannot stand it and seek to spoil our happiness! Of course, Zeus commands and I shall obey, but oh my heart breaks! I saved him and loved him. He is my only companion in this lonely place, but I will see him well provisioned and safely off to the Phaeacian shores."

Hermes took his leave, and Calypso went to find Odysseus. As usual, he was sitting on cliffs overlooking the western sea, weeping for home.

"Come now, my unhappy love. It is time for your tears to cease. Be up about your work, for you must build a raft to bear you to distant shores. There is much to be done!" Odysseus looked at her with bewilderment. For seven long years, he had been begging to be released. Calypso's sudden change in disposition made him suspicious.

"You propose I cross the open ocean on nothing but a raft? It cannot be done without the guiding hand of Zeus! As much as I want to go home, this is madness! I shall not attempt it unless you swear on the river Styx that you mean me no mischief."

Calypso stroked his face tenderly and swore that while she hated to see him go, she would do everything in her power to see him safely home. Together, they prepared for his journey. As they shared their final meal together, Calypso couldn't help trying one last time to persuade Odysseus to stay.

"Am I not beautiful enough for you, Odysseus? Surely your wife is not as beautiful as me. You know I would make you immortal. You could stay here and spend eternity with me!"

Odysseus smiled at her, for he cared a great deal for her despite his yearning for a home. "You are the fairest creature I have ever seen, but Penelope is my wife. I must return to her and restore my house to honor. I thank you for your hospitality these many years, but it is time for me to return home."

They spent their last night without further conversation and with first light, Odysseus pushed his small raft out to sea. For seventeen days, he followed the course Calypso had laid out for him, tracking the stars at night and the sun during the day. On the eighteenth day, he saw the Phaeacian shores, and his heart lightened with joy.

Deep below in his water court, Poseidon returned from the Land of Ethiopia where he had been celebrating a festival in his name. He noted Odysseus in his raft, and his temper flared. He was still angry about the injury to the cyclopes and was even angrier that Zeus had gone behind his back to sneak Odysseus across the sea while he was otherwise occupied. With vengeful satisfaction, Poseidon grabbed his trident and stirred the seas. He called the winds and shook the ground.

Odysseus watched in horror as the storm gathered. He wouldn't make it to land before it hit, and his craft was not meant to withstand such violence. The tempest bore down on him, and waves crashed over the little boat, tearing it to pieces. Odysseus was washed into the sea, and as he was tossed beneath the waves, he began to despair that he would not see his home or wife again.

Ino, a sea nymph, saw his struggles and swam to his aid. "Fear not, Odysseus, for the Fates have decreed you shall once again see your beloved homelands. Poseidon is exacting his revenge, but you shall survive." She tied a sash made of divine cloth around his chest. "This will protect you and keep you safe, but you must swim for shore. Once your feet are firmly on the land, cast this sash back in the sea, so I may reclaim it." In a splash of water, the nymph disappeared, and Odysseus was alone in the dark, stormy seas.

Odysseus followed her instructions and tried to make for the distant shore. The waves battered him and time and time again. He thought he would drown, despite the divine intervention. If not for the sash around his chest and the promise that he was not going to die, Odysseus would have abandoned all hope. For two days, he swam but made no progress toward land. As dawn rose on the third day, Athena stilled the seas and sent a favorable wind to blow Odysseus towards land. Finally, his efforts bore fruit, and he was able to close the distance. Poseidon decided that he had suffered enough and turned his attention elsewhere.

Exhausted and bedraggled, Odysseus washed up on the shores of Phaeacia. He crawled away from the water and had just enough presence of mind left to cast the sash back into the sea before he collapsed on the beach.

Athena watched over him as he slept and sent a dream to the princess of the realm, Nausicaa. In the guise of one of Nausicaa's friends, she told the princess to go to the washing tanks the next day to wash her clothes and those of her family. "You have caught the eye of the great prince and will one day be his wife. You must prepare," Athena told the princess.

When the princess woke, she remembered the dream, and her heart skipped a beat in excitement at the thought of becoming the queen of all Phaeacia. She hurried to find her father and got permission to use the cart and donkey. She gathered all the soiled clothing in the house and with her attendants headed for the washing tanks.

Once the washing was done, Nausicaa and her friends played a game of ball. Athena stirred Odysseus awake. He heard the girls playing and knew he had to make himself known, despite being naked and filthy. When the girls saw him, they screamed and ran - all except Nausicaa, who Athena infused with bravery. She stood her ground and waited for Odysseus to make the first move.

Odysseus had been a king before the war, and he knew a thing or two about princesses. He ignored his nakedness and drew himself up, donning his courtly bearing and manners. "My lady Queen! Your beauty is beyond any these eyes have ever beheld. Perhaps I am looking upon a goddess and not a mortal woman at all! Your father, brothers, and of course, husband must be favored by Zeus to have been given such beauty to gaze upon every day. Would it be in your power, my lady, to give me some clothes and take me to your husband? I am sorry to appear like this to you, but I have been twenty days at sea and must continue my voyage home."

Nausicaa recognized Odysseus' courtly bearing and knew that this was no ragamuffin wanderer. "Sir, you do me great honors, but I am the daughter of King Alcinous. I will take you to him and show you the fine city of the Phaeacians." To her attendants, who had hidden among the carts of laundry, she commanded, "Come, ladies! Why are you hiding? Zeus loves us too much to send an enemy to our shores. Find this man clothes and show him where to bathe. Bring him wine that he might refresh himself."

The women scurried to obey and Odysseus, after requesting his privacy, washed and clothed himself. When he appeared to them once more, Nausicaa knew he must be royal born, for he looked like a god walking among them. "Now then, stranger, come with me to the city, but we cannot go in together, lest gossip spread like wildfire and stain my honor. Wait for me in the temple of Athena until you think enough time has passed for me to return to the palace. Ask directions and present yourself there, but do not go directly to my father. Beseech my mother first, and everything will be taken care of!" With her instructions given, she whipped her mules forward and left Odysseus and her attendants to find their own way to the city.

Odysseus did as he was bid and after passing time in prayer to the gods, he rose to go to the palace. Athena, concerned that the Phaeacians tended to be highly suspect of strangers since they were such a rare commodity on the island, cloaked his passage. She appeared to him as a maiden and offered to show him the way to the palace herself.

"Now then, stranger," Athena said as they neared the great hall, "go straight to the queen and hug her knees humbly. Call her by name, Areta, daughter of Eurymedon, and beg her to help you. She is wise and revered by her people. Gain her favor, and you will see your far distant shores again."

Athena left him at the door of the great hall where Odysseus stood and stared around in wonder. The beauty and richness of this new land astounded him. After he had taken it all in, he made his way to where the queen sat spinning yarn. Athena dispersed the mists that hid him from mortal eyes just as he threw himself down and clasped the queen's knees.

A startled cry at the sudden appearance of a stranger in the court rippled across the room. Everyone gaped at Odysseus as he cried out, "My lady queen, Areta, daughter of Eurymedon, I kneel before you, supplicant and destitute. Please, help me get back to the lands of my people!" As he finished speaking, he sat away from her in the ashes of the hearth as if he were the lowliest beggar in the realm.

Everyone sat in stunned silence until one of the king's advisors whispered to him, "My lord, see how the stranger sits in the dust, but he clearly does not belong there. This may be a god in disguise, perhaps even Zeus himself. I urge you forward. Raise him from the dust and offer him a place at your table. Give him refreshment and treat him as an honored guest."

King Alcinous did as he was advised and helped Odysseus to his feet. As Odysseus was made comfortable, the king declared the next day a holiday and told his advisors to return to their homes for the night. When they were alone, Queen Areta asked Odysseus plainly, "Tell us, stranger, how you have come to us on our remote shores. We do not get many visitors here."

Odysseus answered her simply, though he did not mention his name. He told them about being trapped on Calypso's island and his harrowing journey across the sea. Satisfied with the story, the king and queen promised to help him get home.

In the games the next day, Odysseus was overcome with tears while listening to a bard sing the song of Odysseus and Achilles and the Trojan War. Of course, no one realized that the hero of the song was sitting in their midst. Seeing their guest's distress, King Alcinous ordered the bard to leave off singing and the games to begin. The Phaeacians wanted to impress the stranger, and their best athletes took the field. Odysseus watched politely until Laodamas, the king's son, said, "You are a fit looking man, stranger. Perhaps you would like to try to best our champion, Euryalus? It seems none can best him today."

"Your men are impressive in their form and strength. I do not have the heart for games for mine is too heavy with grief and longing for my home," Odysseus answered.

"That sounds like an excuse to me," crowed Euryalus, whose confidence was riding high. "I think he knows he stands no chance against a Phaeacian!"

Odysseus glared at the young man. "You are clearly mighty in body, but you were not blessed with a mind to match," he snapped. "I have played my fair share of games in my time, and it appears that now I must teach you a lesson in how to treat a guest in your presence."

Odysseus got to his feet and took up the discus. With what looked like casual indifference, he flung it across the field. It sailed over the heads of the crowd and twice the distance as any of the other throws. Athena, in the form of a Phaeacian official, took the measure.

"Stranger, you have bested all here today, and I doubt there will ever be a Phaeacian who can match this throw," she proclaimed.

Odysseus bowed to her, though he did not know it was the goddess of war. "I thank you for your kind words. Is there anyone else who wishes to challenge me? I am no Hercules or Apollo, but I will match strength or bow with anyone here!"

None of the young men stepped forward. The king called up the bard to break the tension with entertainment. Everyone watched as the bard played his lyre and several young women came forward to dance. The atmosphere lightened, and soon, everyone was enjoying the festivities. Odysseus was presented with gifts. Each of the senior leaders brought him gold, and Euryalus gave him a fine sword in apology for taunting him. As the feast was served, the bard began to sing of the Trojan horse and the ruse that saw the downfall of the Trojan empire. Again, Odysseus was moved to tears.

"Enough," King Alcinous barked and held up his hand to stop the song. "This song distresses our guest. Sir," he addressed Odysseus formally, "we have welcomed you as is our custom. I believe it is time for you to reveal yourself fully to us. I promise you safe passage to your home. Tell us now who you are and from whence you came. After all, our ships will need a heading if they are to deliver you there."

Odysseus knew the time had come to tell his story. "I am Odysseus, son of Laertes and king of Ithaca," he began. As the king, queen, and the assembly listened with rapt attention, Odysseus told the story of his adventures since the Trojan War. He spoke for hours, and when he was finished, the Phaeacians again promised that they would see him safely home.

The next day, King Alcinous showered Odysseus with gifts of food, fine linen, wine, and other precious things. He crewed his fastest ship with his best sailors. The queen's attendants laid a sumptuous bed for Odysseus to lie on during the journey. Odysseus gratefully laid down, and the ship slipped out of the harbor in the early morning rays. He fell asleep almost immediately and slept the entire voyage across the sea. The swift Phaeacians crossed the waters in record time. They carried the sleeping king onto his native shore and piled his treasure around him. They hid the gifts with branches from an olive tree, lest they are stolen before

Odysseus could awake. Silently, they pushed back into the sea, leaving Odysseus still sound asleep.

Poseidon had watched the trek from his watery palace. He went to Zeus to voice his displeasure. "Odysseus has been returned home," he complained to his brother. "He was meant to have a difficult journey, and here he has slept the entire voyage! My Phaeacians, born of the sea and blessed with my talents, have piled more treasure around him than if he had returned straight home from Troy!"

"Poseidon, no god has interfered with your plans. The Phaeacians bore him hence with no divine help. I will not stop you from retaliating if they have insulted you," Zeus replied.

"My people have forgotten the prophecies of their fathers," Poseidon groused. "They were told that if they ferried strangers to their native lands that the ship and crew would never again return. I shall make it so if you have no objection." With Zeus' blessing, Poseidon waited for the Phaeacian vessel to draw within sight of their port.

King Alcinous watched anxiously from the shore as the boat came into view. Suddenly, the earth shook, and the waves roared as the floor of the sea rose up and swallowed the vessel. The ship and crew turned to stone. Just inside the port stood a new mountain with the ill-fated vessel and crew perched in their statue form on top.

King Alcinous cried out, "I have just recalled the dread prophecy that foretold of this day. We have offended Poseidon. Quickly, bring out twelve of our finest bulls and let us sacrifice to the Earth Shaker that he might have mercy on us."

As the Phaeacians scrambled to avert the wrath of Poseidon, Odysseus finally awoke on his native soil. Athena concealed him in mists, and he did not recognize his homeland. "Those treacherous Phaeacians. They have deposited me on some foreign shore and abandoned me here! I cannot protect my treasure and have no idea if a race of man lives here or am I on another island inhabited by monsters," Odysseus lamented to himself.

Athena, disguised as a shepherd, approached and Odysseus hailed her, asking what land he was in. "Why stranger, look about you! How can you not recognize these renowned shores? You stand on the Isle of Ithaca," the goddess replied.

Odysseus' heart leaped in his chest, but caution kept the truth of his identity on his tongue. "I have heard of this place but have never seen it with my own eyes. I am from Crete and had to leave my family behind after being forced to kill a man who was trying to steal my Trojan plunder," Odysseus lied.

Athena laughed and revealed herself. "Odysseus, my favorite of warriors, how can it be that after all this time you still do not know me? Can you not set aside your suspicions and plots for a moment? We could pass days away in clever banter, but we haven't the time. Your court is in disarray, and it is time to set it right. I will tell you all that you need to know, but first, let us first conceal your treasure."

Odysseus, who knew Athena the moment she shed her shepherd's guise, fell to the ground and kissed it in his joy. "Pallas Athena, my goddess! How could I know you when you take so many different forms? I suspect I have seen you many times but have been ignorant of it. I thank you for your protection and guidance. Tell me truly, am I really in Ithaca?"

Athena cleared the fog from his eyes that he could look on his beloved homeland. Odysseus wept in joy, but time was of the essence. "Come now, Odysseus! Bring your treasure here that it may remain safe and let me tell you what must be done," Athena instructed.

Odysseus dried his tears and hastily brought his treasures into the cave that Athena had created. She sealed it and turned to the hero. "Your noble wife has fended off the suitors for as long as she can. She's kept them dancing for years with promises and pretty words, but the time has come for her to choose. I will disguise your form that you may walk into your city without being recognized. Seek out your faithful swineherd, Eumaeus, and tarry there while I go to Sparta to bring Telemachus home. Learn about the state of your kingdom, and when your son returns, we will once again see you seated upon the throne of Ithaca."

Athena transformed Odysseus into a stooped backed old beggar and left him to find his way into town. He followed the goddess' instructions, and for several days he stayed with Eumaeus, trading stories and lies and finding out the general state of Ithaca. He discovered that his father, Laertes, was living lost in grief. Eumaeus bemoaned the gluttony and greed of the suitors who infiltrated the court and told the disguised hero that Ithaca was in sorry shape.

Meanwhile, Athena cleared the way for Telemachus to return home safely. His voyage was marked with good omens, and his heart was light as he stepped on to the shores of his homeland. He stopped at the swineherd's hut and was surprised to see an old beggar man in residence. Eumaeus told Telemachus to see to the beggar's needs.

"How can I take care of his needs when I cannot even manage my own house," Telemachus argued, but provided clothes, sandals, and a sword to the beggar.

Odysseus, who was overjoyed at seeing his son, fought to keep up his ruse. "I am sorry to hear of the troubles in your house, young lord! If I were your father, I would not stop until all the suitors were banished or I was dead!"

"You speak bold words, stranger. May the gods hear them that one day my father will return home. Eumaeus, go tell my mother of my safe return."

The swineherd hurried off, and Odysseus saw Athena approaching the small hut. He stepped outside to greet her away from Telemachus' hearing.

"It is time for you to reveal yourself to your son! Make your plans, wily Odysseus. I will come when you have need of me," the goddess of war told him as she restored his appearance before disappearing.

Telemachus stared in wonder as his father, fit in form and radiant in appearance, stepped back into the swineherd's hut. "You must be a god to walk out an old man and return as one in his prime," the young prince exclaimed.

"I am not a god. I am your father and the reason your life has been so difficult," Odysseus said through tears of happiness and grief.

"Nay! It cannot be. Where are your soldiers? Where is your treasure from your conquests? You appear as a beggar. This must be some trick of the gods!" Telemachus stepped back from his father in fear.

"I am your father, and you shall know me. Pallas Athena has changed my appearance, for how else can you explain what you have witnessed here today? See with your eyes and know this to be true!" Odysseus sat and looked at his son expectantly.

Telemachus saw the truth and threw his arms around his father. "Where are your troops? Where is your bounty? Why have you come like a beggar here?"

"I will tell you the whole story in time. For now, know that I am the sole survivor of my company of soldiers and that I have treasure aplenty concealed in a cave on the shore. Tell me quickly how many suitors are in my house and what you know of them.

Our time is short, and we must make our plans." Odysseus listened intently as Telemachus described the suitors. The odds were over one hundred against two, but they would have Zeus and Athena on their side. Cheered by that thought, the father and son fleshed out the rest of the plan and settled in for the night.

The next morning, Telemachus went ahead to the palace while Eumaeus and Odysseus, once again disguised as an old beggar, wandered through the village. Odysseus received insults and kicks from the merchants and nobles but kept a tight rein on his temper. As they made their way to the palace, Odysseus spied an old dog, covered in mud and filth, lying in the ditch. He knelt next to the beast and saw it was his old dog, Argos, who he had raised from a pup. Tears coursed down his cheeks as the dog beat its tail in the mud in recognition of his old master, despite the goddesses' disguise. Odysseus patted its filthy head as it died in the ditch, finally able to rest now that his master had returned.

When they reached the palace, Odysseus went around to the suitors, begging for scraps of food. Most of the suitors gave the old beggar food without any complaints. However, Antinous, one of the most prominent suitors, complained loudly about Odysseus' presence. "Telemachus, why have you let one such as this into the hall? Isn't it bad enough that they infest the streets? Be gone," Antinous shouted and threw a stool at Odysseus.

"To strike a man in the protection of yourself or your property is one thing, but to strike a man for simply begging a scrap of food to ease his hunger is quite another. One is nothing but the other will be punished by the gods. Wait and see, Antinous. You'll die before you wed the queen," Odysseus proclaimed. The other suitors added their condemnation of his behavior, and Penelope cursed him for treating a guest in her house so poorly.

Antinous, stung by the reproaches, saw another opportunity to cause Odysseus trouble later that afternoon. One of the regular court vagabonds named Irus entered the court and was very displeased to see a new beggar in his territory. "Get out of here! This is my place. Go someplace else, or I will drag you out of here kicking and screaming," Irus told Odysseus. Antinous overheard the comment and stirred the contention between the men by calling the other suitors' attention to it.

"Come now! Let us watch our resident beggar, Irus, challenge the stranger. It will be the best sport we've had all day," Antinous called, and the suitors all gathered round to watch the contest.

Odysseus' temper boiled. He was not used to having to bear insults and disrespect. Still, he held himself in check. When the suitors saw him lay Irus out with just one punch, they began to wonder if there was something more to this unknown stranger. The day wore on, and Odysseus suffered more ill treatment from various suitors and even the handmaidens of the house. He bore it all without retaliation until the suitors finally retired for the evening.

As per their plan, as the suitors slept, Odysseus and Telemachus secured all the weapons in the house. As they each went to find their own rest, Penelope sought out the stranger. "Have you heard anything of my lord, Odysseus? He has been gone for so long. I begin to despair that I should ever see his face again."

"He is closer than you think," Odysseus replied and couldn't help but be pleased by the way his wife still pined for him. "I met him on my travels, and he was well. He strives to find his way back to you, my Queen."

Penelope wiped her tears. "Thank you, sir. I am sorry for the treatment in my court today. Please, wouldn't you be more comfortable if you refreshed yourself with a bath? I can have my maids bring water and see to it."
"Nay, lady. That is far too much for a wretch like me," Odysseus replied humbly.

Not to be deterred, Penelope insisted that her attendant, Eurycleia, at least wash his feet. Odysseus relented and the old woman, who had once been his nurse, bent to wash his feet. He watched her fondly and jumped when she gasped and dropped his feet into the basin, sloshing water onto the floor.

"I have seen that scar before. My lord bears one identical to it. I dressed it many years ago after he was hurt hunting with his grandfather," Eurycleia exclaimed.

Odysseus hushed her before she could say more. "It is I, good nurse, but you must say no more. All will be revealed in time."

The old nurse nodded her assent, but she couldn't hide her smile.

Athena, knowing it was not yet time for Penelope to be let in on the secret, distracted her with a vision. She revealed an eagle soaring down into the court and breaking the necks of twenty geese. When Eurycleia had finished her task, Penelope told Odysseus of the vision.

"My lady, this is a good omen. It can only mean that the suitors are soon to be banished from your court!"

Penelope wasn't so sure, but she bade the stranger good night. That night, Athena sent a dream to Penelope, and when she rose in the morning, she dressed in her very finest robes. She went down among the suitors, who all stopped and stared at her beauty.

"My lords, today is the day that I make my decision! I have been cruel to keep you waiting for so long. We will have a contest, and I will wed the victor. Whoever can shoot Odysseus' bow through the rings shall be my husband," Penelope announced, using every bit of her queenly demeanor.

The men scrambled to prepare. Telemachus went first since he was the man of the house. He was unable to even string the mighty bow. Antinous tried and had the same issue. As suitor after suitor attempted to string the great bow, Odysseus slipped out of the court. Outside, he saw Eumaeus and his companion and his chief cowherd, Philoeteus.

"Herdsmen, I have a question," he called as he approached the pair. "What welcome would you give your lord, Odysseus, should he return home this moment?"

Both Eumaeus and Philoeteus assured him that they would be overjoyed to have their lord returned to them, saying it would be an answer to their prayers.

"Your prayers have been answered, my faithful friends! It is I, Odysseus, returned home! See the scar on my leg," Odysseus said boldly and lifted his robe to reveal the tell-tale scar.

Both the men cried out in joy and tried to embrace their long-lost liege. "Now is not the time, my friends," Odysseus admonished them. "I will need you to stand with me, for I am about to take back my wife and my court." He quickly gave them their instructions. They assured him he could count on them.

With the support of his faithful subjects, he once again assumed the air of a beggar and went back into the court. None of the suitors had even been able to string the bow, let alone shoot it.

"My lady, may I try," Odysseus asked.

The suitors scoffed and scorned the beggar, but Penelope held up her hand. "After the treatment, you have received here, it is the least I can do."

Odysseus took up the bow and with practiced movements strung it as easily as if he was stringing a lyre. The suitors gaped and were unable to contain their incredulity when he shot the arrow expertly between the rings. As the arrow soared through the hole, Zeus cast down a thunderbolt. On that good omen, Odysseus smiled at his son and said, "You need not to be ashamed of admitting me to your court, young prince. Now, let the evening's festivities begin!"

Without saying anything further, Odysseus shot Antinous dead. He kicked over the table, scattering food and wine everywhere and threw off his beggar's robe and disguise. "I am Odysseus! The king of Ithaca has returned!"

Eumaeus and Philoeteus followed their instructions. They secured all the palace doors and ushered the women safely out of the hall. Telemachus and his father engaged the suitors and their bow strings sung with arrow after arrow. When their arrows were exhausted, they drew their swords and spears. Athena, in the form of Mentor, fought beside the warriors and infused them with courage. As the battle turned in favor of Odysseus, she transformed into a swallow and watched from high in the rafters, turning any swords or spears away from her champion. Suitors fell one by one until they all lay dead in the great hall.

Odysseus was not done yet. He called the twelve handmaidens who had been unfaithful to Penelope and plotted with the suitors. With ruthless efficiency, he made them clean the hall of the carnage and then hung them for their disloyalty. With his house empty of traitors, Odysseus sought out his wife.

Penelope stared in disbelief as Odysseus stood in the center of the hall, donned in his royal finery. For a very long time, she sat silent, and neither Telemachus nor Odysseus could entreat her to say anything. Finally, in frustration, Odysseus ordered Eurycleia to make his bed ready for him since he is weary from the day.

Penelope stirred. "Yes, Eurycleia, make his bed and stack it high with furs and mantles. Do not make it in my chamber, however. Take his bed from there and make it up in one of the other rooms."

Odysseus glared at his wife. "What nonsense is this? Who could move my bed that I built with my own hands around a living olive tree? How can you expect that it would move?"

Penelope's face lit with a smile. She threw herself into Odysseus' arms, for only her true husband would know about the bed he made. With that settled between, they retired for the night.

The next morning, Odysseus bade Penelope wait in the palace and sought out his father. After much convincing, Laertes recognized his son and wept with joy. However, not everyone was happy that Odysseus was home. News of the slaughter of the suitors had spread across the city, and the families of the fallen men met Laertes and Odysseus on the road back to the palace, demanding justice.

"Thanks to you we have lost two generations of Ithacans! Your soldiers and our sons all roam the dark halls of the Underworld! We do not welcome you home as king." Antinous' father spat the words angrily at Odysseus. Fathers and brothers of the other suitors stood by in support with weapons loose in their scabbards. Rage overwhelmed Antinous' father, and he drew his sword to attack Odysseus, but Laertes intervened and killed him. With blood spilt, the rest of the rabble drew their swords, ready to ensure that Odysseus never again sat on the throne of Ithaca.

Athena, ever watchful over her champion, intervened. "Peace, sons of Ithaca! There shall be no more bloodshed here today." Her voice sounded like a thunderclap. All the men froze in fear.

The challengers took their cue and ran back to the city. Odysseus began to give chase, but Zeus threw down a thunderbolt, stopping him in his tracks. "Enough, Odysseus, cunning warrior and son of Laertes! You will give up the chase or you will know the displeasure of the mighty Zeus!"

Odysseus wisely sheathed his sword and cooled his anger. He and his father made their way back to the palace to begin the process of ruling the kingdom once again.

Conclusion

These stories have entertained and educated people for generation upon generation. Centuries have passed since their creation, yet they continue to fascinate us. The Greek gods and heroes have inspired books, movies, and countless works of art. Hopefully, reading the tales in story format made them even more enjoyable.

Of course, these stories offer more than a pleasant diversion. They give us a glimpse into the lives and beliefs of ancient Greek culture. Like other ancient civilizations, the Greeks conquered amazing odds by simply surviving in an unforgiving and tumultuous time. These stories showcase some of their struggles and from them, we gain an appreciation for the ingenuity and imagination of the age. These tales of triumph, cunning, bravery, intrigue, and love have endured for millennia and will continue to fascinate readers for years to come.

References

A multitude of websites and books were consulted in the compiling of these stories. However, some stood out among the rest!

An extensive collection of translated ancient texts and encyclopedic reference to all things ancient Greek:

https://www.theoi.com

A comprehensive collection of myths and texts:

Anthology of Classical Myths; Translated and Edited by Stephen M. Trzaskoma, R. Scott Smith, & Stephen Brunet

The Key Ancient Texts - though bits and pieces from many, many others were also consulted:

Apollodorus - *The Library & Epitome*

Aeschylus - *Prometheus Bound*

Hesiod - *Theogony* & *Works and Days*

Homer - *Iliad* & *Odyssey*

Epic Cycle Poem

Made in United States
Orlando, FL
25 May 2023

33478035R00221